this is how we love

ALSO BY LISA MOORE

SHORT FICTION

Something for Everyone

Degrees of Nakedness

Open

The Selected Short Fiction of Lisa Moore

NOVELS

Alligator

February

Caught

Flannery

ANTHOLOGIES

The Penguin Book of Contemporary Canadian Women's Short Stories (Selected and Introduced)

Great Expectations: Twenty-Four True Stories about Childbirth (Co-edited with Dede Crane)

this is how we love

lisa moore

ANANSI

Published in Canada in 2022 by House of Anansi Press Inc.
www.houseofanansi.com

House of Anansi Press is committed to protecting our natural environment. This book is made of material from well-managed FSC®-certified forests, recycled materials, and other controlled sources.

House of Anansi Press is a Global Certified Accessible™ (GCA by Benetech) publisher. The ebook version of this book meets stringent accessibility standards and is available to students and readers with print disabilities.

26 25 24 23 22   1 2 3 4 5

Library and Archives Canada Cataloguing in Publication

Title: This is how we love / Lisa Moore.
Names: Moore, Lisa, 1964- author.
Identifiers: Canadiana (print) 20220134014 | Canadiana (ebook) 20220134022 | ISBN 9781487001193 (hardcover) | ISBN 9781487001209 (EPUB)
Classification: LCC PS8576.O61444 T55 2022 | DDC C813/.54—dc23

Book design: Alysia Shewchuk
Cover art: Lisa Moore

House of Anansi Press respectfully acknowledges that the land on which we operate is the Traditional Territory of many Nations, including the Anishinabeg, the Wendat, and the Haudenosaunee. It is also the Treaty Lands of the Mississaugas of the Credit.

 Canada Council for the Arts   Conseil des Arts du Canada   ONTARIO ARTS COUNCIL CONSEIL DES ARTS DE L'ONTARIO *an Ontario government agency un organisme du gouvernement de l'Ontario*

With the participation of the Government of Canada
Avec la participation du gouvernement du Canada | Canadä

We acknowledge for their financial support of our publishing program the Canada Council for the Arts, the Ontario Arts Council, and the Government of Canada.

Printed and bound in Canada

For
Sarah MacLachlan and Melanie Little
Thank you both with all my heart

one

jules
the calls

WE WERE ASLEEP when the phone calls came. We were in
Mexico, Joe and me. It was my sister, Nell, on the phone.
Xavier had been at a party. Nell didn't have the story; she
was getting the story. They said a girl was with him. Not his
girlfriend, no. Nell didn't know what girl. She was gone by
the time Nell got to the hospital.

I'm at the hospital, I'm with him, she said.

My phone ringing and then Joe's phone, both phones at
the same time, very loud.

Ringing and stopping and starting again with the ringing,
mining its way through our tropical sleep. Swatting through
the membrane of mosquito netting. Joe's foot against the
smear of nylon, kicking his way out the slit.

It should be in my purse, I said. Where's my purse?

Joe's phone on the other side of the room, the time difference, why would anybody be calling us at this hour?
Something has happened; we know that before we get to the
phones.

I saw the blue light inside the crumpled plastic shopping bag, pulsing bright, an embryonic pulse.

Hi Nancy, Joe said. His sister Nancy. He had turned on the bedside lamp, he had a hand on his forehead. He was staring forward and the flat of his hand holding his forehead back. I could hear Nancy's voice and it warbled out, off-key, highs and lows all run together. I couldn't hear the words.

It was Nell on my phone. She'd put her number in my phone herself, and the name that comes up is *Nell Best Sister Ever*. That was what I saw on the screen. She told me I had to come home right away.

Get the next flight, Nell said.

Is he going to be okay?

You have to come home, Nell said.

But is he okay, I asked.

They're saying critical, Nell said. They're operating.

You said he was attacked.

He was badly beaten, he was stabbed.

But why?

I mean, I'm down here in the basement, and they're rushing around. They've got scrubs on. St. Clare's. I'm not allowed in there. He's unconscious. Somebody said the doctor is really good. One of the nurses said he's in good hands. Nobody is saying much. They're saying critical, Jules.

But did you see him? Is he going to be okay?

I didn't see him.

Somebody hurt him, is that what you're saying? I asked her.

He's in critical condition, Jules.

Okay, I said. But is he going to be okay?

Before the phone calls, I'd had to drag myself across the

expanse of the big bed to find Joe in order to hold him, while I was sleeping.

I'd been dreaming of home, of Gerry's birthday parties at Nancy's house around the bay — maybe it was the water taxi on the way to the Airbnb. Dreaming of Gerry charging into the ocean, leading us all, parents, children, anybody brave enough. Gerry is Joe's youngest brother and he was forty years old in the dream, no grey yet in the black curly hair, and tanned dark below the T-shirt sleeves. We were running in, the tug of wave, building in height and force, all the adults squealing, shrieking. The children ecstatic, going limp and falling over, or they were plunged under, cocooned in the curl of a wave.

Joe and I keep different hours. I am up at about five in the morning; he stays up until one or two, even on vacation. But he'd turned off the lights in the room and was also asleep when the phone calls came. I'd moved across the bed to throw my arm over him, it really was a giant bed, my fist on his chest, his big hand over my fist.

Then the phones. It didn't make sense. People calling us.

xavier

two stars

XAVIER SAW THE streetlight blink in and out, over a shoulder, over the top of the heads, shafts of light, sharp and then splintering. He could see the side of a cheek, fists, the cuff of a jacket. He knew they were trying to murder him. He was waiting for it. They were landing blow after blow and his face was snapping this way and that, fists, two knees on his shoulders, someone pinning his legs and feet.

Any pain from the knife was delayed. It came long after the knife.

The knife came twice.

He expected it many times more. But the whole thing was interrupted.

He didn't pass out when the boot stamped on his head, though his vision closed to a pinpoint. He could direct the pinpoint, like looking through the keyhole in a door, but it also had a mind of its own. It floated a few inches away from what he was trying to see.

He didn't see the knife. The knife came when he was being

6

kicked in the head. He saw the boot coming and confused the sensation of the knife with the kick to his skull. There was a synaptic misfire and he felt the knife slide through his skull. But it had punctured his jeans and skin and maybe organs and wasn't anywhere near his head. It went deep. He could hardly believe it happened twice but at the same time he believed it.

Xavier heard the sirens. A roar of excitement went up each time the knife sank into him. The roar went up twice and was all the world like waves crashing on a beach, is what it sounded like.

He'd thought his skull was soft tissue and muscle, but that was his gut. He thought the knife went in just above his ear, but that was the steel-toed boot.

Fuck him up, a man shouted. He thought five of them, but maybe seven, there were women running out of the house across the snow.

Men's voices, but a few women were screaming things too. He couldn't tell how many of them but they were huddled in. He was still conscious when they took off. They scattered, back toward the house and the woods behind the house, into cars that lined the road and then the streetlight was white in his squinted-up eye, which he couldn't close.

One eye was swollen shut. The other seemed permanently open, maybe dislodged. Everything visible through the keyhole of his shutting-down vision. There was a ghostly doubling of the snowdrift. All the stars in the inky sky had doubled. Each star was two stars, the second one dimmer, fading.

His sense of depth was wrong. He felt that the sky went up forever, but there was also the sensation that he was sinking through the hard ground with an incalculable velocity.

He was dropping away from the sky and the snowflakes on his face, he thought, had fallen for thousands of miles to find him. They landed, one or two, on his cheek and kept him in the world because they were so cold they burned. The snowflakes were a miracle.

Xavier heard their boots as they ran off and it was a reprieve tinged with mysticism. Something religious, though he'd grown up without religion. An unexpected abandonment after so much attention. But it didn't last.

She skidded across a slick of ice on her knees and put her head on his chest. Her hand on his groin, pressing to stop the blood. Xavier heard her saying his name.

Xavier, Xay, Xay.

She was blubbering. But not hysterical. She was intent. Grunting. There was the rustle of her down jacket. This was her go-to, her way of being. She had one way of being, and it was all huff and intent.

I got you, she was saying. I got you. I got you. I got you.

She was ripping off the coat. She put it over him. She was trying to coax him to do some minor favour, to let her have a ride in the go-cart, to let her have the black gummy bears, she wanted the rainbow gummy worms that came in the paper bag from the store on Queen's Road, with the Missus behind the Plexiglas because they'd been held up with a syringe, some addled and kooky-eyed miscreant with a used needle held in his fist, point out, ready to hammer it into Missus, and the two of them watching by the chip rack, they were maybe eight?, to give her the water balloon, an extra turn on the pogo stick, to do some homework with her. She did his homework.

She was saying: Got to keep you warm.

She kept saying the ambulance was on the way, but there

was nothing except the stars separating and conjoining, growing dim and pulsing bright, more snow, the wind swaying over the top of the drift. The veils of snow the wind dragged with it were glittery when they passed under the streetlight and she said: Here's the ambulance.

She kept saying that. But the ambulance was still a long way off. It was just the two of them and the wind, which was shushing over the top of the snow. It was as though she were trying to comfort the both of them with the huffing, sing-song chant of his name.

Then they were riding in the back of an ambulance together, for the second time in their lives. Like it was becoming a habit, the two of them in ambulances. He was conscious enough to know this was her fault.

What had happened to him was her fault. He had been stuck with her since he was a kid, she was his dim star and he couldn't get shy of her and she was the reason he would bleed to death in a snowdrift in a new suburb near Topsail Beach, far away from his girlfriend and everybody he loved.

The men were her fault, the boot to the head, the stabbing.

Then there really was the ambulance, blinking in and out of view, and that was her fault too because she'd called the cops and they had to move him.

He wanted his mother and father. The thought of his father made him weepy. Because his father had a sense of humour is why he wanted his father. His mother was strident and fierce and a pain in the hole, panicked and shrill, if she were here, he loved his mother, but his father would be joking right now and the whole idea of if his father could be there, if he kept thinking about it, would be his undoing. His sister. The idea of them flicked by and dimmed.

He felt sorry for himself. But he also wanted to make jokes. Be friendly with the paramedics, win them over. He felt an anxiety about the fact that they'd had to come get him in the middle of the night. A ballooning terror that had nowhere to pitch, he didn't know what he was afraid of, and then he knew, he didn't want to inconvenience the paramedics. He regretted going to the party. This came to him as all insights did, with a physical shiver of wonder.

He tried to ask somebody to call his girlfriend.

My girlfriend, he tried to say.

He wanted Violet and felt bereft about her not knowing what had happened and also that she would have to find out what happened. He felt like he was leaving Violet.

Xavier thought that leaving someone by dying was like breaking up through text message.

Leaving should be done in person.

His mother would be angry with him for dying. She would consider it the culmination of every time he had disobeyed her.

He was letting them all down. It was not a sentiment he wanted to be bothered with as the life seeped out of him.

jules
the tell

WHEN XAVIER WAS born we decided we didn't want a name that made him belong to a line, or belong to anything, except Joe and me and Xavier's sister, Stella. Xavier meant "light," one baby-name book said, and that was good enough for us.

We say Xavier or Xay, anglicizing it, hammering out the little hesitation between the X and the rest of the name.

There'd been an argument with Florence, my mother-in-law, who insisted we call him Miles. The minute I told my in-laws I was pregnant, the words not out quite of my mouth, she told me what I had to call him. Miles was her maiden name.

A name, she said, was going to die out of the family.

She had entered into this argument with the same war-room vigour she'd used when we chose the wrong shade of green for our living room. She'd harangued about that paint chip, but we'd held our ground out of spite, out of some absurd desire for independence.

Of course, she'd been right about the paint. Me and Joe and Nancy, Joe's sister, when we bought the house together on Cabot Street. We'd been looking for a blood-dark green, one of those moody, early-nineties shades, austere and earthy. What we got was the opposite, bright and cheerful. A disappointment we couldn't admit or afford to fix.

Choosing a Catholic saint's name was the only way to appease my mother-in-law.

We looked up the feast days of the saints, and our boy was born on the feast of St. Xavier. For a couple of weeks after the birth, Florence continued to call him Miles, trying to make it stick. She fought to babysit him when he was less than a month old and it physically ached to have him out of my sight. She complained to Joe that it wasn't right that she couldn't have him for a few hours. What was wrong with me, she demanded to know. She was the baby's grandmother. She'd raised six children. Then she fed him from the tip of a silver spoon, his first taste of ice cream, said he loved it.

Just before you got here, a little taste, she said. She lifted him close, let her nose touch his. Her eyes closed, breathing in the infant smell. Then handed him over.

You should have seen the face on him when he tasted it, she said.

He's not supposed to have anything but breast milk, I said. I was furious and bitter.

A little taste won't hurt him, she said. She was implacable and softened by awe.

Little Miles, she said.

My mother thought I should have called Xavier after my father, Cyril, who had died when I was sixteen. She didn't particularly like the name Cyril, so she hadn't pushed for it. She would never push, anyway, it wasn't her style. But she had a tell, a way of setting her mouth, the bottom lip pudged out, and a quick wrinkle of her nose. She did that with her bottom lip and I knew she didn't like the name Xavier any more than Florence did.

She'd glanced at my sister, Nell, who had straightened her shoulders, drawn a deep breath, and said she loved it.

Joe had become a father when he was eighteen. They didn't stay together, Joe and Stella's mother, but they shared Stella. She was on his shoulders all over downtown, up to the university, in the library, his big hands cupping her ankles, her two hands clamped to his forehead. Sometimes he had to peel a little hand off his eye. The lope of him through the cafeteria and he had to bend his knees to get through doorways without banging her head.

Then Xavier. We hadn't expected him. Putting the plastic pissed-on wand on the windowsill, wanting it and not wanting it. I could hear Nancy in the kitchen, sliding the roaster in the oven. Her son, Tristan, in one attic bedroom, and Stella across the hall. We did a three-day, four-day schedule, switching the four-day every second week. Stella found a full week in either house too long.

If there was a baby, we could make the storage closet a nursery.

What drama, waiting for the little window to predict the seismic swing of yes or no. The wonder of how things could change; what we couldn't afford. Joe was teaching as a sessional. I taught art to the five-to-seven-year-old set on Saturday mornings, and waitressed. Sold a few paintings, applied for grants.

Brushing my teeth, because it was on the sill, just sitting there, waiting to change my life. Both of us thirty-two, just getting on our feet.

I wouldn't look at it until I was good and ready. Because there were my teeth to brush and maybe some lipstick and I was going to the gallery for an opening, Nancy's macaroni and cheese in the oven, movies for later, Stella had a friend sleeping over. The movies were overdue at the video store and it depended who was on the counter, if it was Maurice and he felt like it, he'd wipe out the debt. His brother made us pay down with every trip. *The Next Karate Kid* under the couch for four years.

Joe upstairs typing, hearing the clatter of what he was trying to write. Calling up the stairs to him.

Saying: Yes.

Going up the stairs two at a time with the pissed-on stick and the little pink plus sign, as if I needed the physical proof, and him standing up like a soldier called to attention. Fists flexing and unflexing, and opening his arms for me to step into. He's a whole foot taller than me, so he has to stoop to put his chin on the top of my head. Neither of us said a word.

Florence had a battery-operated musical knife for cutting birthday cakes and you could program the name of the celebrant. The knife sang the birthday song in a nasal soprano, and Xavier was Miles in the knife and remained that way forever, the password for adding and removing names long forgotten. The voice scratchy and saccharine in a way we should have recognized as a warning, a tell from the future, a hint of what was in store. If you believe that things lie in wait, hidden pockets of joy and catastrophe that the clairvoyant and any old diviner with a forked stick can uncover, then you can believe in the possibility of a really good metal detector with a magical setting that finds what is buried, but coming down the pipe. As if we might have guessed that Xavier's fate would be a question of mistaken identity. Or if not mistaken, just plain wrong. A knife that stabbed my innocent son twice in the gut because the knife had the wrong name.

jules
a downed wire

THE WOMAN WHO cursed Trinity Brophy was a frequenter
of Taylor's Pharmacy at the bottom of the hill. At the end
of each month, when the cheques arrived, there'd be a line
of maybe twenty people waiting for the pharmacy to open.
The summer of the curse, the woman wore a yellow hat with
a floppy brim. She walked up from Water Street every day
past our house, and Joe and I started referring to her as the
Woman with the Yellow Hat, like the Man with the Yellow
Hat in the Curious George children's books.

She had a variety of wigs, but her own hair was thick and
oily, coloured red. That summer she wore a bright orange
lipstick. It spread above her upper lip, just enough to betray
the tremor in her hands.

This was, of course, long before Xavier was attacked at
the party in Topsail. Before he was stabbed in the groin, once,
and then again, the second wound an inch above the first, the
drawing out of the knife between the two stabs also damaging
the flesh, making the total number of cuts four.

Each wound torn twice, the surgeon would tell me later: torn on the way in, on the way out, a serrated knife. A slightly different angle on the way out, more pressure on the blade.

Before the wounds became infected and the infection coursing through him.

Before his white blood cell count went up to seventeen, so high I stopped asking the nurses, before they switched antibiotics. Before he was burning to the touch, a post-surgery complication.

Two nurses, one with short spiky hair, blond with black roots, Margie, who would tell me she was developing a line of skin care products made from seaweed, when I asked what she did when she wasn't working, and the other, Samira, with pale brown skin, arched eyebrows, a coil of shiny black hair, thick and long, held at the nape of her neck with a red elastic, who, while off on maternity leave, had begun investing in penny stocks, had an app on her phone set to arbitrary dates when she would pull out of this or that stock regardless of how it was performing. I asked them both personal questions to keep them by Xavier's bedside. Both in white uniforms, polyester jackets with pockets on the front and short sleeves, matching pants. I could see Samira's fingers tapping against her hip, in the pocket of her jacket, anxious to get through her rounds, trying not to get stuck answering my questions.

They spoke in low voices and sometimes raised the ends of their sentences like a question. It made everything they said sound like a prayer, even when they were describing the colour of my son's pee, which had been collecting in a plastic bag tied to the rail of his bed.

We'd like to see it lighter? Samira said.

They'd both said: His doctor has a good reputation?

Margie said, He's like a saint, revered he is. I could tell her accent was from the Northern Peninsula even before she said St. Anthony.

You're in good hands here, Samira said to Xavier, though he was still unconscious, as she ripped open the Velcro of the blood pressure cuff. Samira Patel, she was from St. Anthony too, her father a doctor there, her mother a school principal. Margie Pritchard, father a rig worker, parents divorced. Mother, I couldn't remember what her mother did.

Before all that.

I was walking home from downtown on the morning of the curse, passing the line outside the pharmacy, and I saw the Woman with the Yellow Hat reach into her handbag and take out a tortoiseshell compact. She flipped up the lid. An oval of sunshine, reflected from the mirror, shivered and wobbled over her cheek and settled in her right eye, making her shut it tight and draw her chin into the loose folds of skin on her neck.

I saw her remove the top of the lipstick and place it on the concrete windowsill of the store. The sill was slanted. The woman put down the little plastic top, and her fingers, a giant ring clumped with rhinestones on each finger and even one thumb — it was a mystery how she got them over her arthritic knuckles — hovered, waiting for the top of the lipstick lid to roll away and fall onto the sidewalk.

Then she spread the lipstick over both lips and rubbed them together, examined them in the compact mirror, moving it up and down to get the right view.

Her faded black leggings, which she wore under all her dresses, sagged at the knees and were pilled with tiny nubs of cotton. The foam soles of her flip-flops had flattened out, become as hard as boards. I'd seen her feet close-up one afternoon when she'd fallen asleep on a bench at Bannerman Park. Our Frisbee had wafted down on the bench near her feet and I had retrieved it without waking her.

I used to see her shopping at the Salvation Army on Waldegrave and she'd try on a lot of glamorous outfits. Prom dresses, or bridesmaids' dresses that she'd buy and wear all day long during the summer. I shopped there too, and all my clothes had designer tags and were made of silk or merino wool or cashmere or one hundred percent cotton.

On the day that she uttered the curse against eight-year-old Trinity Brophy, she was wearing a cocktail dress from the eighties. The material was stiff and opalescent, giant puffy sleeves, a drop waist and skirt of layered flounces. It shimmered and rustled.

The day was already heating up, though there were still gentle gusts of an ozone-smelling cold coming off the icebergs outside the harbour. Trinity came tearing around the corner of Cabot Street and down Carter's Hill with a water balloon.

She was being chased by Xavier, who was also eight, and a girl named Jessica, maybe nine, and Jessica's little brother, Cory, who was probably four.

They each had a water balloon raised above their shoulder. The effort of holding the wobbly balloons in the air waggled their gaits as they turned the corner. They were running lopsided. All three of them aiming for Trinity Brophy's back, but she was too fast. Her long, straight, gold-blond hair flapped between her shoulder blades.

Three water balloons splatted on the sidewalk at the heels of Trinity's new white sneakers. She stopped so fast her sneakers squeaked.

The other kids had spent their arsenal.

Trinity still had her balloon. She saw the water stains from the broken balloons spreading on the sidewalk near her new white sneakers and came to a halt. Even at eight years old, it was clear she would be a beauty. Her eyes were the lightest blue, people commented on the colour all the time. The iris rimmed with black. Freckles over the bridge of her nose, her cheeks tanned gold, her eyebrows gold.

She grated on her teachers' nerves. She'd try to talk to them, louder than the other kids, out of turn, Miss, Miss, Miss, jabbing her arm up in the air, straight and pumping. I could imagine them shutting their eyes and drawing a breath in deep, so their chests got big, and they'd huff with exasperation before answering her. They'd shut their eyes as if she were too much to take in. I'd seen that more than once on the playground.

Nobody spoke about her birth parents, but at least one of them had to be tall. By the time she was fourteen she was a head above me, and taller than Mary Mahoney, who raised her.

Trinity was doing the kind of fast growing that leaves a body without an ounce of fat and robs a child of energy very suddenly so that you come upon them in odd places at odd hours, sound asleep. The kind of growing that kept her constantly hungry, though Mary would have offered her plenty of food. Trinity would lick her finger and stick it in my sugar bowl and put her finger in her mouth, no matter how many times I said other people had to use that sugar too.

The sort of love I felt for Trinity Brophy is nothing like the love I have for my own children, which is stable and uncomplicated. The love I felt for Trinity was inconvenient and random. But it was, is, also intractable. She was just a neighbourhood kid who caught my attention. A childhood friend of my son's. Yes, an intense and consuming friendship, but brief. We don't choose who we love. Lots of kids came and went on that street. Some love just sticks.

I was coming back from a board meeting at the Eastern Edge Gallery on the day that Trinity was cursed, and something of that foul storm ricocheted; hit me too; hit Xavier. The curse joined us like a current of electricity from a downed wire, crackling over an invisible web of its own internal logic.

Each of the children was stuck to the sidewalk, the skin of their burst water balloon shrivelled. Adrenaline and food-colouring from the Mr. Freezes they had in their fists or dangling from their mouths had paralyzed everyone. It was a time when bad behaviour was blamed on additives, or food-colouring.

Xavier's lips and tongue were blue. There's a psychology test or a party trick, where they ask you to say the word *blue* every time they show you a red card. They show you several red cards in a row, and you say *blue*, then they show you a blue card and you say *red*.

I thought his blue mouth and tongue meant my son had been caught red-handed. They knew they weren't allowed to fill up balloons in my house, there would be water all over the bathroom floor. They were in big trouble.

Trinity, on the sidewalk by the pharmacy, after the other kids' water balloons had been thrown, pivoted to stare down Xavier, my son Xavier, with opened-faced glee, and then without warning, like on a basketball court, she faked to the side. She decided to throw her water balloon at the Woman in the Yellow Hat.

The balloon was red and wobbled in the air and burst

noiselessly on the old woman's shoulder. The others in the line for Taylor's Pharmacy stood free from the brick wall with the badly painted mural of a chemist in a white lab coat, a pestle and mortar in his scabrous, flaking outstretched arms. The men and women straightened themselves. The line was jostled.

The Woman in the Yellow Hat had flared a purplish red under the sickly puce shadow cast by the brim of her hat.

The impact of the balloon had knocked one of her giant Velcroed shoulder pads askew. She plucked at the wet fabric of the dress that had suctioned onto her skin, lifting it so it caught a bubble of air and the shoulder pad was dislodged and dropped onto the sidewalk.

She snatched up the pad in her fist. It looked like a sanitary napkin. The shoulder pad caused the men in the line an embarrassment that made them look away. Denuded of just one of the gronky football-player shoulders made the Woman in the Yellow Hat hunched, lopsided. It revealed a raw vulnerability.

But her eyes were bright and narrowed.

She was short of breath and pulled a puffer from her purse and, putting it to her mouth, inhaled so deeply her eyes bulged. I'd bent to pick up the shoulder pad, but she got there first. That's when I noticed the splotch of ink on one of the flounces of the dress.

It was my dress.

I'd owned the dress and given it to the Salvation Army in Stephenville, a ten-hour bus ride from St. John's, when I was going to the community college there. I'd bought the dress at a boutique on Main Street and worn it to a reception for our graduation exhibition. The dress must have travelled through the second-hand stores all over the island for a decade.

The fog was rolling in over the South Side Hills. A spring day that started sunny but the fog, thick as cotton batting, was spreading, across the harbour, engulfing the buildings on Water Street, Duckworth Street, the graveyard of the Anglican Cathedral, crawling uphill toward us.

The dress had been mine.

I remembered the plastic glass with cheap white wine that smelled like a deodorant, the series of ink drawings, nudes, I'd done as my final graduation project. Having sex in the school's photography darkroom, because you could lock the door from the inside, a precaution in case someone tried to bust in while students were developing film. Also, we weren't allowed to have guests of the opposite sex in our dorm rooms.

The clothesline hanging over the pans of chemicals, how we dipped the paper under and let the fluid slosh on top of it, so the image formed itself, rose up in shades of grey to darkest black. How the process, the image coming into being, felt like what was happening to me there, in that tiny town near the ocean, making art, studying art history in a class of twelve students, all of whom might just as easily have signed up for heavy equipment, esthetics (cutting hair), or travel management — coming into being. We hung the photographs with clothespins to dry out. The orange lights, or pitch dark.

My father had died the summer before I started grade twelve. After graduation I left my mother and sister to travel by bus across the province to a town so small I could walk the length of it in an afternoon.

When she stood up with the shoulder pad in her fist, I saw that the ivory-coloured puffer was smeared with the orange lipstick.

She spat on the sidewalk and pointed at Trinity Brophy.

You will pay, she said. You will pay for that. You're going to burn in hell. You mark my words. You will burn.

Then she swayed her finger so that it took in not just Trinity, but also Xavier and me.

All of you, she said. You'll burn for this.

trinity
marooned

A DAY AT TOPSAIL BEACH, when Trinity was seven, the air mattress red on one side and blue on the other and the sun-warmed canvas smelled musty. Her mother's boyfriend was trying to pump up the mattress.

It was a rinky-dink pump, a bright orange plastic casing with black parts. It looked too small between his fat fists.

He was stepping on footholds on either side of the slim little pump, his feet close together and his knees sticking out, he had gladiators, some kind of medieval warriors in chain mail all over his swimming trunks, doing battle with swords and big helmets with red plumes, skirts of leather strips and boots that went up to the knees. Cartoons gritting their teeth. This is what she remembered, though she couldn't remember the boyfriend's face.

It had been a long drive and it was hot in the car. Her mother had said, Stop complaining. But Trinity hadn't said anything. He'd flicked the rearview. She didn't remember his name, but he'd looked at her like she shouldn't be there.

Her mother had said, Let's get her an ice cream.

They were waiting for the store to show up on the side of the road and her mother kept saying it's around the next bend.

Trinity asked would they get to the store soon.

Didn't I say we'd be getting ice creams? What did I say?

Trinity didn't answer. Finally, after a very long time, she said, You said you would get me an ice cream. She had said it under her breath, loud enough for her mother to notice, but not the boyfriend.

He drove past the store when it finally reared up out of the next turn, with a big family coming out the door, three children with ice creams. A father holding the door open and the children parading under his arm. Then, after that family, two girls, teenagers, both with red hair, both with waffle cones and pink ice cream. That was the kind she would have had. Strawberry.

Too late now, the boyfriend said. Her mother didn't want to provoke him, but Trinity had turned all the way around to see the teenagers with their ice creams coming out of the cool, dark store into the blazing sun; they were disoriented from the light and the dust settling from a car that had just pulled off the lot.

The boyfriend was working the little plastic pump, his elbows stuck out. He was bent all the way over, people coming down the path could see his butt crack because the bathing suit was slipping down. The sound of the pump wheezing and sucking. Then he hauled the handle up and slammed it down so hard it cracked.

What do you expect, buying junk, he'd said. He ripped the little tube out and flung the pump across the grass.

That pump was expensive, Trinity's mother said. You didn't have to go and break it.

Her mother dropped to the ground and took the mattress between her outstretched legs and put the little black rubber tube to her mouth, and Trinity watched as she blew into the air mattress with the bright yellow toggle attached and then bit down on the tube to draw in breath through her nose and the corners of her mouth until her chest rose and her shoulders went straight and her cheeks were full, then she exhaled, and her shoulders slumped.

She blew into the rubber tube over and over. Trinity watched as the creases in the air mattress began to soften, unpucker, pudge, and go stiff. Her mother's saliva spread in a little stain on the red flap at the edge of the mattress. Trinity stood by, rigid as a statue because she knew the mattress, which was breathing itself now, puffing as her mother exhaled, was coming to life. It was growing before their eyes. Her mother's cheeks flushed, she was a smoker and she didn't really have the breath for it, but she kept going. Her eyes glittering over the giant red swollen tongue of the mattress that hung out over her chin.

It was the hottest day of the summer. The top of Trinity's head felt hot. Her shoulders felt like they were burning. The beach was full of children with plastic pails and shovels, and some people had thrown nets for capelin. Whole families, people with saris and huge tinfoil containers of food, old people and babies, sitting in a circle, sharing and eating, talking in a language Trinity didn't know. There was a woman lying on her belly on a surfboard, dog-paddling down the shore in only a foot of water.

The sky and the water were the exact same shade of pale blue, so Trinity couldn't tell where the sky ended and the water began. A big white-and-orange boat, far away, looked like it was floating in the sky.

Her mother glanced up and the look said it was a sacrifice, but she was doing it, wasn't she? She was filling up the mattress for Trinity, and it was better than an ice cream.

The boyfriend had gone to the car and brought back two folding chairs with holes in the plastic arms and a net under the hole, where you could put a bottle of beer. He'd opened the picnic cooler with flecks of aqua blue in the white Styrofoam. It made a loud squeak when he unwedged the lid and he got out a beer. The cooler was full of beer and ice cubes.

Her mother stood with the tube of the air mattress still in her teeth and lowered herself into the chair and he'd stood over her, with a beer in each hand, and he slotted one into her cup holder.

Trinity's mother spoke through gritted teeth, clenching the tube. She said for Trinity to straighten out the corner of the air mattress. She pointed at the folded triangle of blue, and Trinity straightened it out.

Eventually, the air mattress was as hard as a rock. Her mother screwed in the yellow toggle, which was attached by a nylon string, or else they would have lost it. She wiped the sweat off her forehead. She was pink all over. Her arms were mottled. She gave the air mattress two firm smacks.

See? she asked. Let that be a lesson.

Trinity didn't know what it was a lesson for, but later she thought it might have been to persevere. It might have been that it is necessary to keep going, to get the job done. Though persevering wasn't her mother's strong suit back then.

Go on, it's cold, the boyfriend said. He lifted his beer toward Trinity's mother, and she picked up her bottle and twisted off the cap. Frost curled up.

Take it, her mother said. Take it down to the waves. Trinity had a pair of red plastic sunglasses shaped like hearts. She'd had the glasses resting on the top of her hair. But now she put them down over her eyes.

Don't get cute with me, the boyfriend said. With your goddamn glasses. She didn't know what he meant, but there had been empty beer bottles rolling around on the floor of the backseat of the car, clinking together every time he turned a corner.

Go on, take it down to the water, her mother said. You wanted to go to the beach, didn't you? Now you're here. This is the beach.

Take that goddam thing down there by the water, the boyfriend said. Where all the children are.

I'll watch from here, her mother said. Go on, you're all right by yourself.

He had spread a blanket on the grass, and he was lying down on his side and he patted the blanket and told Trinity's mother to come down next to him.

I'm all right here, she said. Trinity felt the instant anger in her mother's boyfriend, though there was no physical indication of it. She felt it in the same way she could feel her arms and neck getting sunburnt. He turned over onto his back and put a hand on his shoulder and rolled it in circles, two or three times, as though to get it back in place. To ease it. He was always paying attention to the easing of his muscles, he worked out, he did steroids, he competed. It was his shoulder or a calf. He was always massaging himself.

He said, I want you down here on the blanket.

Will you come down to the water with me, Trinity said to her mother.

You're all right, her mother said. I blew it up for you.

And I told you to get lost, the boyfriend said.

There's children down there, go down with them, her mother said. I'll be down the once.

Her mother had talked about getting in. She'd said they'd hold hands, she and Trinity, and they would run in, no matter how cold it was. They'd make a run for it.

You said you'd get in. Trinity spoke louder now. He wouldn't cause a scene with a crowd watching.

Don't have me speak again, her mother said. This was always the final word on any subject.

Trinity put her arms around the pillow part of the air mattress and tried to drag it, but it was too hard to maintain a grasp, so she pinched the flap along the edge of the air mattress.

I'll be up here, her mother said. Watching out.

Relax, her boyfriend said. Whatever his name was. The boyfriend. Trinity's mother stood up and unzipped her cut-off jeans and shimmied her hips and she let the jeans fall around her feet. She stepped out of them, but the cut-offs clung to one heel and she had to kick to get them free and she almost fell over.

The loss of balance made her look up at Trinity and laugh, but it didn't last because the boyfriend made a noise of disgust.

Her mother lay down beside the boyfriend. He put his hand on her bare stomach and Trinity saw his pinkie slide under the elastic of the bikini bottom stretched across her hip bones. She saw the pinkie inching down like a caterpillar and she saw her mother lift his hand up higher onto her belly. It was the shape of his little finger under the elastic, a black bikini with a print of daisies, that would haunt her whenever the trip to the beach came back to her.

The water was every bit as cold as her mother had said, and when Trinity tried to get on the mattress, one end stood up straight in the air and all the water rushed in and made the red much darker and the whole mattress was wet.

Her sunglasses came off and were tangled in her hair, but she untangled them and got them back on. There were hardly any waves, but she could feel the pull and push. All the colours were several shades deeper with her sunglasses, the spruce along the edge of the parking lot were black. Someone on the beach had a yellow towel, but with the sunglasses it looked a deep orange. The water was green in splotches where the sunlight broke at the edges of the clouds. The water was only up to her knees.

She had managed to fling the top half of her body on the mattress and it folded up like a V around her. She wedged a leg up on the back end and punched the pillow down. A wave tipped it toward her, and she was able to roll on.

She still had her sunglasses; she had goosebumps but it was so hot and the clouds had piled high, violet underbellies and white at the top. She'd inched near a family of three kids and a mother. The mother was laughing and splashing the kids with the flat of her hand. If anyone was looking Trinity wanted them to think she was with the family.

There'd been a girl with a foam mermaid tail that she'd squeezed both her legs into, and she was lying on her belly at the edge of the water, so the low waves broke over her shoulders and she was lifting the tail, which was purple, so it stood up straight behind her, for a photograph. The mother was on one knee with her phone, telling the girl to smile, to put her elbows in the sand and her fists under her chin, to get the hair out of her eyes. Trinity let herself float into the background of the photo.

Soon these sounds were overtaken by the slapping of the water at the edge of the air mattress, and the sun was a weight. The heat was mixed up with the sway and lilt of the mattress as if they were the same things.

The coast guard picked her up. She was halfway to Bell Island, they said. She woke up to a loud slapping and it was waves against the side of a big speedboat. She sat up on one elbow and nearly fell off the air mattress. She was very far away from shore.

She was in the middle of the ocean. She didn't even know how to swim.

There were men telling her not to move, to stay where she was.

One of the men dove over the side of the big boat with a life jacket and he was swimming over, calling out, I got you, but he was still several strokes away. He didn't have her. He kept winking in and out of view behind the waves.

Then the orange life jacket was flung on top of her, cold and wet and flaring and his fist on the edge of the mattress big and bony. His face, so white with the freckles and the blond eyelashes studded with little droplets that flared in the sun, his face so close to her, his breath like cinnamon gum, a wave slapped him gently on the cheek, his face passing through it and he flicked it away and it slapped again. She might have put an arm around his neck, except she was afraid to move.

He gave her the life jacket and told her to put it on. She shifted and the mattress nearly tipped over.

I got you, he said. I got you, I got you.

He said, Put that thing on, don't move. She didn't ask how she could put the life jacket on without moving, because she wanted to obey him. She wanted to belong to him, the earnest, exasperated, shouting huffing face, the glossy mouth and tonsils right next to her face, the white teeth and tanned hand with wet gold curly hair all over the back of it. She felt the words in puffs of breath on her cheeks, I got you, I got you. He was trying to convince himself.

He turned and jerked the mattress hard with each stroke of his other arm.

He shouted over his shoulder, There's Kevin. See Kevin? I got her, Kevin, I got her. I got her. I got her. He said this with each stroke.

Sometimes the water slapped over his head. Or a wavelet obscured him. Then there was just his fist. He was swimming with one arm, he had the edge of the air mattress in his fist and she could see the wavering cream of his legs rippling out of shape with each kick.

Tell her to put on the life jacket, Kevin said.

I told her, the man said.

Don't move, Kevin told her, don't move a muscle. Rob got you. Rob got you. That's Rob there. He got you.

Then they were near the side of the boat, the air mattress was knocking against it. Kevin said to take his hands and he said he was going to count to three and lift her right up over the side of the boat.

Have you got her? Rob asked.

I got you, Kevin said to Trinity. But he forgot to count to three. He just jerked her off the mattress and it bobbed away from her and Rob reached the ladder on the side of the boat, gripped it with both hands and pulled himself up with a big swoosh.

What about the mattress, she said. Her teeth were chattering and she could hardly speak. She was trembling all over.

Never mind the mattress, Rob said. Kevin had her wrapped in a blanket and they gave her a glass of orange juice. They asked her if she'd rather have ginger ale, and she said yes, and they laughed.

Look where you are, Rob said. You're out in the middle of nowhere. He lifted his arms in the air, as if asking her to take in the whole ocean.

She vomited.

Oh Jesus, Rob said.

I'm sorry, Trinity said. She'd put her hands over her mouth, but it had squirted through her fingers. The bag of Cheezies she had and the white bread with Cheez Whiz and fried egg. And the mouthful of ginger ale, acidic, burning.

Don't be sorry, Kevin said. That's nothing.

Kevin will clean that up, Rob said.

I'll clean that, Kevin said. Don't you worry.

I got a cloth here, Rob said.

Rob will have that cleaned up, no time, won't you Rob?

It's cleaned up now sure, Rob said.

I got one like you at home, Kevin said. Little girl. I bet you're seven, aren't you? Get her that bucket there, Rob.

She threw up again but this time in a red bucket that stank of fish.

Okay, let's get out of here, Rob said.

34

She imagined they would crash on the shore they were going so fast. But the boat turned at the last minute and Rob was out and up to his armpits in water and he reached up and Kevin lowered her over the side into his arms. He was swishing through the water and onto the rocky part and he put her down, so she was standing up but it felt like the earth was moving just like the ocean had.

Who owns this child? Rob yelled.

Everybody was looking at her. A crowd had formed. She'd floated over a kilometre and a half and the story made the newspapers, but not her name or picture. There was a picture of Kevin and Rob and their boat.

Her Mom had been making out on the blanket with her boyfriend, and they were both drunk, staggering down over the grassy hill onto the beach of round rocks, but she could see the look on her mother's face just as soon as she broke through the crowd, her mother. Her mother soft and ashamed, but awed by the commotion, the heat of judgment from the crowd, the glare of the water, which was now a solid platter of silver near the shore. What a look of tenderness and shame, which was as close a facsimile of love as the seven-year-old would find for a long time. A look saturated with pity, drunk slackened features, a mildly coercive offering, this pity, a welter of goodbye.

Trinity was taken by a social worker and two police officers that evening. The Torbay Road apartments with the rotating staff who slept sitting up on the couch and who wrote everything down in the morning and who read her the same five storybooks when she went to sleep.

Then she was moved to the group home in Conception Bay South, where she stayed until she was seven and a half, but that place closed down and she moved in with Mary Mahoney on Cabot Street. Her mother moved to the mainland in pursuit of employment. Trinity's file said her mother was cooking in a camp in Alberta, then Yellowknife, then back to Toronto, and they'd lost touch with her. Social services lost touch for a while. Her mother had fallen out of touch.

jules
house around the bay

FLORENCE MILES GREW up in foster care. The woman who became her foster mother was Bride Peach.

This is my mother-in-law. Where Florence came from and, therefore, where Joe came from, my husband, Joe.

And this is our son, Xavier, and everything that happened before I ended up sitting beside his hospital bed. Before the storm of the century. Before we were cursed. What might get us through. The search for why. Why Joe was stranded in Montreal waiting for a plane home, caught in the teeth of a maelstrom, a supernatural void, a whiteout that cancelled all incoming flights for god knows how long. Why I was here by myself. How this happened.

I have to go back before this raucous breathing, the oxygen mask — its croak and caw, the drawing in and out — that Xavier, my unconscious son, had fitted over his mouth and nose to help him along, Samira said, to give him a little boost, an extra bit of oxygen, she said, that's all, we have to go back before all that to find the thread of why.

I'm going to try to stick to the truth, but why is always equal parts truth and speculation. If you blink, why shifts out of focus. In looking for the why of it, I am going to have to call on the dead. This is a story my mother-in-law told me. The way she said it—I can hear her voice—over a dinner with French bread, when Joe and I said we were going to be married. She wanted me to know the different kinds of family there are, an infinite number, arbitrary in shape and form, and I had better be open to them all because it would be my job to hold it together, it was the pact we made, over the sacrament of dessert: whoever came through. Holdfast.

By way of parable she told the story of her own family, of her stepmother. Because if I were to marry Joe, I'd be a stepmother too.

It was a story she recounted often, with only minor variations in fact and tone, but the take-away? What she was actually telling me?

This is how we love.

BRIDE PEACH HAD come up to Caplin Cove from Heart's Desire when she was sixteen years old to marry Mr. Molloy, who lived in the old house set back from the harbour with the river running alongside. The house was surrounded by white rosebushes and two outbuildings and he had cows and sheep.

She had made a stew of rabbit one afternoon and come evening, she'd called her husband out of the barn and told him to sit down to the table. Bride was not a year married yet, and after he was seated, she was gone out to the porch for an armload of wood and heard the thump from inside. She'd come rushing back.

Bride saw him curled up on the floor and put her hand on his cheek and then she ran across the meadow to Grace Yetman's place, Grace, her neighbour, and she told Mrs. Yetman that Mr. Molloy was dead. She had only ever called him Mr. Molloy to other people because he was thirty-four years older than her.

She'd only just got used to saying his first name, Samuel, when they were alone, just before he died.

Grace Yetman wiped her hands and took loaves out of the oven without saying a word. Then she sent one of her youngsters to the wharf to tell the men to go after the doctor and the priest in Carbonear. Then she and young Bride went up the path through the back field. Four other women showed up not an hour later. They had Bride's husband laid out in the living room before midnight.

The priest and the doctor came from Carbonear the next day and said mass in the living room. Grace Yetman told Bride she could come over to her house and sleep on the daybed in the kitchen if she didn't want to be in the house alone with the body, but Bride said she didn't feel it was right to leave her husband by himself.

After they were all gone, Bride went down to the beach, just across the road, and got a stone to put in the foot of the bed. She got it good and hot in the stove. It was late fall coming on to winter, and there was a stack of wood up to Bride's shoulders running along the perimeter of the property facing the river. The wood was dry.

Bride Peach's husband of eight months had taught her how to make bread, though she had to stand on a low stool to lean over the bowl on the counter. He'd left her with the chickens and cows and sheep. He'd had an old plow horse.

He'd never had much to say and it had come down to her reading the smallest involuntary changes in his face to know what he was feeling. She wasn't ever sure, over the eight months they'd spent together, that he was a man of very much feeling. But she developed the skill, during the time they were married, to intuit even the minor flickers of emotion. Sitting up in the chair over the three days before they put him in the ground, especially at night, when the people cleared out, she had the experience of him leaving the world, like the heat dying out of a woodstove if you don't feed it. After the three days, the man was gradually more absent than present, and then she couldn't feel his presence at all. She learned what he had been made of only when he was gone.

They buried him on the day of the first snowfall, in 1906. It was a job to get the shovels into the ground. He was buried between an apple tree and a lilac tree in a pine box in the cemetery on the other side of the main road, looking out over the ocean.

WITHIN A MONTH after Bride Peach's husband's death, another death occurred. In Hant's Harbour, on the other side of the Heart's Content barrens, a man lost his wife and was left with five children to rear up by himself. He called his sister to come over and take care of the youngsters and he headed across the barrens for Broad Cove.

Bride's husband wasn't buried two weeks before the snow was staying on the ground, then it was up around her knees. She wasn't pregnant, nor would she ever be. One night there came a storm the likes of which, people said, hadn't come through in thirty years. The winds were so high the snow flicked past Bride's window in sheets like someone thumbing all the pages of a book, trying to find the spot they left off.

There came a knock on the door and this was Matthew Peach from Hant's Harbour. He'd started out over the barrens because he'd heard about the widow over in Broad Cove and when the snow started, grainy and spiteful, he put his head down and kept coming.

People have lost their way on the barrens in the snow. You can hear their voices, people around there say, when the wind is blowing hard. They are known as the lost souls of the Heart's Content barrens. But there were bits of red rag tied to shrubs along the path and Matthew Peach followed them. Sometimes he was up to his waist, but sometimes the barrens were swept bare, right down to the surface of the rock.

He showed up in Broad Cove after dark and banged on Bride's front door. She had turned seventeen in the eight months of marriage and got through the death and the burial in the big house with the wind howling around it and the snow pinging against the window, falling asleep sometimes next to the coffin, her chin dropping, sitting up straight as a board.

When her head became too heavy and it dropped, she'd jerk awake and the walls of the room would present themselves in the moonlight, the furniture taking shape, the embers in the woodstove breathing bright and dark.

She'd grown up with fourteen brothers and sisters, all of them in one room and never enough food. After the death of Samuel Molloy, everyone thought Bride would go back to see her family, but there were the animals and she had to get the wood in, and she felt sluggish, an unfamiliar slow-wittedness that she saw as a side effect of spending time with the dead. She'd felt a leaching of herself out through her left arm that went numb, sitting up next to the coffin. It was the side of her that didn't face the woodstove. Her arm and her thigh were pins and needles and she'd have to rub them vigorously to get the feeling back in them. She knew this was her dead husband clinging onto her. It was not so much that he wanted her to go with him, but that he wanted to stay beside her. After a time, his grip had grown weaker and then he'd been buried.

She'd shut three of the doors on the upstairs bedrooms and slept in the bed where they had slept together, allowing the dog up with her, which was something she knew Samuel Molloy would not condone. She felt his consternation, even from over the road where he was in the grave with the headstone already iced over and gone under the drifts.

During the storm, when evening had set in, the dog started barking at the front door and there was the knock. Bride went to the window but the snow was coming so fast the footprints up the lane had already disappeared.

She opened the storm door and the candle she had was blown out, but it had lit up the cheek and eye of the man standing there, the snow on the brim of his cap, all over his face. She'd blinked into the dark where he was a floating shape in the orange afterglow of her eyelids. When she opened her eyes, she felt the pang of her pupils dilating and she could see him.

He took off his cap. Standing there on the front step he told her who he was and said he'd heard she was a good woman who lost her husband. The door was torn out of her hand and banged on the clapboard and she looked down the road over his shoulder and saw the lamps come on in every window, one at a time, and then two or three at the same time. Everybody watching out for her, even though she was new there, just the eight months, but they were seeing to her.

He was after losing his wife, he said, and she gone and him with their five children, did Bride think they could get married, so she could rear up the children for him.

So, they were married and she reared up Matthew Peach's children in the house left to her by Samuel Molloy, all five of whom went off to Buchans to work the mines, the youngest one, named Matthew after his father, drove the truck in and out with loads of dynamite. Bride had also taken in her blind mother-in-law, who followed a month after the five children, come up from Heart's Desire. The mother-in-law was crooked as sin and she kept a bottle tucked in her chair and each time she woke from a nap, if young Matthew were home from the mine for a visit, the old woman would shake the bottle at him, staring into the empty space a few feet away from where Matthew Peach stood, saying he'd been into it. Saying she was going to redden his arse for him.

Young Matthew Peach had developed a drinking problem, but he swore it was the looseness in his limbs and the blurred vision that kept him from blowing up the trucks he was taking in and out over the worst kind of road full of potholes and rocks. If he wasn't loaded out of his mind, he'd said, he'd have to think about what he was doing and the whole thing would be blown to kingdom come.

John Morris lived with them too, Florence told us. John Morris was a neighbour. He'd lived with his father in the house behind Bride's house on the lane. John Morris's father was a hard man, and John Morris had a terrible case of nerves as a result. When old Mr. Morris was lost in a gale out on the water, Bride took in young John Morris, who had no knowledge of how to use a knife or fork, according to Bride, Florence said. Bride had to teach him this and other things, but throughout the course of his life, John Morris was a recluse, off in the back bedroom, afraid even of the children.

He was still there when I was growing up, Florence said, and hardly ever went out of doors.

Bride's stepchildren were all grown up and working by 1935, but she'd enjoyed raising them up and did her washing in the river and played games with them down there when they were youngsters. They sent what they could back to Bride, and her husband, Matthew Peach, let Bride keep all the money they sent.

Then, on the seventeenth of the month of December, in 1939, Florence said, four youngsters came up the lane with a woman in a navy-blue wool coat with brass buttons. Four children, three girls and a boy, all of them under the age of eight, each a year apart, or less than a year.

They were foster children who hadn't been placed before the Christmas holidays. There were twelve children in the family in total and the parents, Margaret and Edward Miles, had died within two months of each other in the sanatorium in St. John's and the four youngest had been split up from the other eight. These four had shown up at Bride's for her to take in over the month of Christmas until the new year.

Bride and Matthew were too old for foster children, she was fifty at the time, and he sixty-two, and they didn't have a bathroom, only a commode in the room off the stairs.

But when the social worker came back a month and half later, Bride told her to turn around and go back the way she'd come. She said the children weren't going anywhere. She stood on the front porch with the four children scrubbed within an inch of their lives, and the toddler in a knitted angora hat with kitten ears. It was determined that Bride could keep the youngsters if she put in a bathroom.

She used the money from the first set of youngsters she'd reared, money they'd made in the Buchans mines, and had blue tiles put in and painted the whole room blue because it was her favourite colour. The toilet was beautiful, though they'd had to dig up her garden to put down the barrel they used for a septic tank. She had the parlour with all red furniture and they only went in there Christmas morning or if the priest was visiting.

They had a coffin with blue satin lining for Bride Peach when she died, and the youngest of the children, my mother-in-law, Florence, went into St. John's to live with her older sister on the South Side Hills, where she met up with John Callahan, who was nineteen and going off to the Korean War. Florence was bequeathed Bride Peach's house around the bay because the others didn't want the expense of keeping it up, and they had moved permanently to the new suburbs around Cornwall Avenue and Bowring Park and some of them stayed on the South Side. They vacationed in Florida. Florence sold it to Joe and me for four thousand, overcoming her killer real estate agent instincts for a good sale.

Next to a hospital bed with my son in critical condition, my son unconscious with an infection that might kill him, my son who has been stabbed twice, I'm handcuffing the past to the present.

If this, then that.

I'm beginning again with my mother-in-law, Florence, because she died but she's still around.

Seventeen-year-old Bride Peach had just gone out for the wood and her husband of eight months had fallen over dead, Florence told us. She was talking about her own foster mother. This is a story about mothers. How it has nothing to do with blood or choosing or being chosen. It has to do with being able.

It remains to be seen if I am able.

Before Xavier was mobbed by a crowd, dragged out into a snowbank and left for dead.

Or almost left.

As is seen in the video. As is seen in a video that is mostly dark. Faces not revealed, a video with a single streetlight that winks between the shoulders of men who are drunk, or high, young women who have come out in the snow without their coats, wobbling in the way of young women who have the wrong footwear for the occasion, elegantly tilted and off-kilter.

A bottle is raised in a cheer, and a slosh of clear alcohol glug-glugs out of the lip of the bottle. The edge of the glass catches the streetlight, flares bluish, vodka or gin, a boot meets its mark, and they all turn, more or less at the same time, they look in the same direction.

A woman shoving through, a woman is seen tearing at the shoulders of a circle of people trying to kill my son, it looks like a woman, and then the camera is shut off. The clip is one minute and twenty-three seconds and there's no sound.

jules
god's will

I DIDN'T MEET Nancy, my sister-in-law, until she came home from Quebec for our wedding. One of those sisters whose younger brother becomes her shadow throughout their child-hood. Joe, trailing behind her all the way to school and all the way back. Everywhere together, an inviolate bond, full of uncomplicated tenderness, until she got a boyfriend, a teen pregnancy just like Joe's, only a year before him.

Her mother had enrolled Nancy in a typing course as soon as Tristan was born. When Nancy tells this story she pretends to hammer sticky keys with two index fingers.

She met a new guy, ran an antique furniture store in Montreal, driving to decrepit barns in the Quebec country-side, learning to lift from the knees when carrying oak side-boards, the art of restoration, and how to spot a fake finish. The guy tried his hand at disciplining two-year-old Tristan about table manners, it was a tone thing, a snippy formality in the boyfriend's diction, or the hint of irritation toward her son, that rubbed Nancy the wrong way, and she was on the next plane home. That's when we bought the house on Cabot Street together, Joe and Nancy and me, three equal shares. Florence got us a deal.

Nancy had learned French in Montreal and when she came home with Tristan, she enrolled at MUN and became a simultaneous translator, one of those people who knows what someone is going to say, how they will finish a sentence, before they know themselves, so that she speaks in unison with them. Later she settled with a hilarious guy, Todd, a chef on the rigs, restored a big half-fallen-down house around the bay, near our house in Broad Cove, close enough to the ocean they sometimes wake with the salt on the truck's windshield.

At Gerry's birthday party, the first since their mother died, Nancy had asked me to come upstairs, so I could go through her mother's jewellery. Nobody in that family was interested in the jewellery.

But you'll wear it, won't you? Nancy said.

Gerry was probably sixteen when I met him? I asked her.

The window was open a crack and water had pooled on the sill from the morning downpour. My sandals were wet from walking over the grass, but it was already getting hot. I held the cuff of my blouse in my fist and dried the sill with my sleeve.

Gerry is forty now, she said.

Jesus, I said.

Florence had gone to the priest to ask about birth control before Gerry was born, because the doctor had warned another child might kill her. The priest, of course, was adamant. No contraception.

Florence, my dear child, whatever happens is the will of God, he'd said.

She'd had six children, three lived on the mainland. The eldest two, Rob and Matthew, at ExxonMobil, the third, Veronica, worked in television, then Nancy, Joe the professor, and Gerry, who'd built his own trucking company, seven years after Joe.

Upset the apple cart, Florence said of Gerry.

Nell was bringing Mom to the party. I saw them pull up in front of Nancy's garden. Nell popped the trunk and it wagged up and down. She got out of the car, went around to the back, and struggled to drag out the folded wheelchair. She rattled it and put her foot against the bumper, gave a hard tug. She flicked the chair open, fit the cushioned seat and back into place, pushed it over the asphalt to the front passenger door. Mom flung the door open.

My mother had also asked her priest about the pill, just after Nell was born. The priest of her parish was Father Hickey, who later went to prison on multiple charges of child sexual abuse and died in there.

The Old Colony Club, during a dance. The Mickey Michaels Band was playing. My mother had just come off the dance floor and joined her friend Estelle, who had agreed to hold her drink. Next to Estelle was Father Hickey, wearing a black turtleneck and a navy-blue blazer, drinking a beer, in a tall cone-shaped glass. He was charismatic and hip and depraved. My mother asked him if she could start the pill.

Mom wouldn't be risking her life, like Florence, if she had another child. My mother just wanted freedom. Two kids was enough. And she only half believed in God.

She's fun. That's what people would tell me, people she'd worked with over the years. Once at a restaurant, a handsome man, about my age, sitting with a date, glanced at me. The date went to the bathroom and he said, Excuse me? Can I ask you something? Are you Meg Hallett's daughter?

I said I was.

I just love your mother, he said.

You know Mom? I said.

I worked with her. So much fun. Life of the party. Everybody in the office loved her.

Father Hickey was tapping his foot to the Mickey Michaels Band, according to my mother, and wiped at the foam on his lip with the back of his hand, his eyes darting over the dance floor, the satin dresses with the puffed skirts, the rhinestone tiaras, the gyrating hips. He raised the glass in greeting at this one and that one going past, and told my mother, all the while nodding to the music: The only thing you're allowed to do with the pill is hold it between your knees. She stopped going to church.

Gerry came out the front door of the old bay house, striding across the lawn to help with my mother — Nancy had hung a lime-green see-through nylon curtain over the door to keep the flies out. When someone opened the back door, the hem of the curtain kicked out high and straight like a cancan dancer. Gerry didn't lift it out of the way, just bashed through. It clung to him, sucking onto his knees, his cheeks, his arm, the tail end of it fluttering after him and deflating when he elbowed his way out of it. Anything that gets Gerry wants to hang on. He was broad and strong and tanned, full of freckles, gruff and bursting with a tamped-down, perpetual astonishment.

They were all rebellious, Joe and his siblings. The two oldest had taken off to Alberta as fast as their legs could carry them. Veronica, the one in TV, stayed with the older two, in their apartment in Edmonton, for the first few months away from home, worked in the tar sands, bankrolling a trip to Toronto, got herself behind a camera. They'd been led to believe, all of them, they could do whatever they wanted.

Unlike my mother, Florence believed her children should obey her, and they chafed against it. But while my mother believed in honesty, Florence understood the need for privacy, even tolerated lies of omission, expected them. If she asked a direct question, Nancy and Joe sensed a plot and would obfuscate or outright falsify, guided by instinct about how far to swerve from the truth, how much to embellish. They went out into the great wild world, and when they got home something they'd done had inevitably been uncovered. Having sex, obviously, or selling pot. A bit of shoplifting, a failed math test, a loss of faith, cigarettes, a revelation, a saucy comeback, a small hurt, protest against nuclear weapons, Reagan's Star Wars. Their mother had spies or hidden cameras or intuition.

Gerry had always been more forthcoming, less wily by nature. He did not feel the need to lie. Perhaps because Nancy and Joe, the siblings closest to him, had become parents as teenagers, they understood the calamities the truth could unleash.

My parents didn't ask questions, or resort to intuition, they simply waited, and the enormous pressure of silence made the truth explode out of us. We told them everything. Made sure they knew. We caused them a lot of unnecessary worry. This was how Nell and I were raised. Everything was allowed. As disciplinarians, my parents adhered to the policy of Don't Interfere. The arms-length approach. The let-them-make-mistakes approach. The keep-them-alive-is-all approach. That's how they saw their job as parents.

One of my father's friends from the mainland used the word *dialogue* as a verb. He'd told my father it was important to dialogue at the dinner table, if Nell and I were to ever to amount to something.

This came close, for a short time, to clogging up the easy stream of talk during the evening meal. My father began asking in an uneasy, sonorous tone about our beliefs. Were we one hundred percent honest in our dealings with others? Did we adhere to the idea of turning the other cheek? What were the qualities we searched for when choosing a friend?

But they couldn't maintain dialogue-as-a-verb and they'd break into stories about their days at the office, or what they were going to do about the septic tank, and if the babysitter had been paid; it was a relief to them when Nell and I asked if we could go watch TV.

If they felt forced to weigh in, our parents, by a school principal or the parish priest, they gave us the secret wink, or if the situation were completely out of hand, an eyeroll. It meant they'd play along, but also: We got your back. They embraced our failures but told us, in various ways, that we could do better and we could do no wrong. They seemed to believe that, at any given moment in our childhood, we were accounted for, had already amounted to something, if such a thing were possible.

Gerry was commandeering the wheelchair, thrusting and jamming his way over the bumpy lawn, tilting the back down almost to the ground to leverage the contraption over big stones and sudden dips. I could see my mother's terrified/ thrilled face, her hands gripping tight the armrests.

The decision to cut off her leg was abrupt. There had been a lead-up, of course; they'd tried other things. The veins had collapsed, they'd tried a stent. They'd waited for other veins to grow in the foot, sometimes they sprouted, the doctor said, like the roots of a plant cutting in a glass of water. But her foot grew black. First the toes turned plum, and then black, and colour spread and blisters appeared. Over the period of a few days, she sank into and out of delirium. If the pain medication wore off, she writhed, her fists scrunching the bedsheet. Sometimes she had no idea where she was. My father had died when I was sixteen, so she was alone, except for Nell and me, and her own sisters and all the friends she'd worked with over the years. A mountain of chocolate boxes next to her hospital bed. Delirious, or frightened, or clear-eyed and still, quiet with a new kind of wisdom.

But she was wholly present, even affable, when the surgeon appeared with his team and had her read out the release form. She'd made a show of unfolding her reading glasses, and he was equally theatrical, taking a pen from the pocket of his lab coat.

She signed her name.

Later Nell and I sat on the orange chairs in the hallway, and Nell had her elbows on her knees, her short hair clutched in her fists, staring straight ahead.

What will this mean? she asked. And I could see it unfolding in front of her, like a film. She was riveted, tearing at her hair. I thought she'd pull it out. Finally, she sat up. She smoothed her hair down. Sniffed. Crossed her arms, dug her fists into her armpits. One long leg kicked out straight in front of her, the heel of her boot dug into the floor as if she were in danger of sliding to the floor. She was afraid Mom wouldn't make it through the surgery. The difficulties of learning to walk with a prosthesis. Phantom pain. But Nell had faced down her fears in that moment. She intended to be strong, no matter what. As usual. I had no intention of facing anything before it happened.

We went back in the hospital room and my mother's sister, my Aunt Rachel, was gripping the side of the bed railing, looking down on my mother, whose eyes were closed. Mom was deep in the swim of morphine already.

Now then, Meg, Aunt Rachel said. Now then. She asked us a few questions. She mentioned the parking. She'd had to drive around and around the parking lot. She lifted the lid on one of the boxes of chocolates.

Does this come with a map? she asked. But she picked one and popped it in.

Nougat, she said. Meg, this will be over before you know it. Then she unsnapped her purse so it gaped and took out an envelope with a photograph and handed it to Nell.

She snapped the purse shut and changed the water in all the flower vases. When she was done, she held on to the bar on the bedside again and looked at our mother, intent and silent.

It was her decision, Nell said.

Aunt Rachel was shrugging her coat back on and flicking her shawl.

I'll see you girls tomorrow, she said. She left and the door wheezed shut behind her.

Then they came and rolled Mom away.

The surgeon said, Oh the actual surgery is only half an hour tops, you'd be surprised.

We both sat down in the empty hospital room. Nell was still holding the envelope, and she took the photo out.

It was a picture of my mother with two of her friends

when she was nineteen (one of them is cut off, so we only see a shoulder, the photographer, probably her friend Alice). They're in the mirror of the bathroom at the local CBC, where they were all secretaries.

My mother's best friend, Estelle, side by side with Mom, has her hair in a smooth French roll, seen in the reflection from a side mirror, and a dress made for her at Tony the Tailor's. My mother, just as stylish, but her tongue is stuck out and her eyes crossed, her hair in two childish ponytails, sticking up and curling like ram's horns. This is the expression my mother chose at nineteen or twenty, around 1960, to hurl into an unknown future, and from that long-ago time, it has wafted down into Nell's hands.

When Estelle came to visit after the operation, she said, Your mother has never had a bad word to say about anybody.

And it was true. It was not so much a moral stance, but she was able to hold an infinite number of opinions about a person at once. She didn't like that kind of story anyway, nasty gossip, or the stories where people got hurt or behaved badly. She preferred stories of bravado, the small triumph, the near miss, the unlikely love that ended up working out, and she revelled in the off-colour joke. When my cousin, Rachel's son, visited her hospital room after the operation she put on a face, bright and unhindered.

My pedicures are half price, my mother told him.

Nell passed me the photograph. I'd never seen Mom make a face like this, her head tilted, crossed eyes, the tip of her tongue. The flare of the flashbulb in the mirror hovering like an emissary from the past, a spirit there to remind us what we were supposed to be like, even after she was gone, should she ever go, which Nell and I doubted. This was what she expected of us, this tongue sticking out at the camera, at the surgery, at our fear for her, those crossed eyes. Fun, while waiting for that particular half hour to pass.

Later, when we were packing up her hospital room to go to the rehab clinic, I showed Mom the photograph.

You can have it, Mom said.

You don't want it?

Give me the envelope back. I can use that.

I need the envelope to protect it, I said. In my purse, so it doesn't get bent.

She'd always liked her legs. They were long and strong. Nell had the same legs; I got my father's.

trinity
three good signs

TRINITY WAS SEVEN and a half when she moved in with Mary Mahoney. She arrived on Cabot Street with a pregnant social worker in tow. The three of them had spent a long, awful moment close together in the tiny, all-pink bedroom that was going to be Trinity's. There was a pink quilted bedspread with diaphanous flounces, and matching curtains. Even the ceiling was pink. There were pink fabric carnations in a pink vase. A pink record player with silver corners and silver buckles that looked like a suitcase.

A Disney Cinderella lamp on a pink bedside table. Cinderella raising one white gloved arm to gingerly adjust the tilt of her elaborate hat, which was the lampshade. The bulb in the lamp, which Mary Mahoney switched on and flicked off, was also a fleshy pink, and on that very hot afternoon, it tinted the three of them a heatstroke fuchsia.

They each stepped into the narrow bathroom, one behind the other. A tight squeeze. The cat was inside a covered litter box tucked between the toilet and the bathtub.

That's Butterscotch, let's give him some privacy, Mary said. They each left the bathroom and Trinity followed Mary Mahoney and the social worker down the staircase to the living room. There were plates with gold trim lined up on the mantelpiece and a giant row of Beverly Cleary books held up by two marble book ends carved to look like men, their backs against the books, their heels dug in and shoving from the knees to hold the row of spines in place. The fireplace had been boarded up with a piece of plywood painted with a faux-marble design.

There was a three-tiered silver cookie tray, each tier with a different kind of cookie, all of them crusted with freezer burn. They hadn't had time to thaw properly because the social worker and Trinity had arrived a full twenty minutes early, as Mary Mahoney pointed out.

The social worker had done all the talking, from the moment they walked through the front door, which had been about her pregnancy. The doctor had called it a geriatric pregnancy.

Can you believe it? she asked Mary. I'm only thirty-eight. Mary was watching the heels of the social worker's stilettos press little squares into her porch linoleum.

Those are quite the shoes, Mary said.

It's hard to be on my feet, the social worker said. I find they support my arches. I have very high arches.

Indeed, said Mary Mahoney, taking the social worker by the elbow and leading her off the linoleum onto the thick carpet of the hallway. The social worker looked touched rather than scolded by the gesture, and Trinity had the feeling she was about to cry.

I'm four days overdue, the social worker said. She told

them everything her doctor had said at the last appointment. She'd wanted to give birth in the bathtub, as suggested by two of the birthing books she'd read. But the doctor said it was best to lie on her back, feet in the stirrups.

She had a noisy candy in her teeth, spittle hiss-and-clicking with every sentence. Now that they were in the house she seemed entirely unaware of Trinity or Mary Mahoney, or what they were supposed to be doing together here, which was, as she'd put it in the car, handing Trinity off.

She told Trinity somebody else was supposed to do it, hand Trinity off, but the person had called in sick.

Some chance now she's really sick with this, the first day in a week of fog we seen the sun, she said. And no sun in the forecast for another week.

She'd wrenched her arm over the car seat and jerked around to stare out the back window while trying to parallel park in front of Mary Mahoney's house. Her face between the seats, brow straining forward, her deep-set eyes focused on something behind Trinity, her avid and absent expression. She was pouring herself into the job of parking, giving every ounce of herself to it. The car lurched backwards and jerked to little stops. The back fender bumped the car behind her.

That's nothing, the social worker determined. Let's get this over with, shall we?

She turned off the car, got out and opened Trinity's door, leaned over her to undo the seatbelt, which had a smear of somebody else's raspberry jam. She half lifted Trinity out of the booster seat with a groan that seemed to come from the fireball in the centre of the earth, through the earth's crust, which they had learned about in grade one, up through her spiked heels, and her spine, forcing itself, the groan, muffled, from her hard-set lips. Their chests had been pressed together and Trinity felt the thrum of it.

The social worker led Trinity to the back of the car and examined both fenders. She spit on her fingers and rubbed the other car's chrome.

That scratch has been there for ages, she said. I never done it.

She stood and put down her sunglasses which had been sitting in her thick, unnaturally black hair. She took a quick scan of all the windows on the opposite side of the street to see if anyone was watching.

Then she took Trinity by both hands and bent painfully down on one knee, folded the other knee too, right there on the sidewalk, as if kneeling at an altar, or proposing marriage, so that she and Trinity were eye to eye. She licked her index finger and smoothed one of Trinity's eyebrows.

As if we have time to worry about a little scratch, she said. She spoke with an authority that was heady and clarifying. It made Trinity even more frightened about what was coming.

She knew the social worker wasn't talking about the scratch on the bumper but expressing a solidarity. They were both terrified because they'd found themselves in situations beyond their control.

This would be the way of it for the foreseeable future. The social worker would not lift a hand help Trinity after this moment, but she was here now, they were joined together by the social worker's grip on Trinity's hands. They had shared something, the complicated entanglements of fate, the social worker had been brought to her knees in the hard sunshine, spit washing the child's face, gripping the child's hands, really looking at her, taking her in.

She was saying they each had to accept their situation.

I'm after ruining my stocking down here on the sidewalk, she said. The social worker was letting Trinity know that she was definitely worth the pair of stockings, maybe all the stockings in the world. But she was also telling Trinity that she was on her own, going forward. No matter what was on the other side of the screen door, Trinity would have to make do. All the social worker could offer was a concentrated moment of mutual sympathy. Then, with sudden vehemence, the social worker slapped her own neck. It was as if, like everything else about her body, her hand had acted by itself. The print of her hand on her white neck and there on her palm, a squashed mosquito, which she held out for Trinity to see.

I got it, she whispered. She rubbed the dead insect off her hand onto her floaty dress and got up from her knees. The moment was over. The social worker was rapping on Mary Mahoney's screen door.

They'd done the tour of the house and Mary Mahoney had sat with her back to the window, so all Trinity could really see was the foster parent's hands loosely clasped on her lap and a stillness that was unnerving. Out of nowhere, creeping with stealth, a white-and-caramel cat leapt up into Mary Mahoney's lap.

One of the old woman's hands buried itself in the fur, and her strong, bony fingers arched and dove, over and over, in rhythm with the social worker's speedy, unrelenting monologue about her doctor, who she was convinced was a drunk.

This is Butterscotch, Mary Mahoney said, speaking over the social worker, who didn't stop to acknowledge the interruption, although the old woman had already told them the cat's name upstairs.

Nice cat, Trinity said.

Wasn't nice when I got him, Mary Mahoney said. With the one eye hanging out on his cheek.

They'd had to take the eye, she said. Didn't they? What else could they do? It took Trinity a moment to realize Mary Mahoney was addressing the cat. She'd thought at first it was a skill-testing question.

Couldn't they just stick it back in? the social worker said. Why did it have to come out at all? She sounded plaintive, weary.

Mind you, they did a nice job, sewing it up. Smart, though, this cat. Like the whip. You couldn't get one over on this old fellow.

They'd each fallen into a kind of stagnant pathos, hypnotized by the scratching hand on the cat's back, the knuckles too large, rigorous. The social worker had nearly been swallowed by the couch, she was listing to the side and had to put her arm out straight on the armrest to keep from falling over. It was clear the social worker wanted to get going.

This is my last job, she said. Before I go on maternity leave.

You'll want to get that bath poured, for the birth, Mary Mahoney said. Even at seven, Trinity understood Mary Mahoney was poking fun. It was clear to both of them the social worker was terrified of the birth, and maybe even the motherhood that would follow.

Trinity had never been told about giving birth, as the social worker called it, but she understood motherhood to be an inescapable torment that happened by accident and that "giving" was a euphemism. Doesn't the baby get taken out of her somehow? What does giving have to do with it?

The cat turned its horrible face into a shadow cast by the armchair, and Trinity saw the cavity where the eye had been.

She thought of the stiffness in Mary Mahoney, the timbre of her voice, when she said the cat had needed privacy. It was the first sign that the new home might be better than the last. The tiers of frozen cookies, way too many for them to eat, was the second good sign. It was about show, and Trinity knew the importance of appearances. The cat's missing eye was the third good sign. Mary Mahoney cared about appearances only to a point. She could love something no matter what it looked like or how vulnerable it was.

The two of them sat in silence while the social worker continued with her story about the last visit to the doctor. She suddenly rose up out of the couch and wrenched at her dress, pulling it tight against the medicine ball stomach, and approached the cookies, took a chocolate chip cookie in one hand, and held the other like a plate underneath her chin. She spoke through the crumbs on her lips.

I'm after leaving a few papers in the car, she said. That's all that's left, the papers. Then I'm done. I just have to get the papers, have you sign them, bring them back to the office, and get this thing out me.

She went out the front door, and they could hear the beep of her keys unlocking her car.

Will you help yourself to a cookie? Mary Mahoney asked.

Trinity said, No thank you. They said nothing more, as if they were in church. Then the social worker was back. She laid the papers out on the side table. She stood with her hand on the small of her back.

Sometimes I feel like the spine is going to crack right off me, she said.

Mary Mahoney signed and signed. Then she gathered the papers and knocked the bottom edge of them against the desk and passed them to the woman. She picked up a square of paper towel, of which there were three, next to the cookie display, and she stacked three chocolate chip cookies, two shortbreads, and a date square and handed it to the social worker.

I couldn't, the social worker said. I'm at high risk of diabetes. I'm not allowed to eat sugar.

My guess is that baby will be here in a couple of days. You can eat whatever you like, Mary Mahoney said. The social worker put one of her hands on her belly.

I need more time than that, she said.

Two days, Mary Mahoney said. Not a moment more, I guarantee.

I haven't packed my bag, my hospital bag.

You best get at it. Tell the doctor that if you feel like it, you'll be doing handstands or cartwheels or swinging from the light fixtures while you give birth. It's your birth, you tell him.

He said I'll be in so much pain I won't know what I'm at.

Nonsense, Mary Mahoney said. And with a hand on the woman's back, gave her a little nudge out the front door.

jules
attention

THESE WERE THE things I loved about Joe when we were twenty-three: his thighs in faded jeans, crouched to tie his five-year-old daughter Stella's scarf. The freckles on his pale arms, the moment before he changed lanes, careful, when he flicked his eyes to the side mirror and looked over his shoulder.

The Lada he was driving. I hadn't got my licence yet, and maybe that's significant. We each had the parts the other lacked. But it was unfolding too fast for any sort of tally. We had no idea what it was because we were in it. The Lada was white, and his head touched the ceiling. We were very Soviet spy.

We had to park the car on a hill to get it going — the front doors open — and we leaned into it, our bodies at an angle, the balls of our feet digging into the pavement as we pushed, then jogging beside it, still pushing, but holding on in case it rolled away and jumping inside when the engine caught. Blue smoke we could taste. It backfired and people shifted their curtains to peek out, all down the street. The air-splitting surprise of it seemed the music of our life. Or the music was a cassette of Van Morrison, or Blondie, all chewed up by the car's tape player. Bob Dylan, a hard rain. A hole in the floor on the passenger side through which you could see the asphalt streaming like a silk scarf.

Bought the Lada for fifty bucks and Joe's father said: They saw you coming.

I loved his hair, long and shiny, pulling my fingers through the curls and tangles. The drawings Stella made on newsprint stuck all over walls of his apartment. I loved Stella, for whom I cooked the only dish I was sure of, macaroni and cheese with crushed crackers on top, crushing the crackers with her, the still-pudgy fists, spiky shards of saltines poking through her fingers like medieval weaponry; his books, the Tandy computer, the candles, how he'd folded open a faux-woodgrain vinyl door that led to a walk-in closet from which leaked the supernaturally bright light and verdant stink. Pot bushes, maybe five or six beef buckets full of black soil, I'd press into the illicit jungle and obliterating light to get at the plants in the back with the elegant watering pitcher shaped like a swan, the price tag from the Sally Ann still on the chest of it. The leaves prickly when I brushed them with my hand. The sticky velvet smell on my fingers.

It was very cold, the evening we finally got together. The stars were ice chips. I'd been walking to the Grad House after my art history class, Canadian Landscape, taught by a man who smoked during the lectures, tiny tubes of ash held in the folds of his black scholarly robe, whatever they're called, some of the Brits wore them, flapping around the halls like downed crows, and there was a sheath of ice all over the branches in Bannerman Park, lit up by the streetlights.

Everybody had decided on the Grad House earlier in the afternoon, when we were between classes. A table in the university cafeteria and Joe coming over to bum a smoke. Roberta White trawling her purse for him, putting a smoke in her mouth so it stuck to her lower lip; it wagged up and down as she spoke. She was all industry and business, getting that smoke out.

Telling him we were going to the Grad House for a few beers later on. She jostled the pack so one cigarette jutted up and she held it out to him.

Come with us, Joe, she said. She might just as easily have said, Clear off this table with a sweep of your arm and let's climb on.

I might, he said. Glancing down over all the tables and the lineup at the Snack Bar toward the exit, as if there were someone a long way off with whom he'd have to consult before committing to Roberta. He ran his big, beautiful hands down his thighs and patted his jeans pockets, front and back and his chest, but his lighter was gone, he said. He'd had one, a pink one, but it was gone, and he took the smoke and leaned in to light it from Roberta's cigarette.

I'd known Roberta White in elementary school. She was the first person I knew to have a disco ball at a birthday party. She'd invited the whole class, which set a precedent that was judicious and fair-minded, except not everybody had the means to follow suit. Loot bags were a fortune. So the number of parties fell to about half for the rest of the year.

Everything was spattered with ovals of spinning light at her birthday party. When she opened a present she liked, she'd raise her arms in the air and bring both fists down, mouthing the words *all right*, eyes shut. Then we danced and she did the bump with her closest friend, they had clearly rehearsed, two of them banging hips together, and Roberta hopping and holding out her bum for the other girl to knock with her hip.

Roberta was in her second year, doing archeology. Had he slept with her already?

I just might, Joe said. The Grad House? Maybe, yeah.

Joe let the tip of his cigarette touch hers. Both tips lit up, went dark, lit up. The whole thing so intimate that I was embarrassed to watch it. I picked up my knapsack and started shoving my books inside it so I wouldn't have to look. I stood and my chair, with my heavy winter jacket slung over the back, tipped over and when I tried to catch it, my bag knocked somebody's coffee. Everyone on my side of the table jerking back so it wouldn't spill into their laps, people gathering their papers off the table as the running splats threatened everything. Roberta stalked over to the counter for the napkins.

I was hefting my knapsack onto my shoulders and Joe handed me a piece of paper with a drawing of mine on it. It had been going around the table because I'd handed it to someone who asked what I was working on. A sketch for a painting of Derek, a former boyfriend, his head thrown back, exposing his throat, his chest, one knee coyly bent to hide his genitals, all of it foreshortened, his naked foot larger than his head. A lot of attention to the wrinkles in the bedsheet.

Don't forget your sexy drawing, Joe said.

HERE'S HOW SMALL St. John's is: before I got to know Joe I was a babysitter for his five-year-old daughter in exchange for painting lessons from Sabine O'Regan, Stella's grand-mother on her mother's side.

I was teaching Stella to swim at the Aquarena. I was back in St. John's after Stephenville for the two-year diploma course in fine art at the community college, and on to Nova Scotia College of Art and Design, where I had one semester left for my degree. I was taking time off, subletting a small apartment on Bond, waitressing, dancing in bars until three in the morning, doing the course at MUN.

I made the deal with Sabine because I wanted to keep painting. I'd taken her classes when I was fourteen and fifteen, but my parents had paid for those. I couldn't afford her, so we worked out the deal. She was strict and critical, and I needed to be kept in line.

Sabine was a skeletal woman with steel-coloured curls. Those glossy, tight curls followed the shape of her head so closely she looked shorn and priestlike. When she smoked, her cheeks caved and her eyes widened and she jerked her head to the side to exhale through her nostrils first, then her mouth. Everything was deliberate, and often I knew she was standing behind me in class because a skein of smoke would float over my shoulder. She was the only woman I knew who wore black eyeliner, with a tail at the outer corner of her eyes that made her look perpetually alert.

She'd take the brush from my hand, filling it with paint from my palette. She didn't seem to care what colour, because her eyes never left the street scene, or park, or still life, or whatever I was trying to paint—and she'd draw lines right on top of my canvas so that the space extended or unfurled, a street went on forever toward the vanishing point. It was a desecration that produced depth.

Everyone else in the class was a retired civil servant or teacher or dentist who'd taken up a hobby. They were, those other painters, far better artists than me, because they had the patience to look at the subject for a long time before they touched the canvas. At the Nova Scotia College of Art and Design, realism was definitely *not* the thing. We'd been taught conceptual art, Joseph Beuys, Vito Acconci, June Leaf. Painting what was in front of you was old-fashioned. But Sabine insisted I learn how to do it. She was of a generation who believed in acquiring a skill to fall back on. One should only deviate from realism once you had mastered it. Make something look like what it was, then you could get fancy.

Sabine let me know there was very little indication that I had any kind of talent or skill, conceptual or otherwise, but we both politely avoided that concern. I thought of talent as being like the garlic with the vibrant green shoots I'd seen for the first time at the new health food store downtown—in order to be any good at making art, I'd need one of those half-sinister, stinky things in my chest where my heart should be.

Sabine's house—I'd wait on the couch in the living room for Stella each Tuesday afternoon at three o'clock—was an old Victorian three-storey with Persian carpets and embroidered wool shawls from Kashmir draped over the sofas (they'd done a stint there; her husband, twenty-five years older than Sabine, had been in the British government), hand-painted silk scarves (not tie-dyed) on the lamp shades, an easel in the middle of the dining room, all the furniture pushed out of the way.

There was between us, in the painting/babysitting exchange, an abrupt intimacy. The passing off of towels and swimming goggles, me doing Stella's zipper because it always stuck if not tugged with exactly the right amount of force, a rush for the bus, and on Sabine's side, the refiguring of my painting so it suddenly *worked*, as if she were showing me that perspective was more than an illusion or cheap trick. It was a philosophy: the things we want might be far away from us. Consider the long haul.

Also, that there was no such thing as the painter; when she slashed her own lines across my work, I wondered what belonged to me, and what belonged to her.

The painting mattered, not the painter.

I didn't matter. It's a stinging revelation. I had been brought up to believe I mattered very much. Me and my sister, Nell. We mattered. Sabine had a dimple on one side of her mouth in the uncomfortable moments when she inflicted revelations on her students. In those moments she had an unfaltering, stiff smile, and the dimple was rueful. She could see I thought too much of myself.

It was because I'd grown up wandering around in the woods, reading *Black Beauty* and *Five Little Peppers and How They Grew*, everything by Judy Blume, skating on the lake, riding horses from the local riding school in St. Philip's, mucking out stalls, until my father's construction company went bankrupt. The confidence I'd had was only skin deep; most of me was uncertain.

We were, both Sabine and me, getting in the bargain something of a raw deal. It would take me a lifetime to master perspective, and that was if I stuck with it.

In exchange for teaching me this, Sabine received four hours of solitude in which to paint the commissions that paid her mortgage. She was the only female artist I'd ever met who shouldered a mortgage by herself. Whatever her husband had made had been lost by the time he died, when she was in her late forties. She had books with receipts that she tore out one by one, waving them in the air as if to dry the ink. Her signature was legible, but full of spikes.

She'd painted a number of politicians and sometimes their children and their wives. These portraits relied on chiaroscuro and they were unapologetically complimentary. She couldn't keep up with the commissions. She slapped on lashings of varnish, crackled and yellowed as a Rembrandt, artificially distressed like my acid-washed jeans. A cheek too rosy, hair too shiny. She was worn out trying to fill the orders. Sabine had done two decades of the rosy white men who were Speakers of the House of Assembly. They were all hung too high in the chamber, side by side, all appearing both miffed and wistful. Several had taken off their glasses for the sitting, and near-sightedness made them docile.

Sabine's real art, what she called her *work* at that time, was a series of paintings about dancers, athletes, metal bands, anything where bodies moved, flung themselves at each other, or up into the air. Activities that required strength and grace. One afternoon—back during that first summer I'd studied with her—she invited me to the Arts and Culture Centre, where she was sketching from backstage during a rehearsal. She'd spread big sheets of newsprint on the floor, was drawing on her hands and knees, her head raised, staring forward at the dancers, even as her hand scribbled over the paper with fat sticks of charcoal.

Gesture drawings, sometimes gouging through the paper. She sprayed them with hairspray, the only fixative you could get in St. John's at the time, and I'd watched the particles of spray sift down through the beams of the footlights in silvery clouds.

I felt the breeze when the dancers' bodies cut through the air. They hammered the floor when they landed.

The strong, frantic drawing made Sabine's cheeks flush. Her marks were full of the dancers' muscle strain, clench and stretch, pirouettes, big calves, men lifting women into the air, even tossing them across the stage from one man to another.

I'd seen Joe here and there over the years, at the Ship, at Bar None. But the year I had the babysitting arrangement I started to see him everywhere with Stella. He had her on his shoulders at the Thompson Student Centre. Sometimes he bought her an orange juice at Duckworth Lunch, and a peanut butter cookie. He and Stella's mother, Marianne, were still friends. Then I ran into him at Sabine's house; he was there to pick up his daughter.

That might have been the very moment I fell in love with him, or at least his hair. How he tucked it behind his ear with his big fingers. His chin on the top of his daughter's head while he reached around her with both arms to tug the back loop on her bright red winter boots.

She was beautiful, of course. She was one of those kids with deep brown eyes and springy curls that strangers in the supermarket exclaim over.

Stella was struggling against Joe, she was too hot in the snowsuit, the nylon swishing as she tried to wriggle out of his grasp. It was late in the afternoon and she writhed, bent on making him chase her for the fun of it, or else the whole thing would end in a tantrum. She'd recently given up her afternoon naps. The snowsuit was too small, but they'd wanted to get another winter out of it.

He was so gangly and comfortable in the loose hand-knit sweaters, he had a beret from St. Pierre, which he could get away with — there was the intensity, when he talked about his courses. He looked me in the eyes while talking about the difference between use value and exchange value.

There was a snow squall that day, and when I left Sabine's house, my hair was still wet and smelled of chlorine.

It was hard to think of Sabine as a grandmother, despite the smell of baking gingerbread that wafted from the kitchen. Joe, checking the little knapsack for bedtime stories, the rag doll, a juice box, pajamas and clean socks for the morning. Taking everything out and laying it on the step beside him.

You're the one doing painting classes with Sabine in exchange for babysitting? he asked me, looking up from the little bag as he shoved the things back in.

This is the famous Julie, Sabine said. But maybe you two know each other already?

We've seen each other around, I said. She was leaning against the door frame of the living room, shaking out a match after she'd lit her cigarette. Still flicking her wrist after it was out, a line of smoke from the burnt tip.

I didn't know you were Sabine's student, Joe said.

I'm not very good, I said. I was surprised to find that I didn't want him to know about the painting classes. We were painting lobster pots and driftwood, a killick and a vase of flowers, the folds of the satin cloth on the plinth; there was no talking in the classroom, the silence broken only by the smallest noises. The swish of a brush in a jar of turps across the room; Sabine's heels as she walked around the perimeter of the circle of easels, stopping at each one, until she had materialized behind me. The woman who painted next to me cracked her knuckles whenever she stood back from her canvas to look at her painting from a distance, pulling hard on each finger, first the fingers of one hand, then the other, and then the thumbs.

It was a time when, at every turn, in every other part of my life, it seemed I had to prove something. I had to ride my bike to town, I had to make tips. I had to serve people. I had to finish my degree. But not in Sabine's painting class. It was about laying one colour next to another to see which would recede, which would appear to leap into the foreground—how the surface and depth shifted.

But I realized for the first time, standing in the porch with Joe, that Sabine's approval mattered to me very much. It was meant to be a business transaction, but I loved teaching Stella to swim, watching her handstands in the shallow end, her feet kicking in the air, until she toppled over, and her face when she surfaced, the film of water spilling away from the top of her head, her laughter.

Sabine's eyes narrowed as she watched us—Joe and me.

I've got her little lunch box, she called over her shoulder. All packed for the morning.

I considered forgetting about Joe while I was tying up my boots in Sabine's porch. Someone had broken up with him, and I wasn't sure it was over. I'd heard he was tangled in some drama. The feeling in my chest. The blood pounding in my head. I felt like I couldn't speak a straight sentence. Just a crush. But the intimacy in the porch, the gloomy shadows and whispering of Stella's snowsuit. I'd had a few longish relationships, and some short ones. None of them had started with this thumping. I was blushing. My whole body blushed. Every part of me. Other relationships had been deliberate at first, had required I coax myself into them like diving into a lake. Cold, but nice once you're in.

Besides, there was someone else interested in me, a guy doing engineering who I really needed to give more consideration. Rugby player. I felt certain he was going to lose his front teeth at a game, and I'd given that some thought. We'd gone to a play and out for dinner. He'd made the mistake of glancing at the menu while I was telling a story. He'd also had a belt with canisters for water that he wore when long-distance running, and his preparedness turned me off. I didn't want to go out with anyone who was prepared or distracted, or even the opposite: persistent. He'd called three times after the date. Engaged my mother in conversation when she answered the phone. Even she felt he was too charged up and dogged, though she didn't say it in those words.

She'd said, He seems well mannered, which we both understood to mean not much fun.

Sabine came back with the lunch box and snapped on the overhead light. Maybe she wanted me to get a good look. Stella's mother had another boyfriend. They'd moved in together. Stella split the week between Joe's and Marianne's, alternating three days and four. Both grandmothers took Stella when Joe and Marianne worked. It was hard to imagine a child more loved and cared for.

I was probably the worst student Sabine had ever encountered. I'd done all that schooling. But I hadn't learned to draw. I knew how to solder precious metals in order to make jewellery, we'd had a guest lecturer from Ontario who made vagina brooches in gold each with a tiny diamond for a clitoris, or a garnet or a bit of beach glass. We were all just out of high school when we went to Stephenville. The artist had given a lecture with a slide show and the brooch was enlarged on the screen, the size of a grown man, all the golden folds, the little hood over an emerald clitoris.

It took us a minute.

In Stephenville we'd done an art history survey course, studied the Venus of Willendorf, who looked to me ambushed and gobbled whole by her pregnancy, more an advocate for birth control than fertility fetish, and the cave paintings of Lascaux. The overhead lights off, curtains drawn, a screen with slides, the Impressionists, Expressionists, the melted clocks and sliced eyeballs of the Surrealists, and on up through Robert Rauschenberg's goat's head coming through an old tire, with a broken rope attached. Duchamp's toilet. Michael Snow's *Walking Woman* figures. Rothko. Greg Curnoe, Joyce Wieland's quilts. We'd learned our way around a darkroom. We made terracotta casts of our breasts and asses and fired them in the kiln, hung them on the walls of our studio spaces. The art school was in the buildings of an old army barracks. The water pipes were loud, the radiators banged as if the building were haunted, and there were big windows. The swinging beam from a lighthouse swept through in the evening.

What Sabine offered was something concrete — realism was not fanciful. It was constraining, and I needed constraint. I was all over the place.

She's not a bad painter, Sabine said. There's something going on there. It was a mild endorsement, but I knew what it meant. She thought it was a good idea, Joe and me. Both Sabine and I knew that whatever had happened to me in the porch, how addled and red and suddenly incoherent, might be a lasting condition. It was as if a tornado had entered the porch and picked me up and flung me around in a whirling do-si-do. Of course, Joe had no idea.

Putting my boots on, tugging hard on the laces. I had to get out of there.

Joe was not intimidated by Sabine, in fact he was part of her family now because of Stella, belonging in the midst of the silk scarves and the little French phrases she used now and then, the smell of turps and linseed, the big white stretchers, the fireplace. The charcoal drawings of women flinging themselves across a dance floor, one that showed the toss of a head, the sharp bones of the clavicle, the hockey players smashing into each other, a lead singer gyrating against his guitar.

The last thing I wanted was a guy I'd have to yearn over if he was still interested in someone else.

Yearning was untenable. This was what my own mother had taught me. My father had died, and the most terrifying thing was the brutality of yearning. The grip of it.

It was as though Sabine had taken the brush from my hand again. Making me think about perspective, distance. The long haul.

Maybe you should both come to dinner, she said. I'm having some artists over. Joe, you might enjoy that. It's all Marxism with him, and that — who is it? Foucault. What was the book, *Discipline and Punish*? Parenting self-help book. Joe glanced up, startled. But I knew she was joking.

She meant I should pay attention if I wanted something and I'd have to act and that it wouldn't be easy. Of course, she was right. Because this is a story about my son and how he was stabbed at a party and beaten by a handful of monsters and how nobody chooses yearning, it chooses you.

jules
the swan

THE SWAN HAD reared up against the hot breeze, the webbed orange feet, barely visible in the murk beneath it, churning the placid water into a boiling mass of bubbles which propelled it at a sinister speed to the shore.

It came at Xavier and Trinity and me with its breast thrust forward, wings half raised and spread, a sundrenched white-hot fire, unbearable, until it hit shore when the S of its neck went bolt straight, the beak wrenched wide, hissing.

A hurling missile of spite, the swan shot itself across the apron of gravel that lay at the foot of the grassy slope where people had put down blankets and spread little picnics or toys. Parents grabbing up their toddlers and turning their backs, hunching over their children, the air chopped by the beating wings; parents dangling kids by the armpit, by the back of the shirt, the waistband of their pants, trying to get them out of the swan's path, grabbing up diaper bags, purses, juice boxes, collapsed umbrella strollers—tumbling over the debris of early childhood. Xavier grabbing up his soccer ball.

But it was eight-year-old Trinity the swan wanted; Trinity's little back in her striped halter top, arched away from the open-throated hisses, the dangerous beak; Trinity's head twisted backwards as she ran, eyes wide with terror to see how close it was, and me with her hand gripped in my fist, crushing the little bones, pulling her out of her own gait, discombobulating her escape, making her stumble and almost fall, but throwing her in front of me with centrifugal force, flinging her out of the way at the last minute and turning on the swan, swinging my red sweater at the ball of feathers and fishy stink.

It gave up, not because of me, but because Trinity had crossed an invisible line, she'd neared the top of the embankment, and the swan gave up on her.

The swan stopped under the shade of a maple. The white feathers, dirt-streaked up close, a filigree of algae stuck to it.

It turned with a daintified shudder, shook out its wings, stripped naked of the floaty weightlessness it had in the water; it seemed disoriented and began an off-balanced trundle back to the water's edge.

Once it had glided to the middle of the pond, the swan turned to give us its incandescent profile, a white bonfire, benign as a jigsaw puzzle.

Trinity wiped her eyes, rubbing tears away on my shirt sleeve.

On the way home I happened to glance at Xavier in the rearview mirror. I knew we were both thinking of it, the swan close enough we could smell the boggy funk, the churning wings, the air chuffing toward us. The damp melodrama that lasted less than a minute, or maybe a minute and a half.

I'd known Xavier was beside me. I could have grabbed

him too. In fact, I had tripped over him a little, his foot hooking mine, as he scrabbled up from the grass.

Our eyes met in the rearview and I think we were living through it again together, Xavier and me. It might have seemed an inconsequential moment, had the circumstances of our lives been even very slightly different at that time. Sometimes I think that way about potent incidents — that significance ricochets, searching for a place to land.

Maybe it mattered to the swan I wasn't Trinity's mother when it attacked her. Trinity had needed a magical shield, the kind of force a real mother might provide, or even the kind that Mary Mahoney, her foster mother, could have given her, an airtight contract signed by the director of social services and Mary herself, and whoever else, a guarantee that Trinity would be protected, especially against arbitrary attacks, which she'd already seen a lot of. I was only the neighbour across the street who invited her in to play with my son.

What I'd offered was flimsy, full of loopholes, and the fact that I'd stood between her and the swan was only a matter of happenstance.

The other parents on the hill were brought together in a kind of bashful relief once the swan had turned away from the children. The violent bird, wings spread full span, neck out like a shot arrow, had turned back to stately elegance so quickly we felt foolish for having been startled.

The incident seemed to have been entirely forgotten when we went to look for our car on the parking lot. The kids hadn't wanted to go to the park in the first place, they'd have been happy to stay in the cool living room playing video games. It was too hot, and the day had been an epic journey, the swan a sidebar.

We'd stopped for ice creams and there was a lineup and both children were on the verge of one of those fitful tantrums that mothers never see coming or understand the cause of until the tantrum is full-blown; Trinity and Xavier had been zapped by exhaustion. They'd had too much sun; Xavier had been in the pool, Trinity kicking her legs over the edge, afraid of the water, even in the shallow end, all the splashing and noise, lifeguard whistles, chlorine; the swings, they'd both hung from their knees, upside down on the monkey bars, their faces bright red with blood, Trinity's blond ponytail swishing back and forth in the dust. Sometimes they seemed fused, just one child instead of two. Other times they were ready to annihilate each other.

Xavier's ice cream had dropped off his cone into the dirt and he had demanded that Trinity give him hers. He said that I was his mother and I had paid for it, so now that there was only one left, it should belong to him.

She looked up at me with those eyes, and I said I would get him another one. Everything could be solved this way, I wanted to tell them. We would just get more of everything. As long as I was around, I'd see to it.

People let us back in the line. The entire crowd at the ice cream stand had said *Awwww* when the pink blob dropped into the asphalt. The girl behind the counter gave us the replacement cone for free.

But when I caught Xavier's eye in the mirror, it was the swan we were thinking of, living through again. The terror in Trinity's eyes as she'd glanced back, he'd seen it too, her shifting shoulder blades as she worked her arms, the jiggling string of her halter top on her tanned shoulders, the arch in her back, trying to get away from the beak and how close the swan had been. They'd just wanted to stay in front of the computer monitor playing Mario, or whatever it was, eating Twizzlers. I had put them in harm's way. We were both seeing it again, Xavier and me, just as if we were still there on the hill with the scrambling parents. Trinity had been a silhouette. I'd had to hold my hand over my eyes to see her. The sunlight catching her hair lifting in the breeze, or it was alive with static electricity in the impossible heat of that afternoon, making it look fiery. The edge of the black pond was burning with light. She turned and ran and there were screams around me and the bird was almost on top of us before I knew what was happening, but I had not thought of Xavier.

This was what he and I both knew on the drive home. When our eyes met in the rearview, we had the same thought together: he had been there too. I had not given him a thought.

But he'd got back up on his own and I'd known that would happen.

I hadn't noticed him at the time, or worried about him, or felt any instinct to protect him; this realization came to me as I drove past Corpus Christi Church on the way back down to Cabot Street over Waterford Bridge Road.

I'd thought that nothing would ever get close enough to hurt him. I'd believed he was invincible. I think it was just easier to believe that back when he was eight. The vigilance required to protect something I loved as much as him, to create the forcefield, a wall four feet thick of granite or magic, or whatever forcefields are made of, to keep out the minor inconsequential dangers, the horrors that infect children's dreams, the very bad luck, evil spirits, it was too much when he was little. It was easier to pretend he didn't need me; he would always be okay. But only a fool could have believed such a thing of Trinity. For all her tough-girl act, even at eight, anybody could see she was fragile. Even the bloody swan.

He let his forehead touch the glass and fell asleep.

When we arrived home, Mary Mahoney was standing on her front step.

Trinity was late for her supper. I was, by the dashboard clock, only eight minutes late, but Mary Mahoney was pissed. Trinity would not be allowed over to play for a day or two, a punishment for me rather than Trinity. The sun was already turning the street pink.

I'd told Trinity it would be better if she didn't mention the ice cream. I said it could be our secret, because in truth, it had been too close to supper for ice cream, I'd lost track of time, I said, and Mary wouldn't be pleased. But when I said ice cream, I'd meant not to mention the swan. I didn't say it, though, and I had no such telepathic powers with Trinity Brophy.

I saw that Xavier had a bad sunburn, and a little flame of steam was on the window-glass near his mouth, he was dead to the world. Our brief mind-meld had zonked him out. I wished I could give in like that, simply shut down when I felt like it.

Those days when Mary Mahoney didn't have a migraine, she'd allow Xavier into her house and she made rocky road squares with coloured miniature marshmallows and coconut and chocolate, which were his favourite. But she let me know he was too rambunctious.

She judged Joe and me too. Once we'd put a mattress out on the street and the removal van had come two weeks late. The truth was Joe and I were both working and forgot about it. The removal van wasn't late, neither of us had called for one.

Also, we were in love and having parties and getting drunk and smoking weed and the children were at the parties, and all our friends' children and the kids slept in a heap on the jackets of the guests in front of the TV in the big third-floor bedroom, all of which Mary Mahoney could surely imagine, watching people come and go from her living room window.

There was, in her very posture, such a tight-assed propriety. Even the migraines she claimed to suffer from — the only thing capable of causing her to deviate from her daily routine — were faced with a melancholic stoicism.

Someone had filed a formal complaint with the city about the mattress, and we received a warning, were threatened with a fine. I suspected Mary had made the call.

xavier
shopping cart

THEY WERE IN the middle of a junior high basketball tournament, on a lunch break in Churchill Square, when they found
the cart. It was a long way from the supermarket. The metal
casing for the front wheel was bent out to the side. The cart
useless and rusty. Kenny Burke and Max Hickman leaned it
against a fire hydrant to bang the wheel straight with a rock.
The clang rang out over the parking lot and there were a few
tiny sparks. They took turns whaling on it until they got the
casing for the wheel straightened out.

Xavier was planning to get in the cart and the rest of the
basketball team would push it to the first steep hill they could
find and let him go. They'd known without speaking about
it who would get in the cart. It was clear, as they hammered,
that someone had to fly down the first hill they could find.
Xavier stood apart and surveyed the work. They all knew it
would be Xavier, but Kenny and Max worked silently, and
everybody else watched without speaking.

They'd push him up Bonaventure, past Brother Rice,

where the basketball tournament would start up again after the lunch break, past St. Bon's on one side of the street and The Rooms on the other, and they'd let him go at the top of Garrison Hill. He'd be standing up in the cart, that's the way they all saw it unfolding, his arms out to the sides, wind and sun on his face, the vibrating roar and rattle of it coming up through his sneakers.

He'd abandon the cart at the last second, throw himself onto the asphalt before the cart smashed into the fence that protected the war memorial at the foot of the hill. Or he might somersault over the spear-tipped iron fence that surrounded the memorial or be impaled on it.

They'd been to Subway and got out of hand. Some of the boys had been antic and loud. They'd dropped the wrappers from their sandwiches all over the floor, and William LeGrow tore up the bottom half of his sub bun and smeared the guts of it over the tables on purpose. Mercer was rude to the girl behind the counter, had mimicked her when she told them to leave, his hands on his hips, a soprano pitch. Mercer had shot up, taller than all of them, and his bashful hovering had made him look as though he'd been dismantled and put back together with pieces missing, except when he was on the basketball court. He made up for his hunched shoulders and involuntary barks of nastiness with a physical beauty and grace that appeared only on the gym floor, loping toward the basketball net.

They'd taken fistfuls of drinking straws and torn off the paper sleeves and joined each straw together by fitting one end into the next, until they had fashioned flimsy swords, maybe seven or eight straws in length.

The manager had appeared from the back and kicked them out. William made fun of his beard net. He had a hairnet on his beard, and they were all weak with giggles and snorting laughter at the thought of wearing one of those, or even at having hair on your face. They rose from the table slowly, trying to stab each other with the flaccid swords, banging into each other in the porch, Max knocked a drink off a table into a customer's lap, they all rushed out at once but got jammed in the doorway, were blocking the entrance, until they all fell out onto the parking lot.

A couple of them were almost hit by a car — Eli Molloy nearly was, and Ahmed O'Brien — emerging from the car wash at the back of what used to be the supermarket and the dry cleaner's. Those buildings had brown paper over the windows and the eavestrough hung off one end of the roof. The driver coming out of the car wash was an elderly woman who believed the boys were throwing things at her car.

A police cruiser circled the block while the boys were beating the broken wheel. Kenny Burke had been hammering away, but then he stood, and his arm swung loosely down by his side and as an afterthought, he dropped the rock into the grass near his foot.

They all stood at attention, their eyes on the cruiser, and they each privately connected the police presence with the face of the frail, elderly woman in the car from the car wash, how she had looked through the windshield as though under water, spattered with the shadows of swishing leaves, winking in and out of view, sunken deep in the roomy car, her profile seeping up, all bone, a soft-slewed rage, as she rolled out of the parking lot, nearly hitting two of them who were still trying to whack each other with the straw swords.

The boys stood still as the cruiser passed by them and they remained still until the tail end of it swung around the corner.

Then they ran as hard as they could. They ran as they did on the basketball court, with a synchronicity that made their feet slap the pavement with a single beat that broke up into a thousand overlapping beats and was one single slapping beat again. They ran through the valley, back up the hill behind the stinking brewery, across Bonaventure, back into the school and the gym for the second half of the tournament, already on the floor, when two cops busted in and stopped the game.

Xavier had not been the one with the rock, nor had he touched the shopping cart. He had been standing to the side, like a driver at the Grand Prix who waits for the mechanics to go over the engine before the race. But the feeling was, he'd been the troublemaker. One of the teachers, math, had a gut feeling. He said he knew who was responsible for the vandalism. The teacher was certain, he told the cops, that Xavier was to blame for whatever had happened in Churchill Square.

The math teacher was in the bleachers when the game was interrupted and strode forward to speak to the cops. He had a son on the team and had been yelling throughout the tournament, leaping from his chair, fist in the air, telling whoever had the ball to *Go, go, go.* Screaming foul before the ref had a chance. Xavier listened as the math teacher told the cops about him being disruptive in class, making jokes, the clown, always the one with the big HaHa, the teacher had said.

It's not a HaHa now, he said. The teacher offered the opinion that it was all Xavier's fault. The teacher jutted his index finger in Xavier's face and said, Your days of causing trouble are over.

The cops took notes and said the boys should expect follow-up. They said they'd be getting to the bottom of it. Outside they whooped the siren three times. Xavier slipped away from the confusion in the gym after the cops had pulled out of the parking lot. He ran all the way home, banging on the front door, crying hard, believing the house was about to be stormed by a SWAT team and that he would be dragged away in cuffs.

His mother got a call from another parent who said Xavier had been accused of starting the havoc in Subway and being rude to the girl behind the counter (for his mother this was the worst of the alleged crimes), vandalizing an old woman's car, damaging a fire hydrant and destroying a shopping cart, which was private property, according to the cops. Xavier knew it was Kenny Burke, Kenny who had the stone in his hands when the cops went by. Kenny had even told them, It was me, but nobody listened to Kenny. After supper Colin Mercer called him, told him the principal had said Xavier would be suspended from junior high for at least a week. This proved to be something Mercer had made up.

He had also been the cause, according to Merce, they mostly called him Merce, of the team losing the tournament (the worst of the accusations for Xavier; it was the first loss of the season).

Xavier thought he'd lie awake all night but he was exhausted from the force of the false accusation. He passed into a deep sleep almost at once, but when his mother woke him up the next morning he seemed to have a fever. He was shivering, and his cheeks blazed.

His mother said she'd gone to the fire hydrant and taken pictures, which she'd already emailed to the math teacher and the principal of the school and the police.

I phoned Subway, his mother said, and spoke to the girl

who was behind the counter and to the manager, and I got a physical description of the boy who had been rude and gave them a description of you. They both confirmed you didn't fit the description. They both said it wasn't you. They said it was the tallest kid.

I'm not like that, he said.

Rude to the staff, they said it wasn't you.

I don't do that, he said.

There had been no damage, not a single chip or scratch, in the eye-smarting red paint of the hydrant, his mother told him.

I documented every square inch of it, she said.

I never touched the shopping cart.

I called the cops, she said. I've spoken to one of the officers who busted into the tournament.

I wasn't anywhere near that old lady's car.

The cop was an obnoxious asshole, his mother said.

I didn't do the bun, smear the bun and mustard and tomatoes all over the table, he said. But she hadn't known about the bun.

What the hell?

It wasn't me, he said.

The cop was going through surveillance tapes from four different businesses in the areas: the gas station across the street from the fire hydrant; a surveillance camera on the back of the car wash; a camera in the Subway; and another on the rear exterior of Subway.

It's taped? Xavier asked. The whole thing is taped? He could feel the fear drain out of him. He was light-headed.

You're not worried about the surveillance tapes? his mother said.

I told you, he said. I didn't touch that shopping cart. I didn't touch it. He fell back onto the pillow and slept until late afternoon.

His father called the police officer and left phone messages, as did the other parents on the team. Demanding to know the progress he was making with viewing the surveillance tapes. His mother called too. She told the cop she knew her son was innocent. She knew it because Xavier had said he was innocent, that was how she knew. Xavier listened to her end of the conversation. He had his spoon with Kraft Dinner in his hand stopped halfway between his mouth and the bowl.

He heard her say: Well, you are a very different sort of person than my son. Xavier ate ravenously, spoonful after spoonful, finished the whole bowl in seconds, put his thumb to the edge of the bowl and gave it a gentle nudge away from him, touched his mouth with a piece of paper towel. He realized after he'd done it that it was something his father did, push the bowl, every night for a thousand years.

Afterwards his mother told him that the lesson was that if you're innocent, the truth will out. He didn't think that was the lesson. The lesson was a broken-down shopping cart could leap at you like a tiger and tear you apart, if you turned your back on it. Sometimes bad things lay in wait, and you had to sidestep them.

It was a few weeks after the math teacher had apologized to the whole team (but not Xavier in particular), and had given them all a pop and a bag of chips, and all was forgotten or smoothed over, that Xavier decided to quit the team.

I'm just sick of it, he said.

By that time he was into skateboarding at Mundy Pond. There was a loose group of guys up there, and a few girls.

They nodded to each other and took turns on the ramp, they affected a quiet respect for each other's skill, but nobody would call it a team sport. You didn't have to depend on anyone.

He often wolfed his food at the dinner table, and if there was time before homework, he would play video games. Every so often Trinity came upstairs from visiting with his mother and joined him; they sat on the floor in front of the big screen, each with a controller, and didn't speak, except to grunt at a death, or yell out when one or the other was blown to bits. But she had other friends now, and she went to the Buckmaster's Circle rec centre for gymnastics. She had some friend up behind the Super 8 motel in the housing they had up there. Someone else up behind the mall.

But she had been at the game when the cops busted in. She'd been there with a bunch of girls when they blamed him. When the math teacher said he must have been the one with the rock. That he knew Xavier had been rude to the girl behind the counter.

Trinity was at the game. She left the girls and strode into the centre of the gym and stood in front of him. When the cops approached Xavier. She was standing between him and the cops. Trinity Brophy stood with her arms crossed so they had to talk through her, or around her. Nobody told her to go sit down.

When the cops left the game started up again, but Xavier just went back to the bleachers and got his knapsack and headed out the door of the gym.

jules
proposal

THIS IS TO explain how there would be no marrying Joe without marrying his mother too. Florence.

I'd fallen for her at the dinner when Joe intended to announce we were getting married. I'd said we'd have to tell his parents. He hadn't answered. He was reading Derrida and he'd turned the page. He'd written in the margins with the stub of a pencil that he kept behind his ear.

Florence was fierce and tender in almost equal measure the night we were invited for dinner.

Joe sitting opposite me.

Florence told me how many calories there were in each vegetable on my plate, just before I put it in my mouth.

There's only a couple of teaspoons of olive oil on the baked vegetables, she said. There would be a dessert called Pavlova, which she explained had been invented for a Russian ballerina intent on keeping her figure.

When I'd taken up the antique silver butter knife for my French bread, she told me how much the butter had cost. She talked about a sister in Montreal who ran an art gallery. She shook her head at the folly of this sister, but she said that Vera might be able to help me get a footing on the mainland.

Florence said, Vera puts the stick of bread on the table and they just pass it around and tear off pieces.

We're trying it for the first time, Joe's father said. Florence cut him a look across the table at this minor betrayal.

Normally I'd cut the bread, she conceded, put it in a basket, but this is an experiment.

I could see Joe's father, John, was skeptical when the long baguette was handed to him. He held it in front of him in both fists and glanced up at her.

Just tear it, John, she said.

I don't know, Florence, he said. But he tore the bread.

We passed the baguette and each ripped off a chunk and she assured us they did it this way in France. She'd love to go to Paris, Florence told me, but John was afraid of flying.

All those cities in Europe, I really wanted to see them, she said.

You can go with your sisters, John said.

But I don't want to go without John, she answered, looking straight at me as if I'd put up the argument.

She said real butter was on sale that week at Shoppers Drug Mart on LeMarchant Road; she told me the price of the butter there and the price it was at two major supermarkets in the vicinity. She'd bought nine boxes of butter and she had them in the freezer.

You can freeze table butter, she said. Not everyone is aware. Did you know that?

I said, I didn't know that.

I bought the nine that were left, she said. The flyer comes in the mail and if you get there early enough you can buy the butter for half the price.

The bread had come to her and she held it in both fists, she glanced at her husband, and then just passed it on to Joe without tearing it. She said the carrots were from Lester's Farm and they were the best carrots to be found in the city. They cost more, but they were worth it. She told me how much they were a pound.

They're sweet, she said.

She told me about the gadget on the wine bottle to make sure the wine didn't drip onto the tablecloth. She'd seen a man at Zellers demonstrating it and though it was only September, she'd bought one for each of her sisters for Christmas.

That's a large portion of the shopping squared away, she said. I like to get it done so you don't have to face the crowds.

She'd bought the tablecloth at the auction of a house on which the bank had foreclosed. She just opened up her purse and gave the woman twice what she was asking and the woman was grateful.

You should have seen her face, Florence said.

Florence could walk into a property — any property — and she knew how to make it suit the people to whom she was trying to sell it. She'd lift a hand toward a wall, making a sweeping gesture, telling them they needed to put in a window. She said a white couch. She told them a love seat. She said blue tiles in the kitchen and told them the name of someone they could trust who would install the tiles for a good price. She called semi-gloss an unmitigated disaster. She told them sail-white and the brand and where it was on sale.

She told a story about the priest at Corpus Christi. She'd called him up and said she had a newlywed couple who wanted to buy his house. He'd said his house wasn't for sale.

I told him, she said. It's perfect for this couple and they love it. I'm going to have to sell it to them. I'll get you what you paid for it and find you something twice as nice that'll be a real bargain. You'll come out of it making money.

The embroidery was done by hand, she said. The tablecloth and napkins with French knots that I rubbed between my thumb and finger, the silky grey-green leaves, violet-and-yellow pansies, each petal with a streak of blue-black in the stamen.

Pour salt on a wine stain, she said. Or soda water.

We had decided to get married though we were just twenty-three years old and none of our friends were married. Marriage was decidedly out of fashion. I waited for him to tell his parents throughout the whole dinner. It occurred to me if he didn't tell them, we wouldn't get married. I didn't have enough experience with love to know if the intensity was an indication of how long the thing could last. Or if lasting mattered at all. Brief might be just as good. Brief might burn brighter, for all I knew.

Suddenly, as the gold-trimmed plate with the light Pavlova was passed to Joe's father and the time for bringing up marriage was running out, I was filled with fear that Joe wouldn't say it.

I thought, as his mother passed out the plates of dessert, that I wanted to be married to him, whatever that meant. Later, I'd realize it wasn't marriage at all that I'd wanted — the performance of it, yes; the dress, yes; the heavy silver knife sinking into the fruit cake with icing like concrete, yes.

But it wasn't being married, which might be nullifying. I thought I wanted the stolid agreement, but that wasn't it either. Whatever it was I'd wanted, I had no word for it. Someone said marriage, and I thought, it must be that.

Everything was altering back then.

Once I got a whole wall in an artist-run centre and spray-painted a mural of sea creatures and a sunken ship. I worked with photographs and stencils. The stink of the paint as strong as the euphoria I felt letting loose on that wall.

Leaving Joe to go buy cheese at the corner store, or to go to the university, was like stepping away from a bonfire at the beach. Everything beyond the fire was so dark and then how the boulders formed out of the dark and became solid, and the cold and flankers swirling overhead, how the pupil narrowed or dilated with an ache — that was the way I wanted him, a single-minded ache for a particular heat.

He was getting a master's, he was getting out of Newfoundland, he had a daughter, he had a photographic memory, he'd slept with this one and that one, he was tall, he had a motorcycle.

I had gathered, in the first half hour of meeting his parents, that if, during the dinner with the embroidered pansies, he said we were getting married there could be no retraction.

That's the kind of family they were.

In my family you could say anything and retract anything you liked. You didn't have to mean what you said. Or you could mean it with your whole heart, and still not mean a word of it. I would be given leeway. There had been just my mother and Nell to convince. I'd known I'd be able to roll the whole story out with leisure and theatrics. Telling my family was more fun than actually getting married.

At his house they held off with declarations until they knew for sure.

I'd pressed the napkin with the cluster of French knots under my thumb, as if to press the utterance out of him. I felt a pain in my forehead; it was the effort of willing him to tell them. I saw Joe would be proposing to them. He'd put more effort into the declaration than into any conversation we'd ever had about the subject.

Florence said, There's nothing in this dessert.

Sounds wonderful, Joe's father said.

I cut the required sugar in half, she said. At that John was visibly startled.

Florence, he said. Why did you do that?

None of you would notice if I didn't tell you, Florence said. She worked the silver pie server under the crust. She told me I could eat this dessert without a worry. I wouldn't gain an ounce.

Look, she said. It's all air. She held up her fork with a stiff mouthful on it. I half expected Florence and John to talk us out of getting married so young and felt that might be a relief. Yes, I was willing to be talked out of it. We were too young, that's what I secretly believed.

Joe didn't have to be present when I told my mother and sister, we had both agreed on that without ever speaking about it. We already knew the two families required different handling. I'd told Mom and Nell first, as a test run.

My mother still had the orange-and-black plaid couch and the green velvet chair with the wooden lever on the side that required muscle. Nell lived with Mom during the summers, between semesters in Halifax at law school.

Yank the lever of the velvet chair and the footrest shot out and the back of the chair cranked backwards so you were almost prostrate and it was from this position, staring at the stucco ceiling, I would try to explain about the urgency to marry. The compulsion. My father had been dead for seven years by then.

When it came time to tell them, I'd yanked the lever and I'd said I was getting married, and then I struggled to sit up in the chair, to escape it.

We had two big patio windows in that house, the house my parents had built together, and there were giant squares of sunlight on the shag carpet, and when I told my mother and sister about getting married, I'd paced back and forth between the squares of sunlight. I explained I really believed I would marry Joe, and my sister got up and took two bowls from the cupboard and a tub of vanilla ice cream from the freezer and the Shirriff chocolate sauce, and she let the freezer door slam behind her. She sliced up a banana, half in each bowl. She handed me one of the bowls and she dropped herself into the old armchair I'd left, but didn't pull the lever because she wanted to watch me.

I ate the ice cream while pacing, and when the ice cream was gone, she got out of the chair and took the bowl from me and put both our bowls in the dishwasher. My mother was drinking tea and she held the cup out to my sister and wagged it back and forth and my sister got her another cup. The wind picked up then and a giant cloud doused the squares of sunlight on the carpet.

Joe's mother put down her fork and knife and touched the embroidered napkin to her lips. I closed my eyes and willed Joe to speak.

We've decided to get married, he said.

So, I thought. We will have to go through with it. I had a superstition about ceremonies. Especially ones that involved vows.

Is there a reason? Florence asked.

I didn't know what she meant. My Pavlova was airy, insubstantial.

Some reason? she asked. Florence said the whole idea was awfully sudden. Joe's father had taken up the stick of bread again and I could see flecks of crust spring away as he twisted it apart. I could see he wanted the butter and I passed it to him.

I said: Because we're in love.

His father put down the bread. He had given up on it. He had been determined to enact the folkways of France, a rustic fantasy life they were now going to adopt in Newfoundland, he'd been momentarily game.

But my answer had startled them, the mentioning of such private feelings, the unexpected candour, which was out of the ordinary in Joe's family, because they understood each other without having to blurt things out over the dinner table, and because they believed in coming at the big truths aslant, or recognizing that some things were cheapened by speech, the most delicate and the most powerful things, and that it was better to prove a love than declare it—because of all that, they'd been startled by my innocence in these matters. I was innocent of the will required to produce love, rather than just declare it, and because of this, Joe's father had laid the bread aside, momentarily deflated.

I shovelled a forkful of Pavlova into my mouth so I wouldn't have to speak.

My mother didn't make desserts until much later in life, except an old-fashioned trifle at Christmas time, and then she made two, one soaked with alcohol, and one without, for the children. As she got older the only occasion for dessert was her card club, for which she made something called Sex in a Pan.

Joe told his mother that I wasn't pregnant. I can't remember how he phrased this, because the word *pregnant* was not spoken. Or anything about children. It might have passed telepathically but I'd intercepted it.

While she was waiting for my answer—*Because we are in love*—she'd picked up her fork and knife and held them tight in each fist, she was leaning forward.

When she understood we were enchanted with each other, a limpness came over her and she slumped back a little. She must have known it was the kind of thing that could go tits up, but enchantment she could work with; this was something she understood.

I'd been offered a second piece of dessert and I had accepted it. I was ravenous. Later I realized the offer of a second piece had been a test and I had failed. They commented on my healthy appetite for years afterward.

xavier
responsibility

YOU HAVEN'T LIFTED a finger. You haven't so much as washed
a dish. Your bedroom is a state, and yesterday you didn't get
up. You're fifteen years old and you have one responsibility.

I have more than one responsibility.

You have one responsibility.

Where's the leash?

To get up, that is your responsibility. Get to school on
time. Clean up around here. Do homework. Walk the dog.

I had a double shift. I washed dishes for sixteen hours.

You want a pop from the store later, where's your money?

Where's the leash?

The leash is by the door. That's where it's kept.

Every day after school, before he left again for work,
he'd take the dog through the park and whenever there was
another dog, Fluff tried to rip the arm off him. If two huskies
went by on leashes, Xavier was left with a new understanding
of what an elbow was, what a rotator cuff was.

The dog would drag him from tree to tree and sniff in

short, fast, hard huffs and in-hauls of cold and his breath would come out in little clouds, then he'd move just slightly past the tree and become dignified and rigid. He'd lift a hind leg and piss with regal distain. After this sprinkle he always lurched hard, so that Xavier was jerked like a mime pretending to walk a dog, each joint unlocked, bones wiggling.

His mother had left her earbuds on the side table near the leash. He'd have them now for the day and she would be furious. Ownership of the earbuds had been transferred to him because she had suffered a moment of distraction and put them down in plain view.

This would be the mutual understanding of the earbuds.

She had taken his belt, the leather belt she'd given him for Christmas, which cost a fortune and was bought at the last minute before the stores closed because she had looked at all the presents and realized Stella and his dad had more gifts. Stella was getting a membership at some gym in Montreal. She always had more gifts because his mother had lots of ideas about what Stella needed. Also, she was compensating because Stella said he was spoiled, said their mother was sexist.

Stella had been subjected to broccoli. He had never been subjected to broccoli, that was true. By the time he'd come into the world his mother had lost her zeal for the broccoli wars. There'd been a campaign, when Stella was a kid, his mother got from a book. Put it on their plate, they'll eventually eat it. The smell of a Brussels sprout made Stella gag, but every Tuesday on the side of her plate, three stinking Brussels sprouts. Mondays it was broccoli.

Xavier wouldn't know a Brussels sprout if he tripped over it, Stella said. Her eyes watered just at the memory of the smell. Sometimes talking about it made her gag.

He'd never eaten a Frosted Flake in his life: Stella had that wrong. At Christmas she went on and on about how she'd never been allowed cereal with sugar, and she'd found a box of it in the cupboard. She held it up like she was a crime detective about to unveil a twisted plot.

What's this? Stella shouted. Shaking the box over her head.

I've never seen it before in my life, he'd said.

His mother got Stella and his father whatever she could think of, but she didn't have a clue about what he would like. Every Christmas a leather belt, which she then took over for herself. She'd given him the same belt for his birthday too. She went to Ballistic, the skateboard store he loved, and forgot she'd already bought him a number of belts. It was the only thing of value in the whole store, according to her. The decks all had skulls smoking a spliff, or some other horror mixed with humour that she couldn't condone.

He'd said, Gift card, but she would not do gift cards.

A gift card is impersonal, she said. You are my son, for god's sake.

The belts in the bottom of his cupboard like a nest of vipers.

Three identical belts; he lost two and she took the other one.

He hadn't got up for school until she left, though they'd had a screaming match through his bedroom door and she had called to Alexa and made her play "Bad Moon Rising" and he had said, Stop, Alexa. He was the first person in his class who had an Alexa. He loved showing her off, speaking to her with please and thank you when his friends were over. But Alexa couldn't hear him now because the music was blasting so loud it was threatening to destroy the speaker, hissing static and pops and sputters. He'd bought Alexa with his first pay-cheque so he could listen to whatever he liked, but his mother had started to ask Alexa to play things and she'd messed up his algorithm. After "Bad Moon Rising" he'd had to listen to Joy Division, "Love Will Tear Us Apart," before he threw off the sheets and headed to the shower.

He'd gone through the basket, tossing the dirty laundry all over the floor, and reached the bottom before he understood what had happened to his belt. The belt was, for a time, out of circulation. The belt would find its way back to him; he was watching for it. He tied up his pants with a piece of itchy twine which he cut off the spool in the laundry room with an exacto knife and let his shirt hang out so it wouldn't show.

Then, after school, he was walking the dog like she'd asked him, past the war memorial on New Gower in the driving wind and sleet. A man had collapsed in the middle of the road, at the bottom of Garrison Hill. At first, Xavier couldn't make out what it was because the slanting sun just lit the outline of the man's shoulder and hip, but he yanked out his mother's earbuds and saw it was a man, shouting to him. He was in the middle of the street and the two lanes of traffic on Queen's Road and the cars coming down Garrison cast their headlights on him and wove around. Nobody stopped.

Help me get up, the man shouted. I can't get up. He lay on his side in the slush, his legs moving as if pedalling a bike. He lifted a finger and waved it toward his walker, which was tumbling end over end down the street. The wind lobbed a ball of silver and glint at Xavier, a crumpled bag of barbe-que chips, but at the last second it was wrenched out of his path and got stuck high in the old trees in the garden of the halfway house. He crossed the road in the traffic, dragging the dog, and no one got out to help. The man was very large, and his face, suddenly illuminated in a passing headlight, was mottled with the effort to breathe, a cheek in the slush. His purple mouth open.

I'm dying here, he rasped. Christ sake, help me up.

A woman with a tiny dog on a leash skirted past them and Fluff tried to attack it, the leash out straight, Xavier pulled the dog back and ran after the man's walker. He grabbed at the leg of it, but it skittered out of reach.

Get me up, the man yelled. Take my arm, young man.

I've got to do something with the dog, he said.

He tied the dog to the iron fence that circled the war memorial. They had put new wreaths around the base of the statues, and there were yellow-and-purple irises all the way up out of the earth, and some were weighed down with the slush. He didn't have time to help the man; he had to get to work. He had to get the dog home and he had to get cigarettes at the corner store. But he grabbed the walker.

You want me to pull you? Xavier asked.

I want you to pull me, yes.

What if something is broken?

But the man had rolled onto his back and put his arms in the air. Xavier took the man's doughy, chafed hands with the blue fingernails and dug the heels of his boots into a patch of road that had no ice. He leaned back and took some steps. The walker was starting to skid away from him. The wind had lifted the front legs of the contraption, and the legs tapped around on the ice and the wheels in front twisted this way and that. He couldn't grab the walker, but he had the man's back up off the road. He slammed the side of his boot against the toes of the man's sneakers so he wouldn't slip forward. The more Xavier leaned backwards, the further up the man rose. The traffic had backed up around them, but still nobody got out to help, though they must have known the man was at least three hundred pounds and didn't belong to Xavier in any way and that something was wrong here, because how was this man going to get back to wherever he came from once he was standing? The drivers didn't get out of the cars to help because Xavier and the man were getting to a standing position by themselves, for a second they stood like dance partners hand in hand, until the man lurched at the walker and Xavier held it steady and together they made their way to the sidewalk.

I need a taxi, the man said, but I got no money.

You tried the bus? Xavier said. He looked down the road into the distance but there were no buses on the way. The man was soaking wet. Xavier told the man he would be right back. He grabbed the dog and ran back home.

Xavier busted through the front door and told his mother, Give me some money, I have to give it to a man for a taxi.

His mother stripped off the yellow rubber gloves, smelling of Comet, and started looking for her purse, tearing up the stairs, flinging back the covers on the bed, checking under laundry, all the while arguing about giving him the money. Who was the man? What was he talking about? Give a man money? What man? What was she, a bank? Did he think she was a bank? Xavier was shouting up at his mother from the foot of the stairs.

I had to rush home with the dog, he said. A man fell down, lost his walker, three hundred pounds, and the dog tore the arm off me.

How much money? his mother said. I'm not in the habit

of handing out to whoever comes along, you have money, give him your money.

Enough for a cab, he said. To the west end.

They have a service for people who need public transportation, his mother said. But she was counting out the money.

Come on, come on, he said, rolling his index finger so she'd keep counting.

This is a person, my god, he said. He looked up and their eyes met. People said he had his father's eyes, but sometimes when he looked in the mirror he saw his face was like hers. His Aunt Nell looked like him, people said they were carbon copies.

But there was something Xavier saw in his mother's face, he had to learn, memorize it, every time he saw it. She could look like a stranger. She handed him the wad of bills. Then she screamed right in his face.

Those are my earbuds, she screamed. Her face brilliantly red. He laughed at her and leapt off the two front steps and she reached out to snatch the wires from his ears, he held up the fistful of bills, he flew down the sidewalk kinked up with laughter. He'd had to hold his ribs on one side because he was laughing and shocked by her instant rage, how it made her stiff and straight, the intensity of it. He was joyful; thrilled he could provoke that kind of thing.

Xavier's breath was ragged when he handed the money to the man and the taxi pulled up and he opened the back door and held it against the wind and sleet, then Xavier shut the car door behind the man and he took off past the Anglican Cathedral and down over McBride's hill to get to work, the whole thing a lope with his feet barely touching the ground and music blasting in his ears.

jules

awe

IN THE ROOM where Xavier's surgeon led me there were several large screens and they showed the interior of my son's body. The bones eerily luminous, and here and there burrs of light clinging to the white shafts of pelvis bone. The little sparks were irregularities in the x-ray technology. They looked like comets. The two places where he had been stabbed were grey next to the supernova white of the bones.

They nicked the bladder, the surgeon said. But we sewed that up pretty good in the surgery. I don't anticipate we see complications there.

He tapped the screen with the tip of a pen. Then he zoomed in. And the tear expanded, bursting across the screen.

He leaned in and squinted.

In some ways, we've been very lucky, he said. There was awe in his tone. I was so fucking appreciative of the awe, because it suggested that magic was at play. Something more than just this exhausted man in a dirty lab coat (a stain that looked like mustard on the lapel); some incomprehensible force that seemed to be casting attention our way. The double-bladed irony of a word like *lucky* can reduce me to tears.

People say, Go ahead, cry. I wasn't very good at holding back tears, but I recognized crying as a caprice. Showy and wasteful. It's better to affect an icy efficiency, even good cheer. Nothing to worry about here, folks. Move along, people, move along.

I had already been told about all the wounds, of course. But these pictures felt to me a violation. When did I start to think of Xavier as someone who deserved privacy, even while unconscious? Someone who had a right to secrets from his mother. When did I recognize that just because he had been inside my body didn't mean I could look into his?

THE NURSE SAID only two guests at a time, and for two days our family came to sit with me one at a time. My brother-in-law was at Xavier's bedside now. Gerry.

This was before the snowstorm shut the city down and nobody could get in. Snowmageddon. The hundred-mile winds, the power loss. The immutable dark. Before the state of emergency.

Xavier with all the tubes, pale and unconscious. I'd cried the whole way from Mexico City on the plane. My nostrils were red and chafed and cracked from crying.

I'm cried out, I whispered to Gerry. There was a tissue box on the windowsill, sitting on a heating vent. The tissue sticking out the top was waving in the warm air like a surrender. Gerry handed me the box. I wiped my eyes, blew my nose.

The brown brick building across from the hospital window looked desolate and empty. A metal grille was loose on one of the uppermost windows and it clanged.

The storm's coming, he said.

I got the last seat, I told him, coming back from Mexico.

Xavier had been stabbed three days before the storm struck.

Before the ambulance drivers came to work on skidoos, arriving from Conception Bay South, from Foxtrap, from Manuels, travelling in groups of ten so they wouldn't get lost, before the streets leading to the hospital were just white, with no horizon, infinite undefined space, and all the buildings invisible. The drivers on the skidoos had to be careful not to drive into the buildings that reared up out of the storm. Brick walls only present after you smashed into them.

Everything would be buried in seventy-five centimetres of snow, and still it would keep snowing. It would snow the next day and the next and the next and the next. It would snow forever. The houses shook, water in the toilet bowls sloshed, roofs blew off. The plows were taken off the streets. The city pulled all the plows because the snow was too heavy, the plows broke down under the weight. Then the plows were buried. The windows blew out of the ambulances, one paramedic would tell me. They had to drive with no windows.

I felt it was me. I was generating the storm, making it happen with my rage. The rage was as big as the storm, just as malevolent, tearing out of my chest. Or the storm had entered me. It was inside me, freezing everything, starting with my womb, which was frozen, breaking up like an iceberg, pieces sliding off. It was my womb or my heart, or the balancing fluid in my inner ear. I'd lost any sense of balance. The cold crept through me.

After the worst of the storm, people had bonfires in the middle of unplowed streets and roasted marshmallows and sang songs and put it all up on Facebook and Instagram. The food banks wouldn't open because they were afraid of being mobbed. They demanded security guards, but there were no security guards.

People climbed out of second-storey windows and slid to the ground on their bottoms. Everything was clean and white and buried. People gathered in shovelling brigades and called themselves Snow Angels. They worked to free the front doors of the old and infirm.

Then they brought in the army, all the men and women in uniform, everybody with a shovel, the clumps of snow flying up high enough to reach the tops of the snowbanks. There was a helpline and they prioritized the old, people who had run out of food, people with heart conditions.

New mothers who couldn't breastfeed were out of Similac, because the supermarkets ran out, just ran out. There was no Similac. Someone from the city hall distributed her own frozen, pumped breast milk in little baggies with marks on the side to delineate the ounces. That was on Facebook too.

It kept snowing, but when the violence of it had abated, the shelves in the supermarkets were empty, with nothing left to buy. If you went into the supermarket when it finally opened, after seven days, because they had to open, people were out of food, the lineup ran around the perimeter of the parking lot, and if you got inside and made it to the milk coolers in the back, you found yourself pressed against the body in front of you and a body pressed behind.

We got the phone calls in Mexico, where we'd gone to a conference. Joe's Philosophy and Media conference. I was there for the sun. But I attended the talk by a man from the University of Paris about the yellow vest movement. He showed a hologram of the French president giving a speech.

Macron was full of shimmer the way people are when they're teleported back to the ship on *Star Trek*. The speaker seemed to be pro the yellow vests, but I couldn't be sure, because the simultaneous translator couldn't keep up with him. When I asked him at the coffee dispenser he was so vehement, so charged with passion, he slopped hot coffee on his thumb and spoke in a French so quick, so sputter-clogged I hadn't understood a word.

Joe and I went to Yelapa for a week, after the conference, an hour-long boat ride away from Puerto Vallarta, where we'd been once before, when we'd first got married. Where, it was rumoured, Bob Dylan came to unwind between appearances, during the sixties.

We made love on a bed as big as a boat under a mosquito net with the night breeze on our skin because we'd kicked off the sheet. Just kicking off the sheets was like riding bikes up a steep hill, because we were tangled by then and the sheet was big and it meant making love was languorous because we were already spent. The mosquito netting fluttered in the breeze until all the languor fell away, and there were the fast-swishing palm leaves and the elaborately carved headboard banging. There was no wall on the side of the bedroom that faced the ocean, the waves breaking below.

Some men climbed the palm trees to cut down the coconuts with machetes, and we were up so high on a cliff that the men were almost in our bedroom. One morning men were dangling in the green fronds, the glints of sun on their machetes. We could have reached through the net and touched them, the men, dropping coconuts to other men below.

I'd made it out of there before Snowmageddon. Nell had said it was coming, said there was talk of everything shutting down. I had to race the storm, according to Nell. But Joe couldn't get an airline ticket that would get him all the way home. There was just one seat. We both knew it had to be me, without speaking about it. Joe would have handled everything, been firm with the doctors, if firmness was called for. Joe would be better, calmer. But I couldn't be the one left behind. I'd crack up. So Joe booked the seat for me.

The storm of the century.

But Gerry had shown up before the state of emergency was declared. He'd moved my coat, and had it bunched over his arms, a hot-pink coat, like dipping a ballroom dancer, one of the coat's arms flung out extravagantly, cuff trailing on the floor.

He'd taken the coat in his arms so he could sit down, one cheek on the bed. He tried to cross his legs but that didn't work out, so he stood up again. He was wearing his sunglasses. They were tinted prescription glasses, black as night. There'd been an argument with his mother at Christmas dinner (but that was long before), when she'd told him to take them off at the table.

Sunglasses at the table? Florence asked. I don't think so.

This is me, Gerry had said. He spread his arms, palms up. Offering his true self to his family, on Christmas Day, maybe ten years before Xavier was stabbed.

He put my coat back down and patted a wrinkle out of the arm. Then he took a rotten banana out of a basket on the table. The fruit sat on a nest of green cellophane.

That should go, Gerry said. He tossed the banana through the air and it hit the inside of the metal garbage bucket with a *ding*.

He scores, Gerry said.

I have no idea what time it is, I said.

That banana's been there for a while, he said.

They're giving him antibiotics, I said. That's what all that is, the tubes and everything. Remember that dirt bike you and Joe bought him? He loved that bike.

Xavier was thirteen, Gerry said. Joe got him the bike. I never had nothing to do with it.

I was afraid of him riding the bike, I said. Thirteen. I'd had some fight with Joe, let me tell you. Them coming down the road in your truck, that bike in the back.

What's wrong with a dirt bike? Gerry asked. He looked ready for a mock fight, drawing one fist back, a little wag of the shoulder, jokey, even though we were whispering.

The kid was old enough, he said.

It wasn't even legal, I said. You let Joe borrow the truck to pick up the bike. I was lied to. I was told Carbonear for paint to do the bedroom walls. I was told a sale on paint.

There was a sale, Gerry said. He glanced back at me, startled. I think he was startled; it was hard to tell with the glasses. Why was I drawing him into it?

I mean, he said. That was a while ago now.

He went to the window. He picked up the little yellow-and-white checkered gift bag with the fabric daisies and looked on the bottom for a price. He read out the card from Nancy. And put it back down.

I certainly never lied to you, Gerry said softly.

We both knew that Joe had a different relation to the truth than either of us.

I had believed there was paint on sale, and there had been. He'd bought it just before they picked up the dirt bike, which happened to be the primary purpose of the trip.

I, on the other hand, was like Gerry. We couldn't keep the truth to ourselves, it burst out of us without provocation, it was something we shared, though we recognized it for what it was, a liability. We were easy marks, we believed everything, credulity the easiest kind of generosity.

But it made Joe and me a good match. We shared a single bank account of truth, withdrawing whenever we wanted, and keeping an eye on the credit and debt columns, the total.

There's the start of it, Gerry said. He jutted his chin at the window, making me take notice. Small, spiteful flakes zipping, frenzied.

I just about lost my mind over that dirt bike, I said. We were both suddenly shy of speaking about the harm Xavier might have endured. We both looked at him, newly stricken. The shock of it like a riptide. We were silent. But then Gerry spoke up, pretending to be combative, declarative.

We call Xavier "the Tornado," Gerry said. That's what we called Xavier at our place when he was younger. Broke Louise's favourite figurine, cracked the parasol off this woman in a pink dress. Louise was in a state, bawling over it, the Missus in one hand, the cracked-off umbrella in the other, the Tornado.

He gets that clumsiness from his father, I said.

I never had any say in the bike.

Joe is clumsy too, I said. That's where he gets it.

Remember, he broke the bunk bed? Jumping on it. Burst the side out the inflatable pool. Who gets in a pool with a nail in the pocket of his swimming trunks? A bloody big nail from when I was building the deck.

All the sleepovers, I said.

Nothing wrong with a dirt bike, thirteen years old.

He loved the bloody bike.

I'm just stopping in on my way out of town, Gerry said. Supermarkets shutting down. I need to get back to Louise and the kids before this thing hits. If you need milk, you should get it. Whatever you need. Do you want some milk? I'll leave you a few cartons.

That's when I realized Gerry should have been delivering milk at that hour. He has a route. Gerry owns a fleet of trucks, you can see them all over town with his name on the side in a cursive font. He delivers milk and produce, and years ago he started renting to film crews too. *Gerry Cooper Transport* lined up near the curb and the crew lugging lights and cameras and coils of electric cables, looking like they own the sidewalk. Everybody giving them a wide berth because they're solemn and important and making some kind of illusion you'll see later on TV and it's Gerry's trucks and he's made a fortune off them. But normally he's hauling milk from Central Dairies. It's all the same to him.

The raucous rasp of Xavier's oxygen mask. Recognizing that Gerry had to leave, get back on the road, made me feel bereft. We heard a crash in the corridor, maybe a food tray.

I thought of the attack. The way shadows under the streetlight in the video stretched and twisted, wrenching themselves out of the video frame, the thrash of limbs, the drunken slouching and an arm raised and swinging down, a fist that I believed held the knife. The nurses were bent over at their station, going over papers for the change of shift. One of them, the bigger one, Erin or maybe Ella, had shuffled over in the familiar *shush* of polyester.

She secured the elastic of the oxygen mask over Xavier's ears. Without even turning around to look at me she said:

You got a nice tan. You never got that here. Down to Florida?
Mexico, I said. Do you like Florida?
Loves Florida, loves it. Was down there last winter with
a couple of the girls from work.
She was arranging Xavier's pillows.
We got his blood back, she said. I don't like the look of
the white blood cell count. The doctor will be in to check. I'd
say he's going to want to change that antibiotic.
Is that bad? I asked. Changing the antibiotic?
We got lots to throw at this infection yet, she said. Don't you
worry. The doctor can say better than me. He'll be along now
the once. He got plenty of tricks up his sleeve, the doctor does.

She put the empty bag of fluids into a bedpan and covered it with a towel. She straightened the blanket at the foot
of the bed.

That's better, she said. Nice and fresh. Then she left us
with a swoosh of the curtain.

You got any idea who did this? Gerry asked. What kind
of people?

I couldn't think of who might want to hurt my son. I wondered if it was arbitrary, just had luck. We had been so lucky
all the way through, but everything had turned. I wanted the
good luck back. I was praying even though I didn't believe in
prayer. It just came out of me. The prayer was a single word
and the word was *please*. It was a prayer or an incantation. It
was a petition or a decade of the rosary. Had we done something to provoke this? Were we being punished?

Maybe a year or so after the curse, the Woman with the
Yellow Hat had disappeared from the streets. I am not exactly
sure when. The pharmacy came under new management. Got
a coat of fresh paint.

jules
surprise

FATHER HICKEY IN a grey turtleneck and grey pants with a blue jacket, two police behind him, a policeman in front, leading him into the courtroom. The flare on his forehead from the camera lights.

The video is about ten seconds; long enough for one of the policemen behind him to raise a hand and touch him on the back, or almost touch him. Guiding him forward. I'm surprised by how young he was. I am startled to realize he was younger than I am now. Father Hickey does not look directly into the camera, but his eyes, downcast briefly, glance up and he appears unconcerned.

He was known as a wit, and though his expression is closer to blank than animated in the video, there's the hint of a curious intelligence.

It is cut with another video: Father Hickey, dressed in priest's black with his white collar.

He's standing between Diana and Charles.

Diana is wearing pink polka dots on a white background

and a white hat with a wide brim, a bright pink jacket with white trim. The clip is long enough for her to glance at her feet and adjust her stance as if she's an actor looking for her mark. She is both scrawny and elegant, the dress somehow cool, though I remember the sun on that day baking the top of my head as I made my way through the crowd toward the stage.

Father Hickey drops his program in the chair behind him and also straightens his posture. Prince Charles fiddles with the microphones on the stand in front of him; he turns the two microphones toward each other and waggles them, one after the other, and turns them back out. He is making it look like they are puppets having a conversation. It's a playful gesture, while he chit-chats with the priest. Diana is flushed. I see myself in a striped T-shirt, when the camera roves over the crowd; there are three people between me and the stage.

I was seventeen and working for Parks and Recreation, driving my bike from Cowan Heights to Bowring Park to Bannerman Park, all the parks. I was an "artist mentor." I taught painting on the rainy days to kids in a pool change room in Victoria Park that smelled of chlorine. We performed puppet plays for the parents outdoors on the days it was sunny.

I'd met Gary Halliday at the Ship with my friend Larissa at noon one day in May. Gary was the art director of the Provincial Gallery, from Montreal via Haiti, and was in charge of hiring summer students for the city. I knew his work; we'd studied it in my first-year art history course at the community college in Stephenville.

Larissa sat across from me, wearing shimmery blue eyeshadow and black lipstick. She had a sleeveless pleather vest with the zipper showing cleavage and the top of her red lacy bra. Gary was in a tweed jacket with suede elbow patches and a cheesecloth scarf wound around his neck several times.

I'm getting three coffees, he said, give me a minute. I almost said that I didn't drink coffee, but Larissa gave me a look. I understood that she wanted to impress him, she'd only just been hired as an assistant at the gallery, and she'd put a lot on the line, arranging the interview for me.

When he was at the bar, she sat back with her arms crossed and gave me a wide smile that showed all of her perfect teeth, and spoke like a ventriloquist, without moving her lips.

Just drink it, she said.

Then Gary Halliday was back. He put down the tray with the three cups and saucers, each with two cubes of sugar on the side. I watched Larissa pick up the cubes in her long red nails, and I thought of the smell of nail polish that morning. We'd met up at her apartment before the interview. Her feet had been bare, and she was walking on her heels, cotton balls between each of her shiny red toenails. There were dishes on every inch of the counter, stacked high. The jar of honey was stuck to the Arborite tabletop. She hobbled back to her chair and put one foot up on a seat opposite.

I have to touch up this big toe, she'd said.

But at the bar, she was both smoldering and sincere. She dropped her sugar cubes into the cup with her fake nails, one after the other, meeting my eyes with each *plink*, pausing until I had done the same with my sugar. She had the kind of eyes that dragged themselves wearily from one object to the next, so that when they landed on you, the look was weighted with significance. Each lagging, reluctant glance a parody of a glance, or she may simply have had an iron deficiency that tired her out by mid-afternoon.

Gary talked about the ribbon on the neck of Manet's

Olympia. He'd just given a lecture about the gaze of the Black maid in the painting who offers Olympia flowers. Gary had done a series of paintings about the Black maid that had shown in London and New York. But I was too nervous to work any references to his art into my job interview as Larissa had instructed me to do.

I dropped my sugar cubes into the coffee. Larissa lifted her cup and looked at me over the rim.

She's been at the art school in Stephenville, Larissa said.

I've heard you're also doing classes with Sabine O'Regan, Gary said. He'd balled up his paper napkin and held it loosely over the table, like a soft wrecking ball. He let his wrist swing while he looked for a place to drop the napkin.

What do you think of her work? he asked. I knew that whatever I said about Sabine would determine whether I got the job or not. I understood I was being tested. I had to denounce her. All those hours painting politicians, the maudlin light in the portraits of their wives. The conservative realism, the sentimental lack of wrinkles or warts. But I also knew that wasn't her real work. The real work was the dancers, the atmosphere, things she did with light and compositions that were delicate, her own.

The whole desire to be an artist dropped away from me.

I picked up the coffee cup and the bitter taste was a shock. Why had I not worn black lipstick? I was wearing a white blouse with pirate sleeves and little silky tassels at the collar that had cost a fortune at Reitmans. I'd probably be handing in my resume there by the end of the day. I was disconcerted to discover how much I wanted that job teaching art. I wanted it very much. It hadn't occurred to me that I would be expected to take a stand. I glanced at Larissa, but she was putting her cup down, looking at it as if this little act required her attention. I was on my own.

I'm learning a lot from Sabine, I said. Then, more defiantly: I think she's a powerful painter.

I thought about that afternoon at the theatre when Sabine was on her hands and knees at the feet of the dancers. I thought of the charcoal stick cracking off and how she'd ripped right through the paper but kept on drawing; how she'd crumpled the whole sheet in a fit of frustration and tossed it away from her. Flung it, so that the tumbleweed of paper crashed around in front of the stage lights. And then how she'd captured the elevated ballerina, the strain across the clavicle, the arms flung open, head thrown back, raised up from the floor by some guy who was a strong dancer, part time at the crab fishery. All of it in a few black streaks and shadows on the creamy newsprint.

It wasn't just the drawings that had made me decide it was possible to be an artist, or that had given me the idea I could become one. Made me want to be one. Decided me. It was her face on that afternoon, caught in one of the stage footlights, a silver line of light on the edge of her cheek, her steel-coloured hair, her hard, downturned mouth, the look of someone chasing something.

She'd raised children, she gave lessons, did the portraits of all the potato-ish, dour politicians, grew roses in her little garden. But wild roses that she had transplanted, not the kind of roses from the nurseries that everyone else had. It was how possessed she had been, in that moment with the charcoal on the floor of the stage.

Gary Halliday dropped the napkin and jerked his head to the side, and very slowly rubbed his hand over the stubble on his jaw, then he looked back at me, raised an eyebrow.

She had nice things to say about you, Gary Halliday said.

He was handsome, with large black eyes, high cheekbones, and long dreadlocks. He was a deep blue-black, and lit by the window of the pub, the thick wooden shutters thrown open, the glass filthy with cigarette smoke.

You have the job, he'd said.

I went from park to park and made puppets with the children. We used twigs and balloons and scrunched up balls of paper for the heads. We made puppets with old socks and buttons and pipe cleaners. There were puppets with brown, shrivelled maple leaves for hands, fluorescent pink eyebrows from a bargain store feather boa. We made puppet theatres from cardboard boxes that TVs and stereos had been packed in.

On the day of the royal visit, I'd been issued an identification card with a picture I'd had taken at city hall, which allowed me into the ceremony with Father Hickey. The identification card said I was seventeen and a student employee with the Parks Program. The field was so crowded I had to wedge through with my shoulder, nudging people out of the way, to get close to the stage. I managed to get near enough to the front to see the mild flutter of Diana's dress in the breeze. She'd pressed her big-boned hands down to still it.

The photograph on my identification card has been disintegrating since. But the tan and a flaring innocence is evident, an unequivocal willingness to hang on to the brightness of the flash, to the lithe and zipping rides through the streets of St. John's from park to park, to a belief that everyone has some good in them.

. . .

FLORENCE RECEIVED A call at dinner, and she took it.

I heard her say, Hello Jim. My father-in-law raised his butter knife to silence everyone at the table. We put down our cutlery and bowed our heads to listen. Father Hickey had called to ask her to sell his house. It was the day after his first appearance in court. There were so many charges against him. Children. Young children. Boys. The vile things he had done. How the church fell all around him. Everything we had taken for granted was no longer granted. The turtleneck and his glance at the camera, the lack of remorse, the eager, ugly, sly charm.

The next day Florence beat away the hazard tape around the front door of the house and stepped inside the porch. There were police stationed outside, but they'd let her go through without comment. She started with the basement, as she always did, and found it dry. She opened a door and there was a bedroom with a bed covered in a black satin bedspread. The walls and the ceiling had been painted black, there was a plain wooden cross with a wooden Jesus and it hung upside down. A mirror on the ceiling. An altar draped in black, hidden in the closet.

She blessed herself and said, Sweet Jesus.

Upstairs she found the study with a high-backed desk chair facing a window that looked out onto a substantial garden with apple trees in blossom. In front of the chair was a massive and tidy desk with a blotter and a letter opener with a pearl handle. He had destroyed her belief in the church, but not spirituality. Not love, or charity. Everything else had been destroyed, him and the brothers at Mount Cashel, the other priests, each night on the news another atrocity revealed, men who were guests in her home. Her sons had been altar boys. She still had the communion dresses the girls wore and the white gloves and the little white shoes touched up with polish.

She'd come because she could not forgive them. She wanted to be absolutely sure she could not forgive them.

The chair swung around and there was Father Hickey himself; he had been released on bail. He was holding a crystal tumbler on the palm of one hand, his fingertips and thumb of the other hand resting on the rim of the glass, the hand crouching over the gold sloshing rum like a spider.

Hello, Florence, he said.

stick and poke

TRINITY HAD BEEN visiting at a house on the outskirts of town out off Topsail Road, after the Sobeys Square movie theatres, beyond all the used car lots, a house down a paved driveway that turned into a dirt lane.

She'd gone with a girl she knew from the grade ten after-school math tutorials, Ivy Cull, who didn't need tutoring but liked the quiet of a nearly empty classroom, the teacher up front marking tests, and just a half dozen students rapt by Ivy's ability to figure out problems.

Ivy could touch a math problem with the point of a sharp-ened pencil, enter a trance lasting maybe twenty or thirty seconds, and then write the answer. She'd go back after and jot down the steps for Trinity and the other students, as if showing how she got there. Trinity could tell Ivy hadn't fol-lowed steps to get the answer.

Ivy just knew the answer.

Trinity had passed a few math tests with Ivy's help, then she got a B, and finally a ninety-two percent, before she was invited to the house where Ivy was couch-surfing. After the day's tutorial, on the school parking lot, Ivy had thrown her bag into a grey Datsun truck with sores of rust over the pan and climbed in on the passenger side, rolled down the window, and told Trinity to get in too.

She stood at a distance, gripping the straps of her knapsack. A premonition, or a sudden shift in the breeze that caught up a bunch of dried leaves in a little rustling swirl before hurling them back to the pavement. It was her turn for a trance.

Dave can get you back before six, Ivy said.

This was Dave Costello, an older guy Ivy hung out with because he had a driver's licence. He had a long, narrow face and his teeth were jammed together in the front, overlapping, an incisor the brownish colour of a bad replacement. His hair, drawn into a bun on the back of his head, was thick and long. When he removed the elastic, it dropped over his shoulders, a dark honey colour. Trinity got in, and Dave put the truck in gear and set off before Trinity had done up her seatbelt.

Inside the house there was a TV going and a radio with the news in the kitchen, music in a bedroom, and different music at the other end of the house. A woman who looked to be in her twenties came down from upstairs. She'd just woke up, her mascara was smeared. She was dressed in plaid pajama bottoms and an undershirt, no bra. She opened the fridge door and looked inside for a long time, shut the door and left the kitchen.

Ivy waited until the woman had trudged back up the stairs. She bent to open the cupboard under the sink and removed a scrub bucket behind which she'd hidden a can of Meatballs in Gravy. She opened the can and turned it over into a saucepan and the food plopped out. Once it was spitting hot and the kitchen full of the smell of burnt meat, Ivy put the saucepan in the centre of the kitchen table and got two spoons. They both ate it out of the saucepan.

Trinity washed out the pot. Through the back window over the sink she saw a junkyard of scrap metal. Fridges standing upright with their doors removed, old stoves in avocado and beige and white, piled on top of each other, crushed cars, a mangled baby stroller, a set of wooden kitchen chairs, spindles broken and jagged like bones. A seagull sat on top of a mannequin head.

She'd been invited over, it turned out, to help Ivy bleach a hank of her long, thick hair.

It's one thing I can't do on my own, Ivy said.

In the bathroom, Ivy got out a box of dye she said she'd shoplifted, unfolded the paper instructions, peeled the crinkly plastic gloves off the paper, and laid them on the edge of the sink.

She bit the tip off a plastic applicator and mixed two different formulas in a bottle. She put the gloves on and placed her index finger over the broken applicator tip and shook it, then she handed the bottle to Trinity and told her to squeeze the liquid over her scalp, parting the hank of hair into small bits and getting the dye spread throughout. Then Ivy smeared the goo from her roots all through the big chunk of her hair. She rubbed it in and removed the gloves and they sat on the side of the bathtub to wait.

You want to do it too? Ivy asked. There's enough left over.

Trinity knew Mary Mahoney would not comment, but she would be disappointed. She wondered if she owed it to Ivy, after getting the ninety-two percent in algebra. The high mark had made Trinity think she'd underestimated herself. It had been a revelation.

Ivy tugged up the leg of her jeans to show Trinity a stick-and-poke tattoo, just above her ankle.

It was a pointy heart with the name Terry above it. Ivy had passed out on a couch in the middle of a field party, woke in the sunlight with a tattoo on her ankle. She never heard, first nor last, who Terry might be, or if there even was a Terry.

She twisted on the ball of her foot so Trinity could get a good look at the tattoo. They both stared at it until Ivy glanced up at her, and the ammonia fumes from the dye made Trinity crinkle her nose.

It's no big deal, Ivy said. It's only a little tattoo.

I think I was at that party, Trinity said. She had been wondering if the same could have happened to her. Tattooed with a stranger's name. The horror of it on her face. She had failed to make light of the tattoo and it was a miscalculation. Now she could see that Ivy was quietly furious.

Dave says he knows your mother, Ivy said. She'd cast her eyes down at her hands, which she held out in front of her, the fingers spread, the nails bitten down, a few bleeding, patches of old nail polish. Trinity thought that if she could get Ivy to look at her, they could go back to something less bitter, a collusion or tryst, something that could hold just long enough for her to get the address, but *wouldn't last kissing time*, a phrase that came back to her, from her mother.

It's Dave who rents this place, Ivy said. She put her hands under her bum on the edge of the tub. I told him your name was Trinity and he said must be the same one. Says there aren't many Trinitys around. He knows where she's at in Toronto.

I sell weed for him, after school, Ivy told her. You could do it too. He's a decent guy. I mean, he sells it for someone else, who sells it for someone higher up than him, but I make a killing. Soon I'm going to have enough for a damage deposit. I left the home where they put me. I didn't like it. Why I'm on that couch down there. I'd say, another couple of weeks, I'll have first and last months' rent. I already got the place picked out.

Ivy handed Trinity a plastic water jug and together they rinsed the dye out. She got a hair dryer from a wicker cupboard and bent all the way over, so her hair hung down. She blew her hair dry and flung her head back. She turned her three-quarter profile to the mirror and tilted her head to catch the light. She emptied her face of emotion, so it was blank and wide-eyed, and ran her fingers through it.

I think this colour is pretty, Ivy said. Do you?

Think he'd tell me where my mother is?

After a while, he might, she said. If you sell weed he would. He definitely would then.

Ivy began to put away the stuff she'd used to dye her hair. She tossed the empty bottles into the garbage can and the plastic bag stretched over the mouth suffocated the bang with a soft *whomp*. She caught Trinity's eye in the mirror and the chill went out of her.

Trinity could see the plan had been, all along, to recruit her. Maybe even as far back as when Ivy showed her how to do the math.

Look, Ivy said. It's a good way to make money fast. Only, don't let him drop you off at your house. Say you want to get out at the supermarket, or some other house, and cut through a few backyards.

She reached into the shiny gold bag she used for her

makeup and took out a lipstick. She put it on in the mirror.

You'll be fine, she said. Just don't trust him and don't let him know where you live.

But she was staring into her own reflection as she spoke and seemed to be talking to herself.

TRINITY STARTED SELLING weed for Dave Costello.

Nothing wrong with weed, Dave said. He told her to sell it at the school. There was a big market on the parking lot when everyone came out for lunch. She was still underage and wouldn't go to jail if she were caught.

Worst happens, community service, he said. She met him after school in the parking lot once a week. Gave him the money, minus her share of ten percent, and he fronted her more weed.

He said, No pressure.

She'd heard Dave talking to Ivy about Big Murph, and someone named Little Murph. Ivy told her they were the people directly over Dave.

That's who Dave answers to, Ivy said.

After a couple of months of her selling weed, Dave said Trinity was good at it.

One of the best, he said. You don't smoke the proceeds.

How many you got, Trinity asked.

That's key, starting out, Dave said, ignoring her question. That's why you're able to turn a profit. You focus. You analyze for risks and offer friendly service. Most girls, their profits go up in smoke. Not you. You're too smart. You sock it away, don't you? I don't see you a big spender.

He said she was a grade above those girls. He told her to keep the money good and hid.

Mind you don't let that old bag you're living with find your stash, he said.

He must have followed her, driven by Mary Mahoney's house. Seen her through the window. Or someone had informed him of Trinity's living situation. The casual insult against Mary Mahoney made Trinity's stomach flip and her bowels felt watery. *Old bag.* This woman who had taken care of her. The hairs on her arms stood up, shivers. She was alert but she tried to look unalert.

Dave had only ever been kind, a patter of compliments about her being cool-headed. Once he had a pizza on the front seat, and after they'd done with exchanging the money and drugs, he told her to take a piece.

Go on, luh, he said. I can't eat all that. I got ulcers.

Pineapple, she said. He said he knew she'd like pineapple. He made a fist and jerked it up, in a sign of victory, his eyes shut tight, and he brought the fist softly down on the steering wheel and whispered, *Yes.* I knew it. Don't ask me how I knew. But I *knew*.

He said he recognized in her a particular quality, the ability to make things work out. He said it was an asset. Once, when he was very stoned, he told her she was beautiful, inside and out.

This could be a real good move for you, he said. Work less than an hour a day and you make as much as someone behind the counter at Dominion for eight hours. He pointed out the other jobs, at Walmart, at KFC, the fish plant where his mother worked her whole life, home care where he had a sister hurt her back lifting this one old man in and out to change his bedsheets. His youngest sister had run up all her credit cards and had some guy calling her all the time. She'd have to go to court but for he stepped in. Stepped in and wiped it all out.

Trinity didn't tell him she had made up her mind to only do it for a couple of months. But the money began to seem a defining characteristic of her personality. Knowing she had it gave her confidence. The magical fact of its accumulation. Even the physical heft of it. She kept it under her bed and arranged it with the heads of whoever was on the bill all going in the one direction. She kept the denominations in separate stacks, each stack secured with an elastic band, all of it in the Sleeping Beauty knapsack she'd held tight in her arms the night she'd been taken from her mother. The last night Trinity had seen her.

Mary had bought her an electric blanket for when the weather got colder because of the draft from her window. Trinity turned up the dial on the blanket past nine. After nine there was an icon of a red lightning bolt. As she fell asleep in the suffocating heat, all the houses she'd ever slept in passed through her, the walls shifting, the carpets changing, creaks in the floorboards particular to one or another house of the past. The only constant was the money under the bed. She confused the source of the heat from the blanket with her knapsack under the bed, full of all her money. The money was radiating a sickly but seductive heat and she wondered if it was slowly cooking her organs.

He'd called Mary an old bag. He knew where she lived. She tried to look impassive, but glanced at him to see if he had given this information away by mistake, or if it were a threat.

Big Murph wants you to sell some coke, Dave said. So it had been a threat after all.

It's a way you can make a lot of money fast. We'll drop you at a party on Friday night. Up by Pius Tenth and Gonzaga, that area, fella coming up in oil. Everyone there got money, lawyers and shit. He'll meet you in the kitchen, this guy, the host. You get rid of it as fast as you can and leave. We parcel it fifty bucks a baggie, you take the bill, give them a baggie. You don't talk to anybody. You don't give change. You just take the money and give them coke and you get out of there.

This is short-term, she said. My commitment here.

You need money for something special? A damage deposit? Most girls are just looking for a damage deposit. A couple of months' rent somewhere doesn't have the wind blowing through?

Trinity hadn't seen Ivy in weeks. She'd stopped going to math tutorial. She wasn't sleeping on the couch at Dave Costello's anymore.

A nest egg, Dave said. That the idea?

Where's Ivy, anyway? she said. But he didn't answer.

I'll pick you up, down the street from your house. Have some pizza.

I'm not hungry, she said.

Just have a piece, he said. I bought it for you.

She opened the lid on the small-sized pizza he'd wedged between the windshield and the dash. She began to pick off the pineapple one piece at a time, and flick it back into the box.

Ivy said you knew where my mother was, Trinity told him. I'd like to maybe send her some money from this coke thing. The only reason I'd have any interest in something like that.

After two months of selling weed she had enough for a plane ticket to Toronto, and a place to stay for a couple of weeks. After the coke, she'd stop selling and find a regular job. If she had the address she could go at any time.

mary
the file

THREE MEN HAD come knocking at Mary's door asking for
Trinity, one of them with a gun, which he pointed at Mary's
gut, demanding that she send Trinity down the stairs and out
into the street.

The one with the gun was in his late twenties. He was
standing under the porch light, and close enough the gun
brushed her stomach a couple of times when he swayed.
A vein pulsed at his temple; the cartilage in the bridge of his
nose was sharp and straight. He'd jerked the gun upward so it
pointed at her throat, and forced her to look him in the eyes,
simply by blocking most of the door. He was a head taller
than Mary, but he was on the step below her, so their eyes
met. His, a light brown, red-rimmed and sore. They were
close enough Mary could have wiped away a melted snow-
flake hanging in his eyebrow.

After she'd heard the men get into a truck, both doors
shut, the engine start, she went up the stairs. Her legs were
wobbly, and she'd stopped halfway, holding the rail. She

heard Trinity's mattress creak as the girl shifted her weight. It had begun to rain; it splattered from the eave onto the steel garbage bucket she'd bought to discourage rats. The rain would put a dent in the snow. She started up the stairs again and sat on Trinity's bed. They were both sitting, side by side.

Do you know who he was? Mary said.

Dave Costello, Trinity said. I could hear his voice.

Mary put her forefinger to the bridge of her glasses and pushed them up, bowed her head and shut her eyes. She was trying to avoid tears. They'd found such equanimity, she and the sixteen-year-old girl beside her, and now it was over. She could manage on her old-age pension and the money she'd saved, after the child was gone. But Mary was startled by the swelling emotion.

They sat together on the side of Trinity's bed, both scrunching the bedspread in their fists, both looking down at the floor, speaking only a little above a whisper.

Mary had been called upon once or twice before to stand between a foster child and violence, and she'd experienced enough violence in her marriage, before her husband died, to wonder at the wonky moments between threat and follow-through, rife with unpredictability and clamminess. Those moments of ballooning stillness, a stagnant lethargy that crept into every object, animate and inanimate alike. The sheepish thought, devoid of will or logic, that there might be a valve somewhere, an invisible tap that could release the mounting tension before it exploded, all the while being convinced it would happen anyway, despite any valve or tender phrase or joke. The sluggish wait between the stalling and the punch.

She remembered reading Trinity's file, in preparation to receiving her as a foster child. A girl, seven years old, the mother gone. A stint in a group home in Conception Bay South for a year, and before that the Port Hotel on Torbay Road for six weeks. Her previous ward had grown up and gone, and Mary Mahoney was alone in the world. She thought of that as an accomplishment, though of course it wasn't true, she had the cat. But Child Protection had come to her again. She had a good reputation. This child would be the last. She knew then she might retire after Trinity.

They hadn't shared much of their histories with each other. Both had learned in childhood the advantages of keeping their thoughts to themselves. They valued the simplicity of not giving utterance to every little insight or mood. They shared a poor opinion of shooting off your mouth.

They also knew, since the day they'd met, that their relationship would not last — they could both detect a diffidence in the other that they found a comfort.

Sometimes foster families were fast, lifelong bonds, as was the case with Mary's previous ward. But neither Mary nor Trinity had wanted intimacy or love from this arrangement. Neither of them, Mary felt sure, was disappointed by the absence of that kind of deep feeling, most often too messy to sustain. They'd found something more valuable: silence at the dinner table. They were fluent in silence.

Mary was on her fifth foster child, if you didn't include the newborn infants she'd taken in for periods of two days to a week, before they were placed in more permanent foster homes or adopted; as she grew older, she could not bear the infants being taken from her, sometimes only a few days old they were, so she began requesting older children, who she believed had some instinct for survival that she could never be sure of with a newborn.

The desire to survive was all she required in a child she agreed to take on.

Being a foster parent paid her rent and heat bill. She worked in the school cafeteria every weekday for three hours, to cover other expenses, went to mass on Sundays, and volunteered at the Gathering Place on Sunday afternoons, serving dinner to the homeless or the elderly.

She'd taken Trinity to serve the meals, Mary going with the ice cream scoop, making balls of mashed potato, two on each plate, and Irene Caddigan following with the boiled carrots slathered with margarine. Margie O'Neill, a bright scarf over her bald head, she'd just got over the cancer, followed with a ladle and the pot of gravy.

The women did this part in grim silence, the race against vegetables getting cold. Teenage volunteers brought the plates to the long rows of tables. The voices of the eighty to one hundred guests rose and fell like the waves at Middle Cove. There were things Mary wanted to impart: Generosity was sustaining. Recognize when you have something to give. You will always have something to give. Everything should be piping hot.

What little conversation Trinity and Mary had when they were alone amounted to Mary offering advice in a tone both halting and certain, like a medium taking dictation from a wise, hygiene-obsessed spirit.

Each pronouncement, whether related to the practice of turning rubber gloves inside out to let them dry (blowing into the bunched cuffs so the fingers poked out, one after the other, with a little popping noise, as if each finger were counting off a blessing), the necessity of confession, which she said was a cleansing process, or the safe insertion of a tampon, or how

Trinity should address her teachers if she wished to avoid their attention, these bits of wisdom Trinity absorbed without question. Mary had achieved a meagre independence against the odds, and she hoped Trinity would learn by example.

When the man pointed the gun at Mary's throat, she'd felt the cold rush in around her. The cold had roiled up the stairs behind Mary, and she knew the child must feel it coming under her bedroom door. She thought about the heat escaping. Mary kept the heat low, on the edge of discomfort, only turning it up when she could see her breath in the parlour. She'd purchased a space heater because she'd read they were more efficient than baseboard heating.

She and Trinity positioned it on a chair at the kitchen table while they ate their dinner. The square of wire mesh at the front blew out a dense heat directed precisely at the both of them. For Christmas that year Trinity had bought Mary a pasta maker with money she'd saved from working at Booster Juice. At least that was where she'd said it was from.

They shared a computer, and when Trinity wasn't doing homework they watched cooking shows together, though Mary didn't attempt the recipes.

She'd been flummoxed by the Christmas gift. She'd held it in her hands, slack with confusion.

It's a pasta maker, Trinity said.

Yes, Mary said. I see that much.

It's for making pasta.

Pasta, is it? Mary asked. Isn't that something.

You can make pasta with it. It's got a part where it comes out linguine. A part where lasagna or ravioli. Different settings.

That must have cost you something, Mary said. She was

struggling for the anger she usually brought to conversations about the cost of things but felt stupefied. She wanted to hear the story of its provenance.

The box is damaged, Trinity said. They were after damaging the box in the warehouse, it was soaking wet, one corner of it. But the thing was all in a plastic bag inside, even the little booklet, I said to them, Has this been used?

You got a price then, did you? Mary asked.

Missus took off ten bucks.

They'd made the pasta together on Boxing Day. They watched a video and then Mary was cranking the little handle and the sheet came out thinner and thinner each time they changed the setting.

They ate in silence as usual, but after they were done Mary said it cost more than the boxed stuff, if you figured in the flour and eggs, and she priced it out. The pre-made stuff was cheaper by two bucks.

Trinity had taken the plates to the sink, smug with success.

Good though, Trinity said.

But it was something, Mary said. Wasn't it?

It was fresh, Trinity said.

Yes, it was, Mary said.

The payment for being a foster parent had gone up since Mary had started in that line of work, she'd told Trinity many times. She taught the children everything she knew about money. She believed that money was the bedrock of every relationship known to humankind.

She felt it was important to be up front about the nature of her relationship with her foster children; it was first and foremost a financial arrangement. It was an honesty that guarded against disappointment later, when the nakedness of the exchange was revealed. She believed in working hard and exercising a pliable frugality. The trick was to save and have the good sense to know when an indulgence was appropriate.

I can't afford to heat the street, Mary had finally told the men at her door. They were armed but she was made suddenly brazen by the cold blowing at her.

Sitting beside Trinity on the bed, Mary said she had been cold there in the doorway, talking to the men.

It was a wet cold, she said, and it blew right through me. Right into the bones.

It's a freezing rain, Trinity said.

The cold was like the day we buried my husband down by the lake, Mary said.

He'd been a drunk, a giant red bulb of a nose on him. She'd taken a month off work after he died and spent most of it in bed, and when the month was done, she'd decided to take in children.

Mary had believed the man at the door was going to shoot her, and for a moment the relationship they'd entered into, she and the man, struck her as the most profound and awful in her life so far — two strangers, one taking the life of the other. Meeting his eyes was a form of acquiescence unfamiliar and startling. She lifted her eyes to meet his and was soaked through with spiking fear, her armpits were slick, and the palms of her hands. She felt a bead of sweat run between her two breasts, despite the cold.

He was high and agitated. Mary Mahoney was as sensitive as a Geiger counter when it came to the flux of an inebriation or high.

She felt the man's building rage, though there was nothing in the inky dark and softly falling snow that might have alerted someone to it without previous experience.

She knew without doubt that he was ready to shoot her and that it would be unpremeditated. He had no idea it was coming.

She shifted tack, said if they didn't go away, she would call the police and she said about heating the street, and one of the other men said, Let's go, she's not here.

The man and the two youngsters he had with him, them not much older than Trinity, turned at once and headed down the road. Of course, they were recruiting from schoolyards, the kids who didn't have parents watching out. The ones desperate to belong. Trinity would have been hungry for something like that. The succour of being loyal, breaking rules, the indisputable, blunt authority of violence.

She knew, standing in the doorway with that man, that Trinity was on the edge of the bed, as tense as Butterscotch had been when somebody's dog had chased him up a telephone pole. Trinity would have been listening to the conversation, ready to spring down over the narrow staircase to save her. She'd taught the child to be steady. She believed she'd taught her that.

trinity
giving back

THE TEACHERS WERE saying that Bradley Murphy, when he was eight years old, was out of control. Causing anxiety in the other children.

All of this came back to Trinity, when she was sixteen, in Big Murph's darkened living room, where she'd gone to return the Sleeping Beauty knapsack full of drugs. The coke she hadn't brought to the big party with the oil people, near Pius Tenth School, because she'd been afraid to carry so much. The coke Dave Costello had told her she could sell later. She was bringing that coke back to the owner.

Standing there in Big Murph's living room, she'd seen the little child Murph had been in grade three settle over this teenager in the Adidas jacket.

As if he had felt the recognition dawn on her, he turned from the TV and glanced her way, and then sunk deeper into the oversized armchair.

She'd stood with the bag at her feet. He hadn't met her eyes. He was drawn to the TV show. He may not have recognized her.

The Adidas jacket was the red of a candy apple in the dark of the living room but looked cool to the touch. She hadn't known Big Murph was Bradley Murphy's father, Bradley from grade three. So Bradley was Little Murph.

It was Dave who'd fronted her the drugs. But she'd been afraid to give the rest of the stash back to Dave. He'd tell Big Murph she didn't give it back. Dave Costello would say she'd lost it all at the party when the cops busted in. It was Dave who came to the door, held the gun on Mary. And it was Dave who would go back to Mary's for the drugs, even after Trinity had left. Dave might have people on the mainland. He knew her mother's address but he might not guess that's where she was headed. He might think she was couch-surfing, laying low, hid out in some boyfriend's basement. Trinity couldn't give the drugs to Dave. She'd have to give them to Big Murph herself.

She hadn't expected to see Bradley Murphy ever again. He'd been led away by the cops in handcuffs from their elementary school during grade three, at recess time.

The rest of the class had stood at the front, near the blackboard, watching the spectacle. Usually, two teachers were called to wrestle Bradley to the floor when he acted out, but this time they called the cops and they'd come, two cops.

One of them in a uniform so tight across the chest he looked red in the face. She remembered the cop because he had a red moustache with a single strip of white under one nostril, the moustache so thick the cop seemed to have no upper lip. He'd taken off his hat and held it to his chest to ruffle his hair, but he looked like he was about to make a promise straight from the heart. He ruffled up his red hair vigorously and wedged the hat back on, straightened it by touching the beak with the tips of his fingers.

Brad had taken the stapler off the teacher's desk and thrown it at the window and the pane cracked. The zig-zagging crack had paused for a second, as if making up its mind which way to go, then travelled down to the window frame, a brilliant silver flare, here and there sending off little hair-like shoots. It made a sound as it travelled, a high-pitched *ping*.

Later the police would say they had consulted with higher-ups. A child psychologist somewhere out of province. A specialist in Toronto. Mary read it out of the *Telegram* over the dinner table. They'd both huffed in unison at the words "child psychologist." They'd both taken the measure of a few of them already. Even at eight Trinity was familiar with the questions, the tests, the poster paints and scented markers left out on the child-sized table in the child psychologist's office in case you wanted to paint a picture of your family. They didn't mention any names in the paper. Not even the name of the school.

The cops claimed somebody higher up had said handcuffs were better than a physical struggle, better than touching. They offered Bradley the option.

Bradley, is it? We can force you to the ground or we can ask you to turn around and hold out your hands and you get to try the handcuffs out.

Melissa Fahey said, Get the handcuffs, Bradley. Everyone wanted to see the handcuffs in action. They'd already seen Bradley wrestled to the ground several times. He was acting out on a regular basis.

Somebody else said, Put on the handcuffs.

Trinity had felt anxiety in her stomach. The cops had busted into her mother's apartment once and cuffed one of the boyfriends. Handcuffs were for adults. She felt her stomach flip, or it was the world upside down. Even in grade three she understood that it was a humiliation that wasn't meant for a kid. She'd had a jolt. A revelation. They were just kids. That was her jolt. As if she'd flown out of her body up to a corner near the ceiling and looked down and seen how small they were.

She'd understood it before Bradley Murphy did. Why didn't he just sit down and put his head on his desk?

Now she thought of the cops coming into the oil party up by Gonzaga. They'd got a noise complaint, or somebody at the party had called them about the drugs, or maybe they'd followed Dave Costello's truck. How she'd torn her way through the crowd with their money still waving in her face. She'd figured out where the exits were in the place as soon as she got there. Someone had turned on the kitchen light. There was red wine all over the floor. She knew as soon as the light came on, two fluorescent rings in the ceiling with a frost dome, the dome full of dead flies, a brilliant white light bouncing all over the white kitchen, that it was cops. She'd pushed her way through the crowd, past two cops in their uniforms, coming through the back door. She'd had to turn sideways. One of them had her arm but she wrenched it free from his grip, and then half the crowd in the kitchen was trying to squeeze through the back door behind her and she burst out into the dark garden and ran. Climbed the picket fence into another garden and another garden and a third, avoiding the open street.

They were all loaded, the people at the party. Dave Costello had dropped her off and she'd found her way to the middle of the kitchen as he'd told her to do.

She'd stood near the island in the centre of the room, full of wine bottles, crumpled napkins, and a man who said he was the host asked her who she was. Then word went out and she was swarmed.

Everyone waving fifty-dollar bills in her face. The baggies done up in half grams. The money sometimes smushed against her chest. There must have been a hundred people at the party. Maybe more. They were grabbing the drugs from her bag without paying. Mauling her. A hand on her ass. A guy had put his arm around her neck and was playing with her earlobe, flicking it with his thumb. She'd kept jerking her head away, elbowing people, kicking when she could.

They were pressing in and just as quickly they'd fled and the cops were all through the house, and the lights from the squad cars and she almost lost her boot in a snowbank in one of the backyards. She'd had to put her foot down with just her sock and sank through the glassy crust up to her knee. She reached through the wet, heavy snow to find the boot and fell over to get it back on. A light came on over a back porch and she saw someone in the kitchen window peering out at her and she worked her foot back into the boot and took off.

She ran through the field across from the Confederation Building and down a street to the path by Rennie's River, all the way to Larch Park. She'd crawled into some bushes and just stayed there, she had no idea how long, sitting on a rock. It took her a long time to recognize nobody had followed her. Finally she drew herself back up on the stone, her arms around her knees to control the shaking.

Her bag was gone. They'd taken the money. All of it, every cent, and the coke, whatever she hadn't sold, whatever had been left in the bag. Someone must have cut the strap on her bag.

It was all gone. She was shivering violently, her teeth chattering. It was gone. The sky was getting lighter now, a grey, granulated light, still dark, but more grey than black, and she got up and straightened herself out.

There would be some people heading to work. She had to get back home and get into bed before Mary got up.

The drugs were gone, except the stash she had back at Mary's, under the bed. She'd have to give that back. She wouldn't go through this again. But she knew in that moment she wouldn't give it to Dave Costello. She would return it to Big Murph herself, before Dave came looking for it.

Please don't put the handcuffs on him, the teacher had said about eight-year-old Bradley Murphy. Trinity had felt the acid of vomit in the back of her throat, but she swallowed.

Bradley had turned his back on the cops and held out his wrists behind him. One of the cops strode forward and cuffed him. They could all hear the tightening of the cuffs, the clink of the short chain between.

How's that feel, the cop said. He spoke as if to soothe.

Too tight? Not too tight, is it?

At first it had seemed a game, when the cop suggested it, but when Bradley turned around his head was hanging down and he was crying, and he couldn't wipe the tears away because his hands were cuffed behind his back. He tried to raise his shoulder, but he couldn't get it up to his eye.

Broke the window, didn't you, the other cop said. Now we'll take you for a ride to the station in the cop car.

Everything is okay now, the teacher said. Please take those cuffs off. Don't take him anywhere.

Step aside, Miss, the cop said. They all realized that the calibrated clicking of the cuffs, as the cop tightened them up on each wrist, was the ratcheting of no way back. They had no way back from putting the cuffs on little Bradley Murphy. He would always be, for the rest of his life, a child who the police had handcuffed.

In the living room with the sixteen-year-old Bradley Murphy, she wondered if it was true. That there were arbitrary moments and mistakes that you couldn't undo no matter how much you regretted them. Dave Costello had threatened Mary with a gun. There was nothing she could do about that.

After the handcuffs there had been an uproar, of course; Child Protection had their say in the *Telegram* against the action of the cops. A few doctors from the Janeway weighed in, talked about the psychological damage caused by such an action. But the moment had happened. They'd all seen it. Xavier had been there too, that day in grade three, when the cops put the cuffs on Bradley. They'd been in the same class back then. She thought of Xavier at the basketball game, the two cops who had showed up there, how she'd stood in front of Xavier. Between him and the cops.

And the cops who had come to her mom's apartment along with the social worker, to take her away, her mother putting out a cigarette in the glass ashtray, stabbing the butt down with drunken precision, lit up golden by the little table lamp with the cellophane still on the shade.

Nobody had ever come between Trinity and the cops.

Trinity had thought Bradley Murphy was as good as wiped off the face of the earth after he was escorted out of the school in handcuffs. She'd later heard he and his father had moved to New Brunswick. She'd heard Nova Scotia, but then New Brunswick. It might as well have been Jupiter.

It was possible, of course, that the moment had bounced off Bradley Murphy without leaving a scratch. He might not even remember it. Maybe it was only Trinity who had absorbed the irreparable crack, those handcuffs. She was here, wasn't she? In a living room returning a bag full of drugs, answering to Little Murph and his father.

The chair that sixteen-year-old Little Murph sat in had an autumnal brocade. His hands gripped the armrests, the whitest things in the room, bony fingers emerging from the dark red cuffs of the stolen jacket. His legs were spread wide and the white high-top sneakers engulfed sharp naked anklebones. The TV was muted, but he was watching a car chase over a big bridge and police were coming from both sides, trapping the car in the middle. It was the biggest TV screen she'd ever seen in someone's living room.

It was already dark outside, so only the blues and reds from the flatscreen lit up his face. It had taken her a beat to recognize him.

She had given Bradley Murphy her ham and cheese sandwiches wrapped in wax paper that was folded with creases as sharp as hospital-bed corners.

Mary hadn't used Saran Wrap like the other kids' parents did; she reused wax paper, smoothing it out every day after school. It was easy for him to slide his eyes toward the TV while they waited for Big Murph. He seemed to forget Trinity was there. The only indication that he was aware of her was that his thigh was jiggling.

He'd gone to another school. She had not given him a

thought. But his name came to her and she said it, because she thought it would be better to have him on her side. She said, Bradley.

She might call him up out of the inert marble of those white hands, the hard white cheekbone, the lowered eyelids, the agitated knee. If there was anything soft in him, she wanted to draw it to the surface, the way you pull up an anchor, like the old cinder block Jules and Joe had used to tie on the speedboat at their place around the bay. How the anchor tipped and swayed up out of the muck at the bottom of the pond, light at first and heavier and heavier as it lifted toward the surface, like all things that could flutter up from the depths.

At dawn, the morning after the oil party, Trinity had opened the screen door on Mary Mahoney's house very slowly so it wouldn't screech on the hinges. She held the screen door with her hip as she turned the knob of the front door in tiny increments, listening for the tongue sliding back from the groove. It slid back with only the smallest of noises, a tiny *gluck*.

She pressed the door open wide enough to get through without a sound. In the porch, she'd taken off her boots and hung up her jacket as it had been before she left for the party. The jacket rocked a little on the plastic hanger. She put her fingertips on the sleeve until the jacket was still. She moved from the front porch to the staircase. She knew the places where the floor creaked and avoided them. She had one foot on the first step of the stairs when Mary said her name. Trinity turned and stood in the doorway of the living room. Mary Mahoney was in her chair, Butterscotch in her arms. The cat was purring.

I think you'd better explain yourself, young lady, Mary said.

EVEN BEFORE THE handcuffs in grade three, Murph had thrown temper tantrums and the teachers, who had been trained in safely restraining students who were acting out, soon began to restrain him without waiting for the tantrum to escalate. Even a hint of disruption and they were on him.

Once he had an instrument from a geometry set with two steel points, clutched in his fist and raised over his shoulder, ready to strike, and Miss Donahue ordered everybody out of the classroom in single file. They'd had to line up along the wall and wait. Three teachers arrived, called on the intercom, running down the staircase from the second floor, and filed into the classroom. But they found Murph asleep with his head on his desk. Other than causing disturbances, he often dropped into sleep without warning. Sometimes he couldn't keep his eyes open.

They had him on meds.

He was never physically hurt when the teachers restrained him, except that he must have come to understand there were the kinds of holds he could never get out of, no matter how hard he struggled. After the broken window he was expelled.

But here he was, eight years later.

She was leaving for Toronto in a week, so she was returning what was left of the drugs to Brad Murphy's father. It was all she could do.

Trinity opened the zipper of the Sleeping Beauty knapsack to show Little Murph the contents.

She hoped this was the end of the fear that had been aching in her chest like a torn muscle since the party.

She'd set off down Cabot Street with the knapsack full of

drugs, in the early evening, though it was already dark. She looked back at the house and Mary's bathroom light was off. She hadn't been able to see Mary in the cold black window, but Trinity knew that's where her foster mother was, and she lifted her hand and wiggled her fingers goodbye. She turned the corner of Cabot Street, and Trinity felt as if she had been shot out of Mary Mahoney's quiet, restful, iron-strong morality, her unequivocal sense of right and wrong, her fierce protection, a sometimes cloying, suffocating rigidity, into an entirely dangerous, compelling loneliness, an isolation that might very well kill her.

Murph in the aura of cool television light, just his hands, his cheek, the jiggling knee. Stony, insolent and full of a wonky off-kilter depth, and maybe longing.

Someone on the TV screen got out of the car jammed between an impossible number of cop cars on either side, the size of the screen too big, dwarfing them and their little lives, with his hands up, and all the cops, the ones in front down on one knee, filled the bad guy full of bullets, what a dance the shot body made, like a boneless ballerina, tiptoeing and jerking with every bullet, the soundtrack, if the sound had been on, must have had the syncopation of popcorn popping.

She knew, when the body crumpled to the ground and the camera zoomed out, an aerial shot that made the body look very small, a shot spreading quickly to take in the whole street, that Murph had recognized her as soon as she walked in, knew exactly who she was.

But he'd also looked at her like that in grade three when she'd handed him her sandwiches.

The light from the television slid all over the glossy Adidas jacket. She'd seen a list of stolen property on Facebook with a photo of the kicked-in back door, splintered wood jutting out, a crack across the glass.

Charlie Gorman, who had also been in grade three with them, his father high up in government, on the news all the time, had posted a list of what was stolen along with a picture of him in the Adidas jacket: Air Jordans, an unopened bottle of tequila, wireless earbuds, Samsung subwoofer and portable Bluetooth speaker. A flat gold necklace.

She'd recognized Charlie Gorman's stolen property before she recognized Bradley Murphy.

The necklace had a glint that lay in the dip of Murph's throat and moved back and forth when he breathed.

She had rung the bell and heard a man shout from an upstairs window. Big Murph — there was no doubt — telling her to come in through the back porch. The wind roared in behind her and laid flat the column of steam rising from a pot boiling on the stove. The lid of the pot jumpy and clattering, burping gusts of steam. Moose meat stew. She recognized the dense, gamey tang.

Trinity left her boots on, in case she had to get out of there, but she'd scrubbed them on the mat.

Come in, Big Murph shouted again. Go sit down in the den.

Father, there's somebody to see you, a man said, and it turned out to be Bradley Murphy, being funny, as though she was a neighbour making a social call, or the Avon lady.

Now they heard the door slam in a bedroom above, and someone coming down the stairs and the narrow hall.

Who's this, Big Murph said. Bradley Murphy glanced away from the TV. Big Murph had a gun in his hand. Trinity had never seen a gun before, but she only realized this when she saw it. She had seen the guns cops wore, tucked away in holsters. But she'd never seen a gun out in the open. She couldn't believe it was a gun. It looked too much like a gun. The metal appeared to be black and there were grooves in the chambers, what she imagined to be the bullet chambers or barrels, or whatever they were called. The nose of it was longer than she thought it would be for a handgun. The handle part was covered in two brown plastic panels that had been screwed on either side of the sloping metal. It looked cheap and too heavy.

The only convincing thing about the gun was the way Big Murph kept the nose of it pointed toward the ground, as if there was a need to be careful. As if it could go off by itself. The fact that she was in a room with two men and a gun hit her hard. Trinity realized with a deep weariness that she had been taking care of herself for a long time. She was as alone as alone could be, despite the fact that she'd given this boy her lunch, for the better part of six months in grade three. Trinity had been the only one to talk to him. All the other kids had been thrilled by the drama of his violent outbursts when they occurred, unprovoked, and haunted by them at night. Those outbursts were a rent in the idea that the adults would protect the children. The adults had put handcuffs on Bradley Murphy.

She felt the bang of blood in her temples. Big Murph swayed the nose of the gun toward the bag of drugs in the knapsack that Trinity's mother had bought her for kindergarten a decade before.

She had left Mary's in such an emotional state that she had not thought to transfer the drugs into another bag. It was all she had left of her mother, except a hair elastic. An ordinary black hair elastic that had a little knot of her mother's fair hair caught in the tiny squashed cylinder of metal that held the elastic together.

The gall of you, coming into my home, Big Murph said.

I brought back the drugs, Trinity said. He crouched and tipped out all the packages of coke from the Sleeping Beauty knapsack.

Not all the drugs, though, is it, Big Murph said. He riffled through the Ziploc bags, making a show of counting under his breath.

Not the stuff I lost at the party, she said.

You owe me a thousand dollars, Big Murph said, standing up. She heard his knees crack.

More like fifteen hundred, he said.

I can't sell no more, Trinity said

Here's what I suggest, Big Murph said. You find a way to get me what you owe. He lifted the gun and waved it at her, different parts of her, like he was choosing where to shoot.

Does that seem like a good idea to you? he asked. You got a couple of weeks. A thousand bucks.

Bradley Murphy stood up out of the armchair then and pretended to yawn, or he really did yawn. He stretched into the yawn with his whole body, one fist in the air almost to the low ceiling, one of his elbows drawn into his side, and the yawn ended with a quick intake of breath.

She's all right, Brad Murphy said. I knew her in grade three. Leave her alone.

jules
good run

TRINITY BROPHY HAD been living in foster care with Mary
Mahoney for nine years, from seven years old to sixteen. It
had been a good run. Xavier hadn't had much to do with her
after they both turned ten. There'd been a small rift. Some
minor injustice or breach of faith. Probably they couldn't
have articulated it if they'd tried, or even noticed it happening. They were making new friends; they lost track.

But she'd come over to do homework, talk with me while
I cooked.

I missed the days of having Nancy and Stella in the house,
and felt outnumbered with two men; it was good to have a girl
to talk to—an unwinding of what had happened to us during
the day or all the days. Sometimes I narrated my actions, a recipe
I was following. And that's a cup and a half of flour. Now for
the egg whites. That's what? Four egg whites? Oh, a bit of shell.

Trinity told me her marks.

Sometimes things she'd heard about Xavier. He was the
antic anti-hero in these stories, magnetic crowd-pleaser,

escaping the punishing eye of a teacher by deploying wit or charm. She'd smirk to herself, and then get to work on her math.

I could ask her anything in those days, when she was thirteen or fourteen, but I knew there were winks and folds in every story, things she kept from me.

Then I ran into Mary Mahoney at the supermarket and she asked me if I was giving Trinity money.

Money, no, I said. She'd been going through the green apples, looking for bruises or broken skin. She held an apple up to the fluorescent spank of overhead light.

She seems to have money, Mary said.

SHE CALLED A week after I'd seen her in the supermarket. It was already dark outside.

I'd like you to come over, Mary said.

Right now?

Yes, she said, right now. Then she said goodbye.

Okay, I'm coming, I said. But she had already hung up.

I looked over at her house while I did up my coat. All the lights were off. I called up to the third floor, where Joe was correcting papers, told him I was going across the street. Xavier was playing a video game with his headphones on.

Over to Mary's, I yelled.

Just got to finish these papers, Joe said.

It was only when I got close enough to knock on the door that I caught a glimpse of Mary's face in the window. I tried to open the screen door but it was locked. I waited and heard the lock *scridge* to the side. She stepped back into the living room. I wondered if she'd lost power.

I pulled off my boots without saying anything, letting my

eyes adjust to the dark, and turned through the living room doorway. There was only a single beam of a streetlight coming through a crack in the drawn curtains.

Mary Mahoney, standing in the corner of her living room, her arms crossed, each hand shoved into the opposite sleeve of her cardigan, gripping her elbows. I didn't hear Trinity on the stairs, but I felt her presence behind me, near the door frame.

Stay away from the window, Mary said.

Why are you in the dark?

Tell her what happened, Mary said.

They came for me, Trinity said.

Who came? I said. Nobody spoke. I knew something terrible had happened. I wanted to turn on a light.

Was there anyone out on the street just now? Mary asked.

I don't know, I said. I wasn't looking.

A young man came to the door with a gun, Mary said. Three of them, one with a gun, two of them had knives. I was never so frightened in my life. Him, and two he had with him. Them two, the ones he had behind him, looking at the ground.

Heads bowed down, she said. You wouldn't know but they were in church. Afraid to look up, they was. But him, right up in my bloody face. On the step there, right up to the door, asking for her. Me saying I hadn't seen her, saying she was over to a friend's. Him saying what friend's and I told him she got a lot of friends, and that much is true.

He was pale as the loaf of bread in there on the kitchen counter, Mary said. The one in front with the gun, the teeth on him stuck out like a bloody rabbit. The stink of cigarettes and alcohol. If he were mine, I'd drop him in a bucket of Javex. I said to myself, if he lays so much as a finger on her he'll rue the day he come knocking. She was upstairs.

Two cars passed on the street and we heard the tires slapping up slush. It had been very cold and there was a lot of snow. Then freezing rain and slush. My socks were wet on Mary's good carpet. I unzippered my coat and dropped down into the armchair, though I hadn't been asked to sit.

They'll be back, make no mistake. She owes them a fortune. An absolute fortune. After sneaking out in the middle of the night. She keeps her bedroom door shut, naturally, to keep in the heat. I was asleep, never heard a sound. She, creeping down the stairs, gone out the front door in the middle of the night to a party.

It was the longest speech I had ever heard Mary Mahoney make. I could see the encounter with the gun had transformed her. She looked younger, too bright-eyed, her colour had risen. Her slumped shoulders were straightened, as though the bones had been broken and reset. She appeared to have grown an inch.

Mary Mahoney had done everything in her power to protect Trinity. She'd gone through all the apples in the supermarket, getting the best product for her buck, she'd put up with my son's roughhousing on her good furniture, she'd worn her best outfit to the parent-teacher meetings. Listened to the teachers with her purse on her lap and her two hands folded over the clasp. I'd seen her in there through the little window with the wire grid in the glass; it was my turn to talk to the teachers after her. Mary Mahoney had done everything right, but it hadn't been enough.

I knew she depended on the money provided to foster parents, but she must have been worried, all along, about aging out of the business. It was the only reason, I was certain, she coloured her hair. She was without a speck of vanity. She maintained a scrubbed look, but believed any thought given to fashion was an indulgence, a sin of pride. She wore cat-eye glasses, but they weren't retro, they'd been passed down from an old aunt.

Everything had a careworn patina. The microfibre cream sofa she'd bought from Kijiji was without stain or scuff, except on the skirt, a streak of black tar, from Xavier's sneaker. He'd managed to track in tar, at least five years before, and smear it into the sofa nobody was allowed to sit on.

Trinity herself had always been very tidy, in the way of children brought up by strangers under the eye of social workers. She had a habit of lining up her shoes when she took them off in the porch of my house, toes to the wall on the edge of the bristly welcome mat. The shoes in my house were always in a soggy heap, bleeding slush and road salt.

She's been selling cocaine, Mary said. Cocaine, and the cops showed up. A big party.

I just ran, Trinity said.

She tore the leg out of her jeans going over a fence, Mary said.

Coke, I said. My eyes were adjusting to the dark. Trinity had crossed the room and she sat very stiff on the couch, as if there were a magnetic force pinning her there. Her elbows on her knees, her hands clasped. She was perched on the very edge of the cushion, so that it tilted up, unwedged from the back of the couch, threatening to tip her off it. She looked ready to fly up at the slightest sound.

Somebody took my bag, Trinity said. All the coke in it, all the money.

She has to leave here, Mary said. She's got a plane ticket.

Where's she going? I asked.

They kills people over nothing, Trinity said. I'm after losing all their money.

You went to a party? I said. You were selling coke? I felt the horror of it rinse through me, like when gasoline is poured on barbeque coals, and it penetrates and the match is lit, and the whole thing makes an inward, collapsing bang, more hush than bang. I felt an implosion. So dull and commonplace — drugs. She was in trouble because of drugs. She had been selling and Mary had not known. I had not known.

I wanted to be back in my house. The washer had been going when I left. Joe had put in a wash. And the dryer. Xavier had put his suede sneakers in the dryer. I'd been furious. I'd told him not to do that. The sneakers were going to break the dryer. The pedantic tumble of the rubber soles smacking the sides of the dryer over and over, as if running an infinite distance. Then I was seized with a faraway, hysterical fear.

But where is she going? I said.

I'm going to be with my mother, Trinity said. She had raised her chin a little, and I knew it meant she wasn't certain.

Is that wise? I asked Mary. It came out sounding sharp, even shrill. I was so angry they'd dragged me into it. I didn't want to know about it. I'd been fooling around with watercolours for the last hour. A garbage bag on the dining room table so if I spilled something it wouldn't spoil the wood finish. I'd been working with photographs from the summer, of the river in Broad Cove. The reflection of trees from the opposite bank on the still surface of the water. The stones on the riverbed, visible in the clear water. I loved how all the colours ran over each other. I had been lost in it when Mary had called.

I'm not asking for your opinion, Mary said. I'm asking

you to take her to the airport, she's leaving in a week. She's not safe here.

She was appraising me. We'd only known each other through the children. Our interactions were misunderstandings. In other words, she had always disapproved of me. And I wasn't that keen on her.

I was a good thirty years younger than Mary. In the summer I'd jog, each evening, in neon leggings and a running bra; I had an MP3 player and Donna Summer sang "I Feel Love" at the end of the run, which compelled me into an orgiastic sprint, past Mary's house. I'd glance in her window as I flew past and sometimes I thought I could see, beyond my own reflection, a swatch of her baby-blue polished-cotton blouse, her fashion mainstay, fresh as the day it arrived in the mail, a gift from a previous foster child who had gone on to become a nurse. She sat in the front window, which was otherwise a rippled reflection of clapboard from the houses on the other side of the street. And me, my reflection, my face and ponytail, bouncing over her flat blue chest. Then I'd run across the street to our house, which we'd painted a blazing sunflower yellow, talk about loud. Nancy and Joe and I loved it.

The next time we painted our house we chose black, or what my mother-in-law called charcoal. Nancy had moved out by then. Tristan had gone to university in France and Nancy had moved around the bay with her chef.

Mary Mahoney had been strict, when Xavier and Trinity were small, about when playtime was over. She used the word *curfew* and believed that making things happen at a certain time was a show of defiance against the powers of chaos. We hardly spoke, once the kids stopped hanging around together.

It was chaos that had brought those men to her door. It was chaos that made her stand as straight as rebar in concrete when facing the gun. Chaos had allowed her to give a smile that looked honest and simple-minded, when asked if she knew where Trinity was, all the while hoping the kid had the good sense not to come down the stairs to save her. She had known the men were high, unstable as sticks of dynamite, and even the creak of a floorboard somewhere behind her might set them off.

When the kids were eight, I'd stand at my door and Mary at hers, while Trinity waited for a break in the traffic and ran across the street. The little foster kid, as Joe called her, was always in our sightline — mine and Mary's. She was all pointy elbows and high knees.

Trinity ran across the street as if she were an Olympic contender. It was a performance for Mary. They could agree on obedience. The reason behind not being late for supper was the universe would crush you like an insect given half a chance, and understanding the timing of that particular danceathon, keeping one step ahead of fate, that was their superpower. They were always just one step ahead. I couldn't stand the woman, but I saw that she was graceful. My timing was off.

I'd never seen anything like actual love between Mary and Trinity, but there was something more durable and remote, a sense of inviolate duty toward each other.

I knew that if the man with the gun had forced his way into Mary's house, she would have given up her life to protect Trinity, and, at sixteen, the child would have done the same for Mary. They were family.

But on a sunny afternoon after video games, back when she was eight or nine, or after a trip to Bannerman Park,

Trinity would run across the street and down the opposite sidewalk, past Cheryl Dean's house, the actress, who had later moved to L.A., showrunner for a sitcom, and past Terry Grey's house, the guy who owned the restaurant on Duckworth, where Xavier would have his first job washing dishes, to Mary's small, boxy two-bedroom house, painted an old-fashioned oxblood, where she was holding open the screen door for Trinity.

Trinity would duck under Mary's arm. I'd hear Mary's screen door from my side of the street as it screeched shut behind the kid.

Sometimes I'd see Mary, when I jogged past, reading a book. She'd hold her cat against her stomach, the slothful animal fat and solid as a sack of flour. The cat-eye glasses at the very tip of Mary's nose, her chin tipped up, frowning in an effort to keep the glasses from falling off, her arm out straight with the book held as far from her as she could get it, as if holding things at a distance allowed you to fully comprehend them. The cat a kind of shield against whatever nonsense the author was up to.

The both of us were standing, now. Mary had wriggled her fists free from the sleeve of the sweater. But when she spoke she seemed brazen and unbending.

The flight is at eight in the evening, a week from today. I want you to park down the street, on Carter's Hill by the green house, the one with the garbage bag over the living room window. Trinity will go out the back door of my house and through the gardens. She'll come out by the green house and get in your backseat and you go straight to airport. She's going to Toronto. We'll just hope to Jesus they don't got anybody up on the mainland can find her.

Can't we call the police? I said. They waited in silence for me to realize we couldn't call the police.

Trinity yawned. I'd seen her do this before in moments of distress. Her face morphing, stretching wider than seemed possible, her head tilted back, eyes shut tight, all with a languid slowness that seemed the opposite of fear.

But Trinity's never been off the island, I said. What happens when she gets to the airport in Toronto? Where does she go? My god, she'll be there by herself. She's just a child.

It's not safe here, Mary hissed. Her tight fists trembling at her sides until her hands flew up in exasperation at my stupidity. I thought she might slap me. She'd stepped toward me and I saw in the light from the window that her face was wet with tears. She must have been crying soundlessly ever since I had arrived. Perhaps she wasn't even aware of it.

They had weapons, she said. They came here for her. The child tells me she's been in contact with her mother. She's sixteen, I couldn't stop her if I tried. I got no control over her no more.

They'd been calling me but I never answered, Trinity said. Mary told me not to answer and I never. We never had nothing to give them. I said they'd show up, but Mary booked the ticket. I lost all the money and the coke I had on me. I knew they'd be coming for me. If they come back again and find me, they'll kill me.

Trinity stood up. The feeling in the room shifted. They were waiting for me to understand that the decision had already been made.

Mary doesn't have a car, Trinity said.

I'll drive her, Mary, I said. You want me to drive her, I'll drive her. Whatever you say.

A truck passed the window, and it slashed the streetlight that fell on Mary's face.

She nodded slowly with her lips pursed hard. I had come up a notch in her estimation. But she was not grateful. She believed I had no choice. We all owed things, it wasn't clear to whom or what, not necessarily to each other. She was getting out of the foster business, subjecting herself to a new kind of solitude that, when I gave it consideration — just Mary and the cat — felt vertiginous.

I phoned Nell once I was back in my own house, to tell her what had happened. If she thought Trinity really had to go.

Do you think it's the right thing to do? Put her on a plane? I asked. Nell was silent.

I knew what those kinds of pauses meant when I was talking to Nell. Sometimes I said, Are you there? Even though I knew perfectly well she was there. She wasn't trying to be dramatic, it meant she was shocked, or thinking, or afraid. I was never actually sure what it meant, but the silence had a momentum, like a wave rolling in to shore from a long distance. It annoyed the life out of me. But I knew it was the result of my off-loading the thinking to her. I let her do the heavy lifting in these kinds of situations, the ones involving the law, the ones where a lot was at stake, or maybe nothing. Maybe it would be as simple as waiting in the dark while Trinity made her way through the dead alders behind the houses on Cabot Street.

Nell said, There was a case six months ago, someone murdered over a sixty-dollar drug debt.

There was another pause.

Are you there? I asked.

jules
deluge

XAVIER AT THIRTEEN years old, revving the engine.

Take it easy, Joe said. Joe had given him permission to drive the dirt bike to Nancy's for Gerry's fortieth birthday party. Nancy threw the party every year, an excuse for the family to get together. Gerry, the baby. A big bash.

Over the old railbed, through the grown-over lanes and footpaths. It would take him an hour. They were checking the gas. Xavier made a few circles around the house. I could see him through the branches of the apple tree, popping a wheelie on the front lawn, roughing up the sod. He was going to watch a DVD before he left for the party, or play a video game. He'd show up before the food was served. Before we got in the ocean.

The day had begun with a deluge. I was soaked running from the car to Lorna's Convenience for birthday candles. My sneakers squelched water on the way to the back of the store. Cracks of lightning over Bell Island, splintering the charcoal clouds, jagged lines of it tippy-toeing across the ocean from

Portugal Cove to where we were, Broad Cove, Conception Bay North. A few times big planks of violet light, making everything an x-ray, the white roses garish, a silvery on-off, on-off, and the thunder over the roof so loud we ducked, eyes to the ceiling.

I phoned everybody still in St. John's and told them they shouldn't drive on the highway. I said we should cancel. The road slick with water. The party was at Nancy's in Western Bay. I called Nancy. She said it was clearing already down there. They were going ahead.

Forget cancelling, Gerry said. We're not cancelling.

A half hour later the sun broke out and the steam was rising, a double rainbow from one side of the harbour in Broad Cove to the other, and before noon it was exceptionally hot, already twenty-seven degrees, and people were coming from town in droves.

Later that afternoon, just before the potluck, we'd all get in the ocean. We'd have to get in before we knew what we were doing because it was so cold.

The waves loud when they crashed, a deep thumping. We'd run in wearing our bathing suits, our shorts and T-shirts, our underwear. The kids, grandkids, the dogs barking. Beach rocks tumbling backwards into the sea. White foam, spent, knuckling over the rocks, fumbling with them, drawing back the round shiny ones and us hobbling over the collar of rocks to the sandy apron and we'd keep running until we were up to our waists and then we'd dive under.

We would run out into it, lifting our legs high because it would be so cold. Just sting. The cold would make our legs insensate and hurt our bones until we were numb and couldn't feel anything. The Atlantic in late August.

I'd told Xavier we'd be in the water by the time he arrived. Meet us at the beach if we're not in the house, I said.

Kelp would slither around our ankles and make us stumble, send shivers of a different kind, a preternatural fear of things under the surface, the fronds and nubby seeds, the unseen slither. They say because things are warming up there have been more sharks. Little nurse sharks. A few great whites, but they're not the heat-seeking missiles myth makes them out to be — those broken-nosed hoodlums are way out there, halfway between Portugal Cove and Bell Island. Minding their own business. Garbage guts. There are definitely things to be afraid of, but not quite yet. On this day I am afraid Xavier will fly out of the alders at high speed on the dirt bike and cross the highway without stopping. I know he will do this.

Jellyfish are the worst. One year little Dorothy Rennie with her purple bathing cap, coming out of the water screeching and had to have calamine lotion rubbed all over her belly and one thigh, spoonful of Benadryl.

The swell would lift us off our feet. The surface a blast of sparkles. The waves would pass through us and we'd touch back down on the sandy, stirred-up floor.

The dirt bike was chrome and lime green and there was a lime-green helmet to match, with orange flames over the ears and a tinted visor. I'd watched as they got the bike out of Gerry's truck, and at first it was hard to start. It had a kick-start. Joe was afraid that Xavier didn't have the strength for it. After a moment Joe waved him off the seat and got on to kick-start it for him. He kept it idling, leaning over the handlebars while Xavier got on. Joe stepped aside and the bike took off down the road, two roiling pillars of dust billowing skyward. The dust was a fortress Xavier was outracing, but it closed behind him. He went so far the engine sounded like a buzzing fly, then he turned near the trestle and came back at top speed.

We were both standing in the middle of the lane, Joe and me, and we leapt out of the way as he tore through us and skidded to a stop with a wing of flying stones. The dust settled. Joe ran up the road a bit behind Xavier. And when he turned back to me, I could see he was joyous, as if it were him, at thirteen, on the back of the bike.

But I didn't think he was ready. He's not driving all the way to Gerry's party, I said. He'll have to cross the highway.

I'm ready, Xavier said.

We'll see you there, Joe said.

Yeah, later on, Xavier said. After Xbox.

Don't be on Xbox all afternoon, your cousins are coming.

I'll be there, he said.

Look both ways, I said. Get off the bike and walk it across the highway, I said. Promise me.

I'll get off and walk it.

We'll see him there, Joe said to me.

two

two

jules
last cigarette

SLEEPING IN THE chair beside my son's hospital bed, not
knowing if he would reach consciousness, I woke to the smell
of Camel cigarettes. There was a smoke ring, no bigger than
my wrist, floating in the doorway of the hospital room, lit
by the fluorescent light from the hallway. At first, I thought
it was one of the people who drag their oxygen tanks or IV
poles down the elevator and out the front to smoke in their
housecoats. Getting a last cigarette in before the storm pulver-
ized us. The smoke ring floated down, waggled and became
thin and broke apart.

I knew I was dreaming, but the veracity of it was a
marvel. Sabine came into the hospital room in the painting
smock. I saw that one button near the collar was half in and
half out of the buttonhole. There was a slash of cadmium
red on the collar.

I was aware she'd had to come out of her way, and her
appearance drenched me with hope. It had been an effort for
her to show up, but any show of affection, while she'd been

on earth, had been effortless. Effort was the only flaw in the illusion of her presence. It was how I knew I'd dreamt her.

She raised the cigarette, cupping her elbow with her other hand, to her mouth; it was between two straight, stiff fingers. She turned her head toward it and inhaled from the corner of her mouth, keeping her eyes on me.

We both knew the visit couldn't last long. I knew the brevity of it was going to be hard for me.

Nobody speaks in my dreams, but things are communicated. It's always as if they *have spoken*. I stood up from the chair I'd fallen asleep in, the chair beside my son's hospital bed. Wanted her to hold me, but we weren't the kind to hug.

It was my son lying there beside me. That part was definitely real. I decided to hug Sabine anyway, what the hell, it was my dream, I could do whatever I wanted.

I knew that as soon as I altered the truth of what might have happened, I'd lose her. That was the logic of active dreaming. But I needed to be held. I opened my arms. She stepped into me, holding the cigarette out at arm's length. She'd always been bony. It was ridiculous to hold her; she was embarrassed. She pulled away as soon as was polite and there was the rueful dimple, the half smile that meant I'd asked for too much.

She turned and walked out the hospital room door, and it seemed she was on a moving sidewalk, because though she had turned back to face me, she was drawn away. Smaller and smaller, as in the eyepiece of a backwards telescope. I watched until she'd reached the vanishing point.

I OPENED THE video on my phone. I was sitting beside Xavier's bed, and I held his hand while I watched it. There is a moment:

Xavier's T-shirt is torn from one shoulder like a toga. This shoulder catches the streetlight. His shoulder, round and white and overexposed. The phone camera adjusts to the white of his shoulder and it goes dim and the image winks out as the mob closes in on him, their bodies blocking the streetlight.

The T-shirt used to belong to Joe. Xavier was wearing it when they built the back deck. Joe turning around with a two-by-four in his arms, accidentally tapping Xavier on the bum. Xavier spun around, surprised by the touch, both knocked a little off balance, then pretending to stagger like drunks, clowning, Xavier did a mock one-two boxing move, chin tucked, slow-mo, the fists stopping an inch from Joe's chest. Joe dropped the two-by-four and played an air guitar, hunched over it, flinging himself around by the hips, strumming hard. Xavier holding a pose, fists up near his face, as if he had to peek out at this spectacle from under cover, as if Joe's silent, vigorous rockstar performance required a boxing strategy out of Xavier's reach.

Xavier had gone to boxing classes out by the Shoppers just past Dairy Queen on Topsail Road when he was ten, the smell of the borrowed boxing gloves. The shiny red shorts that came to his knees. Dancing around the living room with earbuds, shooting his fists and letting them rest near his chest. I'd stop to watch him through the French door. He'd make low popping noises, *pow, hah, pow.*

Those moments glimpsed by accident, seen when a family member thinks they're alone, the raw unassembled self, without thought to presentation; I was struck by how gracefully he moved, in tandem with something that wasn't there, the ghost boxer, falling back a step, ducking to the side, the loosely curled fists at rest.

It was around that time he started stealing Joe's clothes. Xavier needed a belt for the pants, he couldn't hold on to a belt to save his life, the waists of Joe's pants were always too big, but they were the right length. The rubbery decal of Che Guevara's face on the T-shirt crackled, flecks of the image coming away.

The men dumped him on the rubble of a snowbank in minus sixteen degrees, staggering back to view their work and falling in on him again.

A young woman, a silhouette, is seen in the video tearing people off my son. A young woman punching her way through, dragging away another person and another. Somebody in the crowd staggers backwards, arms flailing, on a slick of ice.

It's not that the woman has overpowering strength. The mob is drunk and forgetful. Her appearance in the video is accompanied by something happening in the distance. Sirens, it turned out, though there's no sound in the video. The lights of cop cars, the ambulance. Everyone scatters, except the girl, who I can't make out.

They're all screaming, but the video has a spectral silence. The woman hauls the bodies away from my son and as they fall backwards, they are also turning to look into the distance. Then they take off, running over the icy driveway.

I have been thinking about the people who did this to my son. How they got to be the way they are, wondering if they regretted it. The man who drove that knife into Xavier, not once, but twice. I want there to be a reason.

xavier
i got you

TRINITY WAS SLOBBERING all over him and murmuring I got you, I got you. He wanted to say: Your work here is done.

Or: Leave me alone.

Or: Get away from me, for the loving honour of fuck.

They got him in the ambulance. The stretcher rose on the wind, and slipped inside. They'd lifted it, the guys from the ambulance had, and they'd spoken to one another, little instructions, like: Easy, easy now, and Ready. And the word *okay*.

But it was like they'd forgotten him, and the stretcher was animate and arrow-like. It shot into the ambulance on a ribbon of undulating satin, which was the wind. The way the stretcher jiggled around was the paramedics trying to control it. Then Xavier flew from them into the back of the ambulance. Every little jostle hurt him, made it hard to hang on. They knew it, too. He could see the underside of one guy's jaw and it was clamped shut with the effort to be gentle.

Xavier was afraid the guys from the party would come back and finish him off if these guys in the ambulance didn't hurry up. There were the bleats that meant they were backing up and the dip of a pothole and seriously? They were going to meander down the highway like not a care in the world.

He could still hear the wind over the siren and maybe the paramedics had given him drugs because he felt like the wind was drawing some part of him out through the wounds. Maybe all of him.

I had no choice, he said. But he hadn't spoken. He was trying out the idea of just dying and getting it over with and how he would explain it.

And he didn't believe he sounded convincing. He knew he could hang on if he wanted. There was a beat while he decided if he wanted to hang on.

He wanted to leave a message, but when he tried to speak a tooth came out and was there, hanging by a thread of drool on the side of his cheek until one of the paramedics wiped it away. There was a discombobulation between not speaking and thinking he had spoken.

He asked one of the paramedics if he was going to die. But it came out gurgled, just spit and blood. The blood was in the back of his throat, but it was from his nose.

Xavier kept running over the list of people he loved. He had an idea that an accurate tally might give him some leverage with whoever was in charge of the outcome in this scenario. Kennedy-Boland would want him in for work the next morning. Xavier had a job in a video game company that he loved with all his heart, a coveted job, and his boss, Kennedy-Boland, would not be okay with him not showing up simply because he was on his deathbed. Kennedy-Boland would replace him in the bat of an eye. Kennedy-Boland was a big proponent of the goals and outcomes concerning any given scenario, and this situation required: come to work even if it means bleeding to death on the way. Kennedy-Boland wasn't on Xavier's list of who he loved. He had a list, knew it off by heart, but he couldn't get past Violet.

He'd been with her since he was seventeen and now he was twenty-one. What he saw was her fingers on an electronic keyboard that was set up at Walmart. A few weeks ago. They'd moved to the new apartment and they'd gone to Walmart for pillows. Treat themselves. Fresh pillows. She'd halted in front of the electronic keyboard so suddenly he'd banged into her. It was like there was a magnet in her and it drew her to the bench they had set up in front of the keyboard.

She played something so dense and fast it frightened him, tumbled out, notes smacking into the ones that came before, so fast they had little time to spread and crest and crash and draw themselves back.

A man with an infant in a Snugli and another child clinging to his knee had stopped, transfixed, the man nodding with his eyes closed, his shoulder jut-jutting to the music. A full-on rocking that was arrhythmic and stuttering, the shoulder wrenching itself and a hip too, on the opposite side, to the turbulent music. Xavier thought she would stop but it went on. There was a blur where her fingers were supposed to be. Like when you waggle a pencil between finger and thumb and it looks rubbery.

But sometimes there was a pause or beat and her fingers hovered over the keys like arthritic claws, like it was a struggle to hold them still and then she couldn't and they spilled bonelessly all over the keys. Maybe it was two minutes, or three, but she'd been taken over.

Maybe Violet had never told him she could play because she hated it, one of those kids who had been forced to practise. She'd probably vowed never to play again, she was a person who believed in vows, or maybe she had vowed just once, she'd do it once, but only in Walmart, and only if there to buy pillows and only with her true love, and if there was a guy with a jutting shoulder. He didn't know what she had vowed, or why he didn't know she could do that, play like that, but it had made her unknowable and he'd been astonished.

Then she made the gargoyle claws again and slammed them down three times, discordant and nasty, like an old-fashioned movie where three slams lets you know something scary is coming, the sparking wick of a stick of dynamite, or the silhouette of a raised knife on a shower curtain, and when she glanced up at him, the face on her. Him standing there with the two pillows, one in each fist.

He'd never seen that face, a deep and ancient scowl, which broke up almost instantly. She had looked up to find him, and her eyes met his but she wasn't seeing him and then she saw him, and the ugly face was smashed open with a little shrug, and it was her again.

She went faux-limp, like a spaghetti noodle, draped herself limply over the keyboard, and slumped on the puffy bench which wheezed out a fart sound, and she wiggled to make more of the fart noises, loud and airy and gross and hilarious, and the guy with the two children moved on.

Xavier understood then that he would never know her and this was what was required to make it last.

He was all in, he wanted it to last.

He would only know her if he paid attention and she would wink in and out of view forever and he had a revelation, with a shiver, that this was love, though he didn't think the word *love* in Walmart.

He didn't think, *wink in and out of view*. He didn't know when he thought it because everything had been pared from the normal timeline of first one thing, then another. Ever since the knife went in, and he said to himself, there on the stretcher, that he might have only thought the word *love* when the knife sunk in, and he thought it again when the knife sunk in again.

He struggled against passing out because it seemed the same as death; he didn't know if there was a difference, or which was which, because of the new pillows with the blue stripes and medium-soft, either way, dead or alive, he felt he should appeal to someone for help.

He remembered his parents were in Mexico and he hadn't gone yet today to check on their house, bring in the mail, feed the cats.

Suddenly he felt despair. They were too far away.

I want to stay alive, he said. Bubbles of blood in the corner of his mouth. He could taste a rusty foam.

They will know I love them, he thought, and it was like a weight had been taken off his chest.

Violet will know, my mother, my father, my sister, my little niece, Quinn. It struck him as funny, that they would already know, even though he wanted to hang on long enough to communicate this one idea, this thing: he loved Violet. He loved them all, but Violet. What a load of agony that he couldn't tell Violet, that she wasn't there with him.

Trinity was in the ambulance.

He wanted to say: Get her away from me. This is her fault.

The paramedic said to Trinity, Are you family? You can only come if you're immediate family.

She said, He's my brother.

He whispered to her: You're not my family. He didn't know if he'd spoken.

She must have understood even though he couldn't speak out loud, because she put her mouth to his ear and whispered back: Shut up. You're all the family I got.

jules
a kind of family

THEY WERE GETTING Xavier ready for a CT scan. I'd spoken to the doctor when he was on his rounds. He'd said the surgery had gone well, but the infection was a post-surgery complication. They wanted to just take a look. The white blood cell count was twenty-four.

That's high, the doctor said. We want to get that down as fast as we can.

They said I could go with him. The hallway in the basement was freezing, one of Xavier's hands lay loosely on the outside of the bedsheet. I inched my hand under his, so it cupped mine. It was a funny thing, to touch the hand of my unconscious son. His hand was very warm. His face was warm too, I'd put the back of my hand against his cheek.

I wouldn't do it if he were awake. Mothers and grown sons don't hold hands.

At the end of each phone call we say, I love you. Or if he comes over for a visit. He's only a few streets away. He comes over and borrows stuff. Sugar, a pair of clean socks.

He lets me study his face when he's telling a story. He doesn't turn away. Even before this happened, I couldn't get enough of his face. Sometimes when he's telling me a story he's ambushed by giggles and he has to chuff out parts of sentences and he shuts his eyes when the laughter takes over, and then he gets a hold of himself, and continues with the story.

He becomes faux-serious. But he's making fun of how people adhere to the hierarchy of the office and the protocols, sucked into displays of deference to the bosses, who are puffed up with their own importance. He makes fun of himself. How he says, Yes, *sir*, Mr. Kennedy-Boland.

How he rides a line of insurrection with his tone when he says it. Or how he doesn't dare, which is equally funny.

He is equal parts derisive and devout when it comes to Kennedy-Boland, who is only a decade older than Xavier, only thirty-one, but who developed the company, and who is caustic, self-promoting, and splashy with his money. Who has built the company from five employees to fifteen in two years. Who brings them all to the bar across the street and buys a round on Fridays.

And you have to go, whether you want to or not, because it's Kennedy-Boland, says Xavier.

Kennedy-Boland used the word *family*. Or *a kind of family*, according to Xavier, describing the fifteen of them, two of whom are women. He'd bought beanbag chairs and a ping pong table, but nobody uses the chairs. They did at first, and Xavier acted out how they'd all had trouble getting to their feet when the meetings were over.

Kennedy-Boland has fired three people since Xavier got

a job there, seven months ago, and rehired each of them the next day.

Kennedy-Boland's girlfriend was teaching at the university part time; then she got pregnant and the ultrasound said it would be a girl. Everything changed in the office.

Kennedy-Boland put some of them on the job of developing a feminist video game, which meant a lot of pointy breastplates in the graphics. Scantily clad, in metal contraptions, but with extra superpowers, and feminine intuition.

They were tasked with coding feminine intuition, in the board room, which had big windows that looked out onto the harbour, because that's the kind of CEO Kennedy-Boland was. He'd mentioned feminine intuition. Everyone's eyes turned to the two women coders, who'd begun to dress alike, and happened to be both wearing khaki jumpsuits like they were there to repair bomber planes. They'd looked startled and then surly.

But one of them, Joanne, spoke up. Said it would be a good job for Xavier. It was a joke. Everybody with the big laugh. The end of the meeting. Then they'd all struggled out of the beanbags. This is the way Xavier had told it, cracking up, acting out Joanne's sudden shift from startled to suave, professional certainty. Feminine intuition, good job for Xay. Really funny, that was. He was laughing as he told me.

But I'm a feminist, he yelled after them. I *am*!

After the CT scan, it was time to get back into the elevator and the men who got us down here weren't around, maybe because of the storm, they were shorthanded, so I offered to push the stretcher with the nurse. She trotted to the corner of the hallway to see if anyone was coming. She strode back. She had a prominent, sharply curved nose, her eyes were large and close together, her skin very pale. Something about her nose gave her face an unassailable authority. Or I wanted to believe she had authority.

Or it was her darting eyes. Everything about her pronounced and quick. Her nametag said Kathryn. I'd taken in the spelling of it. I thought there was a kind of intimacy on offer when she saw my glance and said to call her Katie.

She said, Okay let's do it.

We got in the elevator without too much trouble and out again on Xavier's floor. She slammed the button for the automatic doors that lead to the ward with her hip and they swung open. Just as we were manoeuvring the stretcher through the doorway of Xavier's hospital room, I saw the end of the IV tube skittering all over the floor with the white adhesive tape, dirty and curled up, hopping all over the tiles.

The needle was hanging out of Xavier's hand, loosened when the tube got stuck on something, perhaps in the elevator. It was no longer taped down but poked straight up out of his skin. I was afraid it had cracked off inside him. I'd been at the head of the stretcher in the elevator and I'd had the pole.

We'd talked about the storm coming in the elevator, whether we believed it would be as bad as they thought. A slew of nurses, Kathryn said, were asked to stay an extra shift. Or however many shifts it took.

Something's coming, Kathryn said. I can tell you that much.

But now she was cold with me. She wanted me out of the way. She snatched the IV pole and it rattled over the floor as she brought it near the head of the bed. Two more nurses came in. I was standing with my fists pressed against my mouth. In a matter of minutes, almost no time at all, they had replaced the IV needle. They'd added new bags to the IV pole, they'd moved Xavier from the stretcher to the bed, they had straightened all the bedding. In the midst of it, Kathryn spoke to me, without turning around to look.

She said: This is not your fault.

I said: Yes, it is.

ferris wheel

XAVIER HAD MET Violet at Thomas Amusements the summer they were both seventeen. He'd seen her around at parties, but he'd never spoken to her. She was working the cotton candy booth. He was with Lily Green, the girl he'd asked to the prom.

His parents had shown up at the meet-and-greet before the prom and he was already well into the gin with his tie loosened, the neck of the white shirt undone. When he introduced Lily and his mother, they seemed unable to speak and unwilling to look away from each other or to speak to anyone else.

He'd made it a habit to not tell his mother anything about his private life. Even when he was little he could see the way she was with Stella's ex-girlfriends. His mother just went on loving these ex-girlfriends, as if she were their mother too, even after the relationships were over, inviting them around, once there'd been two exes of Stella's and a current girlfriend all at the dinner table at the same time. He was determined to avoid that sort of situation.

There were his mother and Lily Green, proving his point. They both stood, very stiff, Lily swinging her sequined evening bag at her side; his mother cupping her elbows and rocking from her toes to her heels.

He saw that his mother was shy. He'd never seen her this way before. She looked dowdy and short next to Lily, who wore an ice-blue satin dress with diamonds cut away at the waist so that her bare skin winked through and the back was gone too, with a few criss-crossing ribbons to hold it onto her shoulders.

They'd said hello and shook hands, but they did not say anything else. His mother glanced around, as if looking for some help. She had a pink cardigan on her shoulders, buttoned at the throat, and a dress with giant blue roses, made of layers of a nylon material that she kept having to smooth down.

Xavier waited for his mother to pull through. His mother who might say anything, who had the capacity to startle with drilling questions, or flummox with shards of raw honesty that made people see themselves in new ways, his mother could only think to ask where Lily got her dress.

Lily had said, Online. A one-word answer that did nothing to crack the bizarre electricity between his date and his mother, both inert, unable to move. Lily was into girls, but she and Xavier had been partners on a science project, and they fell into going to the prom together without really talking about it much, because she was such a laugh.

I expect you to take care of him tonight, his mother blurted. I expect you to make sure, she was telling Lily, that nothing bad happens to him or to you. I trust you in this. Do you think you're able to do that? It was a bizarrely sexist thing for his mother to say. Stella had gone to her prom in a dress that had been strategically ripped and torn, a pair of army boots. It had been necessary to make sure neither of the grandmothers heard about it.

Lily's face instantly became the way Lily's face usually was, full of being up for anything. Her face had been as still as a lake, and glassy with the too-dramatic makeup, because she seemed to think she owed something to the dress, which had cost a fortune of her own money from working the counter at Tims. But his mother had busted out of the doleful stillness that had taken over her face, and instead here was his mother's ordinary rapacious need for intimacy or cutting the crap.

That's exactly what I plan to do, Lily said. I'm going to keep an eye, don't you worry. I has every intention of making sure we has a good time.

He knew it wasn't what his mother was looking for; she didn't care in the slightest if he had a good time. She hadn't considered the contents of the evening, she only cared about it ending with everyone pretty much as they had been when it began, more or less intact.

Xavier could see his mother was realizing this could not happen. They would all change overnight, Xavier and his friends. It was why their parents had spent thousands, in some cases, on the elaborate dresses and suits — they were talismans, shields, weapons, something to get them through it.

But this girl, this Lily, Xavier hadn't even told his mother her last name, with her dress of pouring icy-blue milk and her ridiculous height, and this toothiness — so white and straight and perfect — the teeth contributing lots to the illusion that she was statuesque. Yes, Xavier saw, his mother had decided she might pass her son over to this young woman, who looked formidable and charged, and who had promised to drag him through it.

They'd gone to Thomas Amusements, a bunch of them, before the girls' appointments to get their hair done. He and Lily got off the Ferris wheel and went to the cotton candy stall with the red-and-white stripes and yellow light bulbs all around the window because he saw it was that girl, Violet, working in there. Violet who went to Prince of Wales Collegiate.

She'd held out a cone of pink cotton candy to Xavier and he gave her the money and passed it to Lily. He said they were going to his prom, him and Lily, and then there was a party at the Delta and what time did she get off from Thomas Amusements? They had a room, a bunch of them had chipped in. Would she want to come to the party? They were only staying at the prom until ten. He could meet her in the lobby of the Delta.

He said, You're Violet, right? Violet Penney?

Violet looked over at Lily, who had a swathe of cotton candy in her lips that she'd torn from the cone, the wind had fluttered it onto her cheek and she was wiping it off with the back of her hand.

Come on, he said. Lots of people are going.

Lily's going, he said. He elbowed Lily and she said, Yeah, I'm going, everybody's going. Come on. Meet him in the lobby.

He introduced her to Lily.

So you're his date, Violet said.

Might as well go with somebody, Lily said. Xavier looked at her and she said, What?

Then she said, He's all right. Come to the party. I'll be there.

Violet was holding out the second cloud of cotton candy like a torch.

Okay, maybe, Violet said. Xavier said he'd be in the lobby at ten, waiting for her.

Yeah, said Lily. Me too.

jules
one world and the next

I WAS LOOKING out the window while Nancy pulled out
Florence's rings. I could smell the hamburgers barbequing,
the smoke wafting up. I could see Stella striding across the
lawn with the sunscreen.

The first ring had a fair-sized diamond in the middle and
little diamonds all around. A thin gold band came with it. I put
them on the finger where I wore my father's wedding band.

Florence's wedding and engagement rings fit me perfectly.
She'd had just a speck of a diamond when she and John got
married, all he could afford. But they'd replaced that ring
when she was awarded Real Estate Agent of the Year on the
Avalon. She'd had a jeweller melt her gold charm bracelet
down, all the silhouettes of a boy's head or a girl's, for each of
the children, engraved with their birth dates. The miniature
iron, to show she was a good housekeeper; a Scotch terrier,
because they'd had a dog once, though it was a husky. She'd
worn the melted nugget of gold, embedded with the first diamond, on a chain near her skin.

I wanted the big engagement ring and the wedding band because the febrile intensity of her presence, still, a year after she'd died, was all around me. I wanted something of hers touching my skin, as if that might keep her with me.

I was watching my mother being vigorously jostled by my brother-in-law across the emerald lawn, through Nancy's bedroom window.

I'd measured the door to the bathroom, and I thought the wheelchair would fit, but my mother had brought her leg, if she needed it, with its white sneaker, royal-blue stripes. She hated the leg; the damn thing weighed a ton.

They'd done their best to make it light at the Miller Centre, the physiotherapist sitting on the floor, her legs out on either side of the prosthetic, working with a tiny screwdriver on a minuscule screw in the ankle of the rods and joints that made up the new leg until my mother could walk the length of the room, hanging onto the two bars, to keep her balance.

Shoulders, the physiotherapist had said. And back. Nice and tall. No hunching. You're hunching. There, nice and straight.

My mother, walking toward a floor-to-ceiling mirror, and me shooting video with a camcorder.

She stops to wave at me herself.

Hands on the bars please, the therapist said. Don't get fancy.

Quinn, my five-year-old granddaughter, Stella's daughter, was at the party too, running with a plastic cutlass in one hand, bubble pistol in the other. I'd given her those toys and Stella was furious.

We don't allow weapons, Jules, she said.

It's not a real weapon, I said. It's plastic.

We don't allow plastic, Stella said. Quinn is in Montessori. She was only half joking. Stella organized beach cleanups. She'd been involved in the group who clean up the Waterford River.

Quinn running in the new pink shoes and the shorts printed with pineapples that I'd bought for her at Walmart, her messy cinnamon hair. Stella didn't shop at Walmart either.

I'd already put sunscreen on Quinn. She had such a fair complexion, and she would not wear her hat. But Stella was half running toward her daughter, waving a bottle of sunscreen at her.

Quinn saw her coming and ran in the other direction, pulling the trigger on her bubble gun over and over. Running through the streams of bubbles she shot before her. My mother batting the bubbles away, Gerry rocking the wheelchair over a big rock in the lawn, until one bubble landed on Mom's upturned palm and she lifted it to her lips and blew on it.

Stella had come home from Montreal with a wife and a baby, five years before. Back at school for a Ph.D. in geography at MUN.

I'd asked about the father, but I was told not to ask. I'd thought Harry Hewlett, with whom she'd been best friends since she was twelve, civil lawyer in the Confederation Building, married to a carpenter named Robert. Harry's russet-gold hair and cheekbones. I asked if it was Harry, and she said not to ask. But her tone, I knew.

Also, I just knew it was Harry. Harry had been in my kitchen on the school lunch breaks all through junior high and high school, Stella showing up with a gang, maybe a dozen kids, all of them with packed lunches, there just long enough to eat, beating it back up over the hill before the afternoon bell. Once I'd come across Harry by himself in the living room, a triangle of tuna sandwich held out to the side, staring at one of my paintings. It was the apple tree in front of the house around the bay. I'd used leftover housepaint, lots of pink and white splashes, the thing in full bloom. An old piece of Masonite it had taken about thirty minutes to paint.

Is that the apple tree? he'd asked. Harry used to come out there with us for a week at a time. He and Stella on the trampoline for hours, her bouncing down, him flying up. They slept head to toe, in the bed with the sagging middle, squashed together, still in the bathing suits they'd worn all day getting in and out of the river.

Stella didn't have to say who the father was. The way Harry and Robert showered Quinn with gifts. And they'd started to babysit her once a week. Quinn looked most like Stella, who had given birth to her. Stella's angular frame and chin, her perfect nose.

But she also looked like Stella's wife — all of Sam's expressions and her sashaying walk. Strangers even told Sam: Your daughter looks just like you.

Harry was at the party, too — serving at the drinks table, mixing cocktails. Quinn with the same reddish-gold hair, but it might have been a coincidence. Robert sprawled in a lawn chair beside him with a straw hat covering his face.

Oh this, Nancy said. She had opened the drawer with her socks and bras and underwear, where she was keeping the jewellery that had belonged to Florence. Nancy was in charge of her parents' estate, clearing out the family home, hiring someone to repair the chimney, something with the electrical. Houses decay so quickly once the life goes out of them. They all found it hard to go in there, the family. I'd felt it too, the sense of being watched as you moved from room to room. Not sinister; comforting. But the loss, too, of the great engine of family, of industry, of love and drama, I felt it in the den, with its dark wood panelling and the bookshelves full of Newfoundland history and the biographies of politicians; I felt something of Florence, brushing the back of my hand.

Nancy took a case for eyeglasses out of the drawer. Florence's eyeglasses. The case was faun-coloured, a faux-suede, the gold lettering across the front: *The Visionaries*, Florence's optometrist on Harvey Road. Nancy flicked the lid open with her thumb and inside were my mother-in-law's eyeglasses. She brought them to me at the window.

The lenses were covered in white dust that sparkled in the brilliant sun, grit from the airbag. Florence had died in an accident on the highway. Years later, in Mexico City, I would think of these glasses again, the lenses like silver coins on the eyes of the dead. In Mexico, in front of the cathedral in the main square, I would look down into the Aztec graves — covered with Plexiglas, or some kind of glass, but the view was obscured, the stone walls covered in wet lime-coloured moss, the glass itself jewelled with blots of water that had evaporated from the depths — and I would think of all of this, of Florence's car accident, my mother's leg, my father and Joe's father, and that sheet of plastic between one world and the next.

Quinn had taken off across the lawn. She was gone. Gerry had tilted the wheelchair all the way back again to clear the front step; my mother screamed. They passed under the green nylon curtain that filled with a breeze from inside the house.

Nancy shut the glasses case with a little snap and put it back in the drawer on a nest of stockings and bras.

I wondered if Xavier had the dirt bike out by now. He may have still been playing video games. Or he might have had trouble kick-starting the bike. Or he could be passing the trestle, kids swimming in the river, turning right onto the old railbed. He might not be anywhere near the highway yet.

jules
giving her whatever she asked

I'D PARKED ON Carter's Hill by the green house with the garbage bag over the smashed-out window. The bag rippled loudly with every gust of wind. It sounded animate, something breathing down my back. I had my window down a crack because I wanted to hear Trinity coming. Or anyone else. Mary had seen a truck driving by her house at odd hours.

I'd kept my eyes on the rearview, but she'd opened the back door and got in with her wheelie suitcase without my seeing her. She had ducked down behind my seat and stayed that way until we were out past Airport Heights. Then she sat up.

My boots are soaked, she said. I adjusted the rearview so I could see her face. She was looking out the window. I wondered if she'd ever come back. Or if I'd see her again.

Did you say goodbye to Mary? I asked.

Yeah.

And how is Mary?

Mary is okay, I guess.

And how are you?

Soaking wet, she said. I pulled up near Departures and stood on the sidewalk while she struggled with the handle on the suitcase. It was stuck and finally she shook it hard and kicked at the same time and the extendable handle unlocked and slipped up and she set it down on the sidewalk. Trinity didn't want me to come in; that way I wouldn't have to park. She slung the strap of her purse over her shoulder.

You're going to be late for Joe, she said.

Yeah, he can wait a few minutes, I said. He usually has to talk to students after class.

Thanks for the ride, she said. And I told her to take care of herself. Then she hugged me. She hugged me so hard I felt the buckle on her purse strap dig into my chest.

She turned then and went into the airport. I looked at the clock on the dash. I would be late for Joe. But I wanted to see her check in. I wanted to see her go through security. I knew Mary would want to hear I'd seen her go.

She got her boarding pass from the automated machine close to the doors. An airline representative stood beside her, leaned in and pushed some buttons for her. She pulled the pass from the slot and she must have been asking him what was next because he pointed her to the security area, where a lineup was forming.

A car pulled up in front of me. The driver, a young man, left the car idling and knocked on the big plate glass window, Trinity still standing on the other side, tucking her boarding pass into her purse, she didn't look up, though a man and his wife glanced his way. Then the young man, a kid really, ran in through the Departures doors. Trinity turned and didn't move.

He strode up to her and grabbed her by the elbow, spun her around. They stood less than a foot apart. Then he took her into his arms and kissed her. He kissed her for a long time. They were kissing. The security guard strolling the sidewalk where I was parked noticed the boy's car, still running, was leaning in to see where the driver might be. He turned to look in the window and saw the couple holding each other.

They were standing in the fluorescent blaze of light. The whiteness of the airport. I don't think Trinity could have seen my car, even if she had looked. She thought I had pulled away. But she didn't look.

The boy put his hand up and swished Trinity's long, gold hair over her shoulder, and slowly ran the back of his fingers down the line of her jaw and lifted her chin. He leaned in and kissed her again, and then turned and strode out of airport. He jumped in the car and drove off, ignoring the security guard.

I watched the young man's taillights, he had looked to be about her age, I didn't even believe he could have a driver's licence, all the way up the exit road, to the roundabout, where the red lights disappeared in the dark. Then I saw the security guard waving me out of the way.

ON THE WAY back from the airport — to pick up Joe outside the Arts and Admin building, and either tell him everything that had happened or else never breathe a word of it again, not to him, not to Mary — I thought, as I often did when I was very shaken, of Florence.

Or I felt her around me.

The way she had of raising one eyebrow to emphasize a point. How she had made her way, despite being orphaned. I had thought the young man was going to assault Trinity, and I was ready to jump out of the car, I'd released my seat-belt. But the kiss, in the blazing light, in the middle of all the noise and movement, had been a secret, a seed.

Trinity was gone.

MY MOTHER-IN-LAW'S FIRST job was in an office. This was a story she told about starting out, letting those around you know who you are. She was a secretary. Every morning her boss sent her out for an apple. Florence had to go out in the street and purchase an apple and polish it with a white napkin, a folded pile of which she kept in her desk drawer for this purpose. She took the napkins home and washed and ironed them on the weekends.

Mr. Lawton liked the apple to be presented on a starched, ironed napkin.

Sheets of rain, such a downpour, and she ran into Sister Josephine, a sister of her foster mother, Bride Peach, who had come to St. John's to join the Presentation nuns and went off with the sisters in Peru and came back every five years, and there she was on the sidewalk in the rain. Sister Josephine who called on Florence, when she was back in St. John's, and brought chocolates for the children and once a toy llama with a brightly woven rug on its back, Sister Josephine, after whom my Joe was named. The elderly woman asked Florence what she was doing in the rain.

Only a little cardigan and not so much as a rain bonnet, Sister Josephine said. You'll catch your death.

She told Sister Josephine she was out getting Mr. Lawton's apple, and the old nun told Florence to tell Mr. Lawton to get his own damn apple.

Florence went back to the office and she told him politely,

though she could feel her chin rising in defiance, that she would not be able to get his apples anymore.

Mrs. Cooper, you're fired, he said. She turned her head to the side as if slapped. She was burning with embarrassment for him.

Get your things and get out, he said. There are plenty prettier than you.

But not half so smart, she said. When he'd fired her, she felt the old familiar welter in the tummy, the fish flicker, a part of her and apart from her, moving out of sync with her, felt it for the first time in two years, a fluid kick to her insides, unmistakable, though she hadn't noticed the skipped periods, there were three children under five at home and already, the kick.

And now she was fired.

There was a metal waste basket near the door, and she picked it up and placed it in the centre of the floor without a sound, his eyes were on his desk and he was writing, just as if he had dismissed her from existence.

The boom was loud. He leapt back, eyes popping, cried out for Jesus, drawing his fists to his chest like an infant as if he thought the desk would explode in his face.

She'd been wearing a pearl-grey one-hundred-per-cent-wool pencil skirt with rayon shell and matching waist jacket she'd had made at Tony the Tailor's, the best tailor in town, at the bottom of Freshwater, and she'd also had Mr. Silver, who insisted they all call him Tony, make the St. Pat's Dancers costumes for her eldest, and she was wearing the heels she'd had dyed the same colour as the suit at Ron Pollard's, she would still have the suit sixty years later, not a thing wrong with it, she'd taken care of it, it was a classic and would never go out of fashion, the pencil shape restricting her legs just a bit, and she'd had to hitch it up so the garbage bucket didn't fly as high as she would have liked, but the noise, more crack than boom against the wood panelling of his desk, had been satisfying.

As she left the office with her coat over her arm and her cream box purse and her hat, Mr. White leapt up to hold the door for her and followed her out into the hall. He said it was still quiet, but he was leaving himself at the end of the week, starting his own firm, he'd secured the offices and had two partners, and she could start next Wednesday.

She had been putting on her gloves, and was flexing her fingers into place, making firm fists, but she stopped and took the fabric of one finger into her teeth and pulled it off in order to shake his hand.

While working at White-Galway-MacDonald, she'd studied for her real estate licence in secret, all the while pregnant with her fourth.

She'd kept her real estate books in the basement, in a suitcase. Five children before she was thirty, and the vigilance employed to keep the house clean, to get them all to church, to teach them how to vacuum (move all the chairs out from the table and vacuum under each chair and put the chairs back) and how to scrub (use a pad for your knees) and how to cook (the talk was all of avoiding cholesterol and salt, tossed salad was a new thing, lettuce was new, the tomatoes were unripe, it was all they could get and they didn't know but tomatoes got any better than that). She made sausage curls in the girls' hair before they went off to church and the boys had brush cuts so close their moon-grey scalps showed underneath.

She studied in the basement and made the appointment

for the test, asking one of the teenagers on the cul-de-sac to babysit for a few hours.

She passed with one hundred percent. She walked into the office of one of the smaller outfits and got a job right off the street, but she got a call not two months later from a man who had heard of her work and was starting his own company, a new franchise.

He said he'd make her a partner if she wanted to opt in. She haggled with him until he paid for her desk up front. The partnership buy-in she would pay as she earned rather than up front as he had suggested, likewise advertising. She reminded him she'd turned over a lot of houses in her first two months at the other company, and she didn't have to rent her desk at that place.

There aren't a lot of women in the business, she said. I think you'll probably see the wisdom, once I get going. I can see the home in the house, that's something I can make them see, new couples, people from the university, all their taste in their mouth, the crowd up from the States, the Brits with their daffodils.

She haggled with him about her commission. On all of these things she made him move substantially. She told him about her mark on the exam and she said there was nothing she couldn't sell. She had discovered this in her first two months on the market. She said giving her whatever she asked for would be the best decision he ever made. This would prove to be true.

Four months into the new job, there came onto the market a big commercial property. It would make her a fortune.

Florence told this story a thousand times, but it was one of my favourites. It was a parable about generosity and being afraid of nothing, not even the dead. She could commune with the dead, but they weren't her preferred company. She foresaw things, knew I was pregnant with Xavier before I did. She'd dreamt it.

She had an interested party in the old meat packing plant, but the client could only meet her at night and the building was big, five storeys, and she didn't want to be alone in it with a man, a stranger of whom nobody knew anything because he'd come down from the mainland. There was also the question of ghosts.

The place was known to be haunted. She'd had to cross herself each time she entered the building. She asked one of her associates, Mr. Archie Linegar, who had come straight over from London, England, and was very proper and had the accent and wore a bowler hat, a point of derision with everyone in the office, and a perpetual look of bewilderment—she asked him would he come and just stay in the basement of the meat packing factory until she'd done the viewing.

If anything happened, Mr. Linegar would be hidden in the basement. She felt certain she could call on Mr. Linegar to defend her from forces human and supernatural if required, though he couldn't sell a property to save his life. She had already advised him several times and had even sold his properties for him, all the while trying to make it look like he'd done it himself, though he of course knew the difference. He had a wife who was sick and they had as many children as Florence.

Of course, she couldn't let the client suspect she was afraid of him, she'd told Mr. Linegar. But with him, Mr. Linegar, tucked away among the barrels and cardboard cases in the basement, Florence suspected she'd be safe and have a confirmed sale in a matter of twenty minutes.

The client was excited about the factory, meat packing had been in his family for decades. The deal was settled, but Florence, also excited, suggested the client view the basement, which she knew to be dry because she had gone over every inch of it in broad daylight when she took on the property. It was dry and furnished, with big walk-in freezers. She wanted to show the client every aspect of the deal he was already willing to sign. It was her way.

She had forgotten all about Mr. Linegar, who could hear her talking about the features of the basement and who ducked into one of the stand-up freezers when he heard her pull the cord of the naked light bulb at the top of the stairs. Florence had allowed herself the pleasure of telling the client that the building was rumoured to be haunted, so much she trusted him, so sure of the sale was she by that point. She thought the client would see that the building had heritage features, was a storied building, get a kick out of the ghost sightings, explain it was more than a building, meaningful to everyone who would enter it. A property with a history.

She was also excited about showing the client the inside of the freezer, with the carcasses swinging lazily, the chains creaking, the meat marbled with yellow fat, purple and red.

She flung open the door. And there amidst the billowing frost and dead animals stood Mr. Linegar in his bowler hat. She screamed and covered her mouth and recovering said, Mr. Linegar, sir, what are you doing in the freezer?

Mr. Linegar said: Waiting for you, you damn fool. He stormed past her and the client, up the rickety stairs and out the front door on the main floor. But the sale remained intact.

xavier
joyride

HE'D RIDDEN THE wave of flickering yards of satin into the back of the ambulance, and they floated through a suffocating darkness with the siren going for all eternity. Machines bleating and beeping. They were taking his temperature, blood pressure.

He knew they'd take him out of the ambulance eventually and he wasn't looking forward to it. Moving had hurt so much when they put him in it.

He wanted to tell Trinity to let Violet know what had happened. But he couldn't understand what had happened. The murk of it closing over him.

Xavier was hanging on by a thread, and that thread was Trinity's voice, a low mutter. Trinity haranguing, saying she had him, she was afraid of losing him, asking him to please hang on. Please.

She made it sound like he had a choice.

Trinity holding his hand and her face was close to his on the stretcher. He could feel her breath on his cheek. These were intimacies to which she had no bloody right and she knew it. She was taking advantage. She was crying and he, deep down at the very bottom of himself, found the ability to be irritated out of his mind by her crying. She wasn't the one with guts hanging out all over the place, though he knew she was the cause of it.

He didn't know what she had to do with the attack. But he knew she was the cause of it.

They used to roughhouse when they were little, both of them overexcited to the point of tears. Then he wasn't allowed to anymore.

His mother told him not to quarrel, especially with girls.

You've reached a certain age, she said. That kind of thing is over.

He thought of Trinity in his bedroom with the video controller, blowing everything up. The *bam* and concrete flying, glass shattering and the *beep beep beep* that meant one or the other of them had died. Just over. Turned to a shower of pixels. He had a black curtain on his window so they could see the screen, even on the sunny days.

After he refused to fight back, they weren't friends anymore. They'd only been friends because she lived across the street. Because his mother made him. Because they were inseparable. Because they were so young, they made each other up. They took turns being what the other wanted. They were like siblings. Because she could blow things up. The water balloons were her idea. Water all over the bathroom floor. He'd caught it for that. She came over because his mother bought Mr. Freezes. She helped herself to their fridge. Because she got him in trouble. Because his mother. Because she was only a foster kid with no parents. Because people shunned him if he was with her. Because Mary Mahoney. Because his parents took her around the bay and there was nobody else to play with, and she bounced him so high on the trampoline, all the way up to the leaves. Because he knew something bad would happen. He'd felt it in the dreamy afternoons on the back deck when they played Monopoly and she bought up everything and a wind came out of nowhere, and toppled all the houses and the Get Out of Jail Free cards and the money flew around them and they tried to snatch it out of the air.

Then he found it hilarious she was crying. The irony. She had come through unscathed, and he'd had holes torn into him, and she was the one crying. It struck his funny bone. And he must have made a sound like laughter, or he was shivering violently, because she said, What?

She said, Why is he shaking like that? What's wrong with him?

Trinity still came over, even after he'd have nothing to do with her, but she stayed downstairs with his mother.

Then she moved out of Mary Mahoney's and went to Toronto. He only ever heard tell of her now and then. Somebody said they saw her on a sidewalk in Toronto, at a party in Toronto. Wherever she was, she was gone. *Bam*. Over.

Stop slobbering over me, he said to her.

He thought of her standing between him and those cops in the gym when the basketball tournament came to a halt. He hadn't stood up in the shopping cart, his arms spread wide, flying down Garrison Hill against the wind, and he regretted it. If he was going to die, it should have been that way.

He had been all for it, a joyride, the speed and precarious rock and jitter of it. He'd lost interest in basketball after they blamed him for the shopping cart. After the cops ruined the tournament, the idea of a team seemed to him a big sham. There was no such thing as a team.

But she'd extracted herself from the group of girls on the bleachers and walked across the gym in front of all the spectators, the other team, the silence that had fallen over everybody, the echoey dread in every loud footstep. One of the guys on the other team bounced the basketball, just once, and it sounded like a *bam*.

Trinity had stood in front of him with her arms crossed. Between him and the cops. He could still see the soft juts of her shoulder blades under the oversized grey sweatshirt. All the hatred from those asshole cops, the humiliation, the teacher's finger pointing at him, she stood in front of all of that.

jules
crash

XAVIER ON THAT dirt bike heading toward the gap in the rail-bed where the highway cuts through. He's going at top speed.

Gerry's birthday party in full swing. People shouting memories all over each other, laughter, sunburns, seven dogs and several children. Another wave of guests had arrived, the film people who had rented Gerry's trucks for a TV series they were making. My mother seemed to be chatting up a very handsome actor. Quinn had been stung by a bee. She was wailing. Stella was holding a spoonful of Benadryl, but Quinn had her lips pressed tight, twisting her face away from the spoon in defiance. It wasn't bubble gum flavoured, and that, on top of the sting, was too much to bear.

I was talking to the stunt car driver from the TV series. She was petite and muscled, with a pixie cut. She was eating a hotdog with mustard. She had an Eastern European accent.

Each crash is precisely planned, she said. Every detail. We rehearse for three weeks. Long hours. There's only one shot, because they only want to destroy one car. I can be sitting around on set for fourteen hours and then the whole thing takes thirty seconds, start to finish. But I have to be concentrated that whole time. Even a single stray thought, I'm done.

The tip of her tongue touched the mustard; she considered.

Once I was standing in the road and a car was coming for me at a very high speed, she said. There was a stuntman in the ditch on the side of the road and he had to run out at the last second and grab me in his arms and knock me into the ditch on the other side. It was dark and the car was going as fast as it could go, the headlights were coming for me.

You were just standing there? I asked.

I was in the middle of the road with my arms hanging loose by my sides waiting for the other stunt guy to knock me out of the path of the oncoming car. He didn't come for me. I rolled at the very last second, but it could have cost me my life. Trust is an instinct, not a learned thing, not emotion or thought. It is instinct.

She put some relish on the hotdog.

I've been on fire and I've jumped off skyscrapers and thrown myself through plate glass windows. I'm a person who doesn't like padding, or crash pads, I want to feel the pain, she said.

She chomped the hotdog and made a small groan of appreciation, a murmur that seemed a very private, intimate sound.

For a moment I closed my eyes and tried to imagine where exactly in the railbed Xavier might be. I knew the helmet, if he was wearing it, would be damp with sweat, and the visor was tinted a blue-black and the world would be a darker green than the bright lime of the sun coming through that tunnel of dense vegetation. I tried to will myself into his vibrating bones, the stink of exhaust, the hot metal covering the engine that his knee rubbed against.

You want the pain? I asked. I wondered if it were true. She was talking about stuntwomen and the particular role they play in the film industry, how they were more rare than men, and how there was all kinds of work for a woman who was good at it.

But I was thinking about the pain and its relation to pleasure, and the relation of both to desire. Could you desire pain? And if the desire for pain was fulfilled, did the pain become pleasure?

Her specialty was flipping cars. She'd taken up a paper napkin, printed with poinsettias though it was the middle of summer, and eased her phone out of her hip pocket to show me the clip. I watched a car tearing down a highway with two cop cars coming toward it; the car swerved, hit a guardrail and flipped over on its roof and then back on the wheels and then on the roof again. Then she crawled out the side of it on her belly. The car had been crushed almost flat.

I know it's real, she said. If there's pain I know it's *real*. Do you know what I mean?

I thought: Now is the moment he is flying across the highway without looking. Or now. Or now. Or now.

THE STORM WAS starting and the nurses told me to go home.

Look, Samira said. We're going to take care of this young man. She was pumping up the pressure cuff on his arm. We're going to make sure he's nice and comfortable. She was one of the nurses who'd been asked to do a double shift. I was so glad it was Samira on with him.

I'm going to be here, Samira said. You can go. They aren't letting anyone stay.

What if something happens? What if I can't get back?

Nothing will happen, Samira said. We're going to let this guy get his rest.

I want to stay, I said.

You're going to have to go home.

But the infection is getting worse.

He's got the new antibiotic now. When that kicks in? You'll see, he's going to be fine. I'll call you if anything changes. And you can call, she said. You have the number. Call anytime. I'm going to be watching over him. Everybody here will be watching over him.

There were only a few other souls on the street when I stepped out into the wind. I had to lean my body into it, and the snow was almost knee deep. The pain I felt in my chest was devastating. I had to press my fist against my heart.

Nell called and said she'd tried to buy me a little propane camping stove in case we lost power but they were all sold out.

They also had a run on flashlights, she said.

No flashlights?

Yeah, no flashlights. Instead she'd bought me a rotisserie chicken and a tub of potato salad. She said they were waiting in my fridge. The stores are all staying closed now, she said.

While I was talking to Nell, Joe phoned: he'd made it as far as Montreal.

xavier
the bird

XAVIER'S HEAD SNAPPED backwards and the tinted visor was blackened and smeared, the impact made the bike wiggle and he had to hold the handlebars as tight as he could.

The bike tried to get rid of him.

The bike wanted to fling him over the handlebars and bring up the back wheel, which spun in the air above him and smashed down on top of him. But he didn't let go.

Instead, he was flung to the side. He hit the ground, the wind was knocked out of him. He swiped at the visor and pushed it up and his hand was covered in blood and feathers. He'd hit a bird. A bird had flown straight at him.

Xavier undid the strap on the helmet and dropped it to the ground and he got off the bike. He picked the bike up and kicked down the kickstand, and then his legs turned to water and he fell back on his arse into the grass again. He rubbed his hand in the grass to get the blood off. He crawled to a rut in the road that had a slick of muddy water and he swished his hand in it.

Then he stood, his legs still quivering, his eyes watering, spilling tears, and went back to see the bird. Lying breast up and busted open, its neck was crooked hard in the wrong direction. It was a sparrow.

He'd hit a bird.

Or the bird hit him.

They'd passed through each other. He thought the bird was the world and he had absorbed it.

He thought: This is how we absorb the world. The bird broke through the bone of his forehead and took up residence. The bird became pixels that slipped through the smoked visor and into his skull and dove down from there in a welter of flame and feather and guts into his heart, where it was just beak and the desire to fly. The bird was killed on impact. The world was a slurry of green leaves and moist heat and he was unable to breathe because he had the wind knocked out of him.

The leg was torn out of his jeans and he had several scratches; a cut studded with small stones and a few orange spruce needles, beaded up with bright blood. He thought parts of him were broken, but they were not. His pinkie hurt because it got bent backwards, but he made a fist a few times and there was nothing wrong with his pinkie.

The bird had smashed itself against his head, and it caught fire inside his brain and that little flame went up instantly. The burning flight of it was grafted onto Xavier.

The helmet was smeared with feathers, guts, and blood. Briefly, he thought it was his own brains dripping down the visor. The world went wobbly and then it straightened out and was hyper-bright, and the guck was worse-looking when he removed the helmet; slimy, loose grey-blue sausages, clotted and burst. They must have been the bird's intestines.

He'd grabbed up a fistful of long grass and cleaned the mess off. He lifted the dirt bike from the grass where he'd fallen.

His parents had left him in the house alone. They bickered on the way out to the car because his father wouldn't hurry up and his mother was asking why they could never be on time for anything.

What's the rush, his father had said. It's not a meeting of the UN Security Council, it's a birthday party.

She had two salad bowls with tinfoil over them and a Tupperware container of sweet-and-sour chicken wings. Xavier had peeled back the lid and reached in for a wing, but she'd slapped the back of his hand and told him to drop it.

The wings are for the party, she said.

He'd finally heard their car pull away, and a silence dropped over the house. It dropped, and then the wind waggled the branches of the aspen trees and the traffic on the highway was very far away. He wasn't in a rush to get to the party. What was the rush? He could hear crows cawing to each other. Far away, a lawn mower.

He lay on his bed and he could hear the ocean and one of the branches of the apple tree was rubbing against the glass. The sound of it raised the hairs on his arms. He read an Archie comic cover to cover and napped, and thought a year had passed but according to the clock on the stove in the kitchen it had been forty-five minutes.

He locked the back door and put the key under the rock at the base of the pine tree. Then he headed out to the bike. The vinyl seat was hot. The metal casing felt hot. The helmet made him sweat. He'd drive up Trestle Road, across the railbed, through the grown-over lanes and across the highway. Through Bradleys Cove to the beach in Western Bay. He kick-started the bike and the engine caught and he started slow, but when he got to the dirt road he opened it up. As fast as the engine could go.

trinity
father

SHE'D BEEN IN Toronto for four years, talking to Brad Murphy on the phone and over Messenger the whole time. She'd done upgrading and worked at the Delta, cleaning rooms. For a while she had three jobs, Tims, the Delta, and Pizza Delight. When she was nineteen she could work the bar at the Delta and the tips were good.

Murph had been saying she should come home. He had stints of seeing other people, but even then, they talked for hours at a time.

She'd gone out with a guy named Stan who managed a McDonald's, but after six months he'd said: We're in different places.

She put on a face. It was her glacial look, haughty and side-glancing.

Different places in life, he'd said. He told her he was on track for owning a McDonald's in the next five years, soon as he turned twenty-five. He asked if she knew where she would be five years from now. Did she ever think about her goals?

He said, You never say your goals.

Stan had been going around his apartment putting some stuff of hers in a paper shopping bag with twine handles from a boutique with special candlesticks he'd wanted. A makeup mirror, her curling iron, a couple of books. He'd put the bag down on the glass coffee table. Stan said that he understood her, but he was in a different place. He said he came from a family, they had goals.

You knew that about me, he said. I've been open.

His mother owned and operated a hair salon. Five women under her, cutting hair.

This is what I mean, he said. Look at my mother.

She was surprised how much it stung.

You want me to look at your mother? she asked. The piercing hurt of it was pretty surprising. Trinity hadn't realized she felt anything for Stan at all. She had to hold her bottom lip under her top teeth to stop from saying the things she could have said about his mother.

I want someone who wants the same things I do, he said. He asked her if she knew what he meant.

She didn't know what he meant. Did he mean the candlesticks? They had flecks of gold foil and bits of old text embedded in the wax, Sanskrit, maybe. Did he mean high-tech snowshoes? He had wanted them very much. Over a thousand bucks.

She'd watered the cactus on the coffee table and the water had spilled out onto the glass top and soaked the bottom of the paper bag with all her stuff in it.

Your mother's some kind of painter nobody's heard of, he said. She had mentioned Jules a few times, but she'd never said that Jules was her mother. He'd made the assumption.

Brad Murphy would call on the nights she wasn't sleeping at Stan's, and they'd talk until it was morning. Sometimes Murph was high and spoke shrill and fast, prophesying things like wealth and great power in the underworld. Or he was drunk. Or he was shrunken, inconsolable. She recognized in him the same sort of pain she had.

Trinity had found her mother, though she didn't tell Stan. Her mother was living at the address Dave Costello had given her, with a guy who had beer cartons stacked floor to ceiling in the back porch, a laundry line over a small yard of stinger nettles with a single grey sock hanging on it for the whole six months Trinity visited there.

Trinity's mother said it was better to call her Jill than Mom. They were so close in age. She'd had Trinity when she was sixteen.

Jill had two new tattoo sleeves, and one of her front teeth was badly chipped. But Trinity was entranced by her mother's face, her small hands, her plump breasts. She'd become pleasingly solid, beefy, an off-the-shoulder red sweater she wore. One of those Irish rings.

Just turned sixteen actually, Jill said. You were born on my birthday. Talk about a surprise party.

She loved the way her mother closed her eyes and kept them closed when she blew onto her cappuccino before the first sip. The foam scurrying to the opposite side of the cup, and how deeply Jill breathed in when she first tasted it. Holding the breath and opening her eyes on the exhale of satisfaction. But ladling in the sugar with purpose. Packet after packet.

The night before Jill was leaving to go back to cook in a camp up north, they'd gone out to dinner. Jill had listened to Trinity talk about one of her bosses, about Stan's mother, about Murph. She talked about the poodle who lived in the apartment above her, and how it was left alone all day and barked and barked.

Jill let her talk, with one cheek resting on the heel of her hand, elbow on the table. She had been sober for the whole six months. When Trinity stopped talking Jill asked if she'd been able to stop by the ATM. Trinity took a hundred dollars out of her wallet and handed it over. She was glad to be able to do it. Perhaps handing her mother that money had been her goal all along. Being able to do that.

Her mother put the money in her purse and worked the Irish ring off her finger, twisting it back forth over a wedge of skin, over the knuckle. She was on the road to diabetes, she'd said. Sometimes she retained water.

What about my dad? Trinity said.

We were only fooling around, Jill said.

But what was his name.

There was a guy from Branch, Tommy Power from Branch. That was a weekend camping trip, Tommy Power, around the right time. I was already drinking then, Trinity. Drinking a lot. There'd been a few guys. I don't remember everybody's name from back then. There was a guy Tommy, another guy around that time, Chris. For a while I thought Chris Yetman. But you wouldn't want Chris Yetman for a father. There were a lot of guys around then. I don't know who your father is. It was you and me, Trinity, and I wasn't much good to you. I heard Tommy Power died of cancer.

It was as much as her mother had ever said about a father. She put the Irish ring on Trinity's finger. It was a friendship ring, two hands holding a heart. Or it was a promise ring. She didn't know what kind of ring it was.

SOMETIMES BRAD MURPHY called Trinity when he was driving across the island at night, just so he could stay awake. She'd talk to him until he got to a motel.

He was always going back and forth across the island. He was still selling drugs, she knew that. His father was in jail for two years, with less than a year to go.

Before Stan she had gone out with an Iranian guy named Dana, who she met doing free ballroom dancing classes. A girl she worked with at Pizza Delight made her go. Dana was going to be a surgeon back in Iran. He lived with five other Iranian men, and a Black woman from Haiti. Everything between Trinity and Dana had been too easy. She was used to things being hard, and she'd let her guard down. If she had nightmares, he held her and sang to her in Farsi. He'd always said he was going back to Iran, but there'd been such mutual respect and undiluted care between them, she didn't believe him. She stood him up regularly. She wasn't sure she would survive if she didn't have him. He saw through the feints and jabs. He told her he loved her, and she knew he meant it. She wouldn't say that back. But nothing would dent him. He was happy when she was around, grateful for her presence.

She knew she was in for a big disappointment and just wanted to be able to see it coming.

In the end it had been right there in front of her the whole time. He'd said he was going back to Iran to serve his people. He'd said that all along. Dana graduated a year into the relationship and he got on a plane two days after graduation and was gone, back to Iran.

Stan had picked up the bag with her stuff in it and the

soaking wet bottom fell out. The things she splurged on, things that were important to her, danced on the hardwood at her feet. He was standing there holding the twine handles. She lost the job at the Delta because she'd slept in three times and was late for her shifts.

The guy she went out with next hit her for no reason. She never saw him again.

Then she got a Facebook message from Newfoundland, a woman in Branch who asked if she belonged to the Branch Powers.

The woman said she was a caregiver for a man she thought was Trinity's grandfather on her father's side. She sent a picture of a young man who had died of cancer, and Trinity knew at once he was her father. He looked exactly like her. The woman said Jillian had been in touch with them. She'd contacted them over Messenger on a ride into whatever hick town far away from the camp, where they had internet.

If you come back to Newfoundland, your grandfather would love to meet you, the woman said. Trinity had emailed her mother but got no answer. She tried her mother's boyfriend, but he leaned out an upstairs window without a shirt on and said he hadn't heard from Jill since she left.

She told Murph she was coming back to Newfoundland. He said he had just rented a house with four roommates. She could stay in his room until she found a place.

I'm always gone, he said. You can stay there.

You got a drug problem, Murph.

I'm not like that now, he said. I'm clean.

You're not clean.

I can control it.

xavier
violet

WHEN VIOLET WAS reading a novel and Xavier tried to talk to her, her lips started to move. If he kept on trying to tell her something, she would start to whisper the words. If it was something he really needed to say she would flip the book over on her lap and look up at him as if he had just materialized, or she had no idea who he was.

Some of the books she read had very small print and hundreds of pages and paintings on the covers of women from long ago, or men in top hats. Sometimes they were in horse-drawn carriages with spots of sunlight all over their white dresses.

For a long time he had to content himself with being next to her in the bed while he played video games with earphones; he thought of her reading as an affliction. He began to think, in those times when he convinced her to put down the book, that there was no illness he could not cure.

But then she began reading aloud to him.

There came a time in the midst of all this that he started to listen to the stories. He'd realized the illness was contagious. He started asking her to read to him.

She got in bed with two or three novels and when he got in, they'd be tangled in the bedding, digging into his back or his hip. She said she liked to sleep with them because she imagined they would seep into her head; she could absorb them by virtue of their proximity. She could leach the stories into her dreams if the books were touching her while she was conked out, especially the old ones that had already seeped through decades and sometimes centuries.

She said, Think about all the stories that just got lost.

I'm not the sort of person who thinks up that kind of shit, he said. But he found himself thinking about it.

Her favourite place to read was in bed, wrapped in the eiderdown duvet he'd bought her, with a bowl of popcorn. She put brewer's yeast on it, and the smell was something he got used to. Every pot in the house had little burnt black spots on the bottom from making popcorn; then they got a ride to Stavanger and they bought a popcorn maker at Winners. It was the first kitchen appliance they'd chipped in on together. They both owned it.

She'd been saying about a duvet, so he borrowed a bike and drove out to Kelsey Drive and got it for her. He'd had to tie the huge shopping bag to the bike handles, and he kept banging his knee on the duvet as he pedalled back downtown, swaying into traffic. The way he told the story about the duvet was he'd been willing to risk his life for her smallest whim. He did impressions of the faces of the drivers he nearly smashed into. The way he told it, he'd thrown himself into oncoming traffic just to please her.

He'd wanted to get his mother oven mitts. Jules's oven

mitts had a large burnt hole at the top. The stuffing poked out of a black hole in the quilted fabric. His mother had caught the stuffing on fire and the whole mitt was aflame, the fire alarm yelping. She'd flapped it all over the kitchen until it went out.

The story was emblematic, not only of his mother's slap-happy approach to almost all things that, winningly, had a tendency to work out for her, but of the ways the world could outwit anyone at all, not just his mother, and how it was important to laugh in the face of the little traps and snares the world had set, laugh, and all the while, pay heed.

You need eyes in the back of your head, his Nanny Florence used to say.

Sometimes he came home after dark, when Kennedy-Boland made everybody stay late, and he just got in with Violet and she didn't even wake up. Or when Kennedy-Boland said they had to go for after-work beers to build company spirit.

He'd just hold Violet, and in the middle of the night she'd tell him to roll over and she'd hold him. They could roll over in unison as if they were a single contraption, or as if the whole move were choreographed.

They were going out together three years before they moved into the house. Five roommates lived there, a giant drafty Victorian house attached on both sides and the chandelier, a deck with giant garbage bins and a terracotta Buddha head. A glass table with a hole in the middle for an umbrella, though they didn't have an umbrella.

Brad Murphy found the house, his name on the lease. Xavier remembered him from grade three. At first, they hardly saw him. They knew he had a girlfriend who slept over, but she never showed her face. She came and went at odd hours, even when Murph wasn't there. She was gradually moving in. They knew someone was hogging the shower, using up the hot water, but that's all they knew about Murph's girlfriend.

They'd been living there a couple of months when Violet stopped the movie she was watching and removed her earbuds to talk to him. She said everything that happened at work and what she thought they should have for supper. She said she'd heard Murph's girlfriend's name was Trinity. Someone at Suzy Shier who knew Murph saw him walking through the mall with the girlfriend. Violet said she saw a jacket she wanted on the internet and she was going to put it on her mother's credit card and pay her back when she got paid. She asked him about Kennedy-Boland's girlfriend's pregnancy.

Xavier knew there was only one Trinity. She'd left when she was sixteen and he'd thought that was the end of her. He had believed, at the age of twenty-one, that it was possible for people to leave your life and never show up again.

Trinity must have known he was in the house all along, one of the tenants, but she hadn't ever come out of Murph's room when other people were around. Somebody made a comment, one of the roommates: Murph's girlfriend sleeps a lot.

Someone said: Is she paying rent?

Devin said they were heavy into drugs, her and Murph both.

Xavier gathered from things the others said that she hadn't mentioned that she knew him. After that, if he saw her in the kitchen from the front porch, while he was taking off his boots, he went straight up to his and Violet's room or out on the fire escape to smoke.

Violet was watching a movie on the laptop, an adaptation of one of the novels she was reading. Horses galloping through a forest, a woman in front, a man galloping behind. She took out one of the pink earbuds again and asked him to go start the water for the Kraft Dinner.

Go, she said. And he went.

trinity
branch

SHE HITCHHIKED FROM St. John's to Branch to meet her grandfather. The caregivers who'd written her lived right in the house with her grandfather, they said she'd be more than welcome. They said her grandfather had a car for her. Her father's car. The car her father had before he died.

A husband and wife, who said they felt like they were more than just caretakers. They were her pop's family.

They had Trinity sitting down in their kitchen and the carved wooden plaque the husband made in the garage with words that had been burnt into the wood with a propane torch in cursive and then varnished, saying "The Arse Is Out Of 'Er," and they gave her homemade raisin bread and the grandfather came out. He told her she could have her father's car.

He said he wanted to give her the car. The two caretakers, both in jeans and sweatshirts that Trinity knew had been on sale at Costco last summer because she had one herself from Ontario, the woman leaning against the counter, the man beside her, both of them with their arms crossed, watching for her reaction to the gift, their faces inscrutable.

Afterwards — after the lunch of bread and tea and the talk about what she was going to become, probably a nurse, she'd said, making it up on the spot, or a social worker — the old man gave her a picture of her father, who had died of cancer when he was in his early twenties, and had never known about her existence, never knew he got Trinity's mother pregnant, whoever her mother was, but her father looked just like her, her father did, the cheekbones, the eyes. The resemblance.

She's different around the chin, she must have had her mother's chin they all decided, nobody in our crowd has a chin like that, the old man had said.

He turned to look at the two caretakers leaning against the counter and he said to them: The eyes on her. Just like her father. The cheekbones.

But the eyes, the old man said. He repeated it three times, looking right into Trinity's eyes.

The eyes, the eyes, the eyes, he said. His own eyes got watery. Each time he said it she felt as though she had been blessed.

After that it was starting to get dark and the caretakers suggested that her grandfather was getting worn out and it was time for him to rest, and he had laid his hand on top of hers and patted her hand.

Then he took the key to the car out of his breast pocket, two fingers and a thumb diving deep into the pocket, the whole hand shaky, and drew out the key and put it on the table with a little snap.

The caretakers came out into the cold mist and fast-darkening sky, black clouds over the ocean making the water shine like pewter, down the driveway with her, where she fully expected to be told off for taking advantage of an old man who was dying and that the car rightfully belonged to them, which was what Trinity believed, and that there would be some kind of verbal attack that would ruin the light-headedness she felt about viewing the picture of her father, only two years older than she was right at that moment, and the touch of the old man's hand on her hand, which she could still summon the feel of; she was afraid of them ruining it for her. She drew breath and waited for the assault.

But they said they couldn't wait to get out of there to tell her how grateful they were she'd showed up. They wanted her to know it had meant the world to him, the old man.

The woman caretaker burst into tears, which made them all laugh. She patted the tears away, rather than wiping. Lifted her glasses and patted gently with two middle fingers at the outer corners of her eyes because she didn't want to smear her mascara.

The husband told Trinity that they'd put winter tires on her, and had got the brakes done, and she had the windshield washer full and she was good on gas, she had a full tank because the old man wanted the car done up to the nines for her, and he'd had it cleaned out and the dice on the rearview.

The man said a litany of things they'd done to get the car in the best possible shape for Trinity and the woman talked over him, listing off the same things in a different order, saying she'd taken the old man to Walmart to get the furry dice, and they could have got orange but she said pink was different, you didn't see pink all that often.

They told her the mileage, but it meant nothing to Trinity, and they paused. They were both waiting for her to comment on the mileage. Then they both burst in at once that it was very low mileage on the car, they said, it was like she was brand new, the car.

They said a little old lady must have owned it, but Trinity didn't know that was a kind of joke or cliché about well-kept cars—she thought an old lady *had* owned it. But they said it was only a saying, no old lady owned it, only her father had owned it. The car was in the garage most of the winter, so the salt never got at it. Her father had bought the car brand new off the lot.

Trinity couldn't bring herself to tell them she didn't have a driver's licence, though she'd had a few lessons from Murph since she'd been back; she just got in the car and prepared herself to drive all the way back to St. John's on the highway, terrified of hitting a moose because of all the fatal accidents, but also not caring if that happened because of the old man and his joy at finding her and the car. She had a car.

jules

reaper

I GOT HOME and my face was frozen and wet, my jeans and coat caked with snow. Once inside I realized how loud the wind was. The house was creaking. The cats came down over the stairs and both of them wound around my legs, nearly tripping me. There was no food in their bowls. They'd been licked clean.

I went from room to room, turning the heat on blast in case we lost electricity in the middle of the night. I made cups of coffee for the morning, which I'd drink cold if we lost power. I took the linings out of my boots and put them on the heater.

The wind had picked up and the lights flickered.

The house was three storeys and since the children had left, I'd taken over the dining room so I could paint. I sat in the dining room and devoured half the chicken and the potato salad. I fell asleep at the table, just for a few seconds, my head dropped and I jerked awake. I ran up the stairs and fell into bed. The wind was rattling the window panes.

. . .

I'D WOKEN AT ONE A.M. very thirsty and thrown off the covers. I'd gone into the kitchen for a glass of water, the cats brushing against my legs, and when I looked down the hallway from the back of the house to the front there seemed to be someone standing on the front step, pressing their face to the glass in the door. Someone wearing a black hoodie.

I thought this might be the person who had attacked my son. Someone had come to the house looking for him. They weren't finished. They were looking for money, or somehow Xavier had pissed them off, or it was random.

For a second, I waited for the person to move. Then I opened the second drawer, by my hip, and I took out a big knife and I strode down the hall to the front door. It wasn't a decision. I could have called 911. I had picked up my phone, too, from the kitchen counter where it was charging. I'd torn the plug out of the wall and the plug was still attached, dangling from the charging wire.

I had my arm raised with the intention of slicing through the side of whoever was standing on my front step, then bashing their brains out with the corner of my phone. It was only when I had my hand on the door's lock that I realized it was a reflection of the banister. Xavier's windbreaker was draped over the white wooden ball at the top, a ghost face in the reaper's hood.

I remembered how Florence had been afraid to be alone in her house on the nights after John's wake and funeral. But she'd forced herself, after the reception for close friends and family back at her house. Afterwards, she sent everybody home. It was like meeting someone for the first time, she said, becoming comfortable with John's presence again after he died. She had thought she'd be afraid, but she wasn't. She didn't know if he would be the same dead as alive, but he was himself.

I can feel him, she said. It's a comfort.

Florence had two vertebrae seriously deteriorate over the last six months of her life; they'd been ground down like pancakes. The doctor had said pancakes, and she repeated that when we asked what it felt like — whether it was a sharp or constant pain, whether it throbbed.

They're like two pancakes, she'd say. She'd seen the x-ray. She'd rub her fingers and thumb together, the way someone sprinkles salt, to describe what she'd seen on the x-ray.

There was a powder, just floating in the black, she said. Bits of bone.

Whatever it was, her back developed a hump and she gave me her cashmere sweaters because she said she couldn't wear them.

They accentuated the curve, she said.

The pain could be so excruciating she'd grip the carved wooden armrests on the wine-coloured recliner and her fingers would go white, the dark veins twisting all over the back of her papery skin. She'd close her eyes and lean away from the back of the chair, the touch of stiff brocade unbearable.

In those moments, when the pain coursed through, she'd shut her eyes and look like a monarch forced to change the course of history with a single declaration. But she'd remain silent until the spasm passed. Then, leaning heavily on her wrists, she'd rise from the chair and hobble to the kitchen.

A few times I'd driven over to rub a new cannabis cream on her back. The cream had a mysterious heat that got hotter the longer it stayed on my hand. Even after I'd used soap and water, I could feel a burn or pulse that remained for an hour or so later. It was as if there were an emotion smeared over the palm of my hand, part of Florence, her flitting memories, half formed, that I'd absorbed through the skin, the cream a kind of conduit, like the cold gel they squirt on your belly during an ultrasound that brings up the picture of a fetus. I'd take my hand off the wheel when I was stopped at a red light, and I'd make a fist then flick my fingers open, over and over, to get rid of the pins and needles.

With the doctors she'd been like a child, her features became youthful. A dreamy indolence. But afterwards, even on the way back to the car, her true self took claim and she said they didn't know what the hell they were talking about.

When the kids were small, on Sunday evenings, in the house on Cabot, Nancy and I used to watch films in her bedroom with a bowl of popcorn between us. Joe had gone to Toronto to finish course work on his Ph.D., he had just one semester left, and it was just Nancy and me and the children—Tristan and Stella.

They were films from the video store on the corner of Prescott and Gower, most of them had subtitles, were lush, slow-moving, and saturated with colour.

Nancy's bedroom was also the dining room and the other floors of the house were dark; we worked opposite shifts at a group home during the week and we were going to school and took turns with Tristan and Stella. I was getting ready for a group exhibition in a not-for-profit gallery. I was making flip books with photographs. I was allowed to spread out in the living room. A giant easel, the canvases stacked against the wall, a drop cloth on the floor.

The window went pitch black by late afternoon in the winter and we could see ourselves in the glass, under the covers, the chrome popcorn bowl between us, the faint light from the television flickering over the white duvet drawn up over our knees.

One evening Florence let herself in and must have called to us from the porch but we didn't hear her.

She came down the dark hall and was standing in the door of the bedroom, carrying a giant lily. The leafy stalks shook all over and the gaping white blossoms trembled. That year we were watching Almodóvar and Mike Leigh, *Europa Europa*, *Truly Madly Deeply*, *Wings of Desire*, a run of old Bergmans and Pasolini and Hitchcock.

What's going on here? Florence demanded. Her shock had the kind of heat that was almost visible, rippling the air between us. The flowerpot was covered in a wrinkled pale blue foil that flared coldly in her hands. She'd thought we were lovers. I flung off the blankets and revealed myself fully dressed in jeans and one of Joe's old sweaters.

We're watching a movie, Nancy said. What do you think we're doing?

Nancy was wearing her plaid flannel pajamas. Florence recovered in an instant. She grimly resisted a giggle. She stepped into the shadows, out of the glow from the television, to put the plant down in the corner of the room.

These are from a funeral at the church, she said. I can't stand lilies; they remind me of death. But I couldn't see them go to waste.

There was a loud noise from the television, perhaps an explosion, and Florence turned to look at it and we had turned back too. Nancy back under the blankets. Florence and I were on either side of the wide bed. I had been about to offer Florence a cup of tea, or a glass of wine, because we had half a bottle left over from the dinner party the night before and the truth was, we were still hungover.

I knew she wouldn't accept anything. But for a brief moment, the three of us were absorbed in whatever was happening on the TV screen. It was a dulling out of who we were, an emptying of all the riptide coming and going, dropping off the kids at school, getting to class, to work, cooking meals, having parties, the minor frustrations, and because of the peculiar flickering light cast on us from the television, we seemed to be floating, staring straight ahead, an open-eyed somnolence, and beyond our reflections the infinite blackness of the garden. It was the black void of whatever had already happened and was hurtling deeper still.

trinity
bones

TRINITY WAS DRIVING the car back to St. John's with the picture of her father in the pocket of her flannel shirt. She tried to turn on the lights because it was dusk, but after a few people in the oncoming lane honked, she realized the lights were on high beam and turned them down a notch. They made a faint gold splash rush over the trees and lit up the fog slithering low on the wet pavement. A transport truck passed her and sloshed water over the windshield, and she couldn't see and put on the indicator instead of the wipers. It had only been a few seconds of blur, but the car behind her blared its horn because she'd slowed down. She touched one hand to her pocket, where the picture was.

A photograph of a face that looked like her.

The buzz cut less blond, but the nose. It was her nose exactly, only maybe wider, a little wider. The eyes, like they'd said. The shape of the brow. She pulled over and took the picture out of the pocket and touched the light in the ceiling so she could get another look. The eyes with the pale blue irises, shards of black radiating out from the pupil. This man was her father.

He had the broad shoulders, her shoulders. A grin he was trying to suppress, like there was something he wasn't supposed to laugh at, but he couldn't help it, like he had said something witty and everybody appreciated the joke. He was holding a big glass of milk. There was a streak where the milk had poured over the glass when he'd drunk from it. It was the only thing she really knew about him, the milk and the car his father, her grandfather, had given her. Something of her father. Something he'd saved for and purchased.

He probably had strong bones, all that milk. The expense of it too. They were people who would give their growing boy whatever they thought he needed. If he wanted milk, he would have it. She had seen that in the grandfather, an ability and a willingness to provide. The smile in her father's photograph was with closed lips, but he probably had nice teeth. She could not think of another soul she knew who would pour a whole glass of milk and drink it down.

She drove even though she didn't really know how to drive and she'd lied to her newly found grandfather about having a licence. She was heavy on the gas and she let up on it; the car was racing forward and falling back, until she figured it out. She tried to stick to the speed limit because of the licence. She didn't want to draw attention.

jules
snowmageddon

THE NEXT MORNING the light in the kitchen was all wrong
and the storm was still at its height. I filled with panic. There
would be no way to get back to the hospital. I never should
have left. The windows had been buried. The murky shadows were slanting in the wrong direction. The glass door at
the back was clear of snow. The deck had fallen off during
the night, and when it collapsed it had taken with it the snow
that had built up against the back door. The high walls of the
deck had kept the glass door permanently in the shade. But
now the sun blasted through the murky light in a single column full of dust motes.

I called the hospital, and the nurse who answered said she
would get Xavier's nurse, for me to just hold on a minute.
Then it was Samira.

He's still struggling, she said. It'll take some time for him
to come around.

I can't get back in there, can I? I said. I was weeping.

I'm here, Samira said.

But he's okay?

We're not happy with his white blood cell count. The doctor's not happy about that. He's got a serious infection. But we expect that to go down.

I have to get in there.

Nobody can come in, Samira said. And nobody can leave.

I phoned Joe and told him about the infection. I said that the white blood cell count was still climbing, twenty-five now. They'd changed the antibiotic.

Are you coming? I asked him. I told him about the deck.

What do you mean? he said.

Torn away, I said. Buried. I told him it was still going on, the storm, and I couldn't get out of the house. Nobody was allowed out of their houses.

I called the hospital every hour. They said the white cell count was up some more.

When is the antibiotic supposed to fix it? I asked.

We'd like to see a significant improvement soon, a nurse said. I asked for Samira, but the nurse said that Samira was with a patient.

JOE CALLED AS I was heading out. He said I should stay put. Then he said I should stay on the phone with him if I was going to walk to the hospital. The city was still under stay-at-home orders, he told me, as if he was the one who knew. No visitors at the hospital. The doors were locked against visitors.

I'm going anyway, I said.

He was afraid I'd be buried alive by the plows. He asked why didn't I wait by the phone. He said to take the side streets, but I told him the snow was over my head there and if I sank,

I'd suffocate. The only way to the hospital was by the main thoroughfares. Only the main arteries that led to the hospitals had been plowed. While I spoke to him on the phone, I tried to open the back door. But it was stuck.

Joe was at a breakfast buffet in the hotel where the airline had put him up, next to the Montreal airport. I could hear the clatter of utensils and the murmurs of other diners. I was trying to get the front door open but it was iced shut too. I shouted at Joe, loud enough to hurt his ear.

Why am I dealing with this on my own? I shouted.

Joe said he was trying to get home but there was nothing. Nothing was going to Newfoundland. Our airport was shut down.

A wall of white snow when I opened the front door, with a perfect imprint of the door handle and the mullions on the window and the moulded panels in the steel front of the door. It was like the lid of a coffin.

xavier
roommate

XAVIER COULD NOT fathom how Trinity had managed to rear herself out of his past to show up in the house in which he and Violet were renting a room.

He'd heard his mother on the phone once saying that Trinity was like her own. Back when she was still at school.

Was as good as one of her own.

Felt like her own.

Xavier knew that nobody owned Trinity Brophy. Nobody had ever owned her. She was on her own.

His mother had been talking to his Aunt Nell, the phone on speaker while his mother washed the dishes, though there was just silence from Aunt Nell. It was just before Trinity left town for Toronto. He'd heard Toronto around school. They never talked to each other, him and Trinity, before she left. They'd stopped being friends long before high school. There had been an intensity between them when they were small, they used to roughhouse, rolling across the room, one or the other of them in a headlock. They'd end up in bitter tears, or racked with giggles. Sometimes they fell asleep on the couch in front of the TV head to foot. But she'd left school, and then she was gone.

Trinity had been in the house for weeks, but they were high all the time, her and Murph. She hardly came out of his room. Then she'd swung from a groggy hibernating funk to six shifts a week at Subway and enrolled at College of the North Atlantic. This was after she'd come home with a car. She had three pairs of Crocs, mauve and pink and beige, that she wore in the house.

The first time they talked she blurted out the car had belonged to her father. She asked Xavier did he want to see a picture of him. But she'd taken it out of her wallet and stood looking at it herself.

She'd come down and make toast with the hood of her sweatshirt up, standing still, just waiting for the toast to pop. She'd brought down the butter she kept in Murph's room. He'd hardly been around for a couple of weeks. That was nothing new.

Xavier had come into the kitchen when Trinity was bent over getting something out of vegetable drawer in the fridge, and she stood up and she'd said about the car. He looked at the photo she held carefully by the edges so as not to get fingerprints on it.

That's your father? Xavier said. She nodded and put the photo away.

She said a few things about Xavier and he realized she'd absorbed a lot of about him, had his recent history, the broader strokes.

She turned toward him with the butter knife and asked if he wanted a slice of toast. She said she had made the jam and it was really good, made it at the last place she was.

Where was that? he asked.

You don't know them, she said.

I heard you were in Toronto, he said. She said she had picked the berries on the South Side Hills.

I don't want any jam, he said. He didn't want her thinking they were friends. There had been shouting from Murph's bedroom and things smashing. Maybe that was over, but he and Violet were looking for another place.

She had finished with the toast and her jar of jam, and she put the box of butter under her arm and took up the plate with the toast and a glass of orange juice, juice he'd bought for the house, for the people actually paying rent there. But she was, he saw, undaunted by his refusal of her jam. She stood for one moment and really looked at him. She broke into a big smile.

I used to be taller than you, she said. Say hi to your mom for me.

Then he could hear her Crocs scuffing up over the staircase and he wondered if she would get a little electric shock on the landing as he did, every time he went up the stairs. He heard her scuffing and the front door opened and it was Heather and Devin and Violet coming in at the same time, though they'd all been at different bars, and he wondered if Trinity had reached the landing in time — if she were under the chandelier they'd found in someone's garbage, way too huge for the second-floor landing where they'd strung it up, even got it wired, Devin, who was getting his electrician's papers — if she had made it to the landing in time for the draft from the front door to make all the crystals rattle.

Though lots of the drop-crystals were missing, the chandelier was still bigger than a microwave, maybe more than five hundred crystal pieces, many-faceted, and it showered whoever was on the landing with a downfall of beneficent multi-hued speckles of light, hot pink, purple, white, yellow, when the front door let the freezing wind whirl up the staircase and the whole contraption jiggled and shivered. It might have been the way Devin wired it up that caused the little shock from the worn carpet on the stairs.

He'd thought, at first, Trinity had been pointing out that circumstances had been a lot easier for him, when she mentioned his mother. *Say hi to your mom.* He thought Trinity was reasserting her claim on his mother, now that she was back in town. Reminding him that his mother loved her too. That Trinity was as good as a sibling to him, just like Stella, and Stella's kid, Quinn.

Xavier didn't want Trinity contacting his mother; he felt this with a disorienting vehemence, though he couldn't have said why. But after she had taken a moment to really size him up, letting the butter knife slip into the sink full of water and adjusting the box of butter higher up under her arm, almost in her armpit, where she had a firmer grip, he'd realized she thought they were connected.

He saw that her understanding of their childhood was more convincing than his own.

Trinity's was the version that would endure. It was not an inconsequential encounter from long ago — but something indestructible, fated and full of a clasping disquiet.

I think you're taller than your father, she said and she turned and went up to the room with her toast and butter and juice and jam to study some more.

Xavier listened for the musical clatter of the crystals as the wind blew up the stairs of the creaky old house. He calculated that Trinity had missed the downfall of light speckles from the chandelier that he'd thought of as good luck.

the swan (2)

THE SWAN HADN'T moved of its own volition but was pushed by a little breeze and the movement broke the perfect reflection, a reflection that showed the ridges of folded feather, the curved neck, even the orange beak. The reflection shattered, jagged stripes of white on the black surface, juddering away from the swan in concentric rings, and when the breeze relented the swan was still and the reflection wiggled back into place, perfectly intact, sewn by the liquid seam to the swan's white belly, under which the water was dark and putrid.

Someone threw a stone is what happened.

Trinity saw the stone strike it. The swan was struck on the head, and shook all over, the head flopped, as if the neck had lost all muscle and cartilage.

Teenagers over in the trees. Trinity could see patches, a jean jacket, a blue shirt, chinks of colour in the leaves.

One of them shouted: Got it! A squeal of pleasure.

The slap of their feet on the pavement as they took off. Her mistake had been to turn and watch them go.

The swan rose up. The fury of it, a ball of fire and feather in the low sun, on top of her so that she felt the air hit her back in soft whacks, and she turned and ran.

The swan comes back to her in nightmares, she was only seven or eight, living with Mary Mahoney. But she'd gone to the park with Jules and Xavier.

Once Murph went with another woman for no reason, went off with some woman from a bar, both of them high as kites, and she'd dreamt the swan at the bottom of her bed, wings spread, open beak. It waddled up onto her chest and she couldn't breathe under the weight of it. Suffocating in the feathers and stink, the wet slather of its webbed feet and squirts of green guck as it defecated.

Once he planned a dinner and bought a checked tablecloth at the Dollar Store. He had candles and takeout Chinese and they ate in the backyard at the patio table behind the hedge. He'd bought her a pair of earrings, gold studs shaped like hearts.

Another time, he'd drawn back and punched her in the face, because she was slurping spaghetti noodles at the dinner table and he'd told her already. He'd said, Don't make that noise. He gave her a quick dart in the face. Nearly knocked her lights out.

Now maybe you'll learn, he'd said. When I say something, I mean it.

She'd gripped the edge of the table to force open the aperture of darkness. She'd pulled herself up and made her way to the back porch, she could see three door handles, each one as believable, as solid, as the other, and it was a shell game which was the right one. She tried for one and her hand went right through it. She heard his chair screech back from the table and as though by a miracle, she had the right door handle and was out in the backyard.

She'd got her feet jammed in her boots, in the back porch, but there was no coat and he was saying, Go out there and you won't come back in.

He was saying, Step out of this house and forget it.

She went out into the backyard without her coat and it was very cold but there was no wind because the houses blocked most of it. She was dizzy from the force of what he had done.

She touched her cheek because the bone might be chipped. There was a gouge from his ring which, she needed a stitch, and she went in to tell him.

But he'd locked the door. She was too proud to knock, though she was shivering hard. All the roommates were out, but she didn't want them up in her business anyway. She didn't want Xavier up in her business. Or his girlfriend.

Missus from the next yard opened her door and just stood here. There were two of her, the Missus, stood like twins in the doorway. She waved Trinity forward like a traffic cop.

She had to climb the fence to get to the woman's yard. Up over the bent lilac branch, and she just fell on the ground on the other side.

The woman left her back door open, but she'd turned off the lights. They could usually see into her house from their kitchen window, but she'd turned off the light, so Murph wouldn't be able to see. He might see her tracks through the snow. But he'd probably think she'd gone through the back gate out onto Gower. The woman must have seen the punch because their kitchen was all lit up and they'd been sitting there right in front of the window.

What a dart. He might have snapped her neck. She just sat there with her hands on her face. She never said nothing. The room was spinning.

Just hauled off and gave it to her. It had been dry on the streets and he was pent up. But she never saw it coming. She just sat there, and he started pacing the kitchen, pacing back and forth. He took the chair he'd been sitting on and flung it into the cupboards and still she never moved.

Come off it, he said. I never hurt you that much. He was stood still then, leaning on the counter.

Are you all right? he asked. Then he said he was sorry. He never had no control. He said the spaghetti set him off. He bent down on one knee and took her hand away from her face and the look on him then. He looked afraid. He looked sad. Sometimes she could see everything about him. She knew him inside out. The intensity of his pull; he was always pulling her.

But there were five of him moving in a circle around her. She stood, holding herself upright by pressing the tips of her fingers into the top of the Formica table. She might throw up. She had that thought. Then she made for the back door, out into the backyard.

It infuriated him that she was going out there for all the world to see. She knew if she couldn't say she was okay, that it wasn't bad, that it didn't hurt, he'd know she hadn't forgiven him. It was almost as though he'd hit her just to be forgiven. If she didn't forgive him fast enough, he'd hit her again. Forgiveness was the only thing she had to offer but she didn't have it.

I lost my temper, he said. She moved toward the back door, and she could feel the floor moving under her like a tide, the door was moving away from her, pulled out on a wave that made the floorboards rise up under her. The door was right there but it was also a few feet away. Outside was a black hole, which they had touched on in science, she'd done her upgrading in Toronto and when people graduated they all gathered in the hall and bells rang out over the PA and everybody cheered and clapped, and she knew it was foolishness but she had really wanted it. She couldn't help blushing when she walked down the hall with all that noise and attention. The truth was the idea of a black hole interested her. She had always been good at science. She thought she was smart enough for university. Some people get to go to university and some people don't.

When Trinity got inside the woman's back porch she smelled curry and coffee. Something was roasting in the oven. The woman already had her coat on, her car keys jangled when she patted her pocket.

She gave Trinity another coat, which was not the kind of thing Trinity would ever wear, with fake fur around the hood and no shape to it. It smelled of coconut cream and maybe the woman, something intimate and feminine and aged.

The woman got into the car and turned it on and hit the defrost and got out to scrape the windows. Trinity sat there with her face throbbing. Was the woman ever going to get back in the car and get them out of there?

If Murph found out she was sitting in the neighbour's car it might cause a fury that would kill her and this woman both. She thought the word *smote* from the bible. Up in Toronto she'd gone to church, just to sit there. Not that she believed in anything. *Smote* and *smitten*. *Smitten* from the Harlequins she read after work. She read a thousand of them. He found her on Facebook. Then the phone calls. He said she should come home out of it, and now look at her.

He was probably after ruining her face. She put down the visor to look and what a surprise, a big black bruise all around her eye, so black, like a misshapen pirate patch. He never even hit her eye. There was a flap of skin in a triangle hanging over the pulp beneath the eye from the ring she got for him at Traders. She flipped up the visor. This was a fine state. She was in a fine state now. How was she supposed to go to work looking like this? Tomatoes? Lettuce with that? Yes sure. One look at her and the manager would take her off the schedule. Maybe permanently. The car was going but the heaters were blowing cold air until it warmed up and then it got very warm and she had to open the door and throw up.

She expected him to come around the corner of Gower and bash the old woman's skull in. But the woman just kept going with the scraper. All she had was a few strips cleaned off and Trinity touched the button for her window and it went down a bit, the ice crumpling off it and she asked the woman if she could just leave it.

I think we should get going, Trinity said.

The woman paused, the scraper gripped with both hands. She got back in the car and threw the scraper in the back. She had to hunch over the steering wheel to see out the strip of clear glass, a strip just as wide as two overlapping thrusts of the scraper.

That's him, Trinity said. Coming there now.

When he passed under the streetlight the reflective strip on his camo jacket flared. He was striding forward against the wind, the jacket unzipped, flapping around him. The woman waited for a car coming down the hill behind her to pass.

It was creeping along because the hill was slippery. Trinity wished she hadn't put down the window. Now the ice was off it and he could see in if he tried.

The car behind slid past. The next one skidded to a slow halt behind them to let the woman go. Murph trudged past the car, not a foot away, she could see the flapping jacket.

I can't see the road, the woman said.

Then they were down the hill and turned on to Gower. All the hills would be too slick to get up. It had been a hellish December, and January was supposed to be even worse. She turned to look out the back window. The ice on the back window had cracked in jagged pieces that the wipers shifted around and couldn't flick away. She could see the back of him, a thin shadowy mark writhing out of shape in the cracks between the loose sheets of ice. Then the back of the car slewed to the side and dinged a parked car. Neither Trinity nor the woman remarked on the little accident. The woman kept going.

What I find, the woman said. You have to tap the brakes when you're skidding.

Trinity said, I'm bleeding all over your coat.

The woman said there were paper napkins in the glove compartment and Trinity got one out and put it to her cheek and looked at it, covered with blood, and touched it back to her cheek. She hadn't called Jules when she got back in town because she didn't want to admit she'd been using. She didn't want Jules to know. But it would have been nice to go over to Jules's house and make some dinner together. Maybe she could have visited Mary Mahoney.

The woman drove her up to the emerge entrance of St. Clare's.

Trinity stood for a moment once she was out of the car, the wind hard at her back.

Thank you very much, Missus, she said.

Yes, the woman said. You're welcome.

Thanks again, Trinity said.

I don't need to tell you, the woman said. But the wind took the door out of Trinity's hand, and she headed into the hospital. The emergency room was packed. She patted the back pockets of her jeans and felt her wallet with her ID. She spoke to the woman behind the glass window, gave her information. She made up an address in case they had the cops come after Murph.

Then she was brought to a small room and the nurse closed the door on her, and the fluorescent lights were really bright. The buzzing of the lights seemed to come and go. She might have fallen asleep.

The doctor looked at the gouge in her cheek. He said there was a good chance it wouldn't scar.

He asked and she said the corner of a coffee table. A fold in the rug.

Half an inch higher and you would have lost that eye, he said.

I should be more careful, she said.

Do you have anywhere to stay tonight?

Not really, she said.

I should report this, he said.

That would only make it worse, she said. He said he'd have a nurse call the shelter. He put three stitches in her cheek.

Naomi Centre was full for the night, but the nurse found a bed at Iris Kirby.

She went to the shelter in a taxi. She was given a bed and she just lay there until it was light out.

eight ball

THERE WERE CHRISTMAS decorations all over Duckworth and George Street. It was already freezing cold, but no snow for once. They'd been drinking at Bar None after it closed. He and Violet. People out on the fire escape, banging on the door, and not allowed in, but the music cranked. They'd had to shout at each other, and they were drunkenly playing pool.

Violet scrutinizing the tip of the cue stick with one eye shut. She was playing the role of someone who knew what the chalk did.

She blew on the tip like blowing a kiss.

You ready? he said.

Let's do it, she said. He started to tell her what the idea was.

I know the idea, she said. But she was lining up to smack the eight ball with the cue.

Missus, a guy standing at the opposite end of the table said. He told her not that ball.

What's wrong with that ball, she said.

The black one's the eight ball, he said.

Goes with my outfit, she said.

Hit that one and you forfeit the game, Xavier said.

Go for the red ball, the guy said. All lined up for you perfect.

Xavier lifted the rack, and she tented her fingers on the green felt and what a smash. Balls going everywhere, smacking each other, cascading, glassy cracks, tumbling down pockets, gurgling in the belly of the table.

Her mouth hung open and she yelled to Xavier: Did you see that?

Go again, the guy said.

What? she asked.

Go again, go for the yellow ball, hit her off the side.

Violet became serious, lined up the cue. Her eyes narrowed, stealth. She was nowhere in that look and everywhere at once.

It was a kind of blot at the centre of herself, at the centre of everyone, Xavier thought, the honest lostness, the ability to act without thinking. She was the table and the balls and all the beer and shouting.

She'd had a customer in the café that afternoon before she got off, too touchy-feely. She'd told Xavier about it on the way to Bar None, because she couldn't just tell the customer to stop touching her shoulder. She was doing the communications degree and there was a lot of theory, so she was reading that, and writing papers and going to classes and working to get the tuition together.

It was the kind of touching, not a touch exactly, a brush with the back of the hand, she'd said. Jokey, full of Hey, we're friends, right? Like she was just one of the guys, but he knew, the guy knew, it meant she couldn't say anything, couldn't make a big deal over it. He was a sloppy drunk this guy, came in every Friday.

That's the way it works, she told Xavier. You can't say anything, because it would be, like, What? I just gave you a friendly nudge on the shoulder, what are you so uptight about?

Made to feel complicit, she'd said. There were people coming toward them on the sidewalk, and she jumped up on the plowed bank to let them pass and she was about to slide off, but she caught her balance, jumped down in front of him, hunched against the cold, trudging, her head bent against the wind. She stopped so fast he banged into her, she turned around, most of her face covered by a scarf, but the eyes on her.

Or that it would be impolite to bring it up, she'd said. That's how it works. *Impolite*, she spat the word out. So I tell Marina, the boss, right? And she says let it go. I should just let it go, and it's that way up the whole chain of command, don't make a fuss.

Do you know what I mean by impolite? she asked. She had stopped under a streetlight. He was trying to think of what she could mean, but it turned out she didn't want an answer because she strode ahead of him with her mitts jammed into the pockets of his camel-hair coat — she'd taken it over, and it looked good on her, she was shouting over her shoulder that the guy was a bloody bastard.

But now, draped over the pool table, she was alert, and *smack*, the balls went flying again. Down in the pockets, two at the same time, and another and another.

They were home just after three a.m. and they were hungry. One of the roommates had put the empty box of saltine crackers back in the cupboard. The four waxy sleeves for the crackers had been crushed in the bottom of the box. Xavier pulled one out and held it for her to see. She slumped in the kitchen chair. She put her elbow on the table and rested her forehead on her hand and whimpered.

She said, Starved. I'm starved. I'm starving to death.

He said he'd go get fish and chips, and she said she'd go too but he told her to stay. He was tugging on his coat. They had an electric fireplace and she said she'd plug it in. It would be all warmed up when he got back. He headed out and it was very cold and the streets were almost empty. There were a ton of stars.

On George Street there was a guy in an alley, someone his age, and the guy called out for a smoke.

Xavier said he had a smoke and started down the alley and got out the pack and he held it out and the guy took one. He heard the other four guys in the alley before he saw them.

He turned and saw them moving together and even then, he thought nothing about the guys.

He had been full of the balls banging and all the drinking and he thought of the lights coming on when the bar was closing, and they all looked so wan and Violet's mascara was smudged, and where was her mitt? The mitts he'd bought her. She held one up and waved it at the bartender, asked had he seen one like this, she'd lost her mitt.

The stink of beer came with the lights and it was just them and three or four other customers left. One of the bartenders was turning the chairs upside down on the tables.

He had been lost in her smashing the balls and how they'd tumbled into the pockets, he was pretty sure she'd never played pool before; in the way she cried out for the lost mitt, and a stranger, a woman, said they'd find the mitt. A stranger, just as drunk as they were, summoned an instant intimacy with them, a collusion against the lostness of mitt, and maybe the lostness of all things that went missing at this hour.

I'll help you look, she said. The woman turned on the bartender and said they wouldn't leave the bar until they found the mitt.

Who was she? Her boyfriend waiting with the door open and the snow blowing in, telling the girl in the fun-fur bomber jacket to come on, come on.

She'd turned to him and stamped her foot and demanded he look for the mitt.

We're not going without it, she told Violet.

It must be here somewhere, Violet told her.

I don't ever give up, the woman said

Here it is, shouted Violet. I got my mitt. Under that chair it was. Have I got the two of them? Yes. Let's go. And they'd walked home and she sang "Dirty Old Town," or just one line because that was all she knew.

There were four men coming down the alley, and only then did Xavier realize it was a dead end. He had over a hundred bucks on him. He'd been full of good feeling, share a smoke with a guy at four in the morning, the thought of the greasy chips and the electric fire. The duvet.

In the kitchen, holding out the crinkled sleeve from the saltine box for her to see, they'd both become aware of the emptiness of the house. None of their roommates were home.

They knew the difference in atmosphere, a different weightiness, when the roommates were home and sound asleep. It wasn't just that they couldn't hear them. But their absence made the space different. Nobody was home.

I bet Trinity finished off them crackers, he said.

You could make an effort, Violet said.

What do you mean?

You could be nicer to her, Violet said.

I think we got the place to ourselves, Xavier said.

But I'm starved, she said. He'd been thinking about the duvet and he'd buy some pop, if there was a deal, two litres. He'd jog back and they could heat the fish up in the stove. He hoped she had thought to preheat the oven.

They circled him and took steps in and he knew he'd made a mistake coming into the alley. They were going to beat the living shit out of him and take his money.

Then one of the guys said his name: Xay?

The sounding of his name in the freezing alley.

The guy said, Xavier Cooper?

And Xavier said: Mike? He couldn't remember Mike's last name, if he had ever known it. Mike MacLeod. It jostled the circle of guys who had closed in on him in the alley. They were all glancing at each other. They were bewildered and self-conscious, ready to spring.

Xavier's all right, Mike MacLeod pronounced. How you doing, man? You good?

Mike, Xavier said. He said his name as if to bring him into being. He knew Violet had emptied herself of any thought except making the balls roll in all directions. That's how she did it, even though she'd never held a cue stick before. The crowd around the table had applauded. She had acted without any idea that she was doing it, but she knew in her hands, if that's a thing. Or her muscles or whatever. The stick had shot forward through her fingers as if by itself. The balls went tumbling down.

He had been the same way at the skate park, maybe eight years ago, when the older guys had picked on Mike MacLeod. Acting without forethought.

He was small, they both were, he and Mike. They were the smallest guys in the skate park. Xavier was only thirteen. It was the year he'd hit that bird while he was on the dirt bike. He'd been knocked out of himself. Flew out of himself. And there he was confronting the older guys at the skate park.

But they'd both shot up, him and Mike MacLeod, when they turned fifteen, they were tall now, almost unrecognizable. And Mike's face, shorn of pudge, was sharp, sly. But the eyes belonged to that kid, Mike MacLeod, that the older guys were picking on. He could see the kid Mike MacLeod had been on that day in the park, so afraid, but here he was setting up a scam whereby a guy asks for a smoke from the depths of a dark alley, and next thing a passerby gets the shit kicked out of him by five guys, robbed of everything he has on him.

The older guys at the skate park had been stoned and tattooed and they were violent with each other, knives were a thing then, knuckle dusters, masters of the skateboard, those older guys, and they had turned their attention on Mike, and Xavier had walked into the middle of them and said, Pick on someone your own size.

It was that or some other sentence that meant the same thing, but whatever it was, it came from the same kind of blot that had let Violet send the balls into the pockets. He'd had no idea he would say it. He had been entirely unafraid in a life-threatening situation. He had spoken without forethought, though he was only a kid, only thirteen. He'd never done such a thing before, and here was Mike in an alley at 3:45 a.m., when Xavier was about to be beaten to a pulp.

Good to see you, man, Xavier said.

How you doing, Mike said.

Good, man, good. Mike put an arm around him. Gripped his shoulder. Walked him to the end of the alley. When they were away from the other guys and had turned the corner onto George Street, Mike talked to him in a low voice.

I heard you were in a house with Brad Murphy, Mike said. He's a nasty piece of work, Brad Murph.

You know Murph?

Get out of there, Mike said. You're renting a room? Get another room.

He's not there all that often, Xavier said.

He's seriously fucked, man. If I know that, everybody knows it. Brad Murphy. He gets all fucked up on crack and he's fucked. There's lots of rooms you want a room. I heard crack. I heard Oxy. Needless to say.

I won't say you said anything.

Don't say I said anything. Just, maybe get out of there. Why would you stay there? He's in a bad way, that guy. Behind on payments, fucked in the head. Anyway, it's good to see you, Xavier. Haven't seen you in a long time.

Good to see you too, man. They gripped hands and Mike MacLeod drew him into a hard hug and slapped his back.

Then Mike turned and walked back into the alley.

jules
state of emergency

I'D HAD THE good sense to bring the shovels inside when I got home from the hospital.

I had Joe on speaker and he told me not to slam the door with the snow in the grooves of the threshold. But a massive block of snow fell into the porch.

The flange along the bottom will crack off and the wind will get in, he said.

I am not concerned about the fucking flange, I said. I was trying to shovel the snow off the floor, or slam the door so I could bring the snow to the sink. I didn't know what do with it.

It's important, don't shut the door, he said.

I'm not shutting it, I said. But I could see that the flange had already cracked off.

Get a butter knife or something and make sure the snow hasn't frozen into the grooves of the threshold, or in the hinges, he said. You won't be able to shut the door if it's in the hinges. Do you hear me?

I told him I had to go. I was furious about the suggestion of a butter knife. Where was he, anyway? A goddamn butter knife, on my hands and knees.

But I got the chunk of snow to the kitchen sink and put down a towel and got a butter knife and worked the ice out of the grooves in the foot of the door frame, and along the hinges. Then I tried to shovel my way out again. I reached over my head with the shovel, to get at the stuff on top. It took me more than an hour to clear a path down the two front steps to the sidewalk. Cars were buried. Some houses on the other side of the street were buried up to the second-storey windows. It was still snowing but there were other people out, shovelling. I tried to figure out what was missing. It was the sound of traffic.

I went back to the kitchen and ate more of the rotisserie chicken. The radio said the state of emergency might last for days. People were not allowed to leave their homes. All businesses were closed. Hospitals would allow no visitors.

Joe kept phoning, but I let it go to voicemail. I was angry about the butter knife and the cracked flange at the bottom of the door. I was angry I had to shovel myself out of the house.

Then I saw Glenda, the student who lived next door. I yelled out to her. She was wearing a bright silver jacket, digging out her house.

I asked if LeMarchant Road was cleared.

They must have plowed it because of the hospital, she said.

My son is in critical condition, I said. She stopped and held the red plastic handle of her shovel with both fists and rested her chin on the back of her hands.

Is he going to be okay? she asked.

He was stabbed, I said. She straightened up and took a

mitt off and wiped the back of her hand across her forehead.

They don't know if he'll make it, I said. They're saying he's in critical condition.

My phone was ringing in my pocket. Glenda was probably a half dozen years older than Xavier. She'd come from Ontario in September to begin a Ph.D. We'd met over the back fences because she loved my cats.

Glenda turned and looked down the street with her hand over her eyes against the glare of the sun, white as a faded dime, scoured by the snow. Then she turned back.

I saw him a few times last week — he came and fed the cats, she said. He came outside to smoke. I told him, actually, that's not good for his lungs. He'd come at different times during the day. He was with a girl once. His girlfriend. We stood up talking on the street.

Actually, I couldn't find my key, she said. I was looking in my purse. I was on my way back from a bar. I was tipsy, not loaded or anything. We were stood up talking, him and his girlfriend. She's in the English Department, doing communications.

I haven't met her, I said. I don't even know her name.

They'd been downtown and they were stopping on their way home to bring the mail inside. We talked a good long while, it was well after midnight. He seemed like a nice guy, the both of them were nice, actually. His girlfriend was really nice. They were saying about the music, some band downtown. They'd gone out to dinner first. They were saying what they had, rabbit something. I'm trying to remember where they said they had dinner. I can't remember where he said now, but it was fancy. Oh my god, that was him? The guy in the news.

He's still a child, I said.

They both seemed really nice.

He's at St. Clare's, so I am just going to try to get up there.

Your phone is ringing.

Yeah, I know. It's my husband. I think I broke the front door. What does she look like?

Pretty. The girlfriend? She's pretty with blond hair, a blunt cut, around her jawline. I thought she was really pretty. They seemed in love, to tell you the truth. I mean, I was very tipsy. I couldn't even find my keys, then I was just getting them to hold things, like my lipstick and my wallet, so I could find my keys. A tampon. That was funny. She had on a camel-hair coat and he had his arm around her.

I saw that someone was wading through the drifts down the centre of Cabot Street. He had a shovel over his shoulder. The snow was up to his waist in places. And under his arms in other places. He was making a path.

I looked up into the sky, tilting my head all the way back. My nose was tingling like I was going to cry; I decided to put it off until later. The snow was as fine as sand, and it hung in veils that fluttered and kicked out at the bottom. Glenda was looking up in the sky now too.

It keeps coming down, I said. I started through the drifts in the middle of Cabot Street in the path the guy with the shovel had kicked through.

Be careful, Glenda called after me.

My T-shirt was soaked with sweat and my coat wet with snow and heavy by the time I got to Long's Hill. The road was covered in ice and I kept sliding backwards. There were no cars on LeMarchant, nor anyone on foot. The shape of everything was altered and blazing white, sparkling. The world was unrecognizable. Pure and threatening. Very still, except the veils of snow that bucked and skittered and sometimes dropped straight down.

Then I saw the plows and a long line of dump trucks being filled, one by one, as they drove past the plow with a funnel that spewed the snow into the back of each truck. I walked toward them, and I could feel the street vibrating under my feet. The trucks were deafening.

I tried to call Joe, ducking out of the wind behind a high drift, but there was no answer. He called back and I told him I'd made it to LeMarchant. He was back in the hotel room, trying to re-book the flight. Before he finally got someone, he'd been listening to taped music for more than two hours, with interjections in French and English telling him how valued he was as a customer. I said most of the houses were buried, right to the rooftops.

That's dangerous, he said.

I said I was scared, and my voice went high and wobbled, and he told me not to be that way.

Come on now, he said. You're going to need to get a grip on yourself.

Why, I said. Why do I need a grip?

Because, he said. Okay? Come on now.

I can't help it, I said. But my voice was under control. Then I told him about the flange. I was vindictive about the flange. I wanted to break everything. The flange on the front door is broken and all the wind is getting in.

Great, he said.

I put a towel against the outside of it before I left, I said.

Yeah? Great, he said.

One of the old hand towels, I said.

I can't fly in there for at least three days, he said. They're making me a priority. It's an emergency situation.

The whole island is an emergency, I said. I had started walking again. A hard column of gritty snow, like pebbles, suddenly hammered down on my head, drilling into me. I screamed. A man appeared around the corner of the hill of plowed snow and looked as if I'd struck him. He was still pushing the snowblower, but the spray of snow had jerked to the side.

What the fuck, I yelled. He had small eyes and wide, bovine cheeks and a fluorescent orange toque shoved far back on his forehead. His face was gleaming with perspiration and he was wearing a survival suit.

What's going on? Joe yelled. Are you all right?

Watch what you're doing! I screamed. What the hell? But even as I shouted at the guy, I knew he had no way of knowing anyone would be on the street. Nobody was allowed out of their houses. Behind him in the bow window I could see an elderly woman in a quilted dressing gown, buttoned up to her throat, one hand holding back the curtain to watch his progress, the other holding the collar closed.

That came down on my head, I shouted.

Sorry, he said. Sorry. I have to get my mother out. She's not in good health. He was shouting this over the noise of his snowblower, which he hadn't turned off.

Are you okay? Joe was shouting.

Yes, I'm okay, Jesus.

What happened, he said.

Never mind, I said. I stormed past the man's driveway. Then I was giggling. I was hysterical, unhinged.

Are you laughing? he said. I can't hear you.

Never mind, I shouted at him, furious again. You're not here, are you?

I can't get a goddamn ticket, you wanted the ticket, he said. There was only one ticket and you wanted it and I booked it for you.

But you're still not here, are you?

There's a state of emergency, he said. Maybe you've heard.

I'm in the middle of it, I shouted.

The buffet this morning was shit, by the way. It's thirty-seven dollars plus tax and the coffee is shit. This is the shittiest coffee I ever had in my whole life, it's water, it's just water.

I have to go, I said.

Stay on the phone, he said. But I hung up. It was too hard to talk to him, I needed him so much. I just needed him. I wanted him to take over.

In front of me a man in an orange hazard suit, one of the city workers, was waving at me to get off the road. He'd raised his arm and pointed at the ground, made a circle with his two fingers, and wagged the fingers to indicate that I should walk the other way. I charged forward.

He started a sluggish jog toward me when he saw I wasn't doing what he said. The wind had picked up and he seemed to be driven by it. A huge curved funnel hanging from the back of the plow swung to the side and spilled snow into the back of a dump truck. Once the truck was filled, it moved forward and turned down Carter's Hill. Another truck moved into its place and the funnel shifted again to fill that truck. There were maybe fifteen trucks lined up waiting to be filled with snow. The city had lifted a rule and they were allowed to dump the snow in the harbour. The radio said they had nowhere else to put it.

A record, the radio said. Record amounts. Not in a hundred years.

What are you doing? the man shouted. Nobody's allowed out on the street.

I'm going to the hospital, I said.

They're closed, he said. They're not letting anyone in. His mouth was open from shouting over the noise of the heavy equipment, a grimace that showed his horsey yellow teeth. I saw he was chewing a hard white piece of gum in the back of his mouth; I saw the dents of his teeth in it and I saw him transfer it on his tongue from one side of his mouth to the other. The sun broke through the grey cover and suddenly everything was glittering. There was a band of blue near the end of the street, the snow was still coming down. If I kept going down this road for an hour, I would eventually come to Florence's house. But she had died long ago. And Nancy had sold the house.

They'll bloody well let me in, I shouted.

What? he shouted back.

I'm going through, I said. He turned sideways like a doorman in a fancy hotel and flung his arm wide to let me pass, pulled his stomach in and bowed deeply, a little comic gesture that acknowledged we were the only two people on the empty streets of the entire city, except for the workers in the heavy equipment.

They're only letting in people if they're needed, he shouted. Are you needed in there?

THE FRONT DOORS of the hospital were locked, and there was no one in the glass information booth. There was no one in the lobby. I tried the door. And then I rattled it really hard.

I shouted, Hey!

I banged my fist, first with my mitt on, and then I took it off, but it was so cold my hand started to hurt. Then I went around the back and tried the emergency door and it swung open. The nurse there looked up at me. Snow caked all over the front of my coat.

I have to see my son, I said. He's in critical condition. The nurse put down her pen and put her hands flat on the desk and pushed herself up. She turned and walked through a door behind her. She was gone. But she reappeared, opening the door to the side of the glass booth.

You're not allowed in here, she said. Do you know where you have to go? She pointed down the hall and told me two rights and then the elevator.

I squirted the hand sanitizer into my palm and rubbed my hands together. And pressed the button to get the doors unlocked with my elbow. There was a wait.

Finally, a nurse asked who it was, and I said my name. There was a long silence. They didn't want to deal with me. I waited. Then door buzzed and swung open.

jules
mother

MY PHONE RINGING, Nell saying my name, before all this with Xavier, before Mexico, before the storm, before. The last time I'd had to rush to the hospital for an emergency.

Nell said my name and she asked where I was. She said Mom had had a heart attack. She said they were going to operate. Mom was in an ambulance heading to St. Clare's. I asked if I should go there. I said I was at my front door. I told her I was going. I asked where she was.

I'm going now, she said.

Where will I meet you? I asked.

I'd had a bag of groceries and a takeout coffee and I flung the cup from my hand. I flung the car keys down so hard they toppled from one step to the next. I put down the bag of groceries. It tipped over and a mango dropped and rolled onto the sidewalk.

Nell and me, on a row of chairs in front of the elevators on the ground floor of St. Clare's. Both of us texting on our phones. Every time the elevators opened someone came out that one of us knew. Someone Nell had represented in a divorce; someone in her exercise class. A woman she'd gone to law school with and hadn't seen since then. Sherry Whalen, whose husband was in with an appendicitis. A man who had taken Sabine's classes with me with a bandage over his hand, crimson blood, the stain spreading even as his wife stopped to chat. He'd said it wasn't bad. He'd held up the bloody bandage, as if modelling a new glove.

Then a woman who had bought a painting of mine.

I'm here getting my ears syringed, she said. They do it here, ears, nose, and throat, down the hall. She'd pointed.

We were there for hours before the surgeon came out of the cafeteria with a white Styrofoam cup. He'd stopped in the middle of the lobby and lowered his head and put his hand on the back of his neck. We'd been told to go home, and they'd call us from recovery. We wouldn't be able to see her, they'd said, until she was out of recovery, and there was no sense in hanging around the hospital. But Nell wanted to stay.

I just want to be near her, Nell had said. I'd gone to the bathroom down the hall and as I was coming back out to the crowded lobby, I saw Nell stand and leave her purse gaping open, her phone and her coat on the chair. Then I saw the surgeon with his white coat unbuttoned and his coffee. He was massaging his neck. He had just stopped in the middle of the lobby with everyone moving around him.

He was startled to see us, but he knew who we were, he'd been a couple of years ahead of me going through school. Nell had been in the debate club with him for a while at MUN. He didn't really have to speak, but he was compelled. He looked at the floor as he described the operation in careful detail. It had been four hours. When he said that he gave himself a little shake and checked his watch.

That's a long surgery, he said. He drew a deep breath and blew it out slowly.

We lost her, he said. He looked at his watch again and slopped some of his coffee.

We lost her fifteen minutes ago, he said. We had everything clamped. There were moments when we thought it was going to work out, but things go downhill.

I knew Nell wanted to hear every word he had to say. She was looking intently into his face as he spoke. Her face open and avid.

Nell said, Thank you.

I said, Thank you for trying. But he continued with more details about the surgery.

When things start to go downhill, he said. He made circles with his hand in the air.

There's nothing can be done, I said.

They gather momentum, he said. I glanced over at our coats and purses.

We thought she would make it, he said. I'm sorry. Then he shook our hands. First mine and then Nell's. We returned to the chairs where we'd left our purses and coats, and we put our coats on and even our mitts, but we sat down. I checked my purse but everything was there, my bank card, my phone, a memory stick with the paintings I had planned to submit to the gallery that represented my work, for the provincial procurement program. Today had been the deadline. The memory stick had *Shell* written on the side.

I can't believe it, can you? Nell asked. She started forward in her chair, as if to get up, but she was still. She was trying to believe the situation.

We were just sitting here and next thing, he came out of the surgery, and then this, she said.

I asked if she'd got a parking spot close by. I could drive her to her car.

What should we do now? she asked.

Our mother is gone, I said.

I know, she said. Holy god, Jules. Holy god. Holy god.

Then she got a text from her husband.

Oh, supper is ready, she'd said. Spare ribs. Do you want to come over?

I'm pretty worn out, I said. Then my phone vibrated.

Oh, I said. Supper is cooked for me too. What are we supposed to do?

I don't know, she said. Should we be doing something?

I think we wait, I said. Should we go see her body? I looked then and saw that the surgeon was coming for us.

He said we could come and be with our mother, if we wanted, and we said we did. He led us into the room and said we could have as long as we wanted. We were just to let the nurses know when we were leaving.

He closed the door behind him, and Nell and I went to either side of the bed. Mom looked different enough that we believed she had died. She looked different than when she was simply sleeping. Her expression was not one I recognized, an expression I didn't think I'd seen before. It might have been consternation, or a bemused look, or a settling of features, a tallying of some kind.

She'd been living in Nell's basement apartment for ten years or so. Mom had told me, only a few months before she died, that sometimes before Nell went to work, she would lie down on our mother's bed, lie on her side with her head propped up on her elbow, and tell Mom what she had to do at work that day.

Nell would say if she were going to be in court. Or if she'd be picking up groceries or if she was meeting someone for lunch. Some days she'd ask Mom to ride the lift chair up the flight of stairs from the basement apartment, to the landing where she'd switch to the second chair, installed to accommodate the twist in the staircase, and then get in the second wheelchair waiting at the top of the stairs, so Mom could let the dog out in the backyard.

Nell went through her plans, and whatever gossip she had, and then she got off the bed and straightened her suit and headed off to work and Mom slept for another hour. It had surprised me, the intimacy and ordinariness of it. That my sister would lie down with our mother, exchange these meandering thoughts, and then hop up and go to work. I'd felt a twinge of jealousy.

We each said goodbye to our mother in the other's presence. We'd been in there for almost an hour. Mostly we'd been quiet. A nurse popped her head in and apologized and closed the door. Both of us had a turn crying. Then we went back out into the hallway and found the nurses' station to say we were leaving. That now she'd be in there alone.

Nell stopped in the porch of the hospital and took off her mitts and put them between her knees. She put up the hood of her parka and tugged on the strings, so the fox-fur trim drew in tight around her face. She lifted her chin and made a bow. Then she took her mitts from her knees and put them back on. Someone came through the automatic doors and the wind blew the fur in every direction and she shut her eyes against it.

I wasn't expecting that, Nell said. She stumbled but I caught her arm.

Almost completely dark outside, she said. Our mother is gone.

I know, I said.

xavier
crowbar

MURPH HAD SOLD Trinity's grandfather's car for a freezer bag of pot. He'd wanted a bag and a half, but the guy said no. He wanted coke instead of pot, but the guy said no. This was a story Murph told in the kitchen with Heather there and Devin and Violet, who had just come home from the university. It was not something he would have boasted about, before. Mike MacLeod had been right: he was coming apart.

Trinity was frying bacon. She had her back to Murph. She was holding the plastic spatula that had one side bubbled and melted because someone had left it too close to the burner. She was touching the curls of bacon with the spatula. The whole kitchen was filling with smoke and spittle flew off the pan.

She'd turned from the pan and as she spoke her eyelids drooped down, nearly closing.

That car was a gift from my pop, she said.

The car was a writeoff, Murph said.

The car started and it went, she said. The car was kept up. It was like brand new.

I bought you that bacon, Murph said. You wouldn't be eating bacon if I wasn't watching out. You have a place to sleep. You ever pay a penny rent? Do you think that's fair to Devin here? Or Heather?

Xavier, can you pass the toast, Trinity said. Her toast had popped.

These people aren't friends of yours, he said. Nobody contradicted him. They were afraid.

Heather said, Excuse me, and stepped over Murph's outstretched legs. He mimicked her with a falsetto.

Excuse *me*, Murph said. You're the one down here complaining all the time she uses the hot water.

A bell dinged and Devin opened the door of the microwave and took the steaming burrito out and slammed the microwave door and left the kitchen.

It was just Xavier and Trinity standing and the freezer bag of pot on the table, and they had their backs to Murph, both of them facing the stove.

Move, Xavier said. She moved out of the way and he opened the oven door and took the tray of nachos out and let them fall into a big blue plastic bowl and he got two glasses and his litre of root beer out of the fridge. Murph was high and they were afraid. Xavier wanted to get out of the kitchen and he wanted Trinity out of the kitchen too. But everyone was paralyzed by the news of the car. The car that had belonged to her father.

Murph had seemed okay when they first moved in. But he had an x-ray vision, a narrow genius that could recognize a point of tender, hesitant pride or a raw vulnerability and he'd expose it, in startling ways that provoked sudden, shameful laughter, loosened like a rotten tooth. Devin had already given notice on his room. Xavier and Violet had been looking at places. They'd been to three so far.

Give me a nacho, buddy, Murph said.

Fuck off, Xavier said.

Then Murph took something from the grocery bag at his feet and threw it as hard as he could at Trinity, who had her back to him and didn't see it coming, but Xavier had seen Murph reach into the bag and for some reason he thought it would be a knife, so he ducked, and Murph laughed at him ducking, a high-pitched giggle, and the object struck Trinity softly between her shoulders and it was the pink dice from the windshield of the car. They bounced on the linoleum.

Saved them for you, Murph said. He sounded recalcitrant and misunderstood.

What the grandfather had given Trinity Brophy was not a car but a crowbar. She might get away from Murph before he killed her, that's what Xavier had thought. The grandfather had started something in her, and Murph must have seen it too, something as unbending as a crowbar. That's why he'd got rid of the car.

jules
mother (2)

I'D BEEN IN the car with Mom, doing errands. She'd gone into the dry cleaner's to pick up the suit she would wear to John's funeral, my father-in-law's funeral. Before the amputation.

She was very small in the suit, which was a black, shiny brocade that seemed to move on its own, with gestures separate from the ones she was making, each panel of the jacket shifting out of alignment when she sighed. The jacket and skirt might have fit two of my mother. The fabric shone with a writhing blue-black glare that flashed all over her, catching at the crook of her elbow, sliding along the edge of the stiff collar. There were brass buttons with embossed anchors, embossed nautical ropes coiled around the stems of each anchor, four buttons on each sleeve, two rows of buttons down the front.

It was a sunny day in the middle of winter and she left me in the car with a loonie to put in the meter if the man who gave out parking tickets were to appear. She instructed me to keep a close eye.

Keep a watch, she said. You don't want him coming out of nowhere.

She had taken me with her on this errand strictly for this purpose.

When she stepped out of the dry cleaner's, she was holding the suit high up, and the evening sun, suddenly brightening, struck the film of protective plastic so that the suit became invisible, and the protective plastic sheath shone white and ghostly. The breeze rippled the filmy covering. It was full of static electricity and clung to anything it touched and was wrinkled against the suit, and the long tail of the plastic sucked itself onto Mom's shins, and a corner of it, near the shoulder of the suit, flapped and waggled and smeared onto her cheek, but she turned away from it.

She opened the back door on the passenger side and hung the suit on the handle in the ceiling of the car. It was evening traffic in the dead of winter, and the bright sunshine turned first amber and then violently pink as Mom made her way around the front of the car to get in the driver's seat.

I'd lowered the visor on my side and opened the sliding blind over the mirror to put on mascara, and I saw the transport truck coming, but I'd also caught sight of the stiff collar of the suit and one of the embossed brass buttons, bouncing madly on a loose thread. The transport truck roared past, going too fast, and for the briefest second it blocked the sun and a cold shadow fell over us and my pupils dilated and Mom was no longer a silhouette but visible, the fox fur on her Grenfell coat, her white hair, her hand touching the hood, the slant of her cheek. When the truck had roared past, the boiling red of the sunset struck the button hanging limply now, unmoving, and it glowed like an ember in a dying fire, almost breathing with the sunset light, and Mom had disappeared.

Of course she had simply moved around the hood of the car to the driver's door, but I thought of her arm raised high with the suit, high enough to keep it out of the snowbank, the plastic sheath a white rippling flare, alive, smearing itself all over her.

After she had died it was the button, in the little mirror, burning such a fierce red, so hot and vibrating on the thread, and extinguishing when the thundering transport truck passed, and how she had disappeared from the front of the car where she had halted — this is what I thought of, when I thought of her death, though she would live for another seven years, she would go with Nancy and Florence to Portugal, and there would be the operation and the loss of her leg, and Nell would put in the stair lift, and we'd have Christmases and birthday parties.

My mother at the beach, my mother playing cards. Mom and I watching *Jeopardy!*, shouting the answers. I thought of one weekend in Broad Cove when Florence and John had come out, and Florence's sister, and my mother. They had a bonfire, everybody drinking, singing until they were hoarse. Raising their voices. When they got to Elvis, my mother's aluminum lawn chair fell away as she leapt up; it tottered and waggled back into the blue darkness. She clutched an invisible microphone, flinging the invisible cord out of her path, glanced at them under her brow, did the sneer. The sensual lift of the upper lip, the hedonistic, sexually charged self-parody of Elvis at the height of his career. Mom was doing the sneer and it was funny, her voice deep and syrupy. Florence jumped up to do harmony: *You gave me a mountain this time.* Mom snapping the invisible cord, making it snake over the grass.

honeymoon

AFTER HE'D HIT her. The honeymoon period, as they called it at the shelter. When they try to make it seem like they only hit you because they love you so much. Gifts. They said beware of gifts. They predicted Murph would be full of remorse. Woeful when he came to terms with what he'd done. He'd wince when he looked at the black eye, the pucker of flesh from the stitches where his ring had lacerated her cheek. Wince as though it hurt him more than it hurt her.

She had one foot out the door. But she'd been feeling sick. It was depression or it was gastrointestinal. She was sluggish and sleepless. Couldn't keep things down. It was because he'd hit her. The doctor had said she'd go through a period of depression, and if she did, there was medication. She could make an appointment. If she felt tired, that was probably depression. If she lost her appetite, depression. Her guts were killing her. She wondered if she had a concussion. He'd really done a number on her with that punch. Even looking in the mirror made her sick to her stomach. She knew it was infected and she was running a fever.

She said she wanted to get groceries and Murph said he would take her. He had somebody's truck for the afternoon. The sleet was coming down in tattered ribbons.

But they were driving all the way to the Torbay Road Sobeys instead of the Sobeys on Merrymeeting, which was two minutes away. She watched as the Merrymeeting Sobeys sailed past in the slurry, wiped clear with each flick of the wipers. It made her nauseous.

She said nothing about going out of their way because she could see by the set of his lips and the softness around his eyes that he wasn't thinking of her. He was thoroughly lost, his face naked, his hands loose on the wheel, intent on how slippery the road was.

He was broad-shouldered and without a single ounce of fat. He was a little shorter than her. She'd always worn flats around him, hunched her shoulders. His mouth was full and soft; it suggested a gentleness. A stranger might think gentle. His eyes were bloodshot because he was smoking. But his eyes were light brown and he had lashes like a girl. His nose had been broken, but the small jag to the side in the bridge of his nose didn't harm his looks. It was the high cheekbones and the fact he was windburnt all year long that made him look vulnerable. She knew, had always known, since grade three, that he could be easily broken. He had already been broken, but he had the capacity to break over and over. That was in his face.

When he was soft and unselfconscious like that, she knew he was dangerous. The car was full of pot smoke and the smell of the pine air freshener jiggling on a green thread from the rearview mirror. Whoever owned the truck kept it clean, except for the smell.

She touched her cheek where she had the three stitches. It was still very tender. The doctor had said if there were pus she'd have to come back. He'd said, If it weeps. But she put peroxide on it. Pus meant an infection and that was why she felt so lousy.

There was a crust like varnish across the split skin that came off on her fingers. She wanted to put down the visor and see if there was a mirror but if she looked at the wound he would think she was trying to bring it up, remind him.

He'd said he was sorry, and she'd said it was forgotten. If she put her cheek up near to a mirror to get a proper look, he'd see it as a provocation. But the whole side of her face was hot. Most of the bruising around her eye was yellow now, a mustard yellow, but she put concealer on it, and foundation and blush over that.

He'd made her continue on EI while she was working at Subway, and they caught her, and she'd have to go to court. But when she went to legal aid with her face like that the lawyer advised coming into his office without Murph.

The lawyer said it right to Murph's face, though he wasn't looking at him. She could see the lawyer knew how she got that face and that he wasn't willing to overlook it.

A woman in a pencil skirt walked past them with a bunch of files and Trinity wondered if she could ask for a different lawyer, maybe that woman would look after them. But it had already developed into a situation and it was better not to speak.

The male lawyer had squeaky shoes that creaked with every step, they must have been brand new. The noise of the shoes was a provocation. He said his name was Mr. Collins and the Mr. was a provocation. One of these guys who wants to be a hero. Mr. Collins was short, but she could see he worked out because of the arms on him. There was a tattoo of what looked like octopus arms feeling their way up out of the buttoned-up white shirt, with the suckers on the underside of the mottled purple tentacle showing.

Murph said, She doesn't go in there without me.

This was Murph acting big.

Trinity didn't need a big show in front of the woman with her pregnant daughter, who had to be fifteen, and it was hard to tell by the look of them which one was there to see a lawyer, the mother or the daughter. She didn't need a big show for the secretary behind the glass who had seen it all, obviously, or the woman lawyer, with the rust-flecked tweed skirt and matching jacket. Murph and the short male lawyer both standing with their arms crossed, their feet apart. The two of them were going to make a scene.

She touched her cheek. She got the cheek because she'd slurped her spaghetti. Or because he felt guilty about selling her father's car and he knew he'd gone too far when he did that, and something had changed in her. Or because there was nothing on the streets, it was a dry spell. He was in withdrawal. Or he was planning something. There were things that were irrevocable, and whatever he was planning was one of those.

She'd served up the spaghetti and got them both a glass of water and she put ice in the glasses. She got a few slices of bread out and brought the butter down from the bedroom.

It was as though he had no more idea he was going to strike her than she did. With the ring on. Some kind of ring with an insignia and a little ruby, the edge of it had ripped right through her cheek. Missed her eye, though.

That's something to be thankful for, the doctor had said.

The lawyer asked her what she wanted to do, and she only hesitated for a second because she could feel Murph was going to get himself arrested or just further insulted and there was the possibility he would tear the place up.

She knew that whatever she did could set him off. She had only come to this office — which they'd had to circle around a few times to find the entrance of, and she'd had to run across the parking lot through icy rain and ask the men who were involved with a dumpster which one was the door to legal aid, and one of the men tossing his cigarette and stepping forward to say she had to go around the corner, by that time she was soaking wet — she had only come to find out if there was any way to not have a record for defrauding Employment Insurance, or to say it had been a mistake.

But instead, there had to be this song and dance with Murph, and buddy's shoes, the other lawyer, and the female lawyer, who had come out from behind her desk to lean on the frame of her door with her arms crossed. The pregnant girl didn't even look up from her phone, but the texts were coming to her fast and furious. The texts sounded like the background noise in a horror movie, tinkling in rapid succession little sinister notes.

She felt the cut ooze, she could feel a drip of ooze cutting a path through the makeup.

Murph stormed out and she followed him. He was tearing down the staircase so the metal steps rattled through the whole building.

The reason she couldn't leave him was that she was afraid

he'd come get her. But that was not the real reason. It was because when she was a kid she'd had a terrible sunstroke, they'd said, and she'd found herself in the middle of the ocean, and it was as though there was no other human being on the face of the earth. She knew that terror, and she would not subject him to it even though he was a monster.

He tried to slam the door on the way out of the legal aid building, but it was heavy and wheezed shut with a hush.

If she left him, he would have no one. And she couldn't do that, leave him with no one. Anyone who has been left with no one would never do that to another human being. You'd want to be awfully cynical to do that when you knew what it felt like to find yourself without a soul in the world.

The thing that the lawyer could never take away from her was the ability to forgive herself. She could always forgive herself. But everything costs, and if you turn on the taps of forgiveness, it spills all over the place, soaks everything in its wake, and the truth was, she had not forgiven him and knew she would never forgive him even as his fist had smashed into her face. Yet leaving him required more than she had.

But another thing was true too. She had one foot out the door, and she was leaving him. She was already gone. He would never hit her again. He had crossed a line when he sold her father's car. He had crossed a line the last time he hit her.

Murph went through the stations on the radio with patience on the way to the Torbay Road Sobeys. He listened to a bit of everything, his lips moved to a song here and there.

They drove past the Port Hotel, where she'd been under the care of social services for six weeks when she was seven, before she went to Mary Mahoney's, and she looked at the black windows and the beige siding and she remembered the room and a woman in a flowered sundress sleeping sitting up on the couch. She couldn't remember the woman's name, but she thought her shampoo smelled of peaches, and the apartment smelled of burnt toast the first time she went in there.

She pressed the button and the window went down just a crack and his pot smoke slithered over the ceiling of the car and out the window. There was a cop car pulled up beside them at a red light and Murph glanced over at the cop and looked back at the road. His leg started jiggling. But the light turned green and the cop went ahead of them and turned onto a side street.

They pulled into the parking lot of the strip mall on Torbay Road, and he joined the line to inch toward the Sobeys entrance because it was raining.

He said, I can get you closer. Just wait, for Jesus sake. Don't jump out.

When the car was right in front of the door, he said he'd circle around, and she should stay in the porch and wait for him after she was done. She ran in with the twenty bucks he'd given her and got a full chicken and bag of potatoes.

She'd bought a deep fat fryer at Home Depot, and the roommates didn't like them having it because if you fell asleep there'd be a fire. They were afraid of her and Murph. Xavier was afraid.

She looked around the supermarket, a man laying out eggplants and a woman with only dry goods in her cart. Only dry goods meant she was hired to watch out for shoplifters, posing as a shopper. Trinity waited until nobody was looking and she put an avocado in the inner pocket of her jacket. She came on a bin with plastic lemons with little green screw-on caps and a green paper leaf that said the brand name and she put that in her other pocket. She paid for the chicken and the potatoes and the lady asked if that was all, and for a moment Trinity thought she could see the bulge of the plastic lemon in her pocket.

She said that was everything. The woman asked if she had a points card and she didn't and the woman said cash or debit, but Trinity was thinking, Why this grocery store. Why had they come out of their way?

When she'd got outside of the law office, the wind had rippled the plastic bag with all her papers in it and they'd got wet. Because they stormed out, she would have to make another appointment, and it took forever for legal aid to call you back. She'd have to buy more minutes for her phone. He'd made her scam the EI, and she just wanted to find out a way to make it look like she hadn't scammed them, if there was such a way.

She came out of the Torbay Road Sobeys and the wind was against her. There was a shopping cart rattling backwards all over the lot. She lost hold of the receipt she'd had scrunched in her fist and she hunched over after it, running like a crab, scrabbling after the receipt, but as soon as she caught up with it, the receipt flew up in the air over her head. She was snatching at the air over her head and then it went down on the ground and she was running, because he would be pissed if he thought she'd paid for an avocado or a plastic lemon. She stamped on the receipt with her foot and picked it up and there was a car turning out of the parking space and it nearly hit her, the headlight splintering, and she could see a pink spot floating over the cart corral. But she had the receipt.

Murph was parked by a backhoe at the edge of the parking lot, they were doing some kind of construction. The shovel of the backhoe was covered in snow, and its windshield was a single white eye.

She didn't know why he was looking at a backhoe and then she knew. He was hunched over the wheel, staring up at it. He was going to go after an ATM. She'd seen him watching the video of the last ATM robbery on the other side of town. It had popped up on his phone. The dreamy slackening of his mouth into a thoughtful frown. Her cheek was flaming hot. She jumped in the truck. He looked at her, she was soaking wet from the snow and she handed him the receipt, but the ink had all run and it was falling apart.

jules
fairy

THERE WAS A woman in a chair next to another bed in the room; her daughter had been rolled into the ICU after a long surgery. The woman was from Gander and had nowhere to stay in the city and wouldn't have been able to get there if she did because of the storm. So she slept in the chair. Her name was Geraldine and she had glasses with big, thick lenses and clear plastic frames that had yellowed.

I'd run into her earlier in the day. She was in the little snack area by the nurses' station. The reflection of ceiling lights from the hall on her glasses had made it impossible to see her eyes, but I could see grit where the lenses fit into plastic grooves of the frames. I could see fingerprints.

She'd been making tea and put the bag in a white Styrofoam cup and turned to the water dispenser by mistake, pushing the cup against the nozzle, and when crushed ice spilled out on the teabag, she took off her glasses and pinched the bridge of her nose. Finally, she gave her head a shake.

Oh my, she said, that's another thing ruined.

Best not to keep a list, I'd said.

Geraldine was sleeping in the same sort of chair as me. She was sprawled out, legs apart, feet planted. She was wearing her winter boots. They came halfway up her calf, but the laces were loosened, and the blue synthetic fur was white with road salt. I saw her jerk in her sleep and resettle.

She'd tossed the Styrofoam cup in the garbage with the tea bag and crushed ice. She let herself lean back against the counter, one hand swinging her glasses by the end of the plastic arm. They flicked back and forth on the hinge, and she rocked her head up and down, all her teeth bared, her gums visible, which I realized was the way she cried.

I've only got the one youngster, she'd said. That's her in there. I'm a single mother.

I took the glasses out of her hand before she broke them, and I put one of the lenses halfway in my mouth and breathed hard and wiped the lens in the end of my T-shirt. She became subdued, blinking wetly. I breathed on the other lens and cleaned it in my T-shirt and held them up to the light and then gave them back.

But now Geraldine was sound asleep and there was a fairy at the foot of Xavier's bed.

I realized the fairy was Nell, my sister, at age nine, dressed as a fairy, her pale blond hair flapping as she hopped barefoot over a field of ice and snow that surrounded my son's bed. I had tied sheer curtains to her arms.

I'd been sitting upright in the chair, saturated in sweat because Xavier still wasn't responding to the antibiotics. They said he was slow to respond. And they said he hadn't responded at all. They'd switched antibiotics again, and I asked would all these rounds make him immune, but the nurse just said it was a super-antibiotic this time. I'd fallen asleep and woke to see my sister as she was a thousand years ago when we were children.

My father had bought me a Super 8 camera when I was eleven. It made loud fast clacks, the speeded-up clicking of each sprocket engaging with the perforations in the film.

I had convinced my sister to act the part of a fairy. She'd gone out on the frozen lake in a gauzy dress and I had tied white nylon sheers from her bedroom window to her arms for wings—but her boots!

I'd made her take the boots off because they were from Sears and not like anything a fairy would wear on her feet. I was certain a fairy wouldn't have anything on her feet. And so my sister was hopping around on the ice barefoot.

Nell at fifty: Crown prosecutor, on at least three boards for feminist organizations, a woman who owned two malamutes, both leashes strapped around her waist when she took them for a walk, her blended family, the second husband, and his family of fourteen siblings who embraced her, swimming the channel between Portugal Cove and Bell Island to raise money for mental health and the nursery at the women's shelter so these women could go to work while they were staying there and have someone to take care of the kids, the dinner parties for her second husband's family of forty or more, including spouses and youngsters and cousins, dinner parties with her first and second husbands and all the children and the first husband's second wife, they'd become close friends, and me and my family and wine, she and the second husband working side by side in the kitchen, my mother in the basement apartment, phoning upstairs to ask my sister to program Netflix on her iPad.

This adult, my sister, present already in her nine-year-old face.

Nell at nine years old.

Standing at the foot of my son's hospital bed.

She was wearing a negligee of my mother's, layers of transparent nylon, a pale lime green. My mother had purchased it in the mid-sixties, worn it on her wedding night in Bermuda, and kept it in the cedar hope chest. Perfect fairy costume.

Nell's hair, pale and thick. I'd made a crown of fabric flowers, from the vase in the living room. She wore the crown low over her brow.

Her hair was lifting off her shoulders in a wind, because the hospital room was full of winter gusts. The hospital was swaying slightly in the wind. Geraldine had commented on it, and the nurses.

All over the ICU, poles on wheels with bags of saline swayed and rumbled across the floor to the right side of the room, was it an earthquake? Gusts of snow lifting, twisting, the ICU covered in drifts with a glassy crust that had broken in shards, Nell had sunk to her knees, her footprints were visible behind her, all the way from the door.

The carpet in her bedroom when we were children was bright red and plush. Mine was two-tone shag, mauve and purple. She had a built-in bookshelf, but we had both read everything jammed in there, the Nancy Drews, Hardy Boys, *Stuart Little*, *Charlotte's Web*, *Black Beauty*, *Little House on the Prairie*, *The Secret Garden*, and a hundred others we never heard of again and lost before we had children of our own.

There were two desks, but we'd never used them, except to pile things on. Did our homework at the dining room table.

I'd made my sister stand still with her arms out straight

as a scarecrow while I attached the sheer nylon curtains from the bedroom window to her arms with safety pins.

When we played, she was concentrated and malleable. If she was angry, she shut down and became quiet, like a city in a power outage. She played stoic and bemused to my excitable and shrill. Nell would step in front of me when there was something to be afraid of; otherwise, at that time when I was eleven and she was nine, I was in charge.

I am afraid, and here she is. She has shown up in the costume I made her wear when I was shooting a Super 8 film of a fairy flying across the ice. She hopped across the ice in her bare feet and the nylon curtains billowed behind her like flapping wings and I had to take my eye from the rubber cup at the back of the camera because for a moment it was real; a fairy flying through the dusk toward me.

The woods around my parents' house, the lake with the island we canoed to, mostly wooded, with a path from one side to the other. In the middle of the island was a clearing where we were sure the fairies gathered. But we never found them. The remnants of a bonfire, broken beer bottles glittering the charred wood. A stillness because the trees sheltered us from the breeze.

Heat would collect in the bowl of the clearing, each tree trunk no bigger than a child's wrist, but squashed in close; it was a muggy, uncanny stillness, the call of birds on all sides. There was a small island, too, from which we could walk on a path of rocks hidden just beneath the surface, barely submerged. My sister, when I looked back at her, would appear to be walking on water.

Sometimes, depending on if it had rained, the canoe could ride over this ridge of rocks without scraping the bottom, but we had to hold our breath. If it scraped, I got goosebumps.

I knew the bottom of the lake in front of our wharf all the way to the big island, from swimming with my eyes open. I knew that terrain the way I knew the neighbourhoods in town, how to get from the school to the library, how to get to the ball field across from Churchill Square. I knew the boulders and depths of the lake, where it got too shallow to go in a speedboat, or on water skis. Where the trout were, where the bottom became muddy with long, lime-coloured reeds, each stem wavering with hard buttons of green on the tip.

I'm not sure I know anything with that kind of intimacy now, that kind of familiarity. That knowledge, though I was entirely unaware of it as a child, formed me. It was silent and sometimes I swam through bands of light that had shot through breaks in the clouds, plunging down several feet into the water. It was an impenetrable privacy.

Not only did I never speak about it, I didn't even know I knew it; an entirely useless knowledge, full of light and doubt, full of shadow and the need to breathe, darting fish that startled me and warm springs that flushed up from the deepest parts. I'd tread water over a warm spring, and it felt like a glove that held me loosely. It wasn't a knowledge that could be employed in any way, but it accrued and belonged to me.

One day, in the muggy heat of the clearing on the island, we lay down on the moss and spruce needles and fell asleep. My sister must have stayed there, at the age of nine, and slept all the intervening years, because here she was now in that costume, the flowers a crown in her hair, and her fearlessness; she was standing in a swirling gust, a whiteout, a gritty squall that was scouring through the ICU, burying the whole island and everybody who lived here.

xavier
everything i am

XAVIER HAD TEXTED Violet as soon as he got home and listened for the *ding* of her receiving the text in the upstairs bedroom. But he didn't hear it. She was still out. She texted back, *Another round!*

He'd tugged one ice-stiffened bootlace free and was wagging his leg back and forth to get the boot off. His texts were supposed to be wise and sensible but auto-corrected to something goofy and misspelled. Every text he wrote had a subtext, and the subtext was he cared about her. They auto-corrected to ordinary things like *where's the phone charger?* from *I love you with everything I am*. Freezing rain had covered him in a shell of ice on the walk home and he was crackling out, pieces of ice skittered across the linoleum.

The boot wouldn't fall away from the wet cuff of his jeans. He was drunk enough to stumble all over the other shoes. There were soaked sneakers with holes on the bottom, construction boots, women's leather boots with a faux strap around the ankle, joke slippers that were too big and had horns over the toes like unicorns, Devin's destroyed Adidas chewed by dogs from his parents' house, the sides had busted open. The smell from the wet shoes when you walked in the door, everything covered in white striations of salt. There was a pair of rubber boots with wild stallions running in a canyon full of dust.

Violet sent a bunch of hearts and happy faces and winking emojis, said she'd be home half an hour, max.

Then he was in the hall; Trinity was calling out. He paused outside her bedroom door, looking down at his wet socks. There was a hole over his big toe. He was shocked by how ugly his big toe was, sodden, four or five black hairs sprouting, a baby potato, the toenail too long and jagged.

He touched the wall with his fingertips to steady himself. The wallpaper was two different textures. Velveteen fleurs-de-lys, and when he ran his fingertips over it, he felt pleasant shivers. The sensation was mingled with the love he felt for Violet, who had grown up around the bay, knew how to fish, had a whale touch the bottom of her Pop's boat, burnt everything she cooked, was on the Dean's list and wrote for the university paper.

Sometimes when he thought about Violet, he thought about the river where he'd learned to swim, how he would stand on the boulder in the middle of the little pool and fall backwards into it, how it would unzip to accept him, and how he never tired of climbing up on that rock and crossing his arms over his chest, shutting his eyes, and falling backwards into the water, a muscle that squeezed him, and how after a heavy rainfall he could feel the currents of it tugging hard.

The house was empty, except for Trinity, and Murph wasn't there and she was calling to Xavier to come into her room. He stood outside their bedroom door, Murph's bed-room door, and listened to the house, his hand on the velvet-een wallpaper.

He remembered when he and Trinity had spent their money on gummy worms and were sitting on the couch wait-ing for his father to set up the DVD player so they could watch a movie and she'd taken up a balloon from his birthday party and rubbed it against her hair.

The sound of the balloon rubbing her hair was as close to inaudible as a sound could be, he felt her fine golden hair stand up and float over so that it touched his bare arm. She'd reached behind him and put the balloon on the wall and it clung, scudding a bit down the surface.

The sound went through him.

The fine hair on his arm and the scudding sound, and he rubbed his arm because the tickling was so pleasurable and strange; he could not bear for it to continue. He thought of this as he touched the velveteen wallpaper in the hall outside her bedroom door. The house had once been very grand, and they all knew it was haunted.

The summer before they'd moved in, the police had con-ducted a search, digging out the basement looking for a body because of an anonymous tip. A young woman, a girl, really, a famous unsolved case from four decades past, that's who they were looking for, according to someone Xavier had met at a bar downtown. But they'd found nothing, no remains.

They'd all of them seen something on the stairs; a man with a top hat, Violet said. Devin said a woman in a black dress. They said just shadows, facial features indistinct, and they enjoyed frightening each other with these stories when they got drunk around the kitchen table, but the truth was,

Xavier felt like the scavenged chandelier was a kind of protection against the haunting, if there was a haunting. He'd felt something touch his arm one night, a touch significantly more substantial than a breeze; something very like what happens when you rub a balloon against your hair, a crawling static.

He'd felt it one night when he'd gone to the bathroom, and it had made his heart beat so fast, he had pressed his hand on his chest to slow it down.

After he and Trinity met in the kitchen, she came down from the bedroom more often. Heather would talk to her. If Heather was in the kitchen, she'd speak to Trinity Brophy. Heather was doing social work and selling jewellery in the mall.

If Xavier happened into the kitchen while Heather was there, Trinity could sum him up with a line or two that was always smarting and funny; even Murph understood there was an inviolate bond between them, though nobody understood where it had come from.

Violet kept an eye on it.

Trinity could make Xavier look like a fool, but the attack was leavened with unrequited admiration. She loved him, was the impression everyone had. Or at least she held him in high esteem, a begrudging esteem.

If Xavier thought about her at all, it was the mystery of Murph.

What was she doing with Murph?

Come here, she said. Come into the bedroom.

What do you want, he said. His feet were stuck to the carpet, the ugly, numb toe busting up through the torn cotton of his sock. She was probably out of it. She and Murphy had returned to doing drugs. She hadn't gone to Subway in a while.

Just come in, she said. She didn't sound good. He opened the bedroom door and lifted the blanket they'd tacked up over it, holding it back with his arm. He had a premonition something awful was going to happen if he entered, and he could feel himself giving over to it despite himself. His mother had a habit of using the word *doomed* if they were playing Monopoly or when she was driving on the highway in the rain. She said it with irony, letting her voice quiver and go hollow and deep — the dog stealing the last of the butter off the counter: We're doomed, doomed! as if she wanted to evacuate the possibility of disaster from their lives by naming it.

But he felt doomed as he drew back the curtain on Murph's lair. Trinity and Murph had a thing to stop the draft that lay across the threshold of the bedroom, a long, stuffed snake, crocheted in green wool. Its head was reared in his direction, the red felt tongue stuck out between fangs.

I need you to turn up the heat, she said. She had a space heater which had an on/off switch and a pad you pressed to make the temperature go up and a red-lit digital display as the numbers went up higher and higher and a grille through which you could see bright orange coils. The bedside lamp was at such an angle that her eyes looked like empty sockets.

They'd put plastic over all the windows in the house, made it shrink taut with a hair dryer, and the heat bill was more than the rent for the whole house and they were still freezing. The government was using the term *shock mitigation* about the rise in hydroelectric bills, they were raising the bills in steps, but they would triple, the bills, because of the new dam. The citizens were paying off the dam. This was something his parents ranted about over dinner. Trinity was driving the bill even higher with the space heater. It was all right for her, she wasn't paying utilities or even rent. They would all pay for her space heater.

Each drawer of the dresser was open, all the clothes cascaded from one drawer to the next. There was a big pickle jar that had been full of pennies but Murph had knocked it over and the shiny brown and pinkish coins flared in the tiny bedside reading lamp.

He and Violet had heard the fight in the bedroom below them, a few weeks ago, the jar flying and then the punch of a fist through the Gyproc, and Violet had flung off the sheets and stood like a statue for several minutes, and then she pulled on a pair of jeans and went down over the stairs and banged with both fists on Murph's door and said she was calling the police, and it worked because everything went still in Murph's bedroom.

The snake doorstop had a glass eye, and on a little tray the butter and a kettle and a box of tea and a pint carton of half-and-half cream. He had never been in the room before.

Trinity was on a mattress on the floor and the flannel sheet, red with a print of snowflakes and Santas, was balled up at the foot of the bed.

Turn up the heater, Trinity said. I'm that froze.

She had the duvet with the dried brown stain across the middle — coffee or Diet Pepsi, there were crunched pop cans around the bed — her fists up against her chin, but her teeth were chattering. The whole room stank of cigarettes and dirty laundry. Something was wrong with her. She was shiny with sweat.

Xavier had seen her shoot up once, through a bedroom door that was ajar, at a house party — this was before she got her father's car, seemed to clean herself up. A bedroom in a big house that dwarfed the other houses on the cul-de-sac, at least seven bedrooms and every bedroom full of people, the music so loud the speakers crackled, and he'd looked in and saw Murph sticking a needle in Trinity's arm. Her with her arm held out and looking away, all of it reflected in the big black window that showed a spectacular view, all the lights of the city.

He could see himself too, in the reflection, standing in the doorway, his image smaller, floating over her black hoodie. He'd wanted to go in and tear the needle out of her arm. But they looked peaceful and intent, cocooned against the noise of the party, which was so loud you could feel it through the floor.

He'd seen her down at Distortion on the dance floor too, around the same time. She was banging into people, dancing with her eyes shut, hurting people. A circle of empty dance floor had formed around her. People moving out of her way. Someone had been struck on the temple by Trinity's fist. It was an accident, but the person got off the dance floor; she'd had to sit down. Her friends gathering around her. A couple had gone off looking for the bouncer.

But Trinity kept dancing, a few people yelling what the fuck, her fists clenched, her ponytail flicking up and down like a jack handle, making her bounce higher and higher.

Like when they were kids in the churchyard with the pogo stick and her turn was over but she wouldn't give it back to him. She was determined to stay on for the count of five hundred bounces, but she could only get to somewhere near thirty-five. The pneumatic wheeze of the stick as it jagged to the side and she had to rein it in, keep it under her, her elbows jutted out.

They were supposed to pass the pogo stick to the other person when they fell off. That was the rule they'd agreed upon. It was his pogo stick, because he had all the toys and she had no toys. He'd been nice, letting her use it, though it also meant he had someone to play with, but she would not pass it over. She fell off and said it didn't count, she'd hit a rock, or some other excuse.

Trinity wouldn't give him his turn, and this was always the way with her; he recognized the need in her even when he was eight years old, such a need to be the best, to master the pogo stick, to make it submit to her demands, and she would not give up or hand it over. She would not let him have his turn. The incessant hammering was what had really driven them apart as kids, he thought now. She was too much.

Then the bouncer shouldering his way through, filling out his chest, the muscles in his upper arms, the artful tattoos, the protein-powder-and-steroid-induced sullen anguish of stepping close to Trinity on the dance floor, trying to get her to stop the out-of-control pogo dancing — Xavier had watched it from the bar and felt for the bouncer, remembered it from his own childhood, after his mother had said no more roughhousing with Trinity, or anyone else, that he was too old for that, knowing his mother would be angry if he knocked her off the pogo stick, sending her sprawling, which he had wanted to do very much. But he was also on alert, ready to step in if the bouncer raised a hand to her, ready to come to her aid, because she was out of it and wouldn't be able to defend herself; the bouncer speaking low to her with his hand on her upper arm and her wrenching the arm away from him, staggering backwards so that she almost fell down.

She calling him a big man, you're a big man now aren't you, and the bar, those who hadn't seen her knocking into people — the mood shifting all at once, so the whole bar was against the bouncer, a beautiful girl just trying to dance and him taking her by the arm, his big paw, and she shutting her eyes and continuing with the jumping up and down until the band stopped. She had made the band stop. She had ruined everybody's fun. They were taking a break. Stay around for the next set, everybody.

Trinity had wrenched herself up on an elbow into the light of the bedside lamp, and he could see her eyes. The sharp chin, the light eyes, the pale white skin, the freckles. He didn't find her beautiful, but objectively she was beautiful — he could see that. Her intensity, which was there buttering toast or in a strobe light pogoing on the dance floor, in the filth of Murph's room — her intensity was battery-charged and could dim when the battery wore down, but could also burn for long stretches as bright as anything, and it was exhausting to behold, but that's what beauty was — something to look away from. Or her kind of beauty, anyway.

He watched from the threshold as she was suddenly taken by what looked like a seizure. Her face was stretched, her jaw moved to the side and he saw the pink of the roof of her mouth in the light. She made a sound that was high-pitched and nasal, then the pain seemed to pass over her.

Xavier had the intuition that whatever was happening to Trinity Brophy, it had a grip all over her body, it shook her all through, and dropped her; but it was circling. It was going to get her, she was in a bad way, he saw.

He should just get the hell out of there.

His sister, Stella, would have told him what to do in this situation. He sometimes called her about work when something funny happened or when Kennedy-Boland lost it on him. Stella knew the best way to handle Kennedy-Boland. Xavier had a lot going on. Stress with Kennedy-Boland. This deep and profound thing, this love—it was love—for Violet which, he didn't know he was capable of this kind of thing, this thing which had taken him over.

Stella said it was good that he was in love, told him not to be afraid of it. She would have known what the hell was wrong with Trinity too, but it was way after midnight, and Stella had a kid and a job and he wasn't calling Stella.

He'd had to get on the phone with his mother and Stella yesterday about his father's birthday, there'd been a flurry of texts, and then an argument on the phone about what kind of lawn mower to get. They'd garnered a new respect for Xavier, seemed surprised by his knowledge on the subject, had forgotten he'd had a "business" mowing lawns when he was twelve, he'd shown up at people's houses and said he would do the lawns regularly for half of whatever they were paying the guy they had already contracted, until his mother said he couldn't do that, said it wasn't ethical to undercut, that the other guy might need the money. But he could feel his mother and Stella, as he discussed the engines of lawn mowers and the pros and cons of the different brands, and the needs of their particular lawns, because there was also the house around the bay, he felt them give over to his expertise, be somewhat respectful for a change, though he made sure not to lord it over them, knowing full well it was a fragile respect. He wished he could call them now.

They were his family, Stella and her wife, their kid; his father, his mother.

Trinity Brophy was not his family and not his problem.

His mother held a spiritual belief that some people came into your life, she'd tried to explain this to him, as if through a magic portal or invisible door, a special entrance, and if they arrived that way, you were responsible for them.

A portal? he'd asked. Like, random?

The portal is a metaphor, she said.

But he knew it might as well have been bricks and mortar. There were things his parents believed that were quite simply bullshit. He didn't care how intense Trinity Brophy was, how sick she was or what the hell was going on with her and where was Violet?

He was busy loving Violet, he could have told them. It took everything he had. He had to be good enough for her. Some people are the opposite of a portal, he wanted to say to his mother. Some people are a vacuum, he would have told her. You open that door and you're sucked into oblivion. Trinity Brophy might bring him into her vortex of emptiness if he got too close.

He very much regretted stepping into the room. He willed himself out of the mild paralysis he felt; he tried to think of who Trinity was and what he owed her exactly.

He thought of when he first ran into her again, the first time since she had left town, in the kitchen, her claim to a secret stash of bakeapples somewhere on the South Side Hills.

Big eyes and cheekbones and the hair, as if the overhead light were coursing through each filament, her hair brightly pale. He'd never thought of her as beautiful before now because she only had two expressions, scouring and stoic.

She did this look: her eyelids blinked down slow and it meant she had taken in as much of whoever as she could possibly stand. She blinked, hesitating just a millisecond before opening her eyes, and then only half opening them, to let you know you were unworthy of her attention. She was all flint or spite, even if it wasn't entirely her fault.

Xavier liked people who laughed a lot, who slept deeply, gave in to honking snores, who were self-deprecating in their humour, like he was, who could poke fun at others, yes, but it was a kind of fun that showed the person in a good light too.

He liked people who exploded with laughter, flung back their heads, gasped and trembled, who could see your flaws, yes, Violet saw his flaws, his mother certainly saw his flaws, his father was less judgmental. The guys at work saw his flaws, but he could make them laugh despite his flaws. He could soften everybody up with a kind of physical comedy, an arched eyebrow or a smirk; with his family he could flip a pancake and draw the pan away and stick it back under just in time or toss a knife in the air so it spun around three times and catch it by the handle instead of the blade. He did this kind of thing for the people he loved.

The people he loved didn't blink at anyone with bald distaste. They were not guarded; he didn't owe them.

Trinity was in some kind of pain that she didn't have the threshold for, that's what he was starting to recognize. He had no idea what it looked like when someone was dying from an overdose, but he wondered if this was the early stages, or had she eaten something that had gone off.

The spout was open on the carton of half-and-half cream and he lifted it and sniffed while he looked at her. It was off, and the smell went all the way through him.

Your cream is off, he said. He put it back down on the desk and closed the spout of it.

You should have kept it in the fridge, he said. Cream should be refrigerated, and butter. Butter belongs in the fridge, not in your bedroom. Dairy products, generally, go in the fridge.

As far as he knew they didn't shoot up anymore, it was all pills, and so Murph was constantly saying there was no harm in it. Yes, everybody knew the opioid crisis, but that was British Columbia. There were guns, he knew people who had them, but it was mostly knives.

Fentanyl, yes, off and on, there was fentanyl on the street, he heard about it at work, there were busts in the paper, and he knew a guy had died. Jerome, all the way up in the same class since kindergarten, Jerome had died. Jerome who had a tuna sandwich in his lunch every day of school and became a chef and went off the rails and they found him in an alley. He hadn't seen Jerome in a while, but he'd known him, jumping off the top of the waterfall in Flatrock. The cleft in his chin. A basement given over to a toy train village, and a tattooed sleeve of mermaids and lobster traps. He'd been hired on the rigs but never got out there, because of an overdose. That was the last he'd heard of Jerome. He had it made with this big job on the rigs.

Murph spoke of times when the town went dry and you couldn't get anything and how everybody was jumpy, and then it came in and you could make a fortune. After a dry spell, people would pay anything.

And Xavier believed Murph was going to be moving out soon and maybe taking Trinity with him, and he had time to wonder why that couldn't have happened before this moment when another seizure stole over her and he realized he was now implicated in the whole scene, the spilled pennies and the balloon she'd rubbed on her hair when they were so little and the undeniable fact that his mother also thought of Trinity as his sibling, one of her own, part of their family, someone he couldn't turn away from.

His mother couldn't really see his flaws. Nobody saw them, he kept them well hidden or he didn't have any and this had been a mistake. He'd set up false expectations by being well adjusted or pretending he was.

His mother would think he could act in a situation like this. If he was called upon, he could act.

That's the way he had been raised, his mother would have said. But he didn't think there was any plan in the way he was raised, it was haphazard. They didn't know what they were doing, everything by the seat of their pants.

Yes, they read to him, his mother had read aloud the whole of Harry Potter. She read the fourth book while his father paddled them around a lake in a canoe, the water still except for the plops of small trout, until she was hoarse and she said, Keep going? And he told her to keep going and they'd ended up with really bad sunburns.

His parents smoked dope in front of him, they fought, they cursed and screamed. Once his mother threw a sugar dish at his father, missed by a mile, the trajectory skewed by rage or on purpose.

Once they had a party and his mother got so drunk that she flung his bedroom door open so it slammed against the wall and she climbed onto his bed, crying her eyes out in a blast of joy, demanding if he knew how much she loved him, had she told him?

She broke the bed. One of the legs at the foot of his bed had cracked and he managed to get her out, he was twelve for god's sake, and she had been hugging him and smearing him with tears, had she told him, she kept saying, did he know? How much she loved him?

He'd had to wedge three of the Harry Potter books under the corner of the bed, and she'd slammed the door again on the way out, so hard that the tape gave on one corner of his Biggie poster and it curled over very, very slowly, as if even Biggie couldn't believe the scene in his bedroom and what he had to put up with, even though it was the only time he'd seen her drunk.

They didn't drink very much, his parents, never on weekdays. Sometimes parties or special occasions. It wasn't actually haphazard, the way he was raised. Here is the way he was raised: Don't just stand there, do something.

Should I call an ambulance? he said.

Don't, she said. Could you just stay here? I don't know what this is.

jules
bride peach

FLORENCE TOLD THE story of her foster mother, Bride Peach, many times, and for the benefit of other people, but each time I was present I was meant to take away a different lesson. Everything I came to learn from her was about fortitude and an edict about loving everyone who swept through. If you failed to love someone, you might be scathing toward them or hilarious at their expense, but even then, even if they were distasteful to you, even then, you were expected to attempt something that loosely resembled love.

The first time, at the same dinner when I announced Joe and I were in love, she'd told me the story of Bride Peach because of Stella.

The idea was, though, that you could love any child, whether you were their mother or not.

Another time, we were going somewhere together, Florence and I, and as we walked down the sidewalk to the car, a wind came up and blew so hard against us we were forced to stagger backwards a few steps. Brown leaves and grit from the sidewalk lifted and swirled all around her. She had shut her eyes and pressed herself against the wind. Her handbag flying to the side. She had lost a lot of weight by then and had become fragile, but she set her feet and leaned into the wind and took the necessary steps, one stagger after another, to move to the car door. Once she had lifted the handle, the wind took the door and it cracked back and bounced on its hinges.

And another time she told me the story of her foster mother to let me know she had forgiven me or had accepted that I was a terrible housekeeper and in this way her son had received a raw deal, despite her efforts to guide me. She had accepted that I would never keep a clean and tidy house.

Once she told the story to apologize. She had been doing the baby's laundry and became furious when I had lost a white sock, one of Xavier's white socks, which she had purchased so she could dress him up when she babysat.

She took care of him three mornings a week, so I could paint. She brought Xavier around to meet her friends and her sisters, or to get his picture taken in the mall with Santa, or to get groceries while I worked odd jobs, painting sets at the Arts and Culture Centre or teaching Painting for Children, nine-to-twelve-year-olds, at the Extension Services. Being an artist was something I might trade in for my deficiency in the department of keeping the house clean. Neither of us could imagine how the making of art might have any worth, to anyone, ever, but we both kept a poker face about this, pretending it was a proper occupation. After I'd lost the frilly sock, we both experienced a vertiginous dip in this faith.

It brought us as close to a permanent rift as we'd ever ventured. She didn't speak to me for two days. Then she spoke to me only through Nancy. She told my sister-in-law to tell me to make sure Xavier was ready when she arrived. She didn't want to wait. She didn't want to get a parking ticket.

Through Nancy, I'd said I would buy a new pair of socks. This was defiance and interpreted as such. My losing the sock showed a disregard for the worth of things.

The socks were worth about three dollars, was my point.

And her point was she might never speak to me again over the sock.

Her point was there is a right way to do things. This was to be the non-negotiable contract of our relationship. If I could abide by this tenet, she was willing to look the other way when I failed to achieve appropriate levels of tidiness, or hunt for bargains at the supermarket. She'd even help with the laundry.

In return, if she bought Xavier a pair of white socks, white as the driven snow, as she liked to say, I had to know where both of them were at all times.

Later it turned out she'd had the sock all along. It had fallen behind her dryer. I discovered this when a load of laundry came back from Florence's and the socks were together in a little knot on top of the pile. She was letting me know she'd made a mistake, but it was very difficult to believe that she had lost the sock. In fact, I could not believe it. I picked up the socks in my fist and held them up to her, as if their appearance would astonish her too.

She said, Oh, shut up.

But on the night when I first heard the story of her foster mother, the night we announced we were getting married, my father-in-law, John, winced when she stood. She was going to the kitchen to get him a glass of Coke. As she got older, she would press her fist into the table and wrench herself up from the seat by twisting the fist down onto the tabletop. She had arthritis and the hump was developing on her back and her ankle would give out.

John said, Florence, I will get it myself. But she got it. There was a formality in everything they did that made a heat between them. My mother-in-law was raised by foster parents. But they had lavished her with love.

xavier
back then

XAVIER TOOK THE carton of half-and-half cream to the bathroom and ran the water, pouring the thick clots of it down the drain. Then he went back into her room and hunched over the heater and it already said eighty-four degrees. He could feel it blowing on him, very hot. The air hot on the thighs of his jeans made him think Violet wouldn't love him if he didn't take care of this situation. He was pretty sure Trinity was in a critical condition. He thought she might die. Violet would expect him to act, anyone would expect that.

He couldn't ignore this wall of doom.

His mother wouldn't like it if he just went down over the stairs, put his boots back on and went out in the street and down to whatever bar it was where Violet was having her last drink of the night with her co-workers.

Put the heat up as high as it will go, Trinity said. Then she writhed onto her side and her legs scissored under the duvet and her upper lip drew back as she sucked in air through her teeth.

What's wrong, he said.

Something bad, she said. I don't know. You're going to have to call an ambulance. When she said it his phoned dinged and it was Violet saying they were going to another bar. She told him to go on to sleep, she'd wake him when she got home.

Trinity reached out and dragged a metal wastebasket toward her and puked and the stink of that in the heat made his stomach flip.

Xavier texted Murph and told him something was wrong with Trinity. She finished puking and the clutch of rigidness stole over her again and her teeth gritted, the underside of her jaw was very pale.

You're not texting Murph, are you? she said through the tight teeth.

Her eyes were open and she was looking at him, but then they rolled back in her head and there were only two slits of glassy white and he sat right down on the floor. He honestly thought she was a demon, with her eyes like that. Or she had been possessed and the evil was passing from her into him. He had grown up without any religious education, but his Nanny Florence had been a devout Catholic and she'd had a connection with the spirit world through her dreams, and maybe she had passed that sensitivity on to him, because he was pretty certain he was in the presence of something unholy.

He had to sit down with his back against the wall because that was as far as he could get from her without actually leaving the room, and he couldn't leave the room because she was draining him of the ability to move. She'd sucked the marrow out of his bones and replaced it with a liquid lethargy. A slow-wittedness, brought on by the weltering blasts of warmth from the space heater, and the shots he'd done earlier in the night, and the beer, and whatever the force was, the evil force she had command of and that she was lobbing at him, felt sweet and claustrophobic.

Xavier had just dropped to the floor of the bedroom and then he used his heels to push himself back across the floor, out of the reach of the radiating heat. He understood his relationship to Trinity as magnetic and orbital, tensile and grasping.

There was enough time to remember going tobogganing together when they were eight with his mother and dusk and then a sunset, bitter cold, up by the Fluvarium, on that hill, from which you could see all the way to Cabot Tower and the orange light on Kents Pond, waiting for Trinity to get on the back of the red plastic toboggan. He had made her haul it all the way up the hill.

Then, for a joke, taking off without her, jumping on it while she was prissily getting ready to sit down for her solitary ride. He had flung himself at it and landed on his stomach. The toboggan started to fly down the hill, but she'd run and had thrown herself on top of him, on her stomach, and the weight of her, making it go so fast he lost control.

They really were one person back then.

Don't bother trying to figure out what it was, because it was particular to him and Trinity, this thing between them, it didn't last, so there is no need to pry into it and figure it out. They knew each other, inside out, and what they knew was sacred. It couldn't last.

They were something else now, his phone at thirty-four percent in a big haunted house with someone possessed, her, she was, Trinity Brophy was possessed, now they were this thing wherein she was sucking the life out of him.

She made it so he couldn't leave the room, looking in his direction with those white slits, her eyeballs visible under the almost-closed lids.

Don't, she said.

Yes, I'm texting Murphy, he said. Fucking right I am.

Me and Murph broke up, she said, with her facial features cinched to the side again. She was having trouble breathing and she dug a fist into her stomach. She rolled so her face was in the pillow. The groan coming out of her frightened him, even though it was muffled by the pillow.

He texted Violet and said, *Something is wrong with Trinity.*
Violet texted back: *This just in.*

He texted: *She has to go to the hospital.* And he stared at the phone but no text came back. Then a text came: *Get her to the hospital then.*

And a second text from Violet: *My phone is four percent.*
Another text: *Ambulance.*

The pillow she was groaning into had no pillowcase and was filthy.

Couldn't you get a new pillow? Xavier asked. His voice sounded shrill and high-pitched.

Had no way to get out to Stavanger, she said. Or Kelsey Drive, that's the only place to get pillows. I tried but the bus never came. Then I lost my bus pass.

She rolled onto her back again. She screamed at him, very loud, to call an ambulance, but he had already called it.

The woman on the other end had just answered and he found he didn't know what to tell her, but she was leading him through it with Trinity groaning in the background. Trinity's name, her address, etc., etc.; the woman was so slow, and then he just gave in and was slow just like the woman. If the woman wanted to fiddle with these little details, so be it. She was all he had.

He found that in a small part of his mind he was afraid he'd have to pay for the ambulance since he was the one that called it. He was going over how much money he had in the bank and when his next paycheque was and how much it would be, and if he could sell something, and he was considering excuses so he wouldn't have to go in the ambulance, because, he remembered, he had been drinking and was in no condition for the emergency ward, which would take hours, maybe twenty-four hours, he'd heard stories of long waits, and because she was nothing to him and because he had to work at nine in the morning.

Xavier had to be at work, there was no question. He couldn't go with her, and that was final.

She was Murph's problem. Fucking Murph.

He answered all the questions as best he could. The address, the symptoms as he determined them by looking at her prostrate on the bed trying to squirm out of her own skin. He said appendicitis. Then he asked what happened if one of them burst. But the woman said she was just taking down the information right now. If he didn't know the answers to her questions, he relayed the questions to Trinity and she answered yes or no, and finally said, Just tell them to come on.

After he hung up, he wanted the woman back. Whoever she was, she sounded like she might be as old as his mother. She'd had a smoker's voice, unflustered, almost sultry. He could hear her thinking between her questions. He could hear her typing. She accepted all information without comment. She was hammering the keys. He heard the woman draw in a breath sharply as if she'd cut herself, but he realized it was because she could hear Trinity yelling in the background.

It turned out to be about twenty minutes. When a spasm of pain seemed to have passed, he asked her about the pennies. He was standing with his back to her, looking out the window onto the street.

Mary Mahoney give me them pennies, Trinity said. She said they're going to be worth a fortune.

A drawer got stuck and when I pulled it, the jar fell over.

A drawer didn't get stuck, Xavier said. You let that motherfucker beat you up, is what happened.

Oh, is that what happened, she said. She snorted. But then she became bossy. She was going to order him around.

There's something wrong with me, Xavier, she said.

He didn't like that she'd said his name. It was a way of calling him to account. She was claiming ownership. She was softly reminding him, by speaking his name, by telling him the situation, that he would never find himself, for as long as he lived, dying alone, because he had parents who would take care of him, and a sister, and even his girlfriend, who Xavier believed was the one, there would never ever be anyone as perfect, he'd always be loved because he'd grown up that way, and he'd got used to it.

There were two things he knew for certain. The first was he owed Trinity nothing. The first was that he was not going to the hospital. The first was what about him? The first was somehow she deserved what she got. She was nothing to him. She was Murph's problem. The first was the only people he owed anything to were the guys at work and Kennedy-Boland, who could fire him as fast as snapping his fingers if Xavier was late for work. He'd said he would be there at nine

331

in the morning, and he wasn't getting in that fucking ambulance if it ever arrived.

The second thing he knew, as sure as he was standing there, was that she had said his name and he had been called up as if for a war. There were people had a hold on you, and who knows how they got that hold, he hadn't seen her in years, she had gone off to Toronto, he'd barely spoken to her since they were kids, but it really looked like she was going to die.

Trinity had been bequeathed to him, not forever, but in this moment with the light on the spill of pennies like a fire. And him to her, was the other thing. Because it seemed like she knew him inside out. And she was calling him to account.

Where's Murph, he asked her.

We're after breaking up. I came to get my stuff.

He heard the siren before he saw the ambulance pull up to the door.

He let the paramedics in and he watched as they looked around the room with the ketchup-smeared dishes in the midst of all the clothes, and the glasses and cups with skims of mold over coffee, and the shining flare of pennies all over the floor and the three pairs of Crocs lined up against the baseboard, all in a row.

jules
regret

ON OUR WAY to Mexico I'd run into Rosie Parsons in the airport, working at a Tim Hortons at five forty-five in the morning. I'd put a banana on the counter, and she said my name. Rosie at the Peace-A-Chord in Bannerman Park, Rosie singing at the Ship the night Joe and I made love in the grave-yard of the Anglican Cathedral, Rosie at the sit-in when they closed the women's centres across the country, arrested with fifty other women.

Rosie making CDs every four years. The big oaks and all the gravestones lying flat, sinking into the earth, and me and Joe fucking in the dry leaves and rustle way back then. Her hair now pure white.

We mothers used to call each other to keep tabs on the kids after school, a network of parents, Rosie, Louise Munn, Melody Burke, Jessica Marie Clark, Leela Banerjee, Maureen Dunphy, Mary Mahoney, seven or eight of us, and four or five of the dads, Ross Winter, Glen Johnson, Kevin Riche, and Tom Fury, we'd call each other and say where the parties

333

were, when the cops had shown up, who was in danger of having had too much to drink, asphyxiating on their vomit if we didn't put them in the recovery position when they got home and passed out, and who had made out with whom, what taxi company had dropped off the forty-ouncer so we could call the dispatcher in the morning and give him a blast of shit.

We were vigilant, but we lost some of the children, for at least some of the time, a year or so, especially the boys, to bedrooms in the basement where they smoked pot and played video games, and they treated us with — not hatred, which would have hurt less — but dismay.

We lost some of the girls in more complicated ways. The ones we lost snuck out in the middle of the night and ran away. Sometimes they called but you couldn't keep them on the phone. Sometimes they called and didn't even speak, but you recognized their breathing. They shoplifted and the phone rang, someone had a grip on an arm.

Someone in a uniform was holding them, and what rage we felt on their behalf.

Get your filthy hands off my child.

Or they were drugged in a bar and assaulted, the details of which they kept from us. Or they told us. A date rape drug made them froth and puke, and for days after, they remembered brief glimmers, somebody's hand on their throat, the torn-out crotch of their nylons, blood and a black eye; how you really did see stars, little bursts of lights floating toward them in a dark, seductive void, and at first you could not feel anything but aching and wary.

There was the punch and then there was the pain of the punch, that came later. Or else the rape was an intricate, calibrated coercion that they could not stop, someone they knew but they couldn't speak about it. Or they said no, but not out loud for a court of law, and they lay inert and insensate, like cold stones. Some of them were gay or queer or trans, and whatever they were we were okay with it. Some of us were shocked or miffed or said the wrong things and hurt our kids by not accepting them as they were, but it didn't last, the misunderstanding, there was no choice but to work it out.

But mostly they came back to us, these kids, some of them. They went out in the dark and we waited for them to key in the code at the front door and they spoke to us in quiet tones, standing in the hallway outside the bedroom, just to say they were safe.

To say, yes, they'd been drinking, yes they'd had a wonderful time, yes they'd been with friends, yes they'd danced their arses off, yes there was coke at the party, yes there might have been fentanyl, but on this occasion there wasn't fentanyl, yes they'd been stupid, yes they gave a flying fuck about their parents, yes they were privileged, yes they were spoiled, yes they'd got the shitty end of the stick, and weren't privileged, exactly the opposite, some of them, and they all deserved a good swift kick in the arse, at one time or another, they'd seen friends die from suicide, or from natural, unfathomable causes, they'd seen a few of the friends in the psych ward, yes they'd been chased, yes they'd been victims of racism even though everybody said Newfoundland wasn't racist, it was, of course, yes racism, yes they'd kicked over a sandwich sign on the side of the street, yes they blew all their money, yes they had run for their lives, they had not been believed, countless times they had not been believed when they told the truth, there were no jobs for them and it was our fault, they came across a dying whale on the beach, and the stench reached them before they saw what caused it and they understood the smell as portent and that the world was heating up, they'd seen a former teacher loaded out of her mind, and yes, they were home. Go back to sleep, they're safe. For now, they're safe.

For long periods we didn't like them very much. They didn't like us.

We divided into two groups: those of us who regretted it had all gone by so fast, and those of us who saw that each moment had not gone by, but rather it had all accumulated, like rain sluicing from an uppermost leaf of a tree to every leaf below until it was all there in a single drop on the lowest leaf, clinging but shivering on the serrated tip of the leaf, full of everything that came before.

murph
atm

MURPH HAD A skeleton key and he started it up and the vibration went through him, into his legs, his arse, his chest, his wrist bone, all up through his hand on the stick shift. The cab filled with the stink of exhaust.

It was three forty-five in the morning and not a soul anywhere, but the machine was loud. He drove it across the parking lot, toward the Sobeys in the Torbay Road strip mall. He had the truck he'd borrowed idling near the front window of the supermarket, near the ATM, and he had the ski mask on and the hood up. He had gloves on.

He knew about the soles of his sneakers, they'd check footprints in the snow for wear, nicks, he knew that from a previous B&E when he'd gone to Whitbourne, at sixteen. So that morning he'd gone to the Avalon Mall and bought a brand new pair of sneakers. Not so much as a single scratch on them.

He'd gone to jail for a B&E, and when they let him out the legal aid lawyer asked him if he'd learned from his mistake.

Murph said, Yeah, get a new pair of shoes the next time.

He stopped at the big windows and lowered the bucket, brought it down, more a caress than tap, an indolent nudge. The glass crinkled up and fell in shards and little stars and big jagged pieces. What a racket. There were subdivisions on all sides, and the sound must have travelled into the dreams of everybody asleep in the bungalows, made them stir, and he was ready to get out of there.

He reversed and raised the shovel and rolled forward and the pieces around the frame of the window came down heavily. One piece made the roof of the cab boom, but when it tumbled off, the roof undented by itself with another loud boom. He'd done heavy equipment, but then he got picked up for a DUI and lost his licence for seven years, and the two-thousand-dollar fine, which was accruing interest, and his heavy equipment diploma wasn't no good to him without his licence.

He thought three minutes. But it was already five and a half minutes. The vibration of the backhoe jiggling him all over, the deeper throb of it entered his bones and he was part of the machine. The thrum affected his pulse, or it was his pulse. His heart was pounding in his chest, and in his temple. His hand was grafted to the stick and it tickled through the gloves he was wearing, black polypropylene gloves.

He used both brakes and put his foot to the floor and the whole thing revved and the bucket went up and down, smashing the rubble that fell from above the entrance so he could work the Cat over it.

He felt the cab tilting because the front wheels couldn't get purchase on the debris he'd knocked through, but then the back wheels caught and he rose up, waggled over the pile of debris and down the other side. He scraped the top of the cab on the side of the archway he'd made, and he hunched for fear the whole building would collapse on him.

He brought down the great articulated arm of the backhoe and it clattered on the ground and he could taste a cloud of concrete dust that had risen up and blown into the cab. He scraped the floor of the supermarket with the bucket and slid it under the ATM and he jostled it, cajoled it, begged it into the bucket. The ATM was like a baby in its mother's arms. If machines could beget other machines, then the Cat was a mother rocking its baby, to jolly it up. Then he was reversing and over the debris and he lowered the bucket over the pan of the truck, and very gently tipped it and the ATM dropped squarely into the pan.

There was little wind, and the snow floated straight down in big, delicate flakes. The heat inside the cab of the truck was velvety and dense.

That's when he saw the guys who worked there, who had run out from the back in their kelly-green aprons and hairnets. Maybe they were the butchers, wrapping up the hamburger meat, putting the salmon steaks out on the beds of chipped ice. The frozen turkeys.

They ran to the front of the store and stood in the broken glass, but he made the engine of the truck rev and they took off again, into the back of the store. He hadn't known they'd be there. He felt like this was a crucial mistake, but he was done.

He was gone out the highway, and he saw on the dash the whole thing was nine minutes.

He felt acute terror and such hilarity. He giggled uncontrollably. He was certain he'd never had so much fun in his life. He would never have it again, and that was okay too. The thought of the sheets of glass smashing down and the cost to replace it. Property, you did a lot of time.

But he was also calm. He'd pay off that two-thousand-dollar fine. He'd told Trinity he was going to buy back the car, but she broke up with him. The car was gone. She could forget the car.

He was magnificently still at the soft core of himself; the rest of him was bolts and cogs and grease, and all of that was aquiver. There was a road, not too far out the highway, where he could pull in and fix the tarp over the ATM. Change the licence plate. It was a twenty-five-minute drive to Holyrood, and he had a spot up there, a summer cabin he'd scoped out with his father, and he could hang out there for the night. He'd figure out how to open the ATM up there. The owners hadn't shown up for at least five years, and you could turn on a light and nobody could see you through the trees. The snow would cover his tracks. It was coming down. He heard a *ding* and it was his phone and it was Xavier. It said there was something wrong with Trinity. But she'd left him. He pulled up the driveway and there was his father's car. Out of jail. He'd want a share of the ATM. And the rest of Brad Murphy.

xavier
brother

XAVIER SAW THAT one of the paramedics was Colin Mercer.

Colin, b'y, Xavier said. He was so grateful for this face. It came to him that Colin knew how to teleport them to the hospital without a lapse in time, just as he had moved over the basketball court. Just as he had risen off the gym floor into the air, suspended, and the ball suspended above him and how the ball and Colin Mercer had just hung still in the air with everyone leaping out of the chairs and screaming, especially the women from the cafeteria, who also were watching.

Xavier, Colin said. Xavier. This your girlfriend?

She's Murph's girlfriend, Xavier said. Murph's not here. You know Murph?

Murph drug dealer Murph? Murph with the drugs? Been up on charges?

Yeah, but she's just after telling me she's not Murph's girlfriend anymore, Xavier said. He regretted speaking those words as soon as they were out of his mouth. He should have let Murph stand as the man whose responsibility this was — the room with its stink of vomit and the pennies with the light running over them.

Trinity was Murph's problem.

He wished there was a way to elucidate this strange loophole: he was the one in the room with her and Murph was nowhere in sight, but she was not his concern.

My girlfriend lives here too, Xavier said. She's on her way home from downtown.

Colin Mercer had dropped to one knee and asked Trinity's name. She told him and he swung around to take in Xavier.

Weren't you friends, Colin asked. Back in Mary Queen of Peace? I remember Trinity hanging around with you on the playground.

That was fucking elementary school, Xavier said. She just showed up here. I didn't even know she lived here for the longest time. She was gone away to Toronto. Nobody heard tell of her for five years. I live here with my girlfriend.

You didn't even know she come back, was under the same roof? Xavier could see Colin was excavating an out for him, giving him a way out. Making it clear he, Xavier, was an innocent bystander.

Then Colin Mercer switched tack.

But it was you called the ambulance, Colin Mercer said.

I heard her in here and she said to come in and I could see the state she was in, Xavier said. He waved a finger at Trinity to prove his point.

I texted Violet but her phone died, Xavier said.

Violet Penney? Colin asked.

You know Violet?

She up to the university?

Yeah, communications. Then Colin stopped talking to Xavier. And the two other paramedics came in with a board and he started ordering them around.

Trinity was seized again with an overall muscular derangement. She curled in and her eyes flew back in her head so that they could only see the slivers of white. The plastic sheet on the window seemed to breathe. The bottom half of it had condensation and was wrinkled, coming away from the two-sided tape. The plastic was sucked back against the window and went slack.

Two of the other paramedics were kneeling now, one of them taking Trinity's pulse and asking if she thought she could walk.

I wants Xavier to come with me, she said.

Colin Mercer intervened.

He can't go in the ambulance if he isn't family, Colin said. Xavier remembered a moment on the basketball court when Colin's face was so close that he could feel Colin's breath on his cheek. They had been in the liminal space between knowing you are one person but recognizing you might also be the other person. Xavier had been unable to tell where Colin ended and he began. Colin's breath on his face as intimate as anything he had ever known up to that point. And now Colin was casually handing him an out.

Is she dying? Xavier asked. He'd put his head close to whisper in Colin's ear. Even the rim of Colin's ear was freckled. It had a very fine gold skim of hair, and there was a tuft of gold hair on Colin's chin where he didn't shave properly. Or was it a goatee? He suddenly remembered that Colin Mercer was a jerk, had been a jerk all the time he was in junior high.

He remembered the both of them in an argument on the sidewalk with everybody gathered around them, and it was raining and there was a Kraft orange slice in the gutter, halfway out of its plastic sleeve, and Colin had touched the orange slice with the toe of his black expensive sneaker and said, That fell out of your mother's vagina.

It was such a shocking thing to say that nobody laughed. They had all been on Colin's side, of course, but it was the use of the word *vagina* instead of some curse word, something less clinical and innocent, coupled with the bright orange of the cheese slice, how unnatural the cheese slice was.

He searched Colin's face to see if there were any remnant of the jerk he'd been in junior high, and there was the goatee. But he decided the goatee might be an expression of creativity, the result of an ill-conceived but positive influence along the way. His mother believed that people could change for the better, and the goatee might have been a vestigial characteristic of the Colin from junior high, some part of him he was trying to shed.

You're not related to her, Colin said. She's nothing to you, right?

I hardly know her, Xavier said. Except for we were friends on the playground at St. Mary's Queen of Peace. Then he felt a chill creep over his skin, a premonition that she would die in the bed before they got her out of the house, simply because he had disowned her.

What the hell is wrong with her? Xavier asked the two paramedics at her side; he had determined that though Colin might have been reformed, personality-wise, there was no chance he had the sensitivity required to diagnose a demonic possession, or even a hangnail. He had always been, except for his ability to get a ball in a hoop when required, a total idiot.

She's having a baby, one of the paramedics said.

I'm not, Trinity said. I've got an appendicitis. A burst appendix.

The paramedics didn't say anything more. They were working in silence now.

I had my period, she said. But she sounded uncertain. I have a bit of weight on, that's all.

You're in labour, the paramedic said. Can you walk? We just need to get you down the stairs. Her whole face crunched together then and she made fists, pressed them into her eyes and when she took them away and she said, Xavier you are coming in the ambulance.

Not if he isn't related, Colin said. There was a flush in Colin's face and he was determined to save Xavier, determined because of that moment during the basketball game, or maybe because of the new solidarity of young men everywhere and how important it was for them to turn their backs on this kind of situation, turn together, so they could get a little further ahead and maybe come out on top, even though that was looking less and less possible for them.

Or maybe Colin Mercer felt some loyalty to the code of being a paramedic. There were rules and Merce was a rule follower and it had worked out for him, and he wasn't going to abandon that regime now, and though following rules had never worked out for Xavier, and anything good that had ever happened to him was because he had broken some rule or other and he had faith in breaking every rule he could, he was willing at this moment to convert.

He would follow the rules Merce believed in because maybe there really was a higher order, an arrangement of society, whereby if everybody agreed to follow the rules, they would all benefit, and what the fuck: a baby?

Merce didn't know anything, and that had been clear to Xavier, even out on the basketball court, Merce didn't question anything, that was the problem, had always been the problem, with Colin Mercer, and Xavier said a little prayer, something he had learned from his Nanny Florence, that of course he didn't believe in, and he had been right not to believe, because this was the best God could do? Colin Mercer was the best the universe could spit out in his hour of need? But he said the prayer anyway, in his head. It was the *Our Father*, the only prayer he knew and what it meant was: I will obey.

They put her on the board and strapped her in and the two other paramedics seemed to be working in concert and doing exactly what Colin Mercer told them to do, but they were doing it before Colin told them. It was like dubbing in an old film, Colin looked like he was in charge, but the other two were acting from their guts, following their instincts, not listening to Colin at all. They got to the landing and it was tricky. They were actually stuck for an eternity while they figured out the math of it, the angle and geometry. Xavier was on the steps right behind them. He could catch a look at Trinity's face when one of the paramedics holding the foot of the stretcher shifted his weight. Colin had gone down the stairs before them and once they were moving again, Colin opened the front door and the chandelier shook in the wind. All the light falling and the eerie smashing of the crystals.

I didn't let him hit me, Trinity said.

I'm sorry, Xavier said.

You're a bastard for saying that, she said.

I didn't mean it, he said.

I'm alone, she said. I got no one.

Okay you didn't let him hit you, Xavier said.

I got no one, she said. They'd reached the porch and snow was swirling around them. The guy at the head of the stretcher stumbled all over the shoes.

I got you, the medic said. I got you. I got you. After that they were more intent, and nothing was said.

You didn't let him do that, Xavier said. I shouldn't have said that.

Wow, she said. You can be such an asshole.

I'm sorry, he said.

Then they had manoeuvred her down the front steps and onto the sidewalk. It was really snowing hard now. She had stopped talking. She was caught in another spasm. One of the medics was telling her to breathe.

Xavier was squashing his boots on, and almost tripping out the door. They'd already loaded her into the back. The neighbours' lights were coming on all down the street because of the ambulance.

Are you related to her? Colin asked him again. It struck Xavier that everything had been easy for Colin his whole life. They had a big house with rose bushes along the fence, white roses that dropped petals all over the sidewalk, an honest-to-god picket fence that only came to the knees, and what the hell was that? It was like the idea of a picket fence.

Colin's family had a maid who also babysat, and in the basement, a pool table. In the backyard, Colin's father had built a stone pizza oven, which didn't get used. His mother wore sneakers with her suits and nylons because she walked to work in order to get exercise and to save the planet from carbon emissions. They bought granola bars in bulk and nobody counted how many you had in a single afternoon.

And Xavier had grown up much the same way, he realized. But he had not turned out like Colin Mercer. There but for the grace of god, his mother said all the time, and she meant it could have happened to him, whatever horrible thing it was that had befallen someone in the paper, or someone struck down by illness, or a woman whose husband had left her, those things might have happened to him, except fate had intervened. He had parents who loved him and a sister who mostly loved him but held him to account, god, he'd had everything, just like Mercer, but by some hidden splinter of grace that had worked its way into his soul, or heart or kneecap, wherever, he was not a jerk.

She's related, Xavier said.

You just said you weren't related, Colin Mercer said.

Get in, the other medic said.

I'm her brother, Xavier said. The other medic had gone around to the driver's side. He told Xavier to get in the back.

Fuck off, Mercer said. She grew up in foster care, everybody knows that. She's not related to you.

Just get in the back, the driver said. They had turned on the siren and the lights.

I'm her brother, Xavier said. But he was already in the back.

out of the alders

THE KITCHEN TABLE in Nancy's house was weighed down
with potluck dishes, at least three birthday cakes. They were
telling a story, Joe and Gerry, finishing each other's sentences.
The family had borrowed their Uncle Ted's station wagon
for a summer vacation.

With the wooden side panels, Joe said. Now that was a car.

Roomy, said Gerry.

Why did we have to borrow the station wagon? Nancy
asked. She was getting stuff out of the fridge.

Because of the dirt bike, Gerry said. Joe's dirt bike was in
the back. Going to Salvage for a summer holiday. We took it
out of the car so he could ride it for the last stretch, after we
were off the highway.

Mom was forty maybe, Joe said. Her with the bandana in
the lawn chair. You know that photograph, her in the lawn
chair? With a beer and Aunt Helen was there.

That long dirt road with nothing for miles on the way
to Salvage, said Gerry. Joe and Dan Brennan — Gerry was

telling the story now — were coming behind us on the dirt bikes, and I was what? Six or seven? And I stuck my head out the window of the station wagon, looking back at them, see, Joe and Dan Brennan, our cousin Dan, and Dad was driving and the radio going and next thing Dad's playing with the electric windows because we never had them windows in our car.

Electric windows, Joe said.

State of the art, Nancy said.

Dad, pushing the buttons, Gerry said.

And we're behind, said Joe, me and Dan Brennan on the dirt bikes.

Big clouds of dust going up, said Gerry. And the window comes up on my neck. I'm kicking around on the seat, the bloody window, but they got the radio on in the front. They can't hear a thing.

We see Gerry with the window gone up, me and Dan Brennan, said Joe. We're trying to speed up.

They're trying to speed up, Gerry said.

We were trying to tell Dad.

Me with the window jammed up across my neck, said Gerry.

Dad, trying out the windows, said Joe.

What happened? I asked.

They caught up, Gerry said. I'm here, aren't I?

He raised his beer halfway to his mouth. He paused and rubbed the back of his neck as if seeing the roiling dust unfold, his brother ripping past, pulling up beside the driver's window. Making them pull over.

Yeah, he said. I'm here.

Suddenly I realized Xavier still wasn't there. He hadn't

shown up. And if anything had happened, nobody was home. We were all at Nancy's. The houses were empty.

I'd said no Jesus way to the dirt bike. He was going to be killed, plastered to the grille of one of those fish trucks driving a thousand miles an hour, we'd called the RCMP about the fish trucks, like monsters, tearing down the highway.

He would come flying out of the alders where the old railbed met the highway, Xavier, a tunnel of alder branches whipping him hard, grown together over the top, trapping the heated wet air and the light, lime-green or buttercup-yellow light, and the haze from the evaporating puddles, every part of him full of vibrations and jolting bike.

Xavier going too fast.

THE PHONE WAS vibrating and it woke me. I couldn't find it, the bloody purse I had was a sack and the phone was in the bottom, I could see the light of it. The phone had fallen between the pages of a book.

I took the book out and a spill of sand fell from the pages, sand from the beach in Mexico. We'd gone to a hot spring, Joe and me, someone at the conference had suggested it, a long cave, the walls of which were painted white. There were holes in the rock ceiling here and there, and light punched through.

The water so warm steam coiled up, it was a long, wide tunnel that seemed to be descending deeper and deeper into the earth. Leaning against the white stone walls, couples were making out. Everyone in bathing suits, some of them were having sex, their breathing echoed and bounced around us. There were giggles and murmurs, and groans, plashing of the water, ripples, a few unexpected moments of thrashing in the shadows.

I was in front of Joe and his hands were on my hips. We kept walking forward. At the end of the long tunnel the cave widened like a cathedral or a womb. People were making love in there too. We stood against the stone walls, side by side, the shafts of light from the broken ceiling playing on the aqua-green water, our index fingers linked. We were holding each other that way, aroused but abashed. It was like a womb but it was also a grave.

I glanced over to see if the phone had woken Geraldine, but she was still sleeping. It was Joe.

I've got a flight, he said. Two days from now.

Two days, I said. Two days? Oh my god. It had already been two days since Nell had let me go home; two days of Xavier fighting. The city was starting to dig itself out; the army had arrived.

Has anything changed? Joe said. Is he okay?

Nothing has changed.

xavier
baby brophy

XAVIER DIDN'T TAKE Trinity's hand. He was sitting with his chair pulled up close to the bed, his chin resting on the rail, one hand on the lower rung, and the other above, as if he were climbing a ladder. But he was looking directly into her eyes. Then she told him to go to the foot of the bed and see what was happening. He wished she hadn't asked that.

What he'd seen: the skin of Trinity's vagina tight around an opening wedge of black hair. Her bright red vagina, her blond pubic hair and the fine black hair wet and shining in between.

The wedge of the baby's skull got wider and wider and there was the face. He saw it and couldn't understand it. It was obvious what he was looking at but not obvious to him. He realized there are things you only see a handful of times in your life and you have an obligation to witness.

The little face and the doctor's gloves all around it, blue latex fingers gripping the little head and then a gush of blood. Knowing the baby was dead, but the expression, as if the child

353

had understood she was dying, as if she barrelled toward it. It was the look he'd seen on Trinity's face when they were kids, when they were watching *Muppet Treasure Island* and she'd gone soft with wonder when Kermit the Frog overcame his fear at the prospect of dealing with Long John Silver. A gentleness in her expression he'd only ever seen when she was sleeping, or when she watched the movie.

He thought about how she had been present in his house then, at the dinner table, in his bedroom, everywhere. How she was always slamming the front door.

He'd stood still and then a shoulder blocked his view. One of the nurses. The herd of them in white coats, or smocks with teddy bears, shuffled him out of the way.

He was supposed to tell Trinity what was going on because, though a nurse had offered her a mirror to see for herself, she'd said no, that she wanted him, Xavier, down there explaining. But he'd forgotten about Trinity.

Or, all he could think of was Trinity and what was happening to her and the baby, but he forgot himself and his purpose. His purpose was to describe it.

His impression, which he was having a hard time shaking, was that Trinity was turning inside out and he never should have been put in this position. He was full of wonder and a creeping indignation. He felt he was too young to be in the room. It aged him decades, maybe centuries. He was in thrall to the dead infant, full of profound pity, and he had become stupid and rooted to the floor.

Finally, he turned away from it. A nurse nudged him out of the way; her shoulder against his and a little shove. He went back to the head of the bed and the tendons in Trinity's neck were standing out and little blood vessels broke across her cheeks. Her eyes very bright and it took him a moment to realize she was crying and that was why the colour of her eyes seemed to be much brighter than they usually looked.

The baby's face, he said.

You saw it? she asked. But then she was crunched up with pain again. She was holding on to the railing of the bed and her hand made a big squeak as she pulled herself up to a crouch. She was delivering the placenta, one of the nurses told her.

Somewhere in the last hour or so she'd stopped with the grunts and muttered curses. Now there was only a slow hiss of breath through her teeth. They got the baby out and they were working at the other table, but they confirmed the baby hadn't made it.

Trinity had given birth to a dead baby, four pounds, ten-point-four ounces.

Twenty-three weeks, the doctor said.

Xavier had seen the baby come out. She'd been facing up, and her eyes were shut tight and her hands were little fists over her breastbone and her shoulders were hunched, her little chin turned to the side as if she were admonishing someone. The body slithered out limp after the head. Xavier wanted to call his mother. His mother would often mutter, Take this cup, whenever she had to confront something.

Father almighty, take this cup. Something from her child-hood. Xavier knew she didn't believe in God and neither did his father. He didn't know what they believed or what the cup signified, but he was thinking the words.

The nurse had laid the baby in a blanket that another nurse held for her, and they'd taken the baby to a stainless-steel table on the other side of the room. They said about her not breathing, and the heartbeat, whatever they said, it was communicated to Xavier and Trinity that there was no heartbeat.

He hadn't wanted to look down there, because the baby was coming out, but Trinity told him she couldn't see, and she wanted to know what was happening and the doctors weren't saying anything. They had the masks and they had stopped talking.

Trinity said she wanted to hold the baby before she said goodbye.

We have her in a blue blanket but it was a girl, the nurse said.

Little girl, Trinity said. Should I give her a name?

Nobody answered that question.

I didn't even know I was pregnant, Trinity told the nurse. It was like they had become best friends. She'd already told the nurse that several times, but each time she said it she seemed freshly astonished by the duplicity of it all.

One of the other nurses asked Trinity if she used drugs. But she declined to answer that question.

The nurse had asked Trinity if she wanted a picture taken with the baby. Then Xavier was digging in Trinity's purse for her phone which he'd grabbed off the floor of Murph's bedroom on the way out of the house. Finally, he got it out and she told him the code and there was a message from Murph but he didn't read it. He just held the phone out at arm's length and he stepped in and lifted it up higher.

Can you see her? Trinity asked.

Just hold her up a bit, Xavier said. Okay just put your face closer. Move the blanket a bit?

Can you see her now? Trinity asked. He had tried to take the picture but the nurse who was at the foot of the bed with her arms crossed and her fists tucked into her armpits said that Trinity's hair clip should be fixed.

Xavier looked up from the screen and saw that the pink plastic clip, molded to look like a bow, a little girl's clip, had slid down almost to Trinity's jaw.

You just need a little fixing up here, the nurse had said. She took the clip out of Trinity's hair and smoothed the hair down with two pats and then gathered the lock of hair and ran her fingers over it, and then snapped the clip closed.

Then it looked as though Trinity were taking a deep yawn, but it wasn't a yawn, she was crying without making any noise. Her face was contorted and all the colour rushed out. Xavier waited until that was over and then he took the picture. The camera went into some kind of automatic mode and took several pictures, a gazillion clicks, one on top of the other.

THE PRIEST, WHO happened to be on rounds that evening, came to speak with them.

He stood in white robes with a gold embroidery down the front, on his way to the chapel to say a mass but he'd stopped to see if Trinity wanted a funeral for the baby. She pulled herself up on one elbow when he said it.

An urn and have a mass said in the chapel at the funeral home and they would cremate the baby and have a plot in the cemetery on James Lane. There'd be an attendant who would accompany them to the cemetery, and if the priest were unable to attend the burial, the attendant would say a prayer for the child's eternal rest and lower the urn into a grave.

Were she to go this route, she would receive, after the burial, a velvet box which would contain some of the baby's ashes.

Trinity said she wanted that. She wanted the funeral and the urn and a cremation. She wanted a prayer for her baby.

Trinity was holding on to the rail of the hospital bed while she told the priest she wanted those things, and she asked Xavier to get another photograph, of her and the priest and the baby, who was still in her arms; the nurse, who was standing by looking anxious to take the baby away, said that there might be one last photograph but then they would have to take Baby Brophy downstairs.

After the nurse had taken the baby, Trinity pressed a button that lowered the top half of the bed. She lay flat, looking up at the ceiling. Then she pressed another and the bottom half of the bed rose up high, so her feet were up in the air. She put the bottom half of the bed down again.

I have to get the hell out of here, she said.

jules
you're back

TRINITY BROPHY WAS standing over me. She had made her way through the unplowed streets and the plowed one, LeMarchant Road, and she'd tried the front doors and found them locked, as I had done, and then she went to the emergency entrance. A nurse had let her in.

She didn't bring anything, no flowers or fruit. Everything was closed. She'd passed the snowplows and she'd come through the falling snow. She wasn't dressed warmly enough. The little bomber jacket had nothing to it. She had rubber boots, the kind with insulating linings.

You're back, I said. I knew as soon as I saw her that she was the woman in the crowd. The video of the stabbing, a woman tearing at one of the men, pulling his shoulder out of the way so he stumbled backwards, his arms flung out, and the next man, flinging him with superhuman strength, though of course the men were out of it, drunk and stoned, and it didn't require much strength when attacked from behind, the ambulances and police on the way. She was the woman blotted out by the streetlight behind her, light that splintered and splintered, on the top of her head and on her shoulder until she was just a blot.

I thought you were in Toronto, I said.

She was still standing in the middle of the room as though she couldn't bring herself to look at Xavier.

How long have you been back?

I've been in the house where Xavier lives this long while now. Xavier and Violet and them.

Xavier didn't say, I told her. She dug her fists into the pockets of the bomber jacket and drew a deep breath and let it out slowly.

I was kind of laying low, she said. Dealing with a lot.

You were at the party. You're in the video.

I was living in the house where Xavier had a room, Trinity said. She'd started, but was tentative. She was watching my face. I think she was calculating what I needed to hear and what she could leave out. What it was my right to know. What she owed me, and maybe Xavier. Her involvement. As if she were figuring out her involvement. She was clear with each juddering sentence, but stuck. Halted. As if she were back there, in the snowbank with him. All the sirens and blood.

It spilled out of her then. She could not stop it. As if she needed to convince me. Or just needed it out.

Living with my boyfriend. Murph signed the lease and he rented out the rooms. All the rooms were rented. Xavier never even knew I was there for the longest time. I was staying in the room pretty much. Looking for a place of my own. I found my grandfather, on my father's side. That was the reason I come home.

You were there, I said. That was you in the video.

I called the ambulance, I stayed with him in the snowbank. I was at the party where it happened, but I was in the basement when that was going on. I was down on a couch with some girls, just talking, a rec room they had in the basement and someone come down saying Murph was after stabbing someone. Someone came down and said it and people were texting, my phone was beeping with text after text and I was up over the stairs, fast as I could. I never even knew Xavier was at the party. But somebody said it was Xavier. I ran out and I pulled them off him.

I kept my hand pressed to the wound. The blood just kept coming out through his clothes. I was telling him not to die. I was begging. First I heard Murph had shown up and I was trying to find a way out of there before anything happened. We were broke up. I got a text from upstairs he'd just come through the front door. And a few minutes later, the text it was Xavier, he had Xavier, they'd already had him dragged outside.

I felt light-headed with rage, listening to her. It had not been random. Xavier knew the person who had done this to him. Here was Trinity after all this time. Dark circles under her eyes. Skinny, worn. She'd come back.

It was Murph who done it, Trinity said. Stabbed him. It was Murph. There was no reason to do it. Xavier never did nothing. Murph just took it in his head. He'd been doing a lot of crack. Crack or something else.

You and Xavier in the same house for six months. And this — Murph? He was your boyfriend?

She was just nodding her head. I thought about when I'd dropped her at the airport, thinking I'd never see her again. She had not called or tried to get in touch. I'd wondered if she found her mother. What had happened to her? Mary Mahoney hadn't heard from her either. I knew then that the boyfriend was the guy at the airport, the guy I'd seen through the window, the boy who had taken her by the elbow and swung her around.

Xavier and Violet were looking for another place, she said. Things got bad. Murph found out I was at the party and he was coming downstairs for me, she said. But he saw Xavier first. Whatever he was on. He can flip like that. He knew Xavier had helped me. Xavier was after texting him, saying I needed help, but Murph never came. I was sick and Murph never came. We were broke up by then. It was Xavier who had to help me then. Xavier. I never meant for nothing to happen to him. But it's my fault.

It's not your fault, I said. She had wrapped her arms around herself and was squeezing tight, her shoulders shaking. It was as though my absolving her like that, with just a few words, had drawn away everything that held her together.

Did you find your mother, I asked her. She pressed her lips together and nodded. Then she sniffed.

I found her, she said.

xavier
ashes

XAVIER HAD WORN his coat from Chafe and Sons and a caramel-and-black scarf with a line of bright red through the plaid. The scarf had belonged to his grandfather. He was wearing the scarf that his Nanny Florence had given him a year before she died, and his grandfather's black leather gloves.

Trinity was wearing a bomber jacket and jeans and rubber boots with white felt linings and stallions printed on them. Stallions running in the canyons. They sat in the armchairs in the lobby of the funeral home, waiting for the guy who owned the place.

Then a woman came out from an office and closed the door behind her with a small slam that sent the mini-blinds that hung over the window of the office door swinging. It sounded like a cascade of water. The woman shut her eyes and hunched her shoulders against the noise and then she straightened up and said Trinity's name and asked them to follow her.

The secretary said her name was Chelsea, and she brought them down a hallway and there was a little board by each door they passed with the name of the dead person who was waked in the room. The names were spelled with white plastic letters that were slipped into grooves on the boards.

John Cole had died; Elisabeth Stanley had died; Stephanie Mitchell had died. It looked like, at a glance, they hadn't set up for John Cole yet, the room was empty. Whoever John Cole had been.

They went down two flights of stairs, and the woman, Chelsea, knocked on a door and reached down to pull up her nylon, pinching it between finger and thumb and letting it snap back higher up her leg. She squirmed a bit to get the adjustment to settle. The person inside the office was on the phone. Chelsea was waiting for him to get off the phone. Her head was bent toward the door, listening to the rise and fall of his voice, the cadence of phone talk, negotiation and condolence, firm and tender, rippling like a flag in the wind. She was waiting for him to say, Come in.

She glanced at Xavier and smiled, a faux-exasperated smile. She asked what it was like out.

Overcast, Xavier said.

It's been some winter so far, she said.

She pulled at the other leg of her stocking, the ankle and the knee.

She said to Trinity, Don't you hate nylons? I hate nylons. They're nothing but a nuisance. Then a voice inside told them to come in.

Chelsea opened the door for them and the funeral director asked them to sit down, and she closed the door behind them.

Xavier and Trinity moved toward the chairs without taking off their coats, which they were not invited to do, and after an almost comical hesitation about who would get what chair because they both headed for the same chair and she banged into him, they sat down and had time to really take in the director of the funeral home and the pictures of his family and framed certificates behind him, which Xavier was certain he had printed off from some website, a bible, and, inexplicably, a trophy for championship tennis.

The director said they could not have the baby's ashes until the funeral was paid for in full. He was blunt because he could see what he was dealing with, young people, twenty years old if they were a day, and he'd had a small down payment (he made a show of checking their file, but he'd checked it before they came in because Xavier had made an appointment) and, he reminded them, they'd gone for the most expensive package, he said it ruefully and made a show of shaking his head with, really, a great deal of rue, and he told them that, yes, unless he was mistaken, at every point, they had chosen the most expensive option. He used the word regret.

He said, I'm very sorry.

Xavier watched Trinity sink deeper into the collar of her puffy jacket as the funeral director spoke. Her face got white, except her nostrils, which seemed to flame up, but she didn't cry, nor did she speak. What she was doing was drowning the man in her large, dry eyes. Withering him. Xavier knew it was a very unpleasant feeling. But the funeral director seemed familiar with the tactic, appeared to be armed against it.

He spoke only to Xavier. He hardly looked at Trinity.

This was explained, the funeral director said. Before you signed the contract. He turned the file around for them to see.

Mom has had a difficult time, he said. And she's grieving. We understand that. The death of a child, that's one of the saddest. That shouldn't happen. I wish I could help you.

I want her ashes, Trinity said. But I don't have that kind of money. Can't you make an exception?

The director took his time explaining the nature of exceptions and the sadness his work entailed and the sensitivity he was called upon to display in each case and how there could be no exceptions, even if he had the authority to provide one. The truth was, he was not able to make those kinds of decisions. Like most people, perhaps all people, he had to answer to someone else, and that someone was in Barbados at the moment, and would not have made the exception either.

Xavier said, Can you show a little mercy here, sir?

And after going over the figures once again, and finally cutting six hundred dollars off the expenses of the five-thousand-dollar funeral of a baby who had never seen the light of day, the director and Xavier had arrived at an impasse in their negotiations. They firmly disagreed, and both became entrenched in their positions. The director seemed to feel he had shown mercy; Xavier felt that he had not shown mercy or anything like it.

Xavier believed and articulated quite calmly that there had been no mercy. But it was what the situation required. He said there was a moral imperative at work. This was a phrase, he realized even as he said it, that had come from his mother.

Give her the ashes of her child, Xavier said.

I can't do that, the funeral director said.

Xavier and Trinity walked back downtown. They had to get in the line of traffic because the road wasn't plowed, and Xavier was splashed, his good coat, but he didn't curse. He halted for a moment to wipe off the brown slush on the sleeve of his coat. It was snowing, small flecks hard as salt.

Xavier had been trudging through the slush ahead of her

and he stopped and she banged into him again, like in the funeral home when they were trying the kind of clown-waltz required to sit in the chairs before the director of the funeral home.

I'm sorry, he said. When they got to the Mary Brown's on Freshwater Road, Trinity said she was meeting someone in there. A girl she knew would let her sleep on her couch.

When he got back to the house, Violet had already packed up her books. There were five cartons from the liquor store full of books. They'd found an apartment. A few days before they could move in. All of her clothes from the closet, still on the hangers, lay on the futon.

What happened? she asked.

Nothing, he said. We didn't get the ashes. Violet was punching their duvet into a garbage bag and she stopped. She ran both her hands over her hair and held it off her forehead. She was staring straight ahead at nothing.

Where is he? she asked.

She doesn't know, they broke up. She deleted him. Or blocked him or whatever. Trinity is staying at somebody's house in Mount Pearl.

Somebody who?

Somebody, I didn't ask. I want no more part of this.

I'm afraid of him, Xavier, she said, still staring into space. But then she snatched up the garbage bag and she started punching the duvet down again.

jules
flying

I WAS AFRAID he'd burst out of that path without stopping, without looking both ways, as he had been trained to do since he was a toddler, because even at thirteen, even now at twenty-one, this part of him is what is most pure — the desire to pass through things as though there were a splice in time, as though things can be got through without effort or damage.

It's this part that is strongest in him, and it will only get stronger. It's mingled with a kindness he'd be better off without. The kind part of him is the flame that kindles the daring, the hunger for thrill. The light hot lick of attention. A communing with nature. I knew he would burst through without checking for traffic, and I also believed that I would know when it happened, the moment of it would pass through me too.

But I hadn't known.

Trinity Brophy had said she wanted to give a statement to the police.

I'd asked her once what his first name was, and she said his name was Brad. Then she said, Bradley. But I could tell she had never called him that, or not in a very long time. I knew by the way she had said his name, uncertain, searching, she was done with him. As if she realized he wasn't who she thought he was. That if she had never really said his name, she couldn't have known who he was.

murph
night sky

HIS FATHER HAD taken an angle grinder to the ATM and a wing
of sparks flew up and one of them hit Murph on the back of
the hand and it enraged him. He howled.

His father wheeled around with grinder and Murph had
jumped out of the way.

His father shut the thing off. Then his father saw it had
just been a little spark and mocked him.

Big Murph turned the grinder back on and touched it to
the ATM and the blade snapped. He flung it away from him,
into the trees, flung it down a hill where the snow was deep
and it hissed as it sank into the drift. He shouted at Murph to
go get the bloody grinder.

Get the Jesus thing, he shouted.

I'll get soaking wet, Murph said. His father grabbed him
by the front of the jacket, lifted him off his feet, and gave him
a little shove down the hill.

You're good and wet now, aren't you, his father said.
Murph had beat his way through the waist-high snow and

kicked around until he felt the grinder with his foot and dragged it up. He had to crawl up the hill because it was icy and he kept sliding back. He was careful when he laid the grinder down at his father's feet. He was afraid it was broken, and he would be blamed.

His father picked it up, turned and went back into the cabin. It was very quiet after the door shut behind him. A moment later a branch dropped a hard mound of snow onto the ground and the sound of it made Murph jump. He kicked the ATM and the side of it bent and unbent. A loud boom echoed around the trees.

HE'D GONE BACK to town three weeks after the robbery. He'd stayed with his father until then, in the Holyrood cabin, in case anyone was looking for him. The two of them taking turns cooking supper. They watched the old *Sopranos* episodes on Soap2day, clicking through the screens of business opportunities in their area, ads for cruise ships, and pornographic cartoons until they got the episode they wanted to watch. They watched, each night, on Murph's computer, which rested on his lap, until they fell asleep sitting up. Once he woke to find his father had put a blanket over him. Often his father yelled out in his sleep, curses, threats, violent growls, or his teeth grinding. Once his father said he couldn't take it. He had given enough. He'd begged someone in a small whiny voice to fuck off. Once he shouted at the top of his voice: Come and get me, come on, come on.

The angle grinder his father had was the cheapest one on the Canadian Tire website. They were trying to borrow an expensive one. His father knew someone who had one that would do the job. He'd texted the guy and they waited for the guy to answer his text.

You could get them with some kind of diamond blade and that's what they needed, his father had said. They'd watched videos of demonstrations. The sparks flying up like the spreading wing of some giant tethered bird. Murph read out the description of an angle grinder that was over two thousand dollars.

It can't be real diamonds, Murph said. It must mean something else. He didn't know what it meant, but those blades could saw through anything, if you believed the videos. He figured there was ten thousand in the ATM. No more than that. Maybe significantly less. He'd take half of it and go to the other side of the world, if it meant getting away from his father.

Murph got back to the house in town late in the evening, and they had all left. He called out but there was no answer. He'd switched on the light in the porch, then off and back on, but there was no light, no matter what he did with the switch. He flicked it up and down and then he put his fist through the Gyproc just below the light switch and made his knuckles bleed. He licked the torn skin and could taste the chalky dust of the Gyproc. He tried the kitchen light even though he knew the power was shut off. He used the light on his phone to go up the stairs. They'd taken the chandelier. They'd left the cleaning for him to do. There was nothing left but garbage. There was a stain on the carpet in Devin's room that would cost him the damage deposit.

He texted Devin, but there was no answer.

He went into the bedroom he and Trinity had shared. Her stuff was gone, except for a pink frilly blouse, hanging in the cupboard. He touched the sleeve and the wire hanger rocked back and forth. He pulled on the blouse so hard a button popped, and the shirt slithered limply into his hand and the wire hanger danced around as if trying to escape the closet pole.

His phone dinged and he thought it might be Trinity, but it was his father saying he'd got another grinder. Going at it that night. Telling Murph if he wanted to be there for the grand opening he should head back out.

Then there was a text about a party happening that night. He could at least go to the party and get fucked up. He needed something to stop the pain in his chest that he knew was heartbreak. He checked the news and there was nothing more about the ATM. He kept refreshing the old story. The headline said: Copycat Backhoe Bandit.

He was very cold but he left the house and set out walking with his jacket open to the wind. The guy who texted him about the party was on Leslie Street and he often fronted Murph drugs, so he walked over to Leslie and they did a few lines. The guy gave him several baggies, enough to sell at the party, get himself set up again.

After they were good and loaded and revved from the coke, they called a cab and the guy showed the driver his phone with the address. He paid for the cab while Murph stood outside waiting for him. The music from the party was loud, even out on the street. The whole house thumped from the bass like a living thing. The place was so packed they could hardly get in the front door. Murph was shouldering through when he got another text. It was someone saying Trinity was at the party. She was down in the basement, where they had a rec room.

373

That's when he saw Xavier bent over, getting on his boots. Murph hated the son of a bitch. Whatever was between Xavier and Trinity, that had lasted. It would last forever.

He'd hitchhiked back from Holyrood, and he'd been on the side of the highway after dark. He'd been splashed by a truck and covered in slush and was wet to the skin. His feet were wet and numb. He'd been walking on a part of the road where there was nothing but trees on either side and he'd stopped and tilted his head back to look up at the stars. All the night sky he'd seen on the side of the highway opened up in his chest, a black hole, just as if he had been torn open with a diamond blade.

He grabbed Xavier by the collar of his T-shirt and twisted it around his fist and started to choke him with it. But he wanted him outside, he wanted Xavier to die cold and wet, he wanted to cut him open and throw him down into a snowbank.

jules
i'm here

THE GIRL WALKED up to my son's bed and held the rail. She put her hand out and smoothed his hair. Her lower lip was trembling, and tears began to fall down her cheeks. They fell one after the other, one catching up with the one before it, then dropping. She was wearing Xavier's coat.

Xavier I'm here, she said. I'm here. I didn't know where you were. I couldn't find you, I'm here, I'm here. Xavier, I thought your phone was out of minutes. Xavier, Xavier, I'm here. I'm here. They wouldn't let me in, I've been phoning, I phoned and phoned, they said nobody could come because of the storm. She was smoothing his hair out of his eyes. The tenderness with which she touched him, the intimacy, it was terrifying to me.

She looked up at me then.

I had no idea where he was, she said. It was so frightening. I was thinking the worst, I had a bad feeling. Then I found out he was here, and I came anyway. They said I couldn't come but I came anyway. I got in.

For some reason, I took my purse and held it against my chest. I stood up from the chair, took a couple of steps back and just watched, because I couldn't not watch. She was leaning over him now, her tears were dropping right onto his face. She leaned in over the chrome rail and she was kissing his cheeks.

We spoke at the same time:

You must be Violet, I said.

I'm Violet, she said. But she didn't turn back to look at me. She rubbed viciously with the heel of her hand at her tears.

She said, I had been looking all over, maybe he couldn't charge his phone. He was supposed to come home to the new apartment after the party. This party the guys at his work were going to. Half the time he's out of minutes. He'd gone to that party, I knew that because he called me from the backseat when he was on the way. But I hadn't heard from him after that. I didn't have a phone number for you or his father or his sister or anyone. Finally, Trinity called me. She said he asked her over and over to call me. I'm all this time trying to get in here. They wouldn't let me because of the storm.

She turned to me and we shook hands, but there was an awkward mismatch where we thought hug, or I did, I wanted to draw her close to me, but it was a handshake. We stuttered toward each other and I was going to draw her in, but couldn't. She had an elegance that was not cold, an unruffled quality even as she cried and stopped crying and started again. She was not shy, but comfortable in letting a silence happen between us, though she was doing all the talking.

She was holding Xavier's hand, smoothing his cheek. She kept her hands on him.

She astonished me by lowering the railing on his hospital bed so she didn't have to lean over it when she was touching him. I'd thought the railing inviolate. Then she kicked off her boots and climbed up on the bed and lay down beside him and I had to take a few more steps back. She still had on the camel-hair coat and her tam was squashed in her fist.

They let us both stay there, though you were only allowed one visitor in the ICU. I got another chair for her out of the corridor, and the nurses looked up and saw what I was doing, but I kept my eyes down and they went back to their papers, the counting out of pills in little cups with pieces of paper under them to tell which pills belonged to whom.

I don't know what we talked about in the hours that followed. She told me how she had tried to track down our phone numbers, mine and Joe's, but she couldn't find any phone numbers. She knew we'd been in Mexico and that only I had made it back, because she'd asked the nurses who was in with him, she'd been terrified he was alone. She didn't know what was going to happen to him. She didn't have his sister's number either. Though she'd met Stella in a bar. One night at Christmas, she and Xavier had met Stella, out with the girls from her work, but Stella hadn't told me.

We talked about the storm. We talked about how a part of the roof had blown off her parents' house in Spaniard's Bay. She told me the entire plot of a book she was reading for her English class and that the semester was messed up now because of the storm.

Finally, a nurse came over and said one of us would have to leave. And we said we would, we both said one of us would leave, but the nurse went to check on other patients and we both just sat there.

She told me the movies she and Xavier had watched together and said they watched movies of books they had read aloud to each other, and I couldn't imagine Xavier reading aloud. I felt a stab of pain to realize that my son was an entirely different person for her, and there was a part of him I didn't know. I went to the bathroom, and when I came back Xavier was awake.

jules
wick

THE NURSE, GABRIELLE, opened a packet, and miniature scissors tumbled out onto the sterile napkin. She used the scissors to clip the top off a squirt bottle of clear liquid. She squeezed it all over the two wounds. Xavier looked down at the wounds, the coarse and tattered black edges where the stitches held him together.

Because everything was on the table here, because I could ask anything, I asked if that was an engagement ring she was wearing.

She stopped and held out her hand as if surprised to see the ring there.

Because that wasn't there three days ago, on your last shift, I said. I'm pretty sure.

I got engaged, she admitted. She pressed her lips together and shook her head slowly.

Not used to it yet, she said.

Mom, Xavier said.

Lovely ring, I said.

I know, she said.

Mom, he said. He meant stop asking the nurse personal questions.

Where's Violet, I asked.

She'll be here soon, he said. He smirked because we both realized he'd made a strategic error. He'd much rather I focused on the nurse's love life than his.

His girlfriend was here earlier, the nurse said. Violet? She was here bringing him some breakfast.

How are the wounds? I'd asked. She had the end of the wick in a set of tweezers and it uncoiled from the first wound, stiff and crusty, like a shoestring. This was how they drew infection from the wound. Pus made its way up the coiled wick that was deep in the wound. They didn't want the wound to heal with the infection inside. She dropped the string in the garbage bucket beside her. And glanced up at the door of the hospital room.

There was Joe. He had come straight from the airport. He had his luggage with him.

Hi, kid, Joe said.

Your husband made it back, the nurse said.

Your little holiday all over? Xavier asked.

What about you, lazing around in bed, middle of the day?

Life of Riley, Xavier said.

The nurse had a big square bandage that she held over one of the wounds with tweezers. She let it go so it sat squarely over the puncture.

Those wounds look lovely, she said. I am pleased with the look of them. She folded up the old bandages and removed them from the table tray.

Joe moved up to the bed and took up Xavier's hand. He

took it in his own hand and squeezed it and rubbed his thumb over the back of it and put it back down on the sheet and patted it. Then I lowered the bed rail for him and he grabbed Xavier and held him by the shoulders, his fingers turning white near the tips because he had such a hard grip.

Don't lean on the wounds, I said. Be careful for god's sake. We just got him patched up.

Xavier submitted to this until he finally lifted his hands and put them on his father's back.

You gave us a start, Joe said. Your mother and me. You gave us a real fright.

No walk in the park for me either, Xavier said.

No picnic? I asked.

No fun and games, Xavier said. We both waited, but Joe wasn't letting go.

Hey, big guy, Xavier said. Come on now. Then he patted his father on the back. It was the kind of pat that says, Okay, let go. But also, everything is all right. It's going to be fine.

xavier
the knife

THE PARTY WAS in a monster house in a subdivision in the west end and it was packed with people from all over the city. He had gone out in a taxi with the guys from work.

He'd had a lot to drink and it was time to leave, but nobody was willing to leave with him. Xavier had called a cab that was already an hour late, and he'd called another. He was bent over in the porch in a crush of boots and a pile of coats exploding out of the closet; he'd heard the cops had been called. It was time to go, and the guys he'd come with had probably already left, or they were out on the back deck smoking and it would be a great effort to make his way back through the crowd, people necking in the hallway, people dancing.

Xavier decided he'd walk and hoped to run into the cab on the way. He'd just keep going and he'd phone until the taxi met him on one of these streets named after towns in Ontario and Manitoba and Alberta. He was taking out his phone to text Violet when he felt the fist at his neck and his phone went flying.

For one fleeting moment he thought of the dirt bike when he was thirteen, the crush of bird-bone on his helmet. When he got to Gerry's party he'd looked down, and there and only then did he feel some tickle under his chin and glance down to find the tiny feather on the neck of his T-shirt. He'd plucked it off and he never told anyone. It was between him and the bird.

The fist twisted the collar of his shirt and the fabric cut into his windpipe and he was thrown against the wall. His shoulder went through the Gyprock and it was shocking to see the wall punctured.

Then there came a punch to his gut that knocked the wind out of him. Someone had him by the throat with two hands, banging his head against the wall. His neck had softened and couldn't hold his head. A crowd was forming and chanting. Fight, fight, fight, fight.

It was Murph's face up in his, so his breath and spittle were on him and Xavier allowed himself to close his eyes to see if he could think his way out of it.

A mood that stormed up, overtook Murph, something from his past or from five minutes ago.

Xavier wondered if there was no reason.

There wouldn't have to be a reason. He remembered being in the kitchen and telling Murph to go fuck himself when he asked for a nacho and that might be the reason.

Murph had dragged him out the door and it was snowing. The snow was whirling down in twisting veils from the deepest reaches of the universe. He was tossed onto a bank of snow and there was something going on with his nose, which he wanted to touch but his arms were pinned. Murph had nearly broken his nose, is what happened. A radiation of blinding pain until it was numb and he couldn't feel it.

But Xavier did feel the knife slice up into him. He felt it go in, but he didn't know what he'd felt.

It was a new sensation, it was obscene and staggering. Whatever it was, it was hard to locate or understand. He didn't know what it was until it was drawn out and he was stabbed the second time. He was bewildered by this sensation. When the knife was drawn out the second time, he'd felt himself drawn out with it. Anything you could reasonably call himself flew away.

He'd been down on the ground, he remembered hitting the ground and knowing it was bad that he was down there. They were kicking him, people were screaming, girls were screaming, but he had lost consciousness moments later; and woke in the snowbank. He felt a boot kick his head. He knew it was a boot because he saw it out of the corner of his eye, he saw the foreshortening, the tiny head on top of faraway shoulders and the giant sole of the boot and then he'd gone unconscious, blinked out, and came back to an all over pain that was killing him.

There was Trinity right on top of him. She was breathing in his face. She was saying, Come on. And, Don't do this. She was saying, Please. She was saying his name. First, she was whimpering and breathy but then she went almost still. She commanded him.

She said, I got you. I got you. I got you. I got you. But she made it sound like an order. It went from a sob to something flat and true.

I got you.

I got you.

raising xavier

WE'RE SEEING GREAT improvement, the nurse said. His body is fighting it off. The new antibiotic we've given him.

Your white blood cell count is going down, I told him. He stared off into the corner of the room and I asked him what he could see, because the pain medication was messing with him. We all looked, the nurse and his father and me.

A bird just flew through the room, he said.

That'll happen, the nurse said. He'll see things because of the Dilaudid. But the surgeon said he's doing well.

There's no bird, I said.

She patted Xavier's hand and then she took him by the wrist and bent her head as though in prayer.

That's perfect, she said. Pulse is perfect. That's what you want. I wouldn't be surprised they discharge him end of the week. A week to ten days. Give him lots of water. Make sure he eats. We'll keep giving him some fluids through the IV, get him back to normal. But I'm telling you, he's coming around. If he keeps going like this, I'd say a week, he's out of here. Less than a week.

We won't keep you here no more, she told Xavier.

jules
the next wave

WHERE WAS HE with the dirt bike? But someone said a swim at the beach. We went down over the hill to the beach with our drinks. And we dropped everything in the sand and ran in. All of us ran in together.

I got hit in the face with a wave, and when I blinked one of my contact lenses was askew. It was almost out of my eye, or it had slipped halfway off my iris or a film of water had come between the lens and my eye, and there were drops of water in my eyelashes that broke up the light into spots of violet and blue, spots floating close enough that I could have touched them with my hand, and the cliffs behind the beach became five cliffs wheeling slowly in circles, overlapping at the edges, and the boy on the dirt bike at the top of the cliff, in silhouette, was five distinct boys, each exactly the same, each hovering near the next, and all overlapping with each other, for less than the second or two before the contact lens floated back into place on my eye and I was engulfed by the next wave and dragged under and lifted up. And there he was. There was Xavier on the cliff.

acknowledgements

THANK YOU TO Sarah MacLachlan for the great joyride of working together on this novel, and all my books at Anansi; for your honesty and infinite expertise; for your infallible instincts about what makes a good story; and for the big giant gift of your publishing know-how. Thank you for the steadfast friendship, the dinner parties, and for switching shoes under the table.

Thank you to Melanie Little for editing this book. I feel profoundly lucky to have had the chance to work with you again. You are clear sighted, indefatigable, and brilliant. Thank you for helping me see my way through. Couldn't have done it without you. Thank you, thank you, thank you.

Peter Norman for copyediting and Wendy Thomas for proofreading, thank you for having my back. Thank you so much, Alysia Shewchuk, for my lovely cover, and for making the book look beautiful inside and out. Big thanks to Debby de Groot, Matt Williams, Sonya Lalli, Erica Mojzes, Karen Brochu, Laura Chapnick, Douglas Richmond, Michelle MacAleese, Grace Shaw, Semareh Al-Hillal, and everyone at Anansi.

This novel grew from a short story I published in *Eighteen Bridges*, and I have included parts of the story herein. Thank you to Curtis Gillespie for publishing the story.

Dr. Paul Heneghan, Dr. Judy Rowe, and Dr. Susanne Price — thank you for answering my questions, even as I cornered you in busy hospital corridors, examination rooms, and over text. I feel lucky to have generous experts such as you to call on in times of literary need, as well as all the other times, over the years — thank you!

Eva Crocker, Steve Crocker, Holly Hogan, Larry Mathews, Lynn Moore, and Claire Wilkshire, thanks for reading drafts, for talking me down and talking me up. Thanks for facing significant personal peril in the act of telling me the truth!

Thank you Jennifer Lokash, Danine Farquharson, Robert Finley, Chris Lockett, Joel Deshaye, and John Geck, and everybody in the English Department at Memorial University for your tremendous support.

Thank you to my mom, Elizabeth Moore, for your strength and guidance, for teaching me many things, including how to have fun; thank you to my wonderful father, the late Leo Moore, and my beloved parents-in-law, the late Rosemary and Bert Crocker; Lynn, for all things legal, best sister in the world, and Bob, for being Bob; Emily, Jared, Eva, Theo, and Leo! The fam!

Most especially, of course, Steve: what a life, hey? Thank you.

LISA MOORE is the acclaimed author of the novels *Caught*, *February*, and *Alligator*; the story collections *Open* and *Something for Everyone*; and the young adult novel *Flannery*. Her books have won the Commonwealth Writers' Prize and CBC's Canada Reads, been finalists for the Writers' Trust Fiction Prize and the Scotiabank Giller Prize, and been longlisted for the Man Booker Prize. Moore is also the co-librettist, along with Laura Kaminsky, of the opera *February*, based on her novel of the same name. She lives in St. John's, Newfoundland.